all ab
evie

Books by Cathy Lamb

JULIA'S CHOCOLATES

THE LAST TIME I WAS ME

HENRY'S SISTERS

SUCH A PRETTY FACE

THE FIRST DAY OF THE REST OF MY LIFE

A DIFFERENT KIND OF NORMAL

IF YOU COULD SEE WHAT I SEE

WHAT I REMEMBER MOST

MY VERY BEST FRIEND

THE LANGUAGE OF SISTERS

NO PLACE I'D RATHER BE

THE MAN SHE MARRIED

ALL ABOUT EVIE

Published by Kensington Publishing Corporation

all about evie

CATHY LAMB

KENSINGTON BOOKS
www.kensingtonbooks.com

KENSINGTON BOOKS are published by

Kensington Publishing Corp.
119 West 40th Street
New York, NY 10018

All Kensington titles, imprints, and distributed lines are available at special quantity discounts for bulk purchases for sales promotion, premiums, fundraising, educational, or institutional use.

Special book excerpts or customized printings can also be created to fit specific needs. For details, write or phone the office of the Kensington Sales Manager: Kensington Publishing Corp., 119 West 40th Street, New York, NY 10018. Attn. Sales Department. Phone: 1-800-221-2647.

Kensington and the K logo Reg. U.S. Pat. & TM Off.

ISBN-13: 978-1-4967-0986-8 (ebook)
ISBN-10: 1-4967-0986-1 (ebook)
First Kensington Electronic Edition: November 2019

ISBN-13: 978-1-4967-0985-1
ISBN-10: 1-4967-0985-3
First Kensington Trade Paperback Printing: November 2019

10 9 8 7 6 5 4 3 2 1

Printed in the United States of America

For

Todd and Cindy Everts

May the laughter roll on

Chapter 1

❧

Evie Lindsay
San Orcanita Island, Washington
2012

I knew she was going to be hit by a white truck.

The little girl was skipping up the main street in our small town, several blocks past my yellow bookstore. I was carrying a box of books I'd been reviewing at home in one arm and a cat kennel with Ghost in it in the other. Ghost the Cat loves to go to my bookstore and hang out, so sometimes I bring her. She was meowing with excitement. She's clearly a book lover.

It was early in the morning and sunny. People were up and about, tourists eager to explore the island, townspeople chatting, fishermen headed to their boats, bread lovers entering the bakery, coffee lovers drinking a cup on the bay, the farmers' market open . . . and there was the young girl up ahead with her mother, a red ribbon in her brown hair bouncing about.

I closed my eyes. I reenvisioned the premonition, what I'd seen in a flash when I noticed her. I paid attention to the clothes she'd been wearing, her placement, right in front of the library, a greyhound on a leash behind her, and Mr. Hayes eating a doughnut across the street.

I opened my eyes, saw that the little girl was almost in front of the library, a greyhound was on a leash behind her, and Mr. Hayes was eating a doughnut across the street.

Oh no. Oh no. Oh no.

She was going to be hit soon . . . no, she was going to be hit *immediately* by a white truck.

I dropped the books and Ghost. She squealed and hissed in outrage. I started running up the street, my white summer dress easy to run in, my red flip-flops not so easy.

"Hello, Evie," my friend Gracie called out, but I didn't greet her, I didn't have time.

"Evie," Mr. Jamon croaked, leaning on his cane as I flew past him. "Everything okay, dear? Did you see something?"

I kept running. The girl was two blocks ahead, and I had to catch up. I so hate running. It makes me breathless. Now and then I see people running or jogging, and I think, *My, that looks miserable*. And it is, it *so* is. I tried to breathe and heard a gurgling, choking sound in my throat as my legs started to burn.

The sun was streaming through the towering fir and pine trees, blinding the road up ahead, but I heard it, loud and clear: a delivery truck, rumbling and groaning, the type with huge loads so it can't brake quickly. It turned the corner on top of the hill and barreled down the road toward town, the engine grinding.

I ran harder, faster, darting around Koo and Darrell Jones, who moved out of the way when they heard me panting behind them. I heard Koo say, "It's happening again!" and Darrell yelled after me, "Can we help, Evie?" I heard them running after me.

I could hardly breathe. I need to get in shape, but what a drag that would be. Ugh.

The truck was flying down the street, way too fast, passing the post office, the old white church, the knitting store. I saw the little girl, her eye caught by a dog—a fluffy, white, *cute* dog across the street. She smiled at the dog, waved at it as if it would pick up a paw and wave back.

"No!" I shouted at her as loud as I could, my lungs burning. "No! Don't move!" But she didn't hear me and her mother was distracted, staring into the picture window of my mother and aunts' pink store, Flowers, Lotions, and Potions. The store was filled with the wild, intricate bouquets that my mother makes, the scented potions and lotions my aunt Camellia makes, and the peculiar/sexy/oddly compelling flower photographs my aunt Iris takes.

"No! No!" I screamed again, puffing hard as the girl took that fateful, disastrous step and darted into the street to pet the fluffy, white, cute dog on the other side, her red ribbon flying about, a smile on her face before she was going to be turned into a human pancake.

I saw the truck driver's expression, suddenly panicked as he saw her. He hit the brakes and they screeched, but the brakes couldn't work fast enough.

I flew off the curb toward the truck, lunged and grabbed the girl, yanking her back, stumbling against her weight, both of us crashing to the street, my back and butt bouncing on the asphalt, the air shoved out of my lungs. I pulled my feet in just in time as the truck rumbled past, its brakes smoking, horn blaring.

The girl's back was on my chest and stomach, my arms wrapped around her waist, her head on my collarbone, her red ribbon slinking down my arm. Red for blood. At least there was no blood. I don't like blood. Blood should always be inside of a body, not outside. I was panting, wiped out. I should exercise more and lose some weight, I know this, I do, but it's so boring. And I hate dieting. Garfield the cat had it right: Dieting is die with a *t*.

But still. I could hardly breathe from this short sprint, and that was embarrassing. I would have to make a change in my life. Exercise. Eat more vegetables. That sort of dreariness. But not today. Lord, not today. My aunt Camellia was making a chocolate cheesecake for dessert tonight. I probably wouldn't begin a diet and exercise program tomorrow, either, because there would be leftover chocolate cheesecake and I would not want it to go to waste. Maybe next Saturday I'd begin.

Maybe not.

The girl wasn't moving, but I knew she was okay. I could feel her breathing on top of me. She was shocked, that's all. I sucked in air like a beached whale, my heart protesting my run, first thing in the morning, too!

I heard a scream, piercing, circling around me, then the scream seemed to circle North Sound before it headed out to the ocean, alarming any and all whales and fish. It was a scream of pure terror.

It wasn't me. I couldn't scream. I am too out of shape. The scream was from the mother. She was crying and screaming as she hobbled over to us. She bent over her daughter, cradled in my arms, my dress no doubt hitched up way too high. "Maggie, oh, my God, Maggie. Are you all right? Are you okay? Did you get hurt?"

I felt Maggie nod. "Yep. I'm good."

So casual. "Yep." I was near to dying from running, my legs were almost flattened by truck tires, and the kid, yep, was fine and dandy.

"Why did you do that?" her mother wailed, as if I weren't there underneath her naughty daughter. "Why did you run in the street? You know better than that!"

The girl didn't answer. She couldn't. She had wanted to pet a white, furry, cute dog and now she was lying in the street. She had seen the truck tear past us. She was young, about seven, but she knew what had almost happened to her.

Maggie, dear Maggie, burst into tears. "I only wanted to pet the doggie!"

The mother was now holding her daughter close, shaking, tears streaming out of her eyes, keening over my near-dead body. Dang. I did not want to start my day like this, but whew. That was a close one.

"Thank you." The mother wept, her pale face inches from mine, her tears falling on my face. "Thank you so much."

I gasped again and said, "No problem." But it was a problem, as my poor legs would probably ache for days. I would eat more chocolate to compensate. Maggie's mother pulled Maggie up and was cradling her in her arms, rocking and sobbing.

My friend Gracie, her blonde hair piled up in a ball, sat down next to me in the street, her legs crossed as if she were sitting on my bed and chatting like when we were teenagers. "You had one of your premonitions again, didn't you, Evie?"

I shook my head, sucking air in. "No. I don't have premonitions."

"She did," Koo Jones said, also kneeling beside me. She squeezed my hand. "She started running and dropped her cat before the truck was even in view. We saw it. The cat's not happy, Evie—that one is a hisser—but are you okay?"

I nodded. "No premonition. I saw the truck coming."

Darrell shook his head as he and Gracie and Koo helped me up. Wow. Even my butt hurt from that run. I put my hands on my butt and rubbed. Ouch! Gracie handed me my missing flip-flop as Koo yanked my dress down so the whole town wouldn't see my pink underwear that says "Cats Rule" on the back.

"You couldn't have seen the truck. It was up and around the bend," Darrell said. He's an organic farmer. Sells his crops to our local grocery store and to the other islands. "I feel for you. Those premonitions must be awful. You see something and you have to go save someone. You're a right kind person, Evie. Always helping others."

Gracie ran her hands over my black hair and flicked out small rocks from the pavement. "There. You're good to go. No more rocks in your waves. Hey! Rocks in your waves. That sounded pretty cool. Maybe I should be a songwriter."

"Thanks, Gracie." I had hoped to see Marco today, a tiny sighting, and I would not want rocks in my waves.

The driver ran over, puffing and pale. "Man, I am so sorry. You okay, lady? Is the kid okay?"

"We didn't die," I snapped, my anger rising like a mini volcano. "My legs are still attached."

"The brakes wouldn't work. I kept pumpin' 'em, pumpin' 'em."

"You were going way too fast," I said. "What is this, a racetrack? Who are you, Evel Knievel?"

He looked embarrassed. Ashamed.

"Don't go fast again. Ever." I was pretty dang ticked. "You almost killed that girl."

He hung his head. "I'm sorry," he whispered. "I'm really sorry."

The girl was now jumping and bopping about on the sidewalk, twirling here and there, everything happy! Her mother was leaning against a light post, bent in half, looking like she might lose her cookies, her eyes never leaving the bopping daughter.

"Lucky she had a premonition it was going to happen!" Mr. Jamon croaked out. "She's been having them since she was a wee little girl."

"I don't have premonitions," I said. I knew no one believed me, but it's my standard line.

They all nodded, humoring me.

"Sure, you don't," Koo said. "Sure."

"Not a one," Gracie said. "When you suddenly jumped into the lake in your clothes and swam to the center to rescue my grandmother at the exact moment she stood and fell out of the boat a week ago, it was purely coincidence. How funny you were there at the same time!"

That was a wet one.

"Uh, yeah," Darrell said. "Want some tomatoes? They're ripe. I'll bring them over to you and your mom and aunts tonight."

"Whatever," Gracie said. "You're a bit flushed and you're still panting. Maybe you should run more. For when this happens again."

"Hey," Koo said. "I need a scary book. Did you get any super scary books in?"

"And I need a romance," Mr. Jamon said. "I've got a date on Saturday night, and it wouldn't hurt to take a lesson, right?"

Right. You go, Mr. Jamon, you go.

We all trooped into my bookstore, another friend, O'Dierno Rhys, handing me Ghost, who was unhappy with her disrespectful treatment, but not before the girl and her mother thanked me again and hugged me.

"You came out of nowhere," the mother said.

"Evie does that," Gracie said with a lot of enthusiasm. "She can see the future. It's like she has a crystal ball in her head."

"I think it's those pretty gold eyes of hers," Koo said, slinging an arm around my shoulders, which were beginning to ache from the fall. "Something magical about them."

I rolled my pretty gold eyes. "No, I can't see the future."

Yes, I can.

* * *

I can't always see the future, but now and then, curse it all, I can.

It's been a plague my whole life.

I started having premonitions as a kid. I would see the future for someone. Sometimes it was scary, or bad, and sometimes it was wonderful. It led to a whole lot of mental distress and trying to save people, or choosing not to save people, and committing minor crimes along the way, like breaking and entering, trespassing, small robberies, destruction of property, hiding things people owned like their car keys so they couldn't drive, one time locking my favorite librarian up in her home so she wouldn't get hit by a train, things of that nature.

All of my tiny criminal acts or legal interventions have been to slow someone down so that the premonition will pass them by. So many times in life an accident hits that if you waited one minute, *one*, it would have shot past you. I try to make that minute happen. All the crimes were necessary. I don't regret any of them. I knew what was going to happen to those people— innocent people, often friends, people I loved and cared about— if I didn't.

That's the curse of having premonitions: You know what's upcoming for people.

You may have to become a criminal momentarily to save them.

But I have had one premonition off and on my whole life, starting when I was about five years old.

In that premonition there are two women, one of them me, and one of us dies. I don't know if it's me or the other woman who heads up the golden staircase to heaven. I have not been able to figure this out, which is strange. My endings for my other premonitions are all quite clear, but there's a fuzziness here, as if the premonition doesn't even know precisely who is dead at the end of it.

I don't know who the other woman is. I don't know how old I'll be. I don't know when it will happen. What I do know is that I'm driving on a road, wide enough for only one car, alongside a mountain on my right. On my left side is a steep cliff. The ocean is in the distance, peeking through the pine trees, and there's a whole bunch of orange poppies. I see the oncoming car, and we both swerve, and crash.

Sometimes one car shoots over the cliff, sometimes both cars. Sometimes there's an earsplitting explosion, crackling flames and black smoke bubbling up from the bottom of the cliff, sometimes not. Sometimes we're sandwiched together, teetering over the cliff, up and down, sometimes not. It's blurry, this premonition. Like rain is blurring the full photo, but there is no rain.

It's troubling to know that a car crash, on a cliff, may kill me. Or it may not.

Other than the premonitions? I am utterly, completely normal.

Which means that I'm one hot mess.

Chapter 2

∽

Betsy Baturra
Infirmary
Multnomah County Jail
Portland, Oregon
1975

The young woman screamed, head back, sweat and hot tears dripping down her agonized face into her thick black hair.

The nurse fastened the leather straps around the woman's wrists. She didn't want to do it, but she had to. It was the rule. All prisoners giving birth in the jail's infirmary had to be strapped down, wrists, ankles, and one around the waist. One never knew! A woman could attempt an escape, yes, even one in the throngs of labor, minutes away from giving birth! She could waddle down the hallway, moaning in pain, teeter down the stairs and through the prison yard, without anyone noticing, her hand on her crotch to keep the baby in as she lithely leaped over the barbed wire fence. Escapes were *definitely* against the rules. So straps were always required.

The nurse, Clarissa Hortensen, knew how asinine the rules were. They were made up by men—what could one expect after all? Men thought with their nether regions most of the time. Still. She had to follow the rules or lose her job. She couldn't lose her job. She had four kids, and her clumsy husband had lost his job when he'd broken two vertebrae in his back falling off their roof. She had told him not to get on the roof to fix a hole, but he did it anyhow.

If they had been lucky, this woman would have been in a real hospital. But an unexpected snowstorm hit, the streets were icy, and the prisoner hadn't told anyone she was in labor until it was too late to transport her anyhow. It had also been too late to give her an epidural.

"Let me sit up, let me sit up so I can push!" The woman struggled against the restrictive leather straps as she was hit with another excruciating contraction.

The doctor snapped, "Push, woman, push."

"I can't push right when I can't sit up!" the prisoner yelled back at him, her voice hoarse with pain. "I can hardly breathe!"

"Push unless you want this baby stuck in you forever." The doctor was sweating, too. Dr. Rothney was heavy, in his late fifties, his face blasted with broken red veins.

There were two guards nearby. Both young, both pale and sickly looking. Guarding a murderer awaiting trial giving birth wasn't what they'd signed up for. One leaned over, as if queasy, as the prisoner released a blood-curdling scream again. The other one swallowed hard and stared at the yellowing, cracked wall and tried to think about baseball. They were there to guard the inmate from leaving, but it didn't look like she could get anywhere fast, so it didn't make much sense.

The nurse held the woman's hand. This was against the rules, but no one said anything. Everyone respected Clarissa. Or feared her. Depending on if she thought you were competent or an idiot, and she would tell you which one you were. "You can do this, Betsy. You can do it."

"And if I do?" the murderer, Betsy, panted out. "You're going to take it. You're going to take my baby!" She roared, raw and pained, as another contraction dang near split her in two.

The nurse was tough, but she wanted to cry. It was true. They were taking the baby. Betsy's father, a hypocritical minister, wanted nothing to do with the baby. He had told Clarissa on the phone when she called him and his wife weeks ago about the baby, and told them they could make a claim with the state for the child.

"The girl has sinned," the minister thundered. "She has broken God's law, may Jesus forgive her. She has fallen into sexual sin. She has fallen into the devil's hands. She has committed a crime, and she is bound for hell. We will pray that the Lord removes the evil spirits from within her."

"But do you want the baby?" she'd asked.

"No," the minister said. "It is illegitimate. It is a bastard. We don't want it. We will not bring more of this cursed affliction into—" He stopped then, in the middle of his rant. "Praise the Lord, we are not taking that baby."

Clarissa thought she heard a woman in the background protesting, her voice tearful, but the minister boomed, "Be quiet and obey me, wife," and hung up.

Fortunately, the adoptive parents were waiting downstairs. They had been told that the mother had to give up the baby, as she would be in prison, after her trial, for years. In the highly unlikely, ludicrous event that Betsy was found innocent, the adoptive parents would have to give the baby back to her, as agreed by signed legal papers, but everyone with a brain knew that wasn't going to happen.

"If you don't push, Betsy," Clarissa said, "the baby will die."

Betsy cried then, a gush of tears and hysteria. "I don't want the baby to die," she panted, near hysterical with pain. "I don't want the baby to die. I don't want the baby to die."

"Save her then, Betsy," Clarissa said. "Save her."

Dr. Rothney made a choking sound in his throat. He had worked here in the jail for five years. He hated the job, but it was the only place that would hire him after two—well, *three*—problems at other hospitals. He had almost lost his license but had liquidated his retirement fund, the money that had not been used for gambling and alcohol, and had hired an expensive, effective attorney. He lost his job at the hospital downtown, but here, with lousy pay, they had overlooked his reputation to be an in-house jail doctor.

This young woman had killed a man, that's why she was locked up. But he knew this one's history. He knew about the upcoming trial. He was not convinced Betsy was guilty in the first place. When women killed men, it was usually in self-defense. Like his mother, when she shot her boyfriend in front of him when he was seven years old because he kept slamming her face into a wall.

Between Betsy's shaking legs, Dr. Rothney bent his head. He knew he was a lousy doctor, his alcoholism had a dark, unbreakable grip on him, but he still had a heart. It was covered in regrets and guilt, it was drowned by a painful childhood, but it was still there.

"I want my baby," Betsy cried, chanting to herself as if she'd half lost her mind to pain and grief. "I want her. I love her. I want her. I love her." She convulsed and screamed again, a scream that wound down the corridors of the jail where some women were playing cards, some were chatting, and one was sneaking up on another and then jumped her. The woman who was jumped would end up in the infirmary, slashed with a toothbrush that had been carved into a knife, right across the neck. The woman who attacked the prisoner would end up in solitary, where she would sing to herself about rabbits.

"I love her," Betsy sobbed. "I love you, Rose. I love you. . . ."

Dr. Rothney's eyes filled with tears, but he told himself to buck up. He didn't know how Betsy knew the baby was a girl, but he didn't doubt her. He had checked on her and the pregnancy on several occasions and she was . . . interesting. Almost ethereal. Courageous. He had been brusque with her, though, maybe a little cold, he thought guiltily, not wanting to get involved. Quickly the doctor pushed down his feelings, as he'd done all his life. He stood up, put his hands on Betsy's knees, and ordered, not without compassion, "Push, or you will die, too. Push, Betsy."

Betsy leaned back, sweat dripping, and pushed, not for her but for the baby. It would have been easier if her wrists and waist had not been bound down. It would have been easier if she had been able to sit up, knees bent, but the belt around her prevented that. She pushed. For the baby. Her sweet baby. Their sweet baby. Their love child. Hers and Johnny's daughter.

When nothing happened, and the situation deteriorated to a dangerous, chaotic level, with yelling on both sides, the doctor, after getting a nod of approval from Clarissa, removed the straps around Betsy's waist and ankles so she could sit up and bear down.

The baby's head emerged amidst the mother's guttural screams.

"Almost there, Betsy," Clarissa said, encouraged. "One more push. Huge push. Come on, Betsy."

"She's coming," Dr. Rothney said, red and flushed. "Push! Push!"

Betsy yelled and the guard who had been leaning over his knees, overcome with nausea, tumbled to the floor. The other guard leaned over to check on him, then put both hands to his own forehead. He thought he was going to lose his lunch.

The baby slipped out, head and tiny shoulders, a tummy and legs, but she was quiet, too quiet.

"Is the baby okay?" Betsy cried, collapsing against the bed, her voice exhausted, her body spent. "What's wrong? Why isn't she crying? Is she okay?"

Dr. Rothney took the baby and turned it in his hand, his hands shaking, and gently tapped her back. Lord, he needed a drink.

The baby's eyes met Betsy's. She blinked. Betsy cried, this time with joy tinged with utter, lost sadness. "I love you, I love you, I love you," she whispered. "I love you, Rose."

The baby blinked again at Betsy, still, solemnly quiet, then, after another slap on her back, she started to cry. One wail only, though, as if to say hello, and then she settled back down.

"It's a girl," Clarissa said to Betsy. "But you already knew that." She had seen Betsy several times in the infirmary here because of the pregnancy. They had talked about the daughter Betsy was expecting. Clarissa liked her, even though she assumed she was delusional. Betsy seemed decades older than her years—there was wisdom behind those gold eyes—but she was in mourning for a baby she knew she couldn't keep if she was found guilty at trial. Betsy expected to be found guilty.

Clarissa could hardly wait to go home tonight to her three daughters. She could not imagine giving one of them up. Watching what was to come next for Betsy would rip her heart out. She would hate herself, she knew it, even though she wasn't responsible for what was going to happen. Sometimes women gave birth in here and they were awful criminals, or neglectful and abusive mothers, and their other kids had already been taken away from them, and she was glad the baby was going somewhere else. Not this time.

"Give her to me, please," Betsy begged, sobbing like she was breaking inside. "One time, let me hug her one time. Please. Please."

The doctor knew he shouldn't. It was strictly forbidden. Betsy was in jail awaiting a murder trial. They were taking the baby downstairs to the adoptive parents immediately. But he looked at Betsy, crumpled in the bed, her pale face a mix of tears and desperation and devastation. She was so young. Thick, dark black hair. Thin. High cheekbones. Huge eyes, golden, like he'd never seen before. He needed a drink so bad. God almighty, he needed a drink.

The doctor turned to the guards—the one who had fainted now leaning woozily against the wall, and the other one who looked like he wanted to be anywhere but here—and spoke with authority. "You may go now."

After the guards scuttled out, Dr. Rothney glanced at Clarissa. She nodded and unstrapped Betsy's wrists. The doctor did not bother to strap her waist or her ankles up again, breaking all rules. The doctor gave the baby to the nurse, who cleaned her quickly, wrapped her in a pink blanket, and gave the baby to Betsy while the doctor finished his job between Betsy's legs.

Betsy cried over her daughter, the nurse's hand on her shoulder.

Thirty minutes later someone knocked on the door when Betsy was singing to Rose, a song about a girl who is loved by her mother and dances in a rose garden. "Privacy for the patient," the doctor ordered. The knocking stopped.

Thirty minutes later, while Betsy cooed and sang and told her daughter, Rose, that she loved her, would always love her, there was another knock. "Privacy for the patient! Don't interrupt."

Dr. Rothney felt ill. He knew that he would have to take this baby from the mother soon. He would have Clarissa help. It was going to be an awful scene. It would haunt him, he knew. This wasn't the first time this had happened, but this time it would be the worst, by far.

He hated this job, he did.

He watched Betsy cradle the little girl in the pink blanket, the baby's eyes wide open, the two of them staring at each other. Betsy kissed the baby on her forehead, her little nose, her full cheeks. She was a gorgeous baby, alert, with dark hair and golden eyes—not blue, as usual, but golden, like her mother. It was so strange, the doctor thought, he had never seen eyes that color in a newborn . . . it was almost unheard of. . . .

After forty-five minutes there was another knock. "The parents are waiting."

"Privacy for the patient!" the doctor yelled, irritated, bracing for the excruciating scene to come.

"Oh no!" Betsy cried. "Oh no, please, please! I need more time." She clung to the baby, sung to her, told her she loved her, that she looked like a pink rose.

The doctor wanted an entire bottle of scotch.

The nurse wanted to go home and hug her daughters. She sniffed and tried not to cry.

"I'm so sorry," Clarissa said. "I'm going to have to take her."

Betsy refused, tears running down her cheeks and onto the baby's face, through the black hair that grew soft around her gentle features. "No, no, I am begging you. Let me hold her." She started to get hysterical. The baby never cried as she stared into her mother's eyes, the same as hers.

The doctor ran a shaking hand over his bald head as Betsy begged for her baby.

Dr. Rothney wearily nodded at Clarissa. The nurse went to a cabinet and got a shot ready. The shot was administered when Betsy was staring into the soft eyes of her daughter with such love. "I'll always be with you, Rose," she whispered. "I love you."

Within seconds, Betsy was asleep, her arms slack, and Clarissa took the baby away and gave her to her new parents, who were so happy they cried, too.

Later that night, Dr. Rothney and Clarissa, both emotionally wrung out, checked on Betsy together. Betsy was restrapped to the bed, wrists and ankles, with another strap around her waist.

Betsy had woken up from being drugged and had leaped into hysteria. She screamed, fought to get out of her restraints, and pleaded to see her daughter. She had sobbed, right from the heart, a wrenching, pathetic sound. Clarissa had tried to calm her, but of course it hadn't worked.

Betsy glared at them with a ferocity that took both of them back. Still, they were used to it here. Patients often looked at them with hatred. They had taken her baby from her; there was no other way for her to look at them.

"You," she said to the doctor, "are going to die in two years. Your liver is like a pickle. Your girlfriend is going to leave you soon. She's going to take your guitar collection."

The doctor swallowed hard. How did she know about his liver problem? How did she know he had a girlfriend? How did she know about the guitar collection?

"And you," she said to the nurse, "are pregnant. It's a boy."

The nurse knew that wasn't true. Her husband had a vasectomy three months ago. He'd told her so.

"Your husband lied to you," Betsy said. "Also, your oldest daughter is going to overdose on drugs." Then she softened, some of her anger gone. "She'll be wearing a red dress and knee-high black boots when it happens, so look for that outfit."

That was ridiculous, Clarissa thought with a healthy dose of anger. She had even had sympathy for this girl! Well, that was all gone now. "Don't say that. Don't you dare talk about my daughter like that!"

But the doctor and nurse were both stricken. They knew, even though the trial had not started yet, that Betsy said she had committed murder because she'd had a "premonition" about the man she'd killed. The man was going to kill his son, Johnny Kandinsky, her boyfriend, the father of the baby. The press had had a field day, calling her Premonition Betsy. And Betsy the Beautiful Fortune-Teller. And Crystal Ball Betsy.

"You took my baby away from me," Betsy said. "You took her." Then she began to cry, from the deepest part of her shattered soul.

The doctor and the nurse had the moral sense, amidst their own shock at the patient's premonitions, to feel guilty and sick.

The doctor got super drunk that night and called in sick the next day.

The nurse went home and hugged her oldest daughter extra close.

The doctor's girlfriend left him the same week that Betsy's trial started. She took his guitar collection. He never saw her again. He thought of Betsy and the baby she had lost, and the trial that was being widely covered in the papers. Only the whack jobs believed Betsy truly had a premonition about the father killing his son, her boyfriend. But now she'd predicted, exactly, that his girlfriend was going to leave him and take his guitar collection. Could she really have premonitions?

Guilt washed over him again for his part in taking the baby, and he felt as if he were drowning. Yes, it was his job, but still. He grabbed the fifth of vodka beside him and drank it like milk. Then he stopped. Betsy had also told him that he was going to die in two years, his liver a pickle. He decided he didn't care. He drank again.

Dr. Rothney died as he lived, in pain, lonely, and alone, thinking of his own mother, who had gone to jail for shooting her boyfriend to protect herself, to protect him. On his last day on Earth, exactly two years after the premonition, he thought of

Betsy and her baby and the last beat of his heart was filled with a deep sadness.

Clarissa, the nurse, found out she was pregnant a week later. Her husband had lied to her about the vasectomy. What a selfish, dense man, was her first thought. My God. She had married a man stupid enough to think he could get away with it. She kicked him out, and he spent six months begging her to take him back. He presented new papers showing he'd had a vasectomy. Their fifth child was a gift, a comfort as they dealt with their oldest daughter's drug addiction.

On the night that her husband told her that her daughter was wearing a red dress and knee-high black boots when she ran from the house, Clarissa and her husband frantically searched for her, based on Betsy's premonition. They found her in the back room of a drug house. She almost died. Clarissa did CPR, and the ambulance came.

The daughter later became a kindergarten teacher. Her parents were so proud.

The nurse never forgot Betsy. Her premonitions had come true and she had saved Clarissa's daughter's life. For the rest of her life, the nurse prayed for Betsy.

Chapter 3

〜

I own a bookstore called Evie's Books, Cake, and Tea because that's what I sell: books, cake, and tea. Someone I loved with all my soul taught me to love all three, so it was an easy decision.

I also sell coffee, hot and rich, and the special delicious types: mochas and lattes with whipped cream and frothiness. I sell giant chocolate chip cookies, the size of a kid's face; banana and pumpkin bread; scones and "clotted cream"; and pie, when the fruit is fresh. I buy everything from the bakery down the street, owned by Bettina, a longtime friend of my mother and aunts.

I sell my mother's bouquets. The ones that are labeled, in scrawling black calligraphy, "A Woman's Power Is Nothing to Mess With, So Don't Mess With Me," and "Ladies Need Luck and Wine," and "Play Naughty More, Fret Less" sell quickly.

I sell my aunt Camellia's lotions and potions with names like Lavender Lust, Tulip Tootles, Daffodil Delights, Sexy Snowdrops, and Shasta Daisy Shenanigans.

I sell my aunt Iris's photographs of oddly interesting/sometimes creepy/always gorgeous flowers. Sometimes they seem to be rather phallic to me, or representative of a vagina, but people love them.

People come in to buy books and to sit down for tea or coffee and treats in the café area.

It's a medium-large bookstore. The outside has an old-fashioned, traditional, two-story appearance, yellow with white trim, a picture window where Ghost often sits and watches people walk by, and two faux white pillars by the door.

Inside, the walls are a light yellow and all the bookshelves are white. I have a floor-to-ceiling wall of windows in the back that overlook Whale Bay in North Sound. In the café, there are tables of all colors and shapes and sizes—light blue, yellow, pink, sage green, and purple. I have two long rectangle tables, both painted red, and we pull them together for book clubs and when people come here in groups.

There's also a deck, which people love to sit on so they can watch the ocean, the seagulls, the whales, and any other wildlife that pops its head up.

The ceiling is high, with bare wood rafters. I've hung three huge chandeliers for some fancy bling, all bought when part of an old home fell down in a windstorm and the ninety-year-old owner decided to move because he had fallen back in love with his ex-wife who lived in Anchorage.

I have also hung colorful umbrellas upside down. One wall has white wallpaper with yellow roses because I love roses and need them at home and work. The floors are the original wood and creaky. I will never change them. This building was one of the first built on the island, over one hundred years ago. It was a feed and grain store. It was also a saloon at one time, with a part-time hooker in the upstairs bedroom, and then it was an Italian restaurant that went belly-up. The food was awful.

Upstairs there is a children's book loft on one side, and on the other side is my office, a staff room, and a supply room.

My shop is in the middle of a string of shops on the main street of our town, called Chrysanthemum Way. We cater to the tourists from June to October. It gets quiet around here from November to May, so I work even harder to get the locals in, not only on our island but from the other three islands, during that time. Ways to get people in? Book clubs.

Book clubs social dynamics are interesting. We have fiction and nonfiction book clubs. We have a women's fiction club called Women's Wine and Lit—about twelve people, three of them men. There's the Science Fiction Nerd Book club—about seven diehards, four men and three women. I even have a Classics-Only Group for Serious Readers. Seven women, one man, an ex-literature professor.

Sometimes the people in the book clubs will vehemently disagree. You want an argument? Try a book with a mix of religion and politics together and you can have a literary firestorm. One night a woman smashed her pumpkin bread into another woman's face to "make her shut up." They were neighbors, too. The neighbor with pumpkin bread on her face actually picked up a plate to swing it, but I caught it in midflight like a frisbee.

In a women's-only ten-member weekly fiction book club named Book Babes, the members have been together about twenty years. They come from all of the islands.

They will ardently discuss every aspect of the book from character development to the theme, but they'll later get into "women talk," which is often hilarious. If their husbands/boyfriends only knew what their wives talked about in book club, they'd want to curl up and die.

I, or a member of my small staff, also host a chess group twice a month. One of our members won a junior national's champion. Board Game Night on Friday nights. Trivial Pursuit on Saturday nights. And on Sunday night, after hours, we host about forty people who are starting a new church. The minister is young and smart and doesn't beat people over the head with a Bible. Plus, he loves science and history, and buys a bunch of books from me on both.

We serve all the people in the groups scrumptious cake, tea, coffee, and other treats, and inevitably they buy books and other stuff on the way out.

In short, I do whatever I can to stay in business.

I'm at Evie's Books, Cake, and Tea at least fifty hours a week. I love being here, I love being around books and other people who love books. Books distracted me from a lot of terror and fear and overwhelming guilt during my childhood and beyond, because I could dive into another world and disappear.

I do not like terror, I do not like fear or guilt, but I do like books. I read all the time and have stacks and stacks of books at home that often topple over. It's almost embarrassing how many I have. I could well be a book hoarder, but I know this: Books have saved my life.

"Hello, Mom, hello, aunts," I said, walking into Rose Bloom Cottage, the sprawling, quirky two-story white home that my mother and aunts grew up in. It is eighty-five years old and sits on twelve acres. Part of the property overlooks the ocean, where we have a small beach. You can sit and look at the lights twinkling on the other three islands nearby.

They have an enormous garden, flowers in rows and bunches, and wide borders. Daffodils. Tulips. Irises. Peonies. Lilies. Ranunculus. Hydrangea. Stephanotis. Sweet peas. Foxgloves. Wildflowers. Sunflowers. Delphinium. Gladiolas. Hyacinth. And rows and rows of roses: Claude Monet rose, Lady Diana, Raspberry Swirl, Blue Moon, Painted Moon, Twiggy's Rose, Cinnamon Dolce, Marilyn Monroe, George Burns, Cary Grant, on and on.

They also have a huge greenhouse, where they grow many flowers, and vegetable starts, and an impressive collection of orchids with names like Miltonia, Laelia, Slipper, and Aerides.

In summer and fall, Rose Bloom Cottage is near covered in climbing roses drooping over arbors and arches and trellises, roses that their mother almost frenetically planted in her quest to create a "fairy-tale rose castle." Every year, for months, it's like having pink, red, and white blooming magic swirling all over the house.

"Hello, honey." My mom, Poppy, stood up and hugged me. "I think you need some daisies in your life." She touched my nose. I knew that she knew I'd had a premonition and saved the girl. Hence, the daisy comment, which is her way of saying, "Let's get you into a bubble bath with a mongo-sized glass of wine and a piece of pie so your brain doesn't flame out and explode again as it has in the past, and I love you!"

My aunt Camellia said, bent over the stove and stirring soup, "I'm making you tomato soup." Which in code meant, "Tomato soup will calm your nerves from what happened today with the truck and boost your inner soul's desire to be serene."

My aunt Iris said, "Hello, Evie. How was your day at the bookstore? Did you tell anyone off with that temper of yours?" Which meant, "Let's not get sappy, it's so irritating."

"The bookstore was crowded. No, I didn't tell anyone off today. I resisted." Now and then I can get a little heated at my bookstore with customers. Especially if someone says, "I don't read." I get irritated *thinking* about that comment. *You don't read?* Then what do you *do?* How do you *live* without books, you fool?

"You did not tell anyone, 'Only stupid people don't read'?" my mother asked.

I felt my brow furrow. Sometimes I swear my mother reads my mind. "No. No stupid comments."

"So you created a Zen-like atmosphere," Aunt Camellia said, waving her arms around. "Peaceful."

"Yes. Zen-like," I said.

"You didn't draw blood," Aunt Iris drawled, drinking a beer. "We're proud of you. Violence isn't the answer most of the time. Especially around books."

"I always say no to violence around books."

My mother and Aunt Camellia and Aunt Iris are in their seventies. They have all let their hair grow white, and it is stunning. It used to be blonde. They all have dark brown eyes, like chocolate, but that's where the resemblance ends.

Aunt Iris is the oldest. She's about five ten and sturdy, with high model-like cheekbones. Her white hair has a short and sensible cut.

Aunt Camellia is next. She's about five two with curly white hair that she wears midway down her back. She likes makeup and perfume and her lotions.

My mother is the youngest. She curves. I still see men look at her. She has a welcoming, lopsided smile; her hair is in a bell shape; and her dark brown eyes are huge.

Their mother named them after flowers because she wasn't quite right in the head.

Every day my mother and aunts wear a hat, but not ordinary hats.

Two walls in our home are filled with the most exquisite, interesting hats. Hats from the twenties, thirties, forties, all the way up. Hats with feathers, ribbons, birds, pom-pom balls, sequins, and beading. Hats made from straw. Hats with wide brims and tight brims. Hats that are two feet high, and hats that hang over an eye. Hats with netting, gauze, lace, satin, and silk. Hats that look like they came off the British Royal family, and hats from *Alice in Wonderland* and the Kentucky Derby and Dr. Seuss.

Every day they grab a hat, add a few fresh flowers, and head out the door. They are called The Hat Ladies. They love it.

"We heard you almost killed yourself saving a little girl today," Aunt Iris said. "Shot down the street like a bat out of hell. A stampeding elk. Or a crazy lady, depending on who's talking about it."

"Your spirit is always giving," Aunt Camellia said. "It's a kaleidoscope of generosity."

"My spirit is old and tired," I said.

"Be careful, honey," my mother said. "Please. You were way too close today."

"After your mother heard what you did and how close you came to becoming human roadkill," Aunt Iris said, "she had to go and lay in the back of the shop with a glass of wine or two or more."

"You should try not to worry your mother like that," Aunt Camellia said. I heard the reprimand. My mother nodded. "It's bad for my heart."

"There is nothing wrong with your heart, Mother."

"There could be if you don't stop scaring me."

"You should apologize to your mother," Aunt Iris said. "She looked positively white for hours."

This conversation would have been ludicrous in a normal family. I was supposed to apologize to my mother because she heard I had a close call saving a little girl's life and this made my mother worry and guzzle wine?

I saw my aunts' stern expressions. We are not normal. "I'm sorry, Momma."

"No apology necessary, lovey," my mother said, patting her heart.

I decided to change the topic. "How was the shop today?"

"Busy," my mother said. She pulled out the chair beside me at the long wood table my grandfather built. He used to shoot deer, bring it home, and cut it up right here. Fish he caught from the ocean, and the chickens he kept for dinner were fixed up right here, too.

Above us was an oversized chandelier my grandmother bought in one of her not-so-sane moments from a hotel that was shutting down in Seattle. My grandma liked it because it was a "twinkling light for a magical fairy, surely you can see them flying around the crystals?"

Our family likes chandeliers. We like sparkles. There are even crystal knobs on the light blue kitchen cabinets and on the drawers of their oversized island, which is painted lavender with a granite top. Over each set of two French doors that lead to the backyard, Aunt Camellia has hung a group of faux crystals, "for spiritual blessings and continued happy sex lives."

In winter, they light a fire in the fireplace; in summer, they light candles inside the fireplace. With the French doors open, we can hear the ocean's waves and feel the wind drifting in, soft and smooth.

"We met with a lot of semi-hysterical brides about their wedding flowers," my mother said. "Two called in, we met with two on Skype, and two came in. They're all jittery. Nervous. Only one was relaxed and happy. She didn't seem bright, but she may have been stoned."

"She was stoned," Aunt Iris said. "She smelled like a skunk." Aunt Iris is the blunt and practical aunt. She calls things like she sees them. Or smells them.

"Oh, the joys and spiritual awakenings that occur during wedding planning," Aunt Camellia said, coming over to the table. She pushed a piece of chocolate cheesecake toward me. I would have no more than one or two slices. I deserved it after the running I did this morning. That was exhausting. My butt still hurt. I rubbed my butt.

"Some spirits are awoken in brides that are dangerous and hysterical," Aunt Camellia went on, sitting by me. "I think the blonde one should slather my nerve-calming rose lotions on herself. She had definitely lost her inner peace. She had a twitch in her eye, and she kept wringing her hands and saying, 'I *do* want to get married. I do *want* to get married.' And I said to her, 'Do you want to get married?' and she started massaging her neck and then she squeaked like a mouse and had to go outside and bend over. She called later and canceled."

"I had one on the phone today who was hyperventilating," Aunt Iris said. "Then she started getting absolutely specific about each floral arrangement for her wedding. I hate when the type As get married. They have to micromanage. I don't think she appreciated it when I told her that if she didn't chill out she'd have a heart attack on her wedding day."

"Wonderful image to give to a bride, Aunt Iris."

"I tell the truth." She reached for a second beer. Iris likes beer.

"We're getting into Panicked Bride Season," Aunt Camellia said, "which means we all have to take time each day for meditation and tranquility."

"Yes," Aunt Iris said. "And beer. Or tequila."

"We need to put my tranquility lotions on our wrists for pulse-comfort, and on our necks for soothing our airways, and behind our knees for joint health," Aunt Camellia said.

Yes, lotion solves all those problems according to my aunt Camellia.

"But your sister," Aunt Iris said to me, "she is the perfect bride. No Godzilla there. She simply wants a huge party and dancing."

"Ah yes," Aunt Camellia said. "Jules won't have a normal wedding, thank goodness."

"It will be a glorious day," my mother said, arms outstretched. "Glorious. I will wear my best hat."

Her sisters nodded. I knew they were already sketching out their Jules' Wedding Day Hats.

My sister, Jules, only eleven months younger than me, is getting married on the island this summer, right here at Rose

Bloom Cottage. I adore Jules. We have always been best friends. The only problem is that she lives in Seattle and not here on the island.

"Who is ready for meditation?" Aunt Camellia asked about an hour later.

My mom and aunts were ready, and they started getting up.

"A little cold out there, isn't it?" I asked. I eyed the chocolate cheesecake on the counter. I could definitely have two pieces. The sprinting I did that morning should cover it.

"Nonsense, Evie," my mother said. "Come and relax. You've worked hard."

"Cool air cleans out the negativity," Aung Camellia said.

"Cool air means you can chill out," Aunt Iris said. "After what you did this morning, you need some chill, girl. Here. Have a beer."

I certainly did need some chill, but I don't like beer.

They grabbed their yoga mats. I grabbed another slice of chocolate cheesecake. I knew they'd settle them on the slight rise above the ocean, then they'd strip naked, touch their fingers together over their crossed knees, close their eyes, and meditate.

They believe that outside naked meditation drives the negative away. At least Aunt Camellia does. My mother believes the wind on her skin makes her skin younger, and Aunt Iris believes beer tastes better naked.

I believe those three do many strange things. Sometimes they drink too much in town, and the police chief, Chief Allroy—a longtime friend of theirs along with his wife, Daneesha—brings them home. Sometimes they lead people in raucous songs in the town square. For Halloween they dress up as sexy witches and pass out candy. For Christmas they dress up like Mrs. Claus and hand out candy canes.

They are known for skinny-dipping and jumping off rocks into our two lakes, and they host San Orcanita's Drag Racing Party at the end of the island, which is a popular annual event with a town potluck afterward. You have to dress in drag and drive a homemade go-cart. That annual drunken event happened two weeks ago. Only two people had to have stitches:

eighty-year-old Marge, who flipped her car, and fourteen-year-old Keely, who crashed but won in her age group and was proud of the blood dripping down her face. She took a smiling selfie. The doctor was on hand and stitched them both up right there.

They also host and organize an annual boat race between the islands. Aunt Camellia usually wins.

To put it plainly: They do what they dang well want. All the time. And they invite everyone on the island to do it with them.

I love them.

We all headed out into the dark night, the moon a glowing white ball, the stars spectacular, the rows and rows of flowers they use in their floral business swaying in the slight wind, the scents of a galaxy of roses wafting by.

"Good night," I called out as I headed to what we call the carriage house. I do not need to see them naked.

"Good night, dear," my mom said.

"You're a bit ancient in your thinking," Aunt Camellia called out. "There's nothing wrong with getting close to your soul while meditating in the raw. Rawness brings truth."

"Don't bother her," Aunt Iris said. She always defends me and respects my decisions, even if she does it in a cranky way. "If she doesn't want to meditate, she doesn't have to. A woman should never do something she doesn't want to do. She should say no, then drink a beer."

"It would help," my mother whispered, but I heard it. "She's wound too tight."

"I heard that, Mom," I called out.

"Sorry, dear. But it would."

I knew what she was talking about. I didn't think naked meditation would help at all.

I said hello to all my animals on the way home: two alpacas—Virginia Alpaca and Alpaca Joe; two black-and-white goats—Mr. Bob and Trixie Goat; two horses—Shakespeare and Jane Austen; four cats—Mars, Jupiter, Venus, and Ghost; and five lambs—Padre, Momma, Jay Rae, Raptor, and The TMan.

Sundance, my seventeen-year-old dog, who has gone through

several nervous breakdowns with me, ran right toward me on his three legs as soon as I left Rose Bloom Cottage and stood up on his hind legs for a hug. That golden, furry mutt is my life. I swear he's a human covered in fur.

His fellow dog brothers, Butch and Cassidy, wiggled their tails while I pet them and gave them a hug. They are both shades of brown. I pulled on my farm boots and gloves and a light jacket; checked and replenished all of the animals' food and water; dumped more hay out for the horses; told the goats not to escape again, as they did regularly; promised Jane Austen I'd ride her again soon; and talked with the sheep about how cute they are.

About an hour and a half later, I headed home to the carriage house, my home. The cats and dogs came with me. It was almost time for bed, and everyone would soon be snoring in my bedroom—yes, the dogs and cats mixed together. It is what it is.

I love my animals. They have kept me relatively sane for years.

I went to bed that night and pulled a book off the top of my stack. Then I pulled out the third book down. That was a bad move. The whole stack fell over. I sighed. Book hoarding.

I tried to read but thought this: I had not seen Marco in six days and twelve hours.

It bangs my heart up to see that man, as I know I can never be with him, for the worst reason, but I still want that glimpse. I want to see the smile or hear the laugh.

And after I see him? I take my banged-up heart and go back to being alone.

I try to avoid the house at all costs.

I'll even take a longer route to make sure I don't have to see it, to remember, but I couldn't today. I had to bring Torrance Maricello his books, and he lived on the same road out in the country, so I had to pass it. Torrance is eighty and recently had surgery, and couldn't come in to the bookstore.

The house is tucked back in the trees, in the middle of a field, a little ways out of town. The wildflowers and feverfew and irises would bloom soon, an old willow to one side, a gnarled oak tree in the front. Weeds had overtaken much of the yard.

It used to be charming, a bright yellow home with white trim and a green door. Now it wasn't. I had many memories that were stuck behind the dirty, ragged white picket fence and in the backyard, by the pond. There were memories at the end of a rope swing hanging from the willow tree, in the highest branches of the oak tree, and in a fort that has since fallen down behind the house.

Inside the house, too, were memories. In the kitchen with hand-painted yellow tiles. In a back bedroom painted a cheerful pink.

The pink bedroom didn't match with the blood in the kitchen.

I sniffled as my eyes filled with tears.

What happened there was my fault and I have never forgotten it, never forgiven myself. I had been young, yes, but I had known better.

"Can you believe I'm getting married? Me. Antiestablishment. Antitradition. Anti, what else am I anti?"

"A lot, Jules, you sister-rebel." I held the phone in my hand, Sundance walking along beside me as I headed down to the beach the next night to watch the sunset. I was in my usual uniform, jeans and a purple, hippie-ish top with a ruffle at the hem. I like my clothes flowing. I like embroidery on them, especially if there are roses. I like dangly earrings and bracelets, but I rarely wear necklaces, as they can make me feel like I'm choking. You could say my style is: easy, colorful, flowing, embroidered, and painted island style. With rock band T-shirts thrown in now and then when I'm feeling musical.

Mars, Jupiter, Venus, and Ghost were tumbling behind me somewhere, and Butch and Cassidy had run ahead, barking, their tongues hanging out as if they'd forgotten to put them back in. Behind me, my mother and aunts' daffodils and tulips, ready to bloom, were swaying with the wind.

"Yes. I'm a rebel and I'm getting married. How can that be?"

"You found a biker who matched your coolness. You found love and lust and now you're going to stand in front of a minister and say 'I do.' " I grabbed the baggie in my pocket. There were only a few chocolates in there. Mocha. Divinity. Chocolate sprinkles. I was eating them because of the health value. Dark chocolate helps with immunity and all, or something like that.

"Jay Dove Boy is a minister, he got a paper off the internet that says so, and he's Mack's best friend from when they were nine years old and he's going to marry us and make us one. He says it's the biggest honor of his life and he knows exactly what he's going to wear: his favorite motorcycle leathers. It'll be awesome."

Jules's real name is Julie, but no one ever calls her that. I started calling her Jules when I first started talking, and it stuck. We don't look anything alike. I have black hair halfway down my back and golden eyes, she has long blonde hair and the dark brown eyes of my mother and aunts. She's five eleven, I'm five three.

My sister launched a company ten years ago in Seattle. She did not like school, because she has a mild case of dyslexia and she felt like "a damn failure, and stupid." She was super popular in school because she is like my mother and aunts: always up for a party, willing to dance, game to laugh. But continually getting poor grades in school no matter how hard she tried, no matter how hard she cried with frustration, was simply too discouraging.

But she was always, from the time she was three, an artist. We couldn't believe the pictures and portraits she drew. She utterly loved art, and she drew pictures of me all the time with a huge smile that took up most of my face. At three years old she started calling me her "love-sister."

After high school she worked in a coffee shop in Seattle and created her art at night. She fell in love with motorcycles when she was nineteen because of a boyfriend. She later ditched the boyfriend, not her motorcycle. She painted her own motorcycle with a picture of her as a horse/woman, her long blonde hair flowing, and people loved it. Her business, custom paint jobs for motorcycles, Jules's Daring Designs, was born.

She's painted everything on motorcycles from skeletons wearing jeans to flames to the galaxy to people to flowers to plaids and checkerboards to swirls and twirls. Sometimes people want simply one color, pink or blue or red, and she'll do that. Most of the time, though, they'll ask for more, and the customer and Jules will create a design together.

She is so talented and has a wait time of six months.

Jules has tattoos. She has a pink rose, which is for me, on her left arm. She said she never thought of me as any other flower than a pink rose. Next to the rose, in a bouquet, is an iris for Aunt Iris, a camellia for Aunt Camellia, and a poppy for our mother. She has a small orca with our dad's name, Henry, below that.

She has a heart near her privates with an arrow pointing down (don't ask any questions then I don't have to answer them); a picture of Rose Bloom Cottage on her left shoulder blade; and her fiancé, Mack, and she got matching tattoos of their two motorcycles together, which are on her right shoulder blade. On her right arm she has a tattoo of Mack's face, smiling and sweet, and he has a tattoo of her on his left arm, smiling and sweet, so when they stand next together, their tattoo faces smile at each other.

My sister has three hoop earrings in each ear. She has a small diamond stud piercing above her top lip. She looks wild and free and men love her. She finds many men annoying and condescending and tells them so.

We are so different, and I so love her. I'm going to be her maid of honor when she gets married this summer right here, on our property, the garden in full bloom, roses everywhere. Her fiancé, burly, huge, big beard, tattoos, six foot six, is a pediatric nurse. The kids love him because they can see his heart, as all kids seem to be able to do.

"Evie," she gushed. "Hang on to your hat, hang on to your butt, your maid of honor dress is being made."

"I've got ahold of my butt. Not wearing a hat. What does it look like?"

"I'm not telling you! It's a surprise! Also, I'm pretty sure I know what I'm wearing for my wedding shoes."

"Heels? Flats?"

"It's a surprise!" She laughed. "And I know what my cake is going to be like."

"Should I ask?"

"Nope. It's a surprise!"

I could hear her glee. That's all I needed to hear: her glee. She was so excited to marry Mack. I loved the guy. He was a perfect teddy bear for her, a man with a hard childhood who had left home at fifteen and never looked back. Because of his background he has compassion for others, insight into himself and life, and he knew, without a shadow of a doubt, that Jules was his whole world. "She's my apple pie, Evie," he told me. "My apple pie."

And that's all you need to know when someone is getting married: Does the fiancé think that she's his whole world? His apple pie? If that answer is a yes, ya got a winner.

"I can't wait for your wedding, Jules. I'm going to dance and shake my tail."

"Me too. I'm going to shake my tail. Last night, in bed, after Mack and I, well, you know, and then I started to cry"—she started to cry—"and I told him I couldn't wait until we were married, and he kissed me and said the same thing, and he's so good in bed, and I love him and he held me all night long like he always does . . ." She sniffled. "He's a hugger. He's like a pillow. He's like my blanket. He's warm and snuggly . . . as soon as we get home from work we get right into bed. He makes me feel so much better. After some bang-bang, we get up and he feeds and waters me." She sniffled. I tried not to laugh. Fed and watered!

"I love him so much, Evie. Last week he bought me a sexy sprite outfit. He knows how much I like sprites." She blew her nose. "He even bought the wings and the high heels and fishnets."

I did not know that sprites wore fishnets, but you can learn something each day if you're lookin' for it. I listened to my sister tell me all about Mack in bed while I ate my chocolates at the beach so I can be perfectly healthy for the wedding.

Sundance climbed onto my lap. He's excited about the wedding, too, I'm sure.

Later that night, after I knocked over not one but two stacks of books in my kitchen nook, I thought of Marco, in a tux, waiting for me by the gazebo, as I walked down the aisle in a wedding dress.

That would never happen.

Oh, heart, calm down. Stop breaking. Eat pie.

Chapter 4

〜

"This mermaid didn't have a green tail, like all the other mermaids."

"She didn't?"

"No. Her tail was the color of all the flowers in your mother's garden."

"Purple?"

"Yes."

"Yellow and gold?"

"Yes."

"Did she have the colors of roses in her tail?"

"Pink, red, and white."

"Why was she different?"

"Because she was special. She was a special mermaid with black hair and gold eyes."

"But I have black hair and gold eyes!"

"She looked a lot like you, only you don't have a mermaid tail, do you?"

"No. You're silly."

"I'm going to tell you the story of the mermaid. Her name was Serafina."

"Does she swim in our ocean?"

"She does."

"Where does she live?"

"In her castle, right out there, past our beach. Her garden is made of coral and seashells."

"Can I see her?"

"You can in your imagination."

Chapter 5

⁓

"What do you mean you've never read historical fiction?" I stared at the woman in my bookstore in wonder. "Never?"

She blinked a few times at me in confusion. "Uh. No. Never."

"What do you read?"

"I read romance."

"And what else?" I asked. "What other genres?"

"That's it."

She was about fifty years old. I was darn near stunned. "You have to be kidding. All you read is romance?" Now, I don't have anything against romance. I read a few romances a year. They take you out of life and you're safe in the book: You know everything's going to work out for this couple in the end. No surprises. But what about variety?

"Well. Uh. Yes."

She seemed a bit alarmed by my strong reaction. She should be! This was ridiculous! "I'm sorry, but I am not going to let you leave this store until you find a historical fiction book to read. Here." I pulled out one book, then another, then another. "There's three books. These are all my favorites. Go to that table right there by the window and try them out. Pick one." I looked at her sadly and shook my head. "You need to read something new. You can't read one type of book all of the time, or your brain will drip out of your head and congeal on the floor. Do you want your brain to congeal?"

"Yuck. No. Not today." She obediently took the books and

read the backs, one by one. "I haven't read anything like this since school."

"Then it's time you darn well did." I crossed my arms and glared at her. "You have to read in different genres. You have to keep learning and thinking and learning and thinking. How do you do that if you read in the same genre all the time? You can't. It's impossible."

I needed a piece of carrot cake. This was unbelievable. Stuck in a rut with reading. That should be illegal. Everybody should read all types of books. In fact, we should have a day off each month where everyone is required to stay home and read and read and eat their favorite cake.

She didn't seem startled by my exasperation anymore. She seemed intrigued. "Okay," she said. "I'll do it."

"That's right you'll do it. I cannot have someone in my bookstore who is this rigid in their literary thinking."

She went and sat at a table right by the window, the sunlight streaming in, the tiny island in the ocean beyond a green jewel. I breathed out. I don't know why I get so mad at people about books, but I do. Books should be treasured. Books should be read as regularly as one brushes one's own teeth. I read each day before bed. I read when I have free time. I read when I don't have free time. I read to hold premonitions at bay. I read to laugh. I read for knowledge and information and history. I read to see someone else's perspective or their lives or their challenges and how they beat the heck out of those challenges.

I brought her lemon tea and a piece of pumpkin cake with cream cheese icing as a peace offering because once I simmered down, I felt guilty. Customers should not be attacked. The woman was deep into one of the books I'd chosen for her, and she barely looked up. I sat at her table and ate a slice of pumpkin cake, too. Pumpkin cake has pumpkin in it, therefore it is part vegetable.

"I'm sorry I got mad at you," I said. I had calmed down.

"No problem." She didn't look up from her book. "Thanks for the pumpkin cake."

That woman bought all three of the books I suggested. She will be a happier person now that's she broken out of her literary cell.

Virginia Alpaca was sick.

She was listless, lying on the ground, not moving much, her eyes dull, but then she would get up, then down, then stand up again. She wasn't eating. I bent down and gave her a little hug. Virginia is one of the smallest alpacas I've seen. She is sweet and petite. "Virginia, what's wrong?" She turned those tired eyes toward me. "Are you sick?"

Alpaca Joe leaned over her, as if asking the same question, then he turned and spit on the ground. Alpaca Joe's a spitter. It's like watching a baseball player with tobacco in his mouth, spitting away. "Yuck, Alpaca Joe," I told him. He heard me. He spit again and looked at me. Alpaca Joe can be obstinate. "I saw that."

Virginia Alpaca leaned against me. She was not curious or alert, her normal state. "Okay, Virginia. We have to go and see Dr. Marco."

I tried to breathe through that tingling, happy thought. I wasn't glad that my dear Virginia Alpaca was sick, but I was suddenly all a-jittery at the thought of going to see Marco, my handsome vet, who moved here almost a year ago. I called and made an appointment, then called the bookstore and told one of my employees, Tiala, that I would be late.

"You know Maeve is coming in, right, Evie?"

"Shoot. I forgot. I'll come by." Maeve is the bookkeeper and accountant. I had all the paperwork here at home. I had worked on it last night, then promised myself a mystery book. I ate a slice of raspberry pie while I tried to figure out who did it. I was wrong!

I pulled on clean jeans, lacy white lingerie, and a flowing white cotton shirt with a slightly too-low V and embroidered red roses on the front. I brushed out the tangles in my hair and pulled on gold hoop earrings and red, gold, and yellow bracelets that Jules bought me when she went to Mexico. I slipped my feet into red flip-flops, put on some of Aunt Camellia's pink rose lotion called Let Me Love You, and was ready.

I grabbed the paperwork, then tried not to smile and giggle like a fool at the thought of seeing Marco.

It is fortunate that Virginia Alpaca likes to ride in my truck. I put a rope around her neck and asked her to stand up. She refused at first because she is not feeling well, so I had to go and get a treat. That did it. She stood up. Behind us Alpaca Joe spit and followed us out. I shut the gate on him so he couldn't come, and he bucked and spit more and made grumpy alpaca sounds. He gets anxiety when Virginia Alpaca is gone.

Virginia Alpaca did not look back at all. Sometimes I wonder if Alpaca Joe is a little too possessive and she enjoys her freedom. She climbed in the truck. She's not that big, only 115 pounds, and I pushed the seat way back so it worked. In my back window I could see Sundance in my driveway, already eagerly waiting for me to come home, that sweet dog. I waved, and he barked back, tottering a bit on his three legs.

I drove my truck past Rose Bloom Cottage, noting the red and pink and white roses getting ready to bloom all over the trellises and patios.

I turned down the quiet roads, with all the windows down, passing farms, hills, valleys, and deer in a meadow. The water of the bay shimmered. Virginia Alpaca had her head out the window, like a dog. I parked across the street from my bookstore and said to Virginia Alpaca, "Stay here. I'll be right back." I darted across the street and headed in. I handed Tiala a folder full of invoices, papers, receipts, etc., for Maeve; grabbed a coffee; and waved to two employees, Ricki and Brenz, then headed back out... and ran straight into Virginia Alpaca outside my bookstore door. A group of people were taking photos of her.

"What the heck, Virginia Alpaca?" I asked. "How did you get out? I thought you were too sick to move."

I swear she smiled at me. "Come on, now, you hairy Houdini." She still had the rope around her neck, and I pulled her toward the street. We had to walk slow because she's sick. Needless to say, cars on both sides stopped pretty quick when I went to cross at the crosswalk. I waved to people on their cell phones.

"Can I pet that weird horse?" a little boy asked, holding the hand of a little girl I assumed was his sister, near my truck. His sister was wearing a shirt depicting a gray cat with a long red tongue and a green tutu. He was wearing a Superman shirt.

"You mean this naughty alpaca right here who escaped from my truck?"

"Yes!" He grinned. "Yes. Is he a bad Al Paca?"

"She is a bad alpaca."

He giggled. His little sister meowed like a cat, then they both petted and hugged Virginia Alpaca. Not all alpaca are nice. They can be bad-tempered. But not Virginia.

Other kids ran up to pet her, and I discovered how she wriggled out of the car: Virginia Alpaca had somehow, inexplicably, opened the door handle with a hoof. She had watched me walk into the bookstore and had come to find me. She is an adventuresome soul, and she doesn't like to be alone.

We drove off, Virginia Alpaca's head sticking out the window, people waving and laughing as we drove through town toward my handsome vet.

When I arrived at Marco's vet clinic, there were a number of people with their pets in the waiting room, including a sheep, two dogs, and an iguana, which was lovingly held by a little girl named Bella Mae, who was crying. Bella Mae was wearing a purple shirt with a green iguana on it that said IGUANA LOVER.

"Miss Evie, can you tell me if Mr. Pitto is going to die?"

"No," I told her, knowing this kid and knowing what she was *really* asking. "I can't tell you that. I'm not a vet."

"I know that. But you can see the future with your magic crystals." She sniffed, sobbed.

And there it was. "No, I can't."

"Yes, you can." She stopped crying, and her face scrunched in frustration. She stomped her foot. "Everyone knows it, Miss Evie. Everybody on this whole island knows you're magic. So tell me: Is Mr. Pitto going to be okay?"

The day I start getting premonitions about animals' health and demise is the day I take a sailboat out to the middle of the ocean and sink it while singing, "I'm a crazy fool." I took a guess. "Yes. He's going to be fine."

"He is?" Her face lit up.

"Yes."

Her mother looked at me, relieved. I've known her mother, Jolla, since I was thirteen.

"See? Now can we go home, Bella Mae?" Jolla said. "Mr. Pitto is an iguana. I've told you it's normal for him not to move much."

"No. I'm going to talk to Dr. Marco about Mr. Pitto because he's being too quiet." Bella Mae stomped her foot again and glared at her mother. Then she stuck out the iguana with both hands so he could glare at her mother, too. I thought Mr. Pitto did a fine job of glaring.

"She's exactly like you," I said to Jolla.

"She's rebellious and difficult," Jolla said. She seemed frazzled.

"No, I'm not!" Bella Mae stomped her foot again.

"Hi, Evie," Gerald Stokes said, standing up and walking over to me. Gerald is about thirty-eight. He wants to date me. I am not interested, but he is a good man. Kind. Glasses. Independently wealthy because of some tech company. A startup or something. I don't know.

"Hi, Gerald. How are you?"

"I'm fine. The boys aren't. They ate something they shouldn't have. Bruno likes to eat my socks even though it makes him sick, and his brother likes to gnaw on shoes. They're not bright."

"They don't look too happy." The dogs were unnaturally quiet. "That's what eating shoes does to you, I suppose. And socks. Not healthy."

"No." His face was drawn. He loves those dogs.

"Marco can fix them."

"I know. Say, any chance you'd like to go to dinner?"

"No, but thank you."

"My mom would," Bella Mae said, swinging around with Mr. Pitto held right in front of her. Poor Mr. Pitto.

"Bella Mae, *shhh*!" Jolla said, embarrassed. "I'm sorry."

"Why do you say *shhh*, Mommy?" Bella Mae said, irritated, swinging Mr. Pitto back again to glare at her mother. "I don't like when you do *shhh*. I don't like *shhh*. I'm only telling Mr. Gerald you would go to dinner." She whipped back around to Gerald. Mr. Pitto glared again. Or maybe he was simply getting motion sickness. "She eats pizza. I mean, she can eat a *whole* pizza all by herself. So if you go to O'Dante's for pizza, I'm letting you know. You need to buy one for her and one for yourself. You have to feed her *a lot* and—"

"Bella Mae!" Jolla snapped, standing up and putting her hand on Bella Mae's shoulder. "Stop it. I do not eat whole pizzas by myself, and you don't need to tell anyone that."

"Yes, you do." And there went Mr. Pitto again, but this time he went up, up in the air above Bella Mae's head to make her point. The iguana was now inches away from being a hat. His little feet tried to walk. Or run.

"I'm sorry," Jolla said to Gerald. "I'm working with her on her manners, but she is poorly behaved."

I know Jolla, and she didn't mean it like it sounded.

"I am not behaved poorly." Bella Mae leaned forward and glared once again at her mother, Mr. Pitto swinging in the air over her head. "I am good behaved."

She was going to be a hellion. Exactly like her mother when we were running around in high school doing crazy stuff.

"Bella Mae," her mother said, so stern.

"All I am saying, Mommy," Bella Mae huffed, "is that Gerald asked Miss Evie out and she said no and you would say yes. Why does that make me behaving poor?" She turned to Gerald. "She thinks you're handsome."

"Oh, my God," Jolla said. "Please. Bella Mae, stop."

"My mom is behaved poorly sometimes." Bella Mae now held Mr. Pitto with one arm as if he were a baby, his stomach in the air. He seemed stunned. This was so undignified for him!

"But most of the time: Nice. Want to hold my iguana? Miss Evie says he's going to be fine. She can see the future."

"No, I can't," I said, but it was weak.

"Yes, you can!" Bella Mae insisted, cross again and turning on me in frustration, Mr. Pitto almost flying right out of her arms. "Do you want to go to dinner with my mom and feed her up with a whole pizza?" She turned back to Gerald, who seemed confused, but not as confused as Mr. Pitto.

"That's it." Jolla, blushing, grabbed Bella Mae holding the embarrassed iguana and dragged her out of the waiting room.

"You should think about asking Jolla to dinner," I told him.

"You'll never go out with me?" Gerald smiled. He was cute, but not for me, and I knew he was asking a serious question that needed an honest answer.

"No."

"I like your honesty."

"I don't always like it, but I can't do the whole fake-talk thingie. It makes me feel nauseated, so there it is."

"Okay." Gerald thought about things, his gaze shifting to the window where Jolla was dragging Bella Mae out while Bella Mae held poor Mr. Pitto in the air. This was not a pleasant day for Mr. Pitto at all. If he wasn't sick walking in, he would be sick by the time he arrived home.

"Evie?" Gayle, Marco's assistant, said. "You ready? Marco said to bring Virginia Alpaca out back."

"Yes. See ya, Gerald."

"You broke my heart." He clasped a hand to his heart and feigned dying.

"You'll live, buddy. Go guzzle a beer and watch football or another mind-numbing sport like other men do, and you'll be all better by halftime."

I headed outside to be with Virginia Alpaca, where I'd put her in one of the stalls, behind the clinic, while I waited for Marco.

I tried not to get nervous. I am a tough bird on the outside but not so tough on the inside, hence: breakdowns. Three of them in the past, to be precise. When I'm going to see Marco the result is: jitteriness and gangs of butterflies in my stomach all fluttering around.

I decided to distract myself. I pulled a chocolate bar out of my purse. I would eat only one today. For courage and nutrition. If I had part of a second one after dinner, it would not count as two, because part of a chocolate bar doesn't count.

Marco's property is stunning. He has five acres, and the houses on either side of him are on the farthest ends of their property, so he can't see any neighbors.

He has a view of the ocean, and a dock, where he has his boat. I looked away from the boat as an overwhelming, regretful sadness drifted over me.

Towering fir trees rim the property, but where his home and clinic are, the sun shines right on down. He also has a stable and a red barn, and his meadow is used for animal rehabilitation.

His home is within a short walk to the clinic. I have never been in it. It's a light gray with black trim and about twenty-five years old, but I know that he and one of the only two contractors in town worked nonstop to gut the kitchen and put in new wood floors and take down a couple of walls. I've heard it's modern and filled with light and windows.

I have always wondered what it looks like inside but have not allowed myself to go spy. I've been tempted to spy. I would dress in all black if I could still squeeze into my black jeans, get night vision goggles, grab Jules, climb on the deck, and peer in. I have not yet lowered myself to that pathetic level, but it's tempting. I would like to see him in his natural nude state.

I saw Marco with another horse and his owner in the distance. He was checking the horse's back, his hands gentle but firm. I did not think of his gentle and firm hands on my back, as that would have made the gang of butterflies in my stomach flutter all the harder. I did not think of his gentle and firm hands on my front, either, undoing my lacy white bra, as that would have made me all skittery with passion. I did not think of his gentle and firm hands pulling me into his naked tall body because that could not happen.

My heart ached. He smiled, and my heart ached again. He was smart, deep, insightful, and easy to talk to. Plus, sexy.

I took a huge bite of my chocolate bar. I was here to get Virginia Alpaca fixed. That's it.

I could not fall in love with Marco. And even if I was in love with him already, I had to can it. Stomp it down. Get rid of it.

My premonition about that was quite clear.

I started eating the second chocolate bar in my purse. I would stop halfway through so the calories would not count.

"Hi, Marco."

"Hello, Evie. How are you?"

"Really fine. Very fine. Uh. Oh. Fine." His smile had me melting. Maybe that was both chocolate bars melting in my stomach, but still. It was a delicious feeling. "Virginia Alpaca is sick." *And I'm a little bit glad of it so I can visit you. Does that make me a horrible animal mother? It does. It so does. I love you, Virginia Alpaca!*

"Let's take a look at her."

We went into the clinic's room for large animals. I watched him examining Virginia Alpaca. He was kind and soothing when she became nervous and started moving her feet, swinging her head. He handled her carefully. He palpitated her stomach, checked her respiration and heart rate, asked me a lot of questions about her eating, etc. "I think she has a mild case of colic."

"It's not too bad, then?"

"No."

I sagged with relief. I love Virginia Alpaca. She's a fighter. She's shy and she's bold. She comes up to me every morning to say hello. She's definitely the boss between her and Alpaca Joe. I am sure she is a feminist.

"Thank you, Marco."

"You're welcome. I'll take a blood sample to be sure, and I'll hook her up to an IV and get her hydrated." He did both while I watched him. He was so competent, so soothing. When he was done, he pulled off his gloves, washed his hands, smiled at me. "So how have you been?"

"Good. Working at the bookstore. Taking care of the animals. Making sure my aunts and my mother stay out of trouble. Reading books. The usual."

He smiled at me, but I saw what was behind his eyes. "I don't think anything about your life is usual."

"It is. All usual." Except for the premonitions. I was positive he knew about my premonitions. It was a small island. People talk. My guess is that he thought I was absolutely bonkers or delusional, or he respected my privacy and didn't want to confirm that I am bonkers or delusional.

"I heard your mother and aunts brought the house down the other night at Bennie's bar."

Oh groan. I pet Virginia Alpaca to soothe her, although she seemed calm. I think she has a crush on Marco, too. "You heard about that?" I'd heard what was happening and headed down to drive them home as I knew they would need a sober driver. Everyone in the bar was singing along, swinging beer mugs back and forth through the air.

"Small island."

"They had too much scotch. It's their sinful drink. My mother says it catches up to her when she's not looking. Plus, those three have scotch contests and throw them back like drunken sailors." I shook my head. "I don't know why they do that. They've been doing it since I was a kid, but you would think in their seventies some of this would have slowed down."

"I thought it was hilarious. Heard they got up on the tables and danced to 'Greased Lightning.'"

"It's their go-to dance together. They've choreographed it. It's better, if I'm honest, than if those three dance individually."

"Why?"

"They like to wriggle around a lot. They've got that whole hip-swinging thing down." My aunt Iris, tough as she is, could swing those hips like a twenty-five-year-old stripper. I've heard she still turns on men forty years younger. "It's a bit lewd. Suggestive."

He laughed. "They keep things exciting around here."

"You could put it that way."

"I heard you got up on the bar and danced and sang, too."

"I had to," I said primly. "Family loyalty. And they told me they wouldn't come home unless I sang with them. It was bribery, clearly."

He laughed.

Not only do my mother and aunts sometimes drink too much scotch and dance at one of our two bars, my mother and aunts invent impromptu parades. One parade was "Bring Your Pet." They didn't get a permit, "officially," but the mayor is a long-time friend of theirs and scurried around, found a permit, and stamped it an hour beforehand, then he went home to get his pig, Pinkie. Mayor Than loves Pinkie and refuses to eat her. The streets were closed off downtown for horses, dogs, alpacas, goats, sheep, and cats in cat strollers, many in ribbons and hats and other animal costumes.

Each year we have a Hat Parade, too. To be in the parade, you have to wear a hat. My mother and aunts give out prizes at the end for Biggest Hat. Smallest Hat. Best Hat. Most Radical Hat. Most Scary Hat Without Being Violent. Best British Hat. Best Hippie Hat. Best Crazy Hat. They are the judges, but their own hats and any hat they made are disqualified so that people have a "hope in hell of winning."

They host a lot of parties at our house, where people sing and dance and sometimes skinny-dip in the ocean. One time they had a naked sprinkler midnight party. They turned on two sprinklers, and at midnight all the women got naked and ran through the water. They have poker parties and bunco parties.

"Nah. They don't need to tame it down," Marco said. "They're living it up."

"They live it up, that's for sure, and they haven't been arrested for over a year for disturbing the peace, so that's a plus."

"Certainly is."

"The chief is their friend. He arrests and releases them quickly. It's all a big joke. One time my mother grabbed his handcuffs and she and my aunts arrested him. They drove him home to his wife. The chief thought it was hilarious."

Marco is half Mexican. His great-grandfather moved to California from Mexico. His grandfather was born in California. The sprawling family owns hundreds of acres of farmland in California and a construction business. Marco's father is a college professor in California. He teaches math. His mother is an artist. Marco was born in Newport Beach and joined the military for eight years after high school. He went to college through the military, then went to veterinarian school.

He is six three, with black hair, dark eyes. That over-used saying, "Tall, dark, and handsome," was made for Marco. But he's not a slick gorgeous. He is not a vain gorgeous. He can't help his face. He can't help his broad build. He can't help that he looks like a Mexican cowboy who should be that rough-and-tough hero in a movie. He's even a bit scarred up. One scar is from wrestling with Laredo, one of his four brothers. They crashed over their toy box, and both ended up bleeding from their foreheads.

Another scar is on his lip. That one was from riding his bike double with his brother Manuel. They crashed.

A scar on his neck is from a skateboarding accident. He and Christof were skateboarding off a dirt cliff. He took a bullet in his leg in Iraq, and when he's tired he limps a little. He has shrapnel embedded in his left forearm, so he's had a tattoo painted over it with the name of their family's farm *Campos de Oro*, Golden Fields, to turn "bullet fragments into something better."

He has had some posttraumatic stress issues, he'd told me, from the war. He walks late at night on the island to get rid of the memories he wants to get rid of. He lost his best friend in Iraq, which was devastating. He stopped drinking entirely five years ago because after he returned from Iraq he drank too much because of flashbacks and nightmares and general anxiety from the war. His family, a few war buddies, and three of his best friends intervened.

"I was defensive, angry, told them all to go to hell. Except," he said, "my mother. I would never tell my mother to go to hell. But they were right. I was drinking too much. So I stopped. And

I finally started dealing with what I saw, what I did, what I was ordered to do, in combat in Iraq."

Marco smiled down at me, my hand on Virginia Alpaca, and that smile remelted the chocolate bars I'd accidentally eaten.

"So, Evie," he said. "I'll get Virginia Alpaca all fixed up and she'll feel better. Can you leave her overnight? I'll keep an eye on her, make sure she's eating well, and walking some. If you want to come back later tonight to check on her, that's fine, too."

"Thanks, Marco."

"Sure. If you want dinner, let me know. I'll barbeque steaks." He smiled. He is too gorgeous.

Oh, good Lord, Martha and Mary, and Mother of Jesus. The good Lord should not make men who look like Marco. It's almost sinful, all this rampaging lust I feel. He's like the apple in Eve's garden. I want to bite him. Not hard, of course. A bite-kiss sort of thing. "I don't know. I don't think I can. I have, uh, I can't have steaks. But I'll come by and check on her."

I saw the disappointment in his eyes, like a flash, but he covered it up with another wide and friendly smile. "Sounds good. She'll be ready tomorrow afternoon to head on home."

"Thanks, Marco."

"Anytime."

I felt his eyes on me as I said goodbye to Virginia Alpaca, gave her a hug, and told her to be good.

Bye, Marco. You are the best man I have ever met.

When I climbed in my truck, my eyes caught my face in the rearview mirror. Oh, how embarrassing! I had chocolate in the corners of my mouth! I slapped my hands over my blushing face and dropped my face to my steering wheel. I accidentally hit the horn, and it blared through the property. I popped back up. More embarrassment! Marco waved at me. I waved back as if everything was perfectly fine. I turned on the truck, waved again, and pushed my foot on the accelerator, only for some reason I zipped backwards in reverse. I slammed on the brakes, put the truck in the right gear, drove forward, and pretended yet again that I hadn't done anything ridiculous.

I waved again. Marco waved back.

Oh, woe is me, I am a lovesick fool.

I did not go back and check on Virginia Alpaca that night. I couldn't. I didn't have the courage, and I knew she would be fine with Marco. I was not fine, but she would be fine.

That deep well of sadness overwhelmed me again. Hello, darkness. I will fight you off as I have fought you off a thousand times before. I wiped the tears off my cheeks and ate a chocolate bonbon.

I don't go into the greenhouse often.

Between my work at the bookstore and the work I do for my mother and aunts, helping them cut the outside flowers for their floral business, and taking care of all my animals, I don't have a lot of time.

But they are in the greenhouse often.

More lately, it seems, even though most of the flowers they're using at the shop are growing outside on our property, the colors a petal-filled rainbow floating on island wind. But they're inviting friends over to see the greenhouse, too. They wander in and out, laughing and chatting.

They must have some pretty new plants growing in there. Maybe new orchids?

I live in the "carriage house," which is a short distance from my mother and aunts' home. It was never a carriage house, but that's what we call it because we like how it sounds. It used to be the groundskeeper's cottage when my mother and aunts were young. It's near our small beach, to the right of the greenhouse, and to the left of our red barn. I planted roses all around the perimeter, heavy on light purple, yellows, and reds. I also have a trellis over my front porch, where a pink climbing rose practically drips when it's in bloom.

It's a light blue jewel that had been vacant for years when I moved in. There's about 600 square feet, with a sleeping loft above the main area, accessible by stairs. There used to be a ladder there, but my animals can't climb ladders, hence the stairs. The dogs and cats sleep with me, so that would be a problem.

When I moved in seven years ago, after a van trip around the country to different national parks, and camping in the woods and at the beach, alone, I was broken. I don't like the words "nervous breakdown." It sounds old-fashioned. It sounds like once you have a breakdown, that's it. You're done. You've fallen apart. You're broken permanently.

I was hoping I wasn't broken permanently, but I was a wreck, that is not in dispute. After college, where I majored in English and business because I like both, I went to work for a major book chain. I had worked for four years in the university's bookstore while I was going to school, so I knew a lot about marketing, working with customers, and managing people. First I worked as a clerk at the chain, then assistant manager, then manager, and I was up in corporate in three years. I even wrote a column about books for them, which was in all of their newsletters, because of my book obsession.

I lived in a studio in Seattle, a small space with a view of Puget Sound and the ferries, with Sundance. I've had Sundance since I was twenty. I was volunteering at an animal shelter and fell in love with that dog. He was missing a front leg because someone thought it would be a good idea to shoot it off. He could hardly lift his head, he was so beaten down. He was slow and scared and shook all the time. He was skinny and hobbling, his ribs sticking out.

Sundance wanted to disappear at first. He would sit in a corner of the shelter curled up tight, whimpering. But slowly, he let me pet him. Then he let me hug him for small amounts of time, and finally he trusted me and we became best human/animal friends. I bought him a pink blankie and a stuffed green lizard, and he loved both of them.

When I wasn't at work, we were walking at the park, hiking, going on drives to the country, and camping. Each weekend I had to get out of town, away from the premonitions about people around me that would suddenly zing in.

I was torn between being sane and trying to save people,

warn people about something I saw in their future that was bad, and make decisions on whether I should try to save them and how to warn them. It was the usual chaos. As I often felt the need to warn strangers when I had a premonition about them, I had many people treat me as one would expect when a stranger walks up and warns you of an upcoming disaster: "Get away from me, you freak. Are you insane? That's a horrible thing to say to my wife/father/brother."

I was also still dealing with a grief from years ago that was pulling me down, threatening to drown me, and horror, images set in sand and flames that I couldn't get out of my mind. Alongside the grief was rage, too.

One day, on a hike in the mountains, standing on a cliff and looking down, down, down into a valley, Sundance at my side, I had yet another urge to jump. To simply end the mental torture.

That was not the first time I wanted to die by jumping. There were two other times in my life that I seriously wanted to die and could no longer handle what was going on in my own head. It was a hopeless, black, unending desperation. It happened once as a teenager, once in college when I was twenty-one, and at that moment.

I thought about jumping off various things: Bridges. Buildings. A pier. A mountain. Why a death by jumping? I had no idea. The suicidal thoughts were stuck in my head, on a circle, repetitive and taunting. They scared me, they soothed me. I would rather be scared by thoughts of suicide than soothed by thoughts of suicide.

That day, on the cliff, I felt soothed by it. I could leave all the stress and anger and grief and guilt behind.

As if sensing what I was going to do, Sundance started pulling at the end of my shorts with his mouth. He growled and pulled and barked and growled, pulled, and barked. I looked down at that dog and thought, *I cannot leave Sundance. It'll break his heart.* I stepped away from the edge.

I walked into work at the corporate office of the chain bookstore the next day and quit. I bought an old but well-maintained VW van with a table in the back and a roof that poofed up so you could sleep in it. I sold everything except for my warm, comfortable clothes and all my camping and hiking gear and started driving. I mailed my book collection to Rose Bloom Cottage.

Luckily, it was spring when I started. I went to national parks but hiked and backpacked away from the crowds. I went to quiet campgrounds. I went to the beach. Mountains. Rivers. Lakes. I slept in the van. I woke up when the sun rose, hiked and read books, and went to bed after staring at a campfire.

I met Butch and Cassidy when they limped up to me at a campground by the Deschutes River in Oregon. They were in terrible shape. Starving. Hurt. Pathetic. They had been abused; there were marks and cuts all over their bodies, their frayed leather collars choking them. When I left the Deschutes River for the Wallowa Mountains, they happily climbed in the van with Sundance and me, their wounds healing, their diseases healing.

Six months and three thousand miles later, when I was done camping, and could think again, and did not want to jump off cliffs, when the black fog of desperate depression lifted, I asked my mother and aunts if I could live in the carriage house.

Of course they said yes, but my mother wanted me to live with them in Rose Bloom Cottage. "I've missed you. We can make hats together every night and read books and help your aunt Camellia make her lotions and potions in the basement and go on photography expeditions with Aunt Iris so she can take her odd but lovely flower photos. Do you think some of her flower photos look phallic? I do. Do you think some of her flowers look, well, vagina-like? I do."

My aunt Camellia said, "Let me first light vanilla candles inside the carriage house and pray and use a generous amount of lavender to invite eternal peace to come calling, then the home and I can welcome you with pure vibes," and my aunt Iris said, "I'll put wine in the fridge, don't worry. And a bottle of scotch. Welcome home."

I lived in Rose Bloom Cottage for about a week, and mostly I slept on the new king-sized bed my aunts and mother bought me. It is amazing what sleep can do and what a lack of sleep can do, too. Then I asked if I could remodel the carriage house. Of course they said yes, that they would pay for it, but I refused to let them, and we had a fight, and I was stubborn and so were they, and I finally told them I would rent another home on one of the islands if they didn't stop arguing, and they sulkily gave in.

For three days I hauled dirt and rock at Mr. and Mrs. King's house, an eighty-year-old couple, with their fifty-year-old son, Artie, who was a contractor. In exchange Artie came over and knocked down two walls in the carriage house, taking out the bedroom so I would have an open living space. He raised the ceiling and put up two wood beams with some buddies so the ceiling wouldn't fall in.

I watched Neil Somo's mother for five days, who has dementia and likes to wander around town in her nightgown, while he went to Seattle on business. Neil, who knew how to install wood floors, worked with me to put wood floors in my house. Neil is independently wealthy but quirky. There I was, laying wood with a millionaire.

In exchange for white kitchen cabinets, ten years old but not "modern enough" for a wealthy woman on the island, I checked on her six cats twice a day for two weeks while she went to Paris. After Artie ripped out the carriage house's battered old brown cabinets, he and I hung up the white ones in my kitchen.

I painted all the walls and ceiling white with one of those paint sprayers, except one wall in my family room, where I glued white wallpaper with elegant pink roses because I love my roses.

I paid for new windows and two sets of sliding glass doors, one on either side of the house, so I can watch the sunset and the sunrise as the house is up on a slight hill. I ordered breezy white curtains with tiny light yellow roses.

I ripped out the brown trim around the windows and used a miter saw to make wide white trim. From the wood of an old barn on a friend's property, I made a full wall of shelves, floor to ceiling, for my slight obsession with books.

I found a front door with a half-moon cutout in an antique

shop on the island and painted it red. I found three hanging lights made with dripping crystals at Marv Leopold's estate sale, the fashion mogul who had a vacation home here and died in his bedroom in a frilly pink dress and one of my mother's purple flowered hats with blue jays.

I painted the new stairs to the loft/my bedroom white and the floorboards upstairs white. I went for a jean material to block out the light at night through the two windows. I bought a white comforter with embroidered red and purple roses and a bunch of pillows by Ellie Kozlovsky with roses painted in all colors.

My mother and aunts hunted around in their attic and gave me an antique library card cabinet that I put next to the front door. I piled more books on top, and below it. It had been used in the town's library at one time, and the cards to locate books were still in it, so it was my kind of furniture piece.

They also gave me a blue weathered antique wardrobe their mother owned. She liked to curl up in it, shut the door, and sing. I added shelves to it and used it in the kitchen as a pantry. They also gave me a pew from a church that collapsed from age outside of town. They remembered their mother sitting at that church and humming rock songs while the minister spoke. Their father had to take her outside if she refused to quit.

I placed the pew against one wall in my kitchen nook and piled more books under it for storage. I painted sawhorses dark blue and put a butcher block counter over the top for a table. I bought two leather couches from an estate sale when ninety-four-year-old Colonel Ralph Kalama died. They had that cool used look to them. From the rafters over the leather couches I hung three model airplanes that my father had made as a kid, and nailed up two of his fishing poles on either side of the shelves for my books. I hung one large crystal from Aunt Camellia above each window and the sliding glass doors. I could not miss out on possibly receiving a hot sex life from those crystals.

Aunt Iris found me two wine barrels—"Wine makes life sweet," she said—which I used as side tables by the leather couches, and I used an old wooden sea chest of my grandfather's for the coffee table. The chest opened up so I could pour more books in.

My mother gave me her favorite light blue vase. "To remind you to always have fresh flowers, dear. Bring beauty to your life, as it will not always come to you on its own." As soon as the roses bloomed each year, they were in that vase. Light purple. Pink and yellow. White. Burgundy. Bright red. That vase was never empty. Roses brought peace, hope, and color to my life like no other flower.

I hung six amazing hats on one wall that my mother and aunts had made me, and I hung family photos in the short hallway to my bathroom. There were photos of my mom and aunts in hats, photos of my parents on their wedding day, holding Jules and me as babies, and me on top of my dad's shoulders. I bought a white clawfoot tub from an estate sale and created a bathroom/spa.

I saved up, then drove down to central Oregon to buy a commissioned collage by Grenadine Scotch Wild. It was a painting of Rose Bloom Cottage. I'd sent her fabric from my mother and aunts' dresses and she made tiny pillows out of them for the porch swing. I sent her one of my dad's ties and she made a sheet on a clothes line with it. I sent her a charm in the shape of a motorcycle for Jules and she used it as a door knocker. She added an abundance of roses, using faux petals. That painting has the place of honor in my kitchen nook.

I repainted the exterior of the carriage house a light blue, the shutters black, and the trim white.

It was a cottage by the bay, the water lapping against our beach.

When I finally got myself and my house together, and could eat and breathe normally, I opened my bookstore with money that I had saved for years, as I am a naturally frugal person. My motto: If something bad can happen, it will. Hence: Save your money.

Not a fearless way to live, but there it is.

I saw the rent for the building on Chrysanthemum Way and knew I could not pay it. I offered half. The owner took it. He lived on the mainland and wasn't too concerned about money. I painted the inside; rolled up yellow rose wallpaper; bought boxes of books; and set up the shelves, café, and cash register. I brought fresh roses in regularly to sit next to the cash register and in my office. I was happy there. I am happy there.

It's not that I'm scared to leave the island again. I'm scared of what will become of my brain if I do. This is my place of calm. It's my place of sanity. It's my home.

I am an Island Hermit, and I will probably leave this place as dust on the wind.

It's not a bad way to go.

"Greetings, Evie. Let's have 'em."

"Hello, Mr. Jamon." I brought out four books from behind the counter at the bookstore. "I've chosen them especially for you." We were busy today. Every time I have a sale and give a free cup of peppermint or chamomile tea away when customers purchase a book, we're busy. Today the cake was peppermint mocha lava, advertised in the window, so we were pretty full.

He looked at them, grunted. "Not bad, Evie. Once again, not bad."

Mr. Jamon is eighty-five years old and owns a small fishing company. He lives up on the top of our highest hill in a log cabin his own father built as a family vacation home. The father owned two newspapers in Washington. I've seen the log home from a distance but have never been up there. He's a bit of a hermit. I relate to him, hermit to hermit.

In the last ten years he's built up a fishing business and employs about ten men and women. He pays incredibly well. All of his fishermen and fisherwomen own homes on the island and drive nice cars. They love him.

"What do I need more money for, Evie?" he said to me about five years ago. "I'm eighty years old. But I can provide jobs for families, so I do."

But "fisherman" only covers his last job. Up until he became a fisherman, he was the president of the publishing empire his grandfather started and he expanded.

We're friends, and he is also friends with my mother and aunts. Mr. Jamon has quietly donated money to the schools on the islands, the small hospital, and he's bought up land all over the islands and put it in trust, so it will never be developed.

Mr. Jamon goes through one or two books a week. His interests run anywhere from biographies, particularly of presidents and leaders around the world; memoirs, particularly of Hollywood actors and actresses; science, particularly the history of space travel; history, particularly World War II. Also physics and politics and occasional spy novels. Recently he has become interested in romance books, "for love," he told me, "the eternal hope even when you're my age. Romance isn't dead and neither am I!" In short, he's my ideal reader.

"I'll take them." He tapped his cane.

"Let me give you some spice cake with cream cheese frosting. Bit of cinnamon in there, too."

"I can't say no to that."

He sat down in the café to eat, and I sat with him. I always do. It's rude to give someone cake and not eat with them. Plus, the spice cake had zucchini in it. Zucchini is a vegetable, therefore the cake is healthy.

Chapter 6

〜

Betsy Baturra
Multnomah County Jail
Portland, Oregon
1975

Late that night, after Betsy's baby, Rose, was taken away, she hemorrhaged in her jail cell. A new doctor coming on shift had sent her back to her jail cell after the birth, still bleeding profusely onto a pad, shackled at the wrists and ankles. The two squeamish young guards, reeling from all that screaming and what happened between the prisoner's legs, led her back.

The infirmary had been crowded. The woman who had been jumped by a fellow inmate and had her neck slashed with the toothbrush/knife bled quite a lot and needed stitches. Three other women had gotten into a fight. One had her head bashed against a toilet. The other took a broomstick to the eye. The third tried to slug the first woman, slipped, and somehow broke an ankle.

So there was no room for a woman who had given birth with, apparently, no problems. Of course, no one had checked on Betsy again after Dr. Rothney and Clarissa left in a huff after she told them what would happen to them in the future, with the doctor's girlfriend stealing the guitar collection and the nurse being pregnant by a lying husband.

Betsy's body was aching, her spirit and mind shattered. At

first, huddled on her cot in her cell in a ball, when the bleeding grew heavier, she didn't want to do anything to stop it. They had taken her baby. They had taken Rose. She would undoubtedly be found guilty in her upcoming trial and be in jail for twenty years, maybe more. The newspapers were in a frenzy about her and Johnny. Young lovers, they said, wanting to steal Johnny's father's money. She was the ring leader, the liar, the manipulator! They were criminals! The public outcry was high. These youths today are out of control! Drugs and more drugs!

There was only a slim chance she would get out for good behavior, so what was the point? Why live? Why try? So she let the blood between her legs run, she let the fever shake her, she let her body die.

But her roommate, a woman named Rainbow, as she told Betsy, "because I invented colors," cried out for help, and when help didn't come, Rainbow started reciting colors in alphabetical order, her voice shaking as her tears fell, "Lime green. Mauve. Scarlet . . ."

In the midst of her devastation, her loss, Betsy thought, *Why is Rainbow here? She's sick in the head. Why is she in jail?* No one came when Rainbow repeatedly yelled for help. The guards told her to "shut up," so she went back to her color recitations, her body trembling. Two hours later, when one of the guards finally ran a check, Betsy was passed out, cold, white, dying, and accepting of her death. Rainbow had wrapped her body around Betsy to warm her up. She held her close, whimpering, repeating colors to comfort Betsy.

When a guard finally did her rounds to check on prisoners, she was initially mad because Rainbow should not be in bed with Betsy! Women may not sleep together! That's against the rules! Then, when Rainbow sat up and pointed at the blood all over the mattress and on Betsy's jail scrubs and even on Rainbow and Rainbow said, "Blood red," the guard finally hit the alarm.

She rushed in and told Rainbow to move. Rainbow told her that she saw black when she looked at the woman. "Black in your heart," Rainbow cried. "I kept calling for help and you all ignored us like gray slugs. You're a black-hearted woman."

"Oh, God," the guard said, realizing the severity of the situation, then swore. She slapped Betsy to get her to wake up as Betsy was clearly fading out, and Rainbow lightly hit the guard in the face with three fingers in protest. Rainbow did not believe in violence—she was in jail because she stole a roasted chicken and donuts because she was starving—but she felt the guard needed a punishment.

The guard turned and hammered Rainbow, and Rainbow fell back into the wall, her head banging against the cement. Rainbow sobbed out, "Azure blue. Banana yellow. Lavender purple."

"Wake up! Wake up!" The guard shook Betsy hard, her white face still. The guard was shocked at all the blood soaking the mattress. Other guards ran in, and Betsy was whisked off to the infirmary, blood trickling behind her, the mattress stained with Betsy's life.

Later, after the doctors and nurses leaped to take over caring for Betsy, moving with frantic practice, the guard came back to punish Rainbow for hitting her. The guard slipped in the blood on the floor and fell on her back. Rainbow said, "It's karma. It's coming for you like midnight black. Gunmetal silver. You're an infected lime green color now." This enraged the guard because she believed in karma, too. She had Rainbow put in solitary for a week.

Rainbow whimpered as she was led away and said, "Betsy is golden yellow."

Betsy woke up in the infirmary again, tied down, of course, wrists, ankles, waist, a different doctor leaning over her.

"What happened?" she asked. It was morning, she could tell by the light. Maybe afternoon.

"You hemorrhaged. You lost a lot of blood."

The doctor was a woman. She had a kinder face than the nurse standing there, who looked impatient, her face scrunched like a bulldog's. Tears welled up in Betsy's eyes again. Rose.

Rose. Rose. She would never see Rose again. Never. She wanted to die.

"You'll stay here for a few days."

She nodded through her tears.

"You'll need to build your strength up. Why didn't you ask for help?"

"Rainbow did. My cellmate. No one came."

"I'm sorry." She knew who Betsy was. She knew about the case. "Your trial starts soon, doesn't it?"

She nodded. What did it matter? Her baby was gone.

Taken.

Lost.

Never to be held or kissed again.

Betsy again wished she was dead.

Betsy had the same premonition the next night in the infirmary that she'd had since she was five years old. In the midst of her delirium, as her fever spiked up and down, again and again, she was lucid enough to grasp it.

She was driving her car on a winding, too-narrow one-lane road. The sunlight was behind her, the sun setting through the tall, swaying fir trees. There were orange poppies on both sides of the road.

She curved to the left, toward the side of the mountain, distracted by the steep cliff to the right and not wanting to go over.

A truck was coming toward her. She swerved her car to the right, closer to the cliff, but in that short expanse, with the tight road, there was no chance of not hitting the truck. She hit the brakes to lessen the impact, terror filling her heart, as the back of her car fishtailed. There was a woman inside the truck. She could not see much more than that.

The truck and the car smashed together with a reverberating, echoing bang, metal on metal, glass shattering, brakes shrieking, tires twisting.

One of the vehicles went over the cliff. She thought it was hers, but the premonition ended in a blur. It could have been the truck. It could have been her car. But this particular premonition shifted sometimes; it was the only one where the scene altered. One of the women died, she thought. Probably. There was an air of death. She didn't know who it was, though, or if it was both of them. It was fuzzy, and her premonitions were never fuzzy.

Was it she who died?

Or did the other woman die?

Was it her fault that the other woman died?

She couldn't live with that.

She took note, yet again, of the scene. The weather. The time of day. The place. The poppies.

She could change the outcome of premonitions with other people; she could interfere sometimes, she had done it her whole life. Because of the fuzziness, did that mean the end result of this premonition was undecided?

And, if she changed the premonition for herself, if she reacted quickly to save herself from crashing into the truck, and she didn't die, would the other woman die? That wasn't fair, it wasn't right. She could never hurt anyone like that.

If this was set in the future and she was older—she thought, because her hands, on the steering wheel, were all she could see of herself and looked older—and the other woman was younger, the younger woman should live, not her.

As she lay miserable in that grimy infirmary, the leather straps tight, her body throbbing, her fever spiking up again, her legs hot and sticky from blood and sweat, she tried to sort things out through the excruciating depression in her mind.

If the premonition was correct, she was out of prison. She was not here. She ended up on a winding road near fir trees and orange poppies.

Maybe she would not die in prison.

Even if she wanted to.

Chapter 7

～

I have a lot of animals, I know this, I do. I am not an animal collector. I am not an animal hoarder.

I simply love animals.

Jane Austen, my brown horse, was almost dead when I saw her on the western edge of the island on a farm. You could see her bones. My friend, Amy, saw her and called me. The farm was owned by a mean son of a gun named Doc Haurley. Doc used to be a doc, but he lost his medical license and was sued because he was a negligent, drunken doctor. He was a urologist. One man ended up wearing a colostomy bag the rest of his life. Another woman ended up incontinent. One almost died.

When he was in town, he was regularly rude and drunk and mean.

So my mother, aunts, Amy, and I stole Jane Austen. We knew that Doc was off the island because we asked his neighbor, Mr. Jennings, if he would keep an eye out. Mr. Jennings, who had offered to buy the horse from Doc Haurley because he was so upset about her condition, agreed to be our coconspirator.

Mr. Jennings called us when he knew Doc was headed off the island, and we headed over as stealthily as we could hauling a horse trailer. I called to Jane Austen. She didn't move, her head down, bones out. We went over to pet her. She jerked away, frightened. I gave her an apple and called out gently, and she ate it right up, then another apple, and a third. We led her to the trailer by dropping hay along the way. She, slowly, with what seemed like great pain, got in.

We drove her in the trailer to a vet's on Lopozzo Island, as Marco had not arrived yet.

The vet was appalled and called the animal cruelty line. The vet said Jane Austen was suffering from a long list of things she never should have suffered from. We left her with the vet for several days. The animal cruelty inspector came out, took photos, and Doc Haurley was arrested. He went to court and was fined and put on probation. His other animals were taken from him, including his prized but abused hunting dogs, which Amy and Mr. Jennings adopted. He also had to pay the vet's bill for all of the animals, which was substantial. He was not allowed to own animals again.

We took Jane Austen home. I named her Jane Austen because I love Jane Austen and have read all of her books twice. If there was a time machine, which I am not embarrassed to say I do dream about, I would get in it and go and be Jane's friend.

Within a month Jane Austen was a new horse. She was heavier, shinier, happier. When I walked the property, she followed me around like a dog, only there was no leash. We fed her hay and apples, and she liked her salt lick. We fixed up the barn and gave her a lovely stall, but most of the time she was outside, as she liked watching the other animals.

Shakespeare was rescued because the vet called us from Lopozzo Island and asked if Jane Austen wanted a gentle horse friend. Jane did want a friend! We named him Shakespeare because I read Shakespeare out loud in college each time I was trying to avoid paralyzing anxiety or panic attacks or a horrible scene filled with sand and flames that kept burning through my mind. There was something about the cadence that calmed me down.

Shakespeare was an old racehorse that was going to be quietly turned into glue. We went and got Shakespeare. Then Shakespeare and Jane Austen fell in love. They played in the meadow, they ran, they strolled. They do not write plays or books, but their love is true.

Mars, Jupiter, and Venus were feral, diseased, and weak, and I took them in. I found them in a box off the highway at a rest area about forty-five minutes north of Seattle, where I'd stopped to get coffee. People's cruelty to animals can be shocking. I found Ghost when I was twenty-four outside my apartment complex in Seattle, mewing, shaking with cold, and wet. No one ever responded to my ads or the local pound about Ghost.

The lambs had been used in medical experiments. I found out about them from a friend who lived in Seattle and worked in the medical field. All the lambs were going to be put down.

"I'm coming," I told her.

I found my black and white goats wandering around the is-land. I kept seeing them, and one day I called them to me. They came. They were friendly. They were silly. They were emaciated, their hair matted. I put up signs, asked around, no one ever claimed Mr. Bob and Trixie. They're mystery animals.

My animals and I are one big family. I go outside, we walk and talk. I watch them play. They greet me when I come home. They are naughty, hilarious, loving.

It's like having an animal circus around me at all times. The dogs and cats are inside and outside; they go in and out through a tiny door right next to my front door. Both goats wander into the house now and then because somehow, someway, they're able to figure out how to get out of their pen. The lambs stay outside, but they'll come up on the deck and look in the win-dows and prance around when they see me as if they're thrilled they found me. They have, clearly, forgotten that they saw me fifteen minutes ago. I'm like the gift that keeps on giving.

The horses stay outside for the vast majority of time, but if I open their paddock, sometimes they'll come up on the deck and stick their heads in through the open front door.

I love my animals, and when I'm around them I feel better, calmer.

They remind me about everything innocent and kind and car-ing in life.

* * *

The Book Babes, the ten women who regularly meet on Wednesday evenings from six o'clock to eight o'clock at my bookstore, are serious readers. If you are dead or unconscious, you're excused from reading the book. Otherwise you have no excuse with the Book Babes.

Tonight they were discussing the plot of a book in which a woman ran naked along a river because her anger management counselor told her to do something out of her comfort zone to shake out her anger. The woman accidentally ended up entangled on the ground with a handsome man, the moon shining down on them, an owl hooting.

"I would run my butt down a river naked," one woman said, "to get rid of my lingering anger with you-know-who." Oh, the Book Babes knew exactly who Lynn was talking about. It wasn't a cheating husband. It wasn't someone who took off with her money. It was her sister-in-law, that witch. Always flashing her money and her rings and her silly, shallow lifestyle. So annoying!

"You would?" another replied. "I doubt it. I think you kind of like hating her."

"I'd do it. Make me." The woman is not a runner. I heard her describe her own body type one day as "dough woman."

"I dare you," said the online college professor with pink streaks in her hair.

"I dare *you!*" she told the professor. "You're the runner. Plus, you can't stand your daughter-in-law."

"That's because she hates my cooking. Says it's not organic enough. She has all these allergies, too. Can't eat meat. Can't eat dairy. How do you say it? Glue-ton? Glug-ting? Gluten! That's it! Can't eat that stuff, either. I swear she can eat only carrots."

"I would run naked if no one saw." I blinked. The woman is seventy-three.

"If Eunice does it, I'll do it. I can't run fast, but I'd participate. I have a lot of anger in me because my father was a bourbon slamming, wife-beating, kid-slapping son of a gun. You'd think my anger would be gone with him being dead and burning in hell for five years, but I still got it."

"I'm angry that my kids don't come to see me," huffed LouLou Meiers. LouLou was the wrong name for this woman. "LouLou" is the name of a fun and sweet woman who likes to party. This one served in the military for twenty-five years and always talks like a drill sergeant.

"Maybe if you didn't scare them so much and always tell them to address you as ma'am instead of mom, and if you didn't wake them up at the crack of dawn for running and exercising when they're here visiting, and if you didn't insist that they fold their sheets like they're in boot camp, they'd come by more."

"Humph," LouLou said. "Up early, make your bed right, exercise your body so you can exercise your mind. Go to bed early. That's how I raised 'em, that's how it's going to be when they return for visits."

"It's not working, LouLou."

LouLou appeared baffled. Why would anyone not want the discipline of a military life?

"Let's do it," a mother of five said. "I'm mad because my teenagers are awful. They are wild and sneak out of the house and drink alcohol and are probably having sex. It's a small island, you would think I could find them screwing around, but no. So. Tonight. At the lake. No one's around."

"I'll do it. My menopause is a raging red bull inside of me. Have I told you about the vaginal dryness I'm experiencing? I need gel or oil or something for it. My aunt told me to put basil leaves on it. My cousin told me the skin of a banana would help. It didn't."

There was some interest in talking about vaginal dryness, but soon they were back to the naked run.

By God and by golly, they did it. I heard about it later. Nighttime. Naked. Running. Jogging. Walking. Around the lake. They invited me and I said I had a lot of work to do at the bookstore, woe is me. Plus, I'm not going to do something I hate to do, like running. The only time I want to run is if a bear is chasing me.

As for the book? Most of them liked it. But one of them thought it was a "ridiculous and unrealistic look into a half-cocked woman's first-world problems. Annoying. Irritating. Honestly, I wanted to hit her. Let's go back to a classic for next week as this book made my brain rot."

Seeing someone's future, especially if it's bad, is totally distressing.

Part of it is because if I can prevent it, I have to plan. I have to figure out how to do it, when to do it. It often involves keeping a vigilant eye out for when the premonition is coming. I've learned to look at people's clothing in the premonition, which is how I can try to identify when something is going to happen.

As a kid, once I accepted that I wasn't *causing* the bad event to happen, once I understood that other people couldn't see the future, it was even more terrifying.

As an adult, it's still terrifying.

You can save someone, or leave them to their fate.

You can interfere, or not.

It's often a moral nightmare.

I suppose some theologist might say, "Leave fate to fate." Or "Don't interfere with others' lives." Or, the one I like least, "It's God's will."

That is easy to say perched atop a philosophical, fundamentalist, or religious mountain.

But when you know that Mrs. Keeton, who is your favorite librarian, or Antonio Juarez or little Jason Chambers is going to *die* if you don't do something, if you don't say something, and they are loving people with many people who love them who will be crushed if they are killed, and who knows what horrendous reverberations will strike amidst their family and friends, you act.

You have to.

I had to.

Most of the time.

But sometimes I don't do or say anything, and I have to emotionally and intellectually make decisions that I don't like to make. Sometimes, for example, if I see that someone is going to die soon of a terminal illness, and there's nothing I can do to change that, I say nothing.

I have also declined to help, to intervene, several times because the person was absolutely awful and the people around that person would be better off without him or her.

Sounds harsh, doesn't it?

Who am I *not* to interfere when I see doom coming for them, even if I think the world would be a better place without them?

I don't know. It's like playing God, but I am an imperfect God.

I can see incredible, happy news coming for people, too. I see their laughter, their relief, their families celebrating. I love those, and whispering to someone who is in pain now about what will come for them later, bring them joy, is a relief to them and me. It lightens life's load.

But almost each day I have to go and stand on the edge of the ocean, near my carriage house, feet in the sand, and watch the waves to maintain my calm and prevent "the shakes," which happens when I get overstressed.

Sometimes it works, sometimes it doesn't.

Like life in general. Sometimes it works, sometimes it doesn't.

I saw Marco two days later at his clinic. Butch hurt his foot. He was limping. He chased after a squirrel, and the squirrel won. Marco got him all bandaged up. Butch licked him when he was done.

We had long moments of gazing into each other's eyes. I saw in his eyes . . . attraction, I thought. Interest. Confusion. Sadness. And questions. Lots of questions. I had the answers but couldn't share them with him. I had shut him down many times when he gently asked to go on a hike or lunch or dinner . . .

Afterward I went and bought an ice-cream cone. Peppermint and chocolate chip are so good next to each other.

Then I went to my beach and cried my eyes out.

I stopped crying when Mr. Bob and Trixie Goat appeared.

"How did you two get out of your pen again?"

Mr. Bob kicked his legs up, taunting me. Trixie head butted him. I swear she smiled at me.

"I can hardly breathe, Evie."

"Yes, you can. Sit down, Jules." It was late, I was in bed, and I put aside two books I was reading, a memoir and historical fiction, while I balanced my phone in my hand. Sometimes I like to mix and blend my books. When I placed the books down on top of a stack of books, the stack fell over. Dang it. That had happened in my kitchen nook today, too, next to the library filing cabinet. A whole stack toppled over.

"I can't breathe, Evie. I'm pacing."

I heard Jules trying to get her breath. "Everything's going to be okay, Jules. It is."

"But I'm getting married. M.A.R.I.E.D. Did I leave out an *R*? I think I did."

"Do you want to get married?"

"Yes, I do. I would give up my motorcycles, my house, and all my tattoos to marry Mack."

"So you're worried about the day of the wedding?"

"I don't know. Maybe." I heard her gasp. "I'm going to have a panic attack. I hate panic attacks. Oh no. Here it comes. It's like a wave, you know? A tsunami of fear and breathlessness and you have to fight back the tsunami. Oh no. Oh no."

I thought about what I could do to get her to calm down. Panic attacks are the worst. You feel like you're dying or losing your mind. I don't know which is worse. "Tell me why you love Mack."

"He's acrobatic in bed," Jules gushed, her breathing still short. "I mean, that's not the only thing. But look at him. Lots to cuddle." She took a deep breath. "Lots to love. I love how big he is. Everywhere big, if you know what I mean. But I can handle it! He thinks he's fat, but I think he's a huggable bear."

"What else?"

"He's romantic." She wasn't panting anymore. "When we're

in bed, he takes his time, you know? Sometimes I'm, like, let's do a quickie because I have to go to work and paint a bike, but he's like, no, baby, let's have some fun. And pretty soon I'm late to work."

"And what else do you like about him? About his personality?" I tried to stress the word *personality*. Not bed. Personality.

"He's sexy. I mean, the way he thinks about me, about us, how he kisses me and holds me. And I like how creative he is. Always thinking of different things we can do in bed. He brought home these fun sex toys the other day. We have enough for, like, a month now."

I'd try to ask things in a different way. "Is he generous? Is he kind? Is he thoughtful? Is he protective?"

"Yes. Absolutely generous. When we're in bed he always lets me have my woo-woo first. He says he's a gentleman and it's always ladies first. When I need to have another one, he's very welcoming about it. And he's kind and thoughtful." She was breathing, calming down. "He knows that I don't like sex first thing in the morning, so he always lets me get showered and have my coffee first, and he's protective because he always makes sure that all the curtains are closed before we have sex on the kitchen table or the island in the kitchen. He says he doesn't want any of the neighbors seeing his beautiful fiancée."

I gave up on the personality questions. "You sound better now, Jules."

"What? I am." She breathed deep. "Wow. Way freakin' better. I'm so happy. I can't wait to get married and be Mrs. Jules. It's going to be the best day of my life. Mack says the day we're married is going to be the best day of his life, too. We decided how many kids we're going to have over Chinese food last night. Know how we did it? We were eating naked in bed, and we broke the chopsticks up and sat knee to knee and threw the pieces up in the air. All the pieces that landed in the little triangle you make when you've got your legs crossed, that's how many kids we agreed we would have."

"And what was that number?"

"Eight." She sighed. "I can't wait 'til we're married. Hang on, I'm going to show you my wedding shoes! I can't keep it a surprise any longer!"

She texted me a photo of her wedding shoes. No satin heels for her. No white ballet shoes. She was going to rock it in a biker way.

"You're going to be the sexiest bride ever."

"I know, right?! Wait 'til I get in bed with Mack in these. He'll lose his mind."

Well, Mack might lose his mind, but, even better, my sister had lost her panic attack.

Chapter 8

〜

"Serafina spent her days with her four brothers and four sisters."

"What did they do?"

"They explored the ocean. They swam through ancient sailing ships. They found treasure chests buried deep beneath the waves. They explored coral reefs. They jumped with the dolphins in parts of the ocean that no humans go to. They swam through caves to lagoons."

"And none of her brothers and sisters had a tail like hers? With colors from the flowers in Mom's garden?"

"No. They all had shiny green tails, normal mermaid and mermen tails."

"Where were their mom and dad?"

"They lived in an undersea castle altogether. They loved their children very much. They were surprised that Serafina had such a colorful tail. No one else in their family had anything but a green tail, but they told her it was special and they told her that they loved her."

"Are mermaids nice?"

"Yes. But one merman wasn't nice."

"Oh no. What happened?"

"Are you ready for the scary part?"

"Yes. I'm brave. Tell me."

Chapter 9

∽

It was my grandmother, Lucy, who planned and planted the lush, winding gardens around Rose Bloom Cottage. Lucy was a sweet, loving, absolutely delusional woman. She was mostly sane for the first few years of her marriage, if only somewhat eccentric and quirky, then she seemed to slip more each year, my mother and aunts told me.

My mother and aunts took care of their mother starting at an early age, as their father owned the grocery store in town and worked a twelve-hour day. Their mother often wandered off. Now and then she stole a boat and snuck off the island, which required every person living here at the time—and there weren't that many—to go search for her, along with the Coast Guard. She had thick black hair, an olive complexion, and dark brown eyes like my mother, sister, and aunts.

I've seen photos of her, and she was stunning. She was half French and half Greek, and she liked, now and then, to think that she was magical. "I'm part fairy," she told her daughters, "and you are, too."

Who knew what Grandma Lucy suffered from? They didn't have all the labels then that we do now. My mother and aunts' best guess was that she was somewhere on the bi-polar spectrum.

"With a twist of fantasy," my mother said.

"With a dollop of magical thinking," said Aunt Camellia.

"She was loving and gentle and flat-out crazy," Aunt Iris said.

My grandma died when she was forty-eight. She jumped off the cliff at the south end of the island. Two fishermen were in their boat below when they saw her running across the top of the cliff in a flowing pink dress, pink ribbons in her long black hair, her arms outstretched. Lucy never stopped as she leaped off the edge. They swore they heard her laughing, even when she was under the waves.

The fishermen, I was told, were absolutely traumatized as they pulled her broken body out of the water.

Lucy loved flowers. She loved her garden. And when she was in her garden, planting, digging, pulling weeds, creating pathways and different garden rooms with shrubs and trees that still stand today, she was peaceful. She was focused.

She knew where a small wood bridge over a rock river would look best. She knew where her garden needed a trellis and a red bench down a curving path. She knew where the vegetable garden would thrive. She knew where a pond should be built for lily pads and where a blue bistro table should be placed under a willow tree for reading books.

When she gardened, Lucy wore a straw hat, a flowered dress, and her red boots, which still have the place of honor to the right of the front door. She smiled and sang while she worked. She was a master gardener, everyone said so, and her garden is one of her legacies.

Lucy is why my mother and my aunts love flowers, too. They loved their mother. If she wasn't having a bad day, or a bad week, where she would cry and moan under the covers of her bed with the lights off, she would hug them, sing to them, and make up intricate fairy tales. She did not get meals on the table. She did not do housework, she would disappear for days on end in the woods, she would swim naked in the middle of the day with others around, and she believed she could heal people with a touch.

"She would pick bouquets for people all over the island," my mom told me. "Dad would drive her around to deliver them to people in need. She said she looked for people who needed a smile. She would put on a flowered dress and a tutu and sparkling glitter on her face and tell everyone she was the flower fairy."

"When Gene Sheldt lost his wife, she brought him flowers each week for two months," Aunt Iris said.

"When Jory Lefts was ill, same thing," Aunt Camellia said. "For months."

"When Abigail's husband left her with three kids, she brought the little girls each a bouquet every Tuesday all summer."

Everyone loved her. She may have been on the mental health spectrum somewhere, but the spectrum was a generous, kind spectrum.

"There was not a drop of unkindness in her," Aunt Camellia told me.

"It's why everyone loved her, everyone took care of her, and us," my mother said. "The neighbors often brought us meals. Cookies. Pies. Cakes. They wanted to help. Mom would greet them at the door in a princess dress and wand, welcome them in, hold their hands, smile."

"That's why the three of us were never teased in school about her," Aunt Iris said. "Even when she would walk to town naked with one of our dogs on a leash."

"Even when she wore wings," my mother said.

After high school, one by one, they all left for college. In fact, they were in college when their mother took a flying leap off a cliff. They have all told me how guilty they felt: If they had stayed on the island, would their mother have jumped? Probably not, they thought. And the guilt never left.

"She loved us, we knew that," my mother said. "Was it so hard to bear, having all her girls gone, that she couldn't stand it anymore? Could she not endure the battle in her head any longer? I have cried during a hundred black nights trying to answer that question."

"Guilt has plagued my soul," my aunt Camellia said. "My soul will never be able to remove that stain of responsibility in leaving her, of abandoning her, of not being there for her each day, when I knew she was ill."

My aunt Iris was direct: "The vision of her jumping will never leave me. Because behind her I see myself, pushing her."

And yet I have also listened to my mother and my aunts talking about their mother, how they intellectually knew that they shouldn't feel guilty, how they were not responsible, how they did everything for her, and were they never to go to college? Never to leave the island? Lucy had their father, who loved her, cared for her, as best he could. She had friends and neighbors she had known for years. My mom and aunts came home to visit all the time, including all summer to work in the family grocery store, in shifts, so someone would always be with Lucy.

My mother became a nurse, her interest in medicine, in healing her mother, sparking that interest, but then, as she traveled the world, following my dad in the military, where she often couldn't work, she started her own small floral business. She loved arranging flowers and making bouquets, as she had with her mother, so that's what she did.

My aunt Camellia owned a huge nursery and a mail order bulb business outside of Seattle. "I wanted to calm people's spirits, soothe their angst, comfort them in their need, through flowers and gardens." Again, you can see my grandma's love of flowers in the business Aunt Camellia started. She sold it for a huge profit when she moved to the island ten years ago and changed her career to become a "Lotion and Potion Pixie."

Aunt Camellia was married for two years, but her husband, as she says, "turned the other way and decided that I did not have the right plumbing," and never married again. When her husband was trying to pretend he wasn't gay, they did get pregnant twice, but Aunt Camellia miscarried. Then something happened, she won't say what, and she was no longer able to have children, which broke her heart.

There have been a number of long-term boyfriends for Aunt Camellia. "I like romance, and there is nothing wrong with bringing a new spiritual romantic partner into your life, regularly, every three years or so for a new physical and mental awakening. Tra la la."

Aunt Iris is a botanist. She traveled the world for decades, studying plants and flowers through her job as a university professor. Her husband of forty years, Arvid, was with her when he died in Kenya of a heart attack, and she's missed him every day since. Her love of photographing flowers came from Lucy. She photographs them from under the stem, or with half the flower in the frame, or drooping. They're lovely, but people always stop and stare and try to figure the photo out. Somehow the flowers look emotional, sad or alone or joyous, or as if they're going to straighten up and talk to you.

Even their business reflects Grandma Lucy. The inside of Flowers, Lotions, and Potions is painted pink, the ceiling a lighter pink. They play country music, rock, or classical depending on their mood. In the center is a round antique table where a huge bouquet is always flourishing.

They'll hang tiny people dressed in ethnic clothing from branches stuck in the middle of a bouquet of sunflowers. A sign will read, "Let's make our world welcoming." Or they'll hang red Valentine hearts from the ceiling in front of a wildflower display, with photos of their Hollywood boyfriends attached: Jimmy Smits. The Rock. Keanu Reeves. Robert Redford. Denzel Washington. Morgan Freeman. "Who Is Your Hollywood Boyfriend?" a sign says, and people are invited to write down names on hearts.

They might have a pink tulip display, but then they'll have birth control packets attached to bamboo shoots. They'll make a sign that says, "This Is Birth Control Awareness Month. Remember That Health Insurance Pays for Viagra, So It Should Pay for Your Birth Control! Call Your Senators and Representatives Today!"

They'll make "political statement bouquets" before an election. Two years ago they hand-painted a lovely sign with red letters next to a calla lily bouquet. It said, "Don't Vote for a Dick." The person running was named Richard. He lost.

A minister protested about one of their flower displays because it was titled "The Glories of Being a Feminist."

"Feminism is a threat to marriage," he intoned, so piously.

"A man who wants to dominate and control his wife is a threat to marriage," my mother snapped at him, his quiet, cowed wife standing beside him. "Pretty soon the wife won't take it anymore and she'll leave her balding, paunchy, middle-aged husband for someone smarter and handsome." She eyed the middle-aged minister's bald head and bulging stomach. "It does get tiresome in bed to sleep with a man who has a medieval attitude about women."

The quiet, cowed wife then laughed to her sanctimonious husband's surprise.

My mother and aunts say they'll always be together, "unless," as Aunt Camellia says, "I find another lover. Then you two are going to have to leave, or at least move to the barn when he spends the night so I don't have to worry about you listening in. I should make a lotion called Sexy Lotion. Or Nighttime Naughtiness. Or, simply, Lust."

"It would sell," Aunt Iris said. "Sounds like it'll appeal to a carnal audience, particularly to people like us in our horny years."

"You could make a lot of money," my mother said. "Maybe I'll find a lover, too. Sorry, dear." She glanced at me.

"It's okay, Mom." My dad had been gone a long time. She deserved a lover.

"I think I'm up for a lover," Aunt Iris said. "It's unlikely I'll get pregnant, no matter how exuberant I get with my new man. But if I did get pregnant, I would know it was an act of God and I would know that the second coming of Jesus Christ was in my uterus. I would then act accordingly and stop drinking wine and scotch and I would stop smoking an occasional cigar and I'd quit eating pie for dinner and eat more carrots. God," she groaned, "that sounds awful."

"I'd love to see you knocked up." My mother laughed. "White hair and a huge stomach."

This started a conversation on getting pregnant at seventy and how a body would hold up.

They're hilarious.

They are their mother's daughters, and Lucy's love for them burns brightly, still shining from every inch of her magnificent island garden.

*   *   *

Every year I fill a number of pots on my front porch with white geraniums right when summer is starting. I like white, and the white geraniums look sharp next to two white roses I have on either side of my porch.

I couldn't find my trowel, so I headed over to the greenhouse. I knew I could find one in there. My aunts and mother were keeping lights on in the greenhouse because they were growing more seedlings, as usual. And orchids. They love orchids. They love exotic flowers, too, the ones you'd find in Africa or Hawaii or Thailand, so they needed warmth and lights.

I opened the door. Inside the greenhouse, right in the middle, there's a circular table with a mosaic top. My mother and aunts made the mosaic together. It's the three of them, three sisters, only they've turned themselves into fairies, wearing silver and gold wings and flowered hats, sitting at a table drinking tea and eating pink cake. They are quite artistic.

There are four black iron chairs with red pillows around the table. They also have a shelf filled with books, poetry, mugs, and art supplies.

There were seedlings, pink plumeria, birds-of-paradise, yellow hibiscus, and orchids. I stopped to admire the orchids, the lavender, pink, pure white, purple, coral, scarlet, and butter yellow colors that blended right in the middle to make flower miracles.

I headed toward the back where I knew they had a bucket of tools. Then I stopped. Right by the lights.

Whoa.

Oh, whoa.

I said some bad words. I could not believe this. I put my hands to my head.

It's like dealing with rebellious teenagers sometimes, it really is.

"I want to give you this book." I held out a heavy coffee table book on Italy to the couple in front of me. She looked to be about seventy, her husband about seventy-five.

"I beg your pardon?" the husband asked.

"I want to give this to you. I overheard you talking about wanting to see Italy one day, and I think you should have this book. It's on me. I'm the owner here, and I want you to have it. No charge."

They glanced at each other in confusion. Was she serious? Should we do it? Is it wrong to take it? Should we pay her?

Take the book, I thought. *Take it. Book the trip you've always wanted to go on.*

I turned the pages of the book and showed them Italy. Venice. Rome. Florence. I showed them photos of mountains and streams, charming villages and ancient cities, pizza and wine. "Please. Take it."

"Oh, we couldn't," the husband said, his voice gravelly, his smile gentle. "We'll pay for it, if you think we should have it that much."

"I insist." *Take the book.* "Maybe you should plan that trip to Italy." I smiled. Encouragingly. Hopefully.

The wife smiled. "Herman. Maybe we should."

Herman's eyes lit up. "Maybe you're right, honey."

"We've always wanted to go. We've talked about it for fifty years. The kids even say we should go."

"We like pasta," Herman said. "And we like wine and bread, Rubina."

"It's our time, honey," Rubina said softly. "Our time. Six kids. Decades of work. We should go."

They smiled at each other. Herman raised his eyebrows at her. She nodded her head back. They walked out with a mystery for Herman, a biography on Abe Lincoln for her, and my free Italian book.

They came back in the store three days later and bought two travel books on Italy. They were so excited. "We're going," the wife gushed. "We called a travel agent and we're leaving in one week."

The husband rocked back on his heels. "We're old, but we're not too old."

"We're young enough to have an Italian romance, right, Herman?"

He laughed.

"Thank you," they both said to me.

"You pushed us to jump on the dream," Herman said.

"And now we're going to Italy!" Rubina raised her fists in victory. "For one month!"

I bagged their purchases as we chatted. They looked at each other with such love. How many people get that?

Herman would be dead soon. I saw his body in my premonition, wracked with disease in the hospital. He would die during the Christmas holidays. I saw a tree in the background, the stockings, and how he had collapsed.

Rubina would have the memory of their Italian trip forever. That meant something.

That night I had dinner with my mother and aunts. We sat on their back patio, pink, white, and red roses soon to be in full bloom like a wave of glory on the trellis above. I could not bear to bring up the dreaded, ridiculous subject. I was confounded that I had to bring it up at all. It had been a long day at the bookstore, then I'd come home and taken Shakespeare and Jane Austen on a ride. I was not up to it. I sighed.

Aunt Iris told me, "When we were younger I took off my bra and swung it around my head and launched my belief in feminism. Equal rights, that's all feminism means. Equal rights for women."

"That was a wild time," my mother said. "Protests. Marches. Demonstrations."

"What?" I put down my fork.

"We danced and took off our shirts and drank too much and sat and talked with other people and learned from them," Aunt Camellia said, flipping her white curls back. "We launched our feminine enlightenment. We grasped our own freedom, our power, our voices."

"You never told her about all this?" Aunt Iris said.

"Not in graphic detail. I am her mother," my mother said. "The sixties were an uncontrolled, changing, revolutionary time."

"And amidst all that," Aunt Camellia said, "we had to dance. We had to celebrate. And we had to get angry at what was going on." She raised her fist and shook it.

"We had to sing," my mother said. "And find ourselves. Find ourselves within a society that had repressed women. We had to find our place and our role and what *we* wanted, not what we were told to want."

"We had to grow and learn and change and think," Aunt Iris said. "We had to break barriers. We had to deal with men who wanted to keep us down, to keep us in traditional roles that would smother us, keep us from becoming who we wanted to become."

"I never knew this," I said, as they chatted on about Vietnam. Marches they participated in. Civil rights. Social issues.

"We learned about our sexuality during that time," Aunt Iris said. "We finally talked about that taboo subject. Who controlled our bodies? Us, or a man who had control over us? We learned we weren't bad girls for liking sex. So many of us had been raised in a puritanical era that said if you had sex before marriage you were a slut. It was very damaging, misogynistic, and cruel."

"It led to women feeling horrible about themselves," Aunt Camellia said. "Me included, when I was younger."

"So I shed my fear of sex," Aunt Iris said. "And I walked away from the 'good girl rules' of sex, which were written by patronizing, paternalistic men who lived by a double standard. Being a 'good girl' was so dreary, so dull. By the way, I'm not going to tell you which band leader I slept with during a three-day concert even if you beg."

"Who was it? I'll beg!" I said. "Totally willing to beg."

"Why should I tell you?"

"Because I'm curious. I shouldn't be. But I am. I want to know."

She raised her eyebrows at me, then she tilted her head and looked proud of herself. She told me whom she'd slept with.

"You're kidding." I leaned forward. He was famous.

"No. I did. It was fun. He wanted to see me again."

"Did you?"

"No. Because the next night there was another band, and I slept with another man in that band."

"Who?" My gosh. What was going on here?

"Why should I tell you?" Aunt Iris asked, one eyebrow lifting.

"Same reason. I'm curious."

She told me.

"You're kidding."

"No. Why do you keep asking me if I'm kidding? Do you think I'm lying, young woman?" She tsked. Then she grinned, then tried not to grin, then grinned again.

"Romantic memories," Aunt Camellia gushed.

"I think it was lustful memories," my mother said.

"Romance. Lust. Whatever." Aunt Iris moved a hand back and forth. "I'm glad I have them."

"Those memories are delicious," Aunt Camellia said. "I still get a kick out of my love affairs here and there."

"They make you smile when you go to sleep at night," my mother said.

"This has been a surprising and entertaining conversation, and I've learned a lot about you three," I said. There is so much that we don't know about our own mothers and aunts. They were younger, they were us, and yet . . . we know only what they've chosen to share with us, to talk about.

"No one is who you think they are," Aunt Camellia said. "We all have different sides to us, and some sides we hide from everyone. We're different people at different times in our lives, too. Plus"—she winked—"there are the secrets."

"All women have secrets," Aunt Iris said. "Some juicier than others."

"Let's talk about . . ." I named the rocker she slept with. "Was he . . ."

"Oh yes." She rolled her eyes. "He was heavenly. Totally worth it. I still have his records. You know that song 'Iris on the Wind'?"

I nodded.
She raised her eyebrows at me.
Oh, my goodness.

Torrance needed more books, his surgery keeping him house-bound, so I had to go by the house with all the memories again. On my way to Torrance's, I turned my head away so I wouldn't have to see that abandoned, falling-down home, but on the way back to town, it was as if I couldn't *not* look. I felt my eyes fill with tears, and I stopped across the street.

The yellow was faded, the white trim dirty, the green door tilted. I wasn't surprised that no one new had bought the home. What happened there couldn't be erased, it was part of our island's history. More tears spilled out as if they'd been waiting for me, waiting for a weak moment so the grief could sneak out. Because that's what grief does. It sneaks out on you when you're having a weak moment.

So much laughter in that house, so much fear, so much violence.

So much blood.

My fault.

Early Wednesday evening, after a busy day at the bookstore, the summer sun headed on down amidst soft pink and orange streaks, I checked on all my furry family members. I was in a light blue summer dress that stopped mid-thigh with eyelet trim and blue earrings made from silver hammered metal. I had matching silver hammered metal bracelets on. I like to dress nice in case I run into Marco in town or at my bookstore, oh, be still, my foolish beating heart.

I slipped off my sandals and pulled on my red boots to take care of the animals.

Jane Austen and Shakespeare hurried right on up to the fence for their apples, but the goats, Mr. Bob and Trixie Goat, were outside of their pretty goat home, staring at me, wagging their tails. They were between two rows of black-eyed Susans and sunflowers. They grinned, the bells on their collars ringing.

"How did you get out, Houdinis?" They are insufferable. I have no idea how they escape their pen and leap the fence. None. They wanted to be petted, and I gave them some alfalfa, then I tried to get them to go back into their home. They refused. I chased them. They outran me, then turned to taunt me. I grabbed the alfalfa and a handful of hay, threw it in their yard, and they scampered in and I locked the gate. They're not that bright, just bright enough to escape.

The cats wound themselves around my feet, popping in from all over the property as if they were transmitting through cat radar that I was home. I went over to the lambs' homes, and they all clipped on over, right in line: Padre, Momma, Jay Rae, Raptor, and The TMan. I pet their heads and said hello.

Butch and Cassidy bounded out of the house through their dog door, tongues wagging. "Hi, guys," I said. "Where's Sundance?"

As if they knew what I was asking, they started barking and running toward the house, then back to me, then running toward the house. I ran behind them, past the wild flowers and the verbena and Jupiter's-beard, knowing something was wrong. This had nothing to do with a premonition, but you know to follow a dog who is barking and turning around to make sure that you're following.

And there was Sundance. Groaning, on his side, panting, on my porch. He obviously had been trying to make it down the steps, probably to say hello to me.

"Sundance," I said, getting on all fours, feeling my eyes fill with tears. "Sundance, honey."

He panted, then grunted, and his eyes rolled back. "Oh no. Oh no." This was bad. I picked him up and ran toward my truck, tripping at his weight. Sundance is a big, heavy, furry dog, and I love him, but he's built like a dog tank.

I had to put him down on the ground to open the passenger door. Butch and Cassidy both licked him, the cats about ten feet behind. They obviously did not do well with emergencies.

I gently put Sundance in the front seat, then ran around and jumped in the driver's seat. "It's okay, Sundance," I said, my voice breaking, petting his golden furry head, his stomach heaving up and down, his eyes wide with fear. "It's okay."

I drove down our long driveway to Robbins Drive, then down the winding street through the main part of town, past the blue bay and my yellow bookstore on the left and into the hills, then back out toward the ocean. I turned at Marco's driveway, the sun headed down when I pulled in front of the clinic. "Hang in there, Sundance, it's okay."

There was only one other car there. A teenage girl was leaving the clinic, cradling her cat.

I ran around the truck, trying not to cry, and grabbed Sundance. He was panting, making choking sounds.

The teenage girl, Tari, ran for the door and held it open for me, her cat in one arm, elongated like a cat rubber band, as she struggled to hold him and the door. The cat had a disgusted look on his face, as if he couldn't believe this undignified thing was happening to him. I ignored it. I had an emergency.

"Thank you," I said.

Gayle wasn't there, but I could see Marco in the back of the clinic.

"Marco!" I called out. He saw my face and came running, opening the door to the reception area.

"Let me have him," he said, and gently took Sundance out of my arms.

He took a limp Sundance into an exam room and laid him on the table. He was gentle, and efficient, and Sundance lay quietly, with only a few whimpers.

"I think he's swallowed something," he said.

"Oh no. Will it kill him? Can you get it out?"

"Let's X-ray him." On the X-ray he saw something that shouldn't be there and induced vomiting. It wasn't pleasant, poor Sundance. Marco pulled something out of his mouth.

Oh dear.

And there was the evidence.

So embarrassing.

Sundance had eaten one of my pink lacy panties.

I groaned.

Marco laughed.

"I think you'll need new underwear."

"Oh dear."

"Let me know if you'd like me to buy it for you."

For heaven's sakes. "Why did you have to say something so sexy?"

"Ah. Was that sexy?"

"Stop that sexy smile."

He tried to frown. He looked intimidating, intimidating but so sizzling hot, darn him, then he laughed. That man turned me on so much I wanted to lie down on the grass outside and catch my breath while fanning my flushing face.

"I don't know what to say to that one," I said.

"Say yes."

I rolled my eyes at him, then turned toward Sundance, who bounded right over to me with his three-legged wobble as if to say, "There! You can have them back now!"

"Have you had dinner?" Marco asked as I pet Sundance and told him never to do that again.

"I haven't even had lunch," I said. "The bookstore was busy today. I had a group in for their monthly meeting, and I joined them. The Scientific Nerds group. They were discussing new research in genetics, and it was interesting. It appealed to the nerd in me."

"I heard about them. There's a number of retired scientists and tech people living here, isn't there?"

"Yes. Anton Husk lives here, too." Anton was, apparently, famous in the nerd science world. "Have you met him? He walks around in red pants and a black hoodie most days. He wears sunglasses even on overcast days because he has social anxiety and he says it helps him to stay calm if people try to talk to him."

"I've met him. We went fishing together on my boat. His father was a fisherman, and he worked with him for years in Alaska. He definitely relaxed when we were all out on the water."

He pet Sundance again. He was a gentle man, but tough, too. "I'm hungry. Want to come over to the house and have dinner with me? Sundance can come with us. He seems a lot better."

"Oh no. I couldn't."

"Why? I mean." He put his hands up. "I'm sorry. No pressure. I haven't eaten for hours, and I actually have turtle soup."

"What is turtle soup?"

"Mrs. Gradenni made it for me. I healed her Persian cat. There are no turtles in it. Vegetables. Chicken. I think. I'm not sure. But definitely no turtles, so don't ask why it's called turtle soup. It does have a green color to it. . . ."

Soup sounded delicious. I knew Mrs. Gradenni, and she made amazing soup. But could I eat with Marco? Could I control myself? There was, for sure, a bed in that house. "Thanks. Yes. I'll have some soup and eat you." Oh, Lord. "I mean, I'll eat some soup. By you. With you. Turtles and soup, but I realize there are no turtles in the soup."

Please shut up, please stop talking.

Marco smiled at me, his eyes indulgent, amused, friendly.

"Great. Let's go."

"Yes. Let's go and eat turtles. Uh. Well. Turtle soup." I laughed as if I'd deliberately made a joke. But I hadn't.

Try not to fall more in love with him, Evie. Try.

And close your mouth.

"Tell me more about your life growing up with a father in the military," Marco said. I told him I was born in Portland, Oregon, how we lived in the Middle East for three years when I was a toddler, then four years in Germany, and four years in Washington, DC, and Georgia before moving to the island.

"My father worked for the military, for the government . . ." I paused because I didn't quite know when my father's job switched from military to a *different* sort of job within the government. "And he traveled a lot, but my mom and Jules and I were here." He had a lot of questions, but they didn't seem nosy to me. They seemed . . . interested. Kindly interested.

It had never been lost on me that my beloved father was a

military man . . . as was Marco. But they shared many of the same characteristics that any normal woman looked for: Kindness. Intelligence. Humor. Protectiveness. Maturity and insight. Experience. Courage. Dedication and a strong work ethic.

We ate the turtle soup with no turtles in it in his kitchen as we chatted. Marco had a rustic yet modern open home with views that spilled out everywhere toward the ocean, as I'd imagined. His four dogs, all rescues, hung out with us, too, Sundance having made a miraculous recovery. They were fairly well behaved, one more naughty than the others. One tried to sit in my lap. I let him.

"You were brave to serve, Marco."

"I was proud to serve, still am. But it was tough." He hesitated, then said, "After I served, I know I told you this already, but I had a hard time for a while. I still do. I still struggle. But it was years ago and it's better now. When I got out of the military, I traveled. I went to Vietnam, Thailand, Laos, parts of Africa."

We talked about his travels and I, the island hermit, lived vicariously through his adventures. "Why did you become a vet?"

"I like animals. They're innocent. They are not dangerous like humans are. The wild ones may eat other animals, but it's nutrition based, right?" He smiled. "I like healing them. I wasn't interested in being a vet until I served in the military. I planned on going to medical school. But then I saw too much death. Too many horrific injuries. I have seen enough human pain to last forever. Some of it, even though I try, I'll never forget." He looked away for a minute, and I could tell he was trying to get control of his emotions. He sighed, blinked, and I knew he'd gone to the battlefields and come back. I wanted to hold his hand, because I wanted to comfort that hurting, courageous giant, but I didn't have the guts.

"I have always liked animals. There were stray dogs in Iraq. It was pathetic, the condition they were in. We fed them, tried to help. But some had rabies and had to be put down."

"That's terrible." I meant it. Tears came to my eyes. I hate hearing about sick or hurt or unloved animals.

"It is. It was. So after my service I traveled then became a vet in Portland, then I came up to the island on a bike trip with my brothers"—he smiled at me—"and it was beautiful. I had a vet practice in Portland, but I was tired of the noise and the traffic and all the people, and I wanted to live closer to nature. Then I met someone in a bookstore called Evie's Books, Cake, and Tea, and thought she might want to be friends."

Whew! I felt myself blush. Lord, I am way too old to blush, but there it was. I remembered the day Marco and his brothers trooped in as if it happened this afternoon. They were all in their bike pants and shirts, tall and rangy and masculine, and right from the start I was attracted to Marco. He had smiled and I was done in. He walked toward me and I wanted to get naked in my own bookstore. He towered over me and I wanted to hug him.

We stood and stared at each other, smiling like fools, his brothers snickering in a friendly way behind him. I finally muttered a "Hello. May I help you find a happy?" Which was ridiculous. And I coughed and said, "May I help you find a book?"

"Yes, thank you. You can help me find a happy and a book."

Marco was as handsome as a sexy devil, and he was pure man. Pure male.

He asked about nonfiction books I liked, and I stumbled all over myself and showed him my favorites. He bought five books, which was funny, as his brothers quietly laughed, because he was biking and didn't have much room for the books, but he took them anyhow.

He came in twice more for books on his trip, buying five more books each time. I offered to mail them to his home in Portland. He said yes, and I mailed them off. He e-mailed me a thank-you later, and I responded. It was friendly banter back and forth, a couple of phone calls, but I started to draw back, not answer his e-mails.

I was surprised—no, shocked—when he decided to move to the island and let me know he was coming. I got him in touch with a competent realtor, suggested places he might like to live.

He said to me, "I'm looking forward to seeing you . . . and how about dinner when I get there?"

And I had to tell him that I wasn't dating at that time. That was true. I don't date. But the reason I couldn't date him specifically was completely different from why I don't date in general. Completely different and completely tragic.

It was awkward and I felt horrible, and Marco was polite and kind, and still moved out to the island anyhow, so I knew he did love it here.

He was engaging and funny and interesting when he came into the bookstore to see me or when we accidentally met in town or when I saw him as a vet. He was never overbearing. He wasn't pushy. He was his gorgeous and sexy and understanding gentlemanly self.

About a month after he came to the island, he tried to take me out again. "I know I have asked you before, but I thought I would try again. We can be friends. No pressure. Just dinner. Or fishing. Or we can read books by the ocean and I'll bring cake."

He knew I liked cake. My heart squeezed as I stared into those dark, soft eyes. I wanted to eat cake with Marco! "No, thank you."

"All right. Well, if you change your mind."

"I'm sorry, Marco. I can't date you." I winced. I shouldn't have said "you."

"Would you like to tell me why?"

"I'm not . . . I can't . . . I'm not into dating right now."

"Okay. Would you be into dating later? Say in a month or two or a year?"

"No, I don't think so."

"I understand."

He didn't. He didn't understand. He couldn't. I saw that he was disappointed, I saw that he was hurt.

How could he possibly understand the reason I couldn't date him? What I saw, clear as a lightning blast, that first day I met him in my bookstore, handing him one nonfiction book after another?

"Well. If you would like to go on a hike or out on my boat in a nondating situation, as friends, would you let me know?"

"Yes, I will."

There was more silence.

Dang. Double dang. I wanted to cry. I thought I might have seen a wet sheen over his eyes, too. I made a choked and inelegant sound in my throat.

"Evie?"

"Yes." I was trying not to sob like a fool in front of him that day. I am not a pretty crier. I get all red in the face and my eyes swell up and I often start to hiccup and then that can cause me to wet myself a little bit, I have no idea why. So I'm a wet mess all over.

"Please bring your animals to me when they're sick or hurt," Marco said. "I do want to help them, heal them. I don't want this to be awkward between us. I'll pretend I never asked you out if you pretend the same thing."

"Okay. Let's do that. And I'll probably see you soon." I sniffled ingloriously.

"I'd like that."

I tried to forget that I couldn't date Marco as we talked for three hours that night at his home, the conversation flowing and funny and deep, all at the same time. It was so easy to get lost in him, lost in us. He was a man in all senses of the word. You could trust him. You could rely on him. He was confident, but never arrogant. He had a history that had hard things in it, so he didn't expect other people to come perfect with no history.

He wouldn't want to know all of me, though, would he? The often anxious, obsessive, now and then depressed and worried person that I am who would find being a hermit to be a pleasant occupation? The woman who had a lot of animals she talked to as if they were people, who slept with three dogs and four cats, who had to be alone a lot to keep her head on straight, and who had a passion for books that was an inch from hoarding? Plus, the *other* stuff . . . groan.

I wanted to take my blue summer dress off my head and throw it behind my shoulder and jump the man.

Do not do that, Evie, I told myself. *No. Keep clothed. No bopping-about nudity.*

I longed for Marco.

I wanted to be with him. I wanted to hold him, and kiss him, but I remembered that chilling, bone-rattling premonition that day in the bookstore when he first walked in. I see what happens to him.

I cannot risk it. *He* cannot risk it.

Chapter 10

❧

"We made a bouquet today in the shape of a pig's face using pink roses," my mother said. "It was about three inches tall and twelve inches wide. I used black-eyed Susans for the eyes and red carnations for the bow on her head. We put it right up on Facebook and our web page, and everyone loved it. We had many pig-loving people write in saying they wanted the same bouquet delivered to them or people they knew on the mainland, but you know we only deliver to the islands."

My mother and Aunt Iris and Aunt Camellia and I were eating four-cheese garlic pizza on the deck of Rose Bloom Cottage, pink and red roses ready to bloom off the trellis, their scent light and sweet. Pizza is part of a healthy diet, so I made sure to have an extra slice. Lord knows I could die tomorrow, perhaps eaten by a whale, and I'd definitely want to make sure I had another piece of four-cheese garlic pizza in me before I headed up the golden staircase.

"I saw it," I said. "I heard about it from a customer. It was a sweet pig, personable."

The bouquet was labeled "Check your meat! Make sure you are getting your bacon from farmers who are kind to their pigs! Oink!"

"The other bouquet that was particularly popular," my mother said, "was the one Iris made. She used a piece of plywood, then glued fake grass over it and spelled out 'Tina Sorbel Sucks' with tiny glass vials and daisies. It was exquisite. Inspired!"

"Please tell me that you didn't put that one on Facebook or your website," I asked, dreading the answer and the possible defamation. The tulips were blooming, row after row of flower bliss. Iris had been busy photographing them, straight into the petals to that luminescent mystery in the center, from the stems up, in bunches and singles, upside down, at odd angles, and odd designs. They were almost like tulip people.

"Oh, yes, we did," my mother said, her shoulders squared. "For business and marketing reasons."

"We did it because of Karma," Aunt Camellia said, waving her arms. "What goes around comes around. Karma drifts around people like the wind." She moved her arms wildly. I think she was trying to imitate blustery wind and not a seizure.

"And we posted it because we're vengeful," Aunt Iris said, "when our friends are hurt."

"Who was the bouquet for?" I asked. There was a reason for this mean bouquet, by golly.

"It was for Kora Liponski over on Lopozzo Island," Aunt Iris said, her disgust apparent. "Her husband left her last week for that manipulative dragon. The lout. The spider. The worm. Her sister ordered Kora the bouquet to show sisterhood bonding."

"And the manipulative dragon who seduced the husband was Tina Sorbel," I said.

My mother and aunts nodded. I groaned. Poor Kora. Tina was prissy. Awful. Manipulative. She was a piece of work. However, she could be a sexy piece of work for a man dumb enough to fall for the vulnerable act she had perfected over the years, where she pretended that she needed protecting. Tina needed protecting about as much as a rabid viper.

"She did wrong," my mother said. "Taking another woman's man!"

"Hopefully her intestines will twist," Aunt Camellia said. "I don't like to get violent about people's intestines—I believe that one should wish for happiness and peace for all—but Tina deserves it. Kora and Vance have five young kids. Five. Tina has a black soul poisoned by her selfishness, and Vance has the brain of a skunk, but Vance was Kora's skunk and Tina shouldn't have taken the skunk. The skunk was Kora's to shoot, not Tina's."

"Tina Sorbel doesn't even seem like the type of woman who would like sex, so it's hard to picture a torrid affair here," I said. "She's too concerned with keeping her lipstick on straight and her hair brushed. She looks like an overgrown Barbie."

"I don't think she took Kora's husband for the sex," Aunt Iris said.

"She took him for his horses," my mother said.

"You're kidding."

"Oh no," Aunt Iris said. "Those horses are racing horses. He takes them off the island a couple of times a year. She loves traveling and wearing those fancy, silly hats to the horse races."

"Those hats don't compare with ours," Aunt Camellia sniffed. "We make our hats with the intent to bring smiles to others, to make them laugh, to bring creativity and color to their day."

"No comparison," my mother sniffed, too. "We make our hats with love."

"We will never make Tina a hat, or a bouquet. We will not even sell her one daisy," Aunt Iris said. "Can we agree on that simple, rational solution?"

"Agreed," my mother said. "She took Kora's husband, and that makes her not hat or flower worthy."

"She's on The List," Aunt Camellia intoned. She enthusiastically drew Tina's name in the air with an imaginary pen.

My mother and aunts have a Flower Black List they keep— it's short—with the names of people who have wronged others.

My mother and aunts will give hats away to friends who are going through hard times to cheer them up. And sometimes they'll sell their hats in Flowers, Lotions, and Potions for charity or for school fund drives. They also donate hats to other worthy charity fund drives. But if you're on the Flower Black List, you're on it for good, shame on you and your meanness.

I decided that tonight I would bring up one more teeny, tiny subject to see how they would react. "I've noticed more people coming in and out of the greenhouse."

None of them answered, and the atmosphere suddenly felt charged. I almost laughed. My mother squirmed and reached for her wine. My aunt Iris suddenly found that she was extremely interested in the small wood bridge near the willow trees in the distance. Or maybe it was the pond with the red bench. My aunt Camellia hummed, the song rising and falling dramatically.

"What a wonderful place to grow your exotic flowers. From Hawaii and South America and Delaware." Exotic flowers. *From Delaware.* I almost laughed again. "And your orchids. Why, your orchids must be in a delicate full bloom."

My mother squirmed once more, rolled her shoulders, slugged down more wine.

My goodness! The willow that Aunt Iris was fixated on must be fascinating.

Aunt Camellia's humming rose to a high, near-shrieking pitch.

"The greenhouse is particularly, uh, perfect, for the plants and flowers that are more . . . difficult to grow outside," I said. "The ones that need special care."

Squirm. Stare. Hum hum hum!

"More wine?" my mother said, and got up.

"I'll get it!" Aunt Camellia and Aunt Iris said. They all three darted into the kitchen, chairs scraping the deck, to get more wine.

I laughed, then tried to muzzle it under a cough. There was already wine on the table. I had one more slice of cheese and garlic pizza. If I met my maker tonight I'd want to have a full stomach. We had a lot to talk about.

The bookstore was busy the next day. Tourists streamed in. Part of the reason was that I had an employee standing outside giving away samples of apple cider caramel cake. It was the treats that drove them in. I don't blame them. I believe a treat a day keeps the doctor away. I also had my tea specials up on a board at the door: Honey Lavender and Cinnamon Chai.

But who couldn't love a shop called Evie's Books, Cake, and Tea? The finest things in life, right? They loved sitting in the café area and looking out over the bay. They loved the deck. They loved the bouquets I sold for my mother and aunts today labeled "Men Are Dense, Like Cheese. Buy Your Own Bouquets" and "A Woman's Place Is Wherever She Damn Well Wants It to Be" and "Laugh More, Laugh Loud, Drink Beer."

They loved my aunt Camellia's lotions and potions, called A Lady's Secret and Carnal Coconut and Soothing Seduction.

And they loved my aunt Iris's puzzling/somewhat suggestive/now and then a little creepy flower photographs that made you stop and think and tilt your head as you tried to "get it." One of her purple flowers definitely resembled a penis, and two other exotic red flowers together definitely resembled breasts. She had turned many of her photographs into cards, and they flew out the door.

I met with customers and tried to get them to buy piles of books they would love. I am not bragging, but I know my books. I can find any book for anybody. And I can usually figure out what they might like to read that they had never *thought* to read. Books are my business. I am their book gal.

But in between customers and loading up shelves with new books and rearranging displays, when I had a minute, I thought of Marco. I knew I loved him. But there could never be a future because of what I knew, what I had seen, would happen between us.

I could not let that happen.

And that made the inside of me feel lonely and cold.

I touched a yellow rose petal in the bouquet on my office desk. I would eat a raspberry rose cupcake to warm me up, then I would have some honey lavender tea.

The Book Babes were back.

They were discussing a book in which a woman watered her cheating soon-to-be-ex-husband's Corvette with a hose.

The discussion had morphed into what was appropriate in terms of revenge if a husband cheated. They decided . . .

1) Don't do anything that would get you arrested. Jail would not be fun, and there might not be book club.

2) Driving his jointly owned midlife crisis car into the ocean while cackling would be okay.

3) Cutting out the crotches of all his pants was also acceptable.

4) Going to visit the mistress at work and announcing yourself like this in a loud voice to the receptionist would also be acceptable: "I am the wife of Dave Miller and I want to talk to his girlfriend, Marni Smith, about why she is banging my husband."

5) Stalking him, taking incriminating photos, and then mailing them to his mother and grandmother was a smart idea.

6) Going to Hawaii after the breakup and having a brief vacation affair would be a splendid postdivorce event as long as one had the affair-ee take a blood test to check for all STDs and one used condoms, just in case.

Always interesting to listen to the Book Babes.

"I still miss Dad every day."

My mother's hands stilled. We were in our garden, snipping flowers here and there for her shop, the sun high, the wind soft. We were both in garden boots and hats. Mine was a baseball hat, hers was straw, wobbly, with a white ribbon tied below her neck.

"I do, too."

"He's been gone for so long, but that pain still hits me when I think of him." Sundance bent down with me as I snipped a bundle of purple tulips. Butch and Cassidy wrestled nearby.

"Me too, honey."

Often my father, during his career in the military/government, would return to us pale and tired. A couple of times he came home with an arm wrapped or a bandage on his head, or he would be limping. He would take calls privately, so we couldn't hear, and sometimes, as we were stationed in various locations, cars would come and get him and whisk him off in the middle of the night. He wouldn't talk much about what he was doing.

I would climb on his lap, his green eyes smiling at me, his brown hair cut short, and say, "What did you do on your trip,

Daddy?" And he would say, "I missed you and your sister and your mother."

And I would giggle and say, "No, Daddy. What did you do? Tell me!"

And he would say, "I thought about coming home and reading you stories and chasing Jules on her bike and holding your mom's hand."

And I would giggle again and say, "Daddy! When you were gone, what happened?"

And he would say, "Let's ask your mom to bake us a cake. You know I love cake and tea. Then we'll read books together."

And we would ask my mom, and she was so relieved to see him, so happy to have him home, I could tell even then, as a young child, that she would bake us a cake. White chocolate coconut cake. Hummingbird cake. Dark chocolate candy cane. We would eat cake, drink tea, and read books together.

"I always appreciated how you and Dad tried to help me with my premonitions and how you tried to help other people. You two taught me how to change the timing so that the premonition would pass them by, and I loved you for it. I don't know if I ever told you that, but thanks, Mom."

"Of course, honey." She gave me a hug. My mom always hugs me. "We wanted to help them, but mostly we wanted to help you. From a young age, we had to have the most serious of conversations with you about what to say, what not to say, when to act, when not to." She shook her head and wiped the sweat off her brow with her purple garden glove. "I was discussing ethics and morals with a five-year-old."

"The worst was when I had premonitions about Dad. Remember that time I saw an explosion behind him and he kept walking over a bunch of rocks, as if he hadn't heard it? And he wasn't in his military clothes."

"I remember that when you told your dad, his face went grim."

"He asked me a lot of questions, and I told him what he was wearing and what I saw."

"You saw him in a desert. You said you saw him by buildings made of sand and you saw guns. 'Guns as long as jump ropes,' you told him."

"Another time I told him I saw an explosion in a tower and I saw a whole bunch of jeeps with guns on the back. I cried and cried, and Dad held me. Then he asked me specific questions, and I told him that he was going to run behind a black truck and get straight down on his stomach and the truck was going to get hit by a bomb and he was going away on a stretcher on a helicopter with a lot of blood."

"That premonition saved your father's life."

"It did?" I was stunned. Sundance leaned against me. He likes to be close. "Why didn't you tell me?"

"Because you were nine years old. We didn't want to scare you. But your father never forgot it. That incident played out in the Middle East. He actually saw a black truck and he made sure that he, and the other men he was with, did not go behind it. The black truck was blown to smithereens."

I sat with that one shocking story for a while.

"Dad didn't want you to know because it would have been so upsetting."

"I feel upset now." I took a deep breath and bent to cut a few orange-pink roses. "I know we've had this discussion before, but I don't understand why me. You don't have premonitions, Aunt Camellia and Aunt Iris don't. Jules doesn't. I'm all alone with this curse."

My mother's hands stopped for a second, and she took a deep breath.

"Mom? What is it?"

"Nothing. I'm admiring these roses. Aren't they particularly beautiful this year? I love yellow roses with a touch of red, don't you? And look at our Dr. Marie Curie roses. So delicate, and she was so brilliant."

She wasn't thinking about roses or Dr. Curie. I saw her hands shake.

"I don't know why you have this gift slash curse," she said, her voice pitching up, high and squeaky. "I don't."

"I wish I could go to a support group. We could call ourselves The Future Crazies. Or The Premonitioners. Or, We Know It All. I wish I knew someone else who I could talk to. It would be helpful to have someone in the family older than me, wiser, who saw these things, too. She could tell me how to be as normal as possible and not haunted all the time by the things I see coming down the pike and can do nothing to stop. How to deal with the guilt, and not being able to fix something, or to help. The knowing is hard. Plus, trying to help people on the fly is exhausting."

The other night I had to sneak into Millie Coons's barn. The only way to sneak up on her house was through her back fields. It was a long walk, and it was dark. I had had a vision of her falling off her riding mower and getting her leg run over. Somehow the seat became loose, and when she stood up to see what the problem was, she fell off, and whack. Her leg was a bloody mess. She was out in the field all alone, too, into the night, crying. So I went into her barn and fixed the seat. I didn't want to tell her, because I don't like advertising about my premonitions, even though we're friends and only a couple of years apart in school.

Anyhow, it was a long walk, and I was darn tired when I got home.

My mother stood up, her head bent down.

"Are you okay, Mom?" I reached for her hand. "Mom? What's wrong?"

"Yes, I'm fine. Not too wrong. Nothing wrong. Fine and dandy. Too much coffee. You know what too much caffeine does to me."

No, I didn't. What was she talking about? She drank six cups of coffee a day. It never had this effect. "Mom. Are you sick? You look pale."

"I'm perfectly healthy." She took a shuddery breath. "Tell me. How is Sundance doing?"

Sundance? What the heck was going on?

"How is Sundance, Evie?" She said it firmly, and I knew to change the topic, so I told her that Sundance was as loyal as ever, and I pet his head. "Also. Kara Lighthouse is going to have triplets. They'll be early but they'll be fine. Don't tell anyone. She doesn't even know."

She smiled. "That is the kind of premonition you need to have."

Later, though, walking to my blue carriage house through a column of foxgloves and delphinium, I wondered about that conversation. It upset her. It worried her. It made her go pale. But why?

Sundance put a ball in my hand, which was my cue to throw it. Butch and Cassidy ran after it, too.

Sometimes I wish I were a dog.

The red car was coming straight at me.

The sunlight behind it momentarily blinded me. It was a tight road, one lane, mountain to my right, the cliff to my left. I hit the brakes. The other driver was looking away; she didn't see me at first.

I pulled my truck as far to the right as I could go, but it was too late. The other driver's car fishtailed as she hit the brakes, but it still barreled toward me.

The impact was fast and hard, my air bag exploded, my body jerked back. The metal crunched, the windshield split and shattered, and smoke spilled from the engine. The premonition had changed again, fluid, versatile, confusing.

At the end, as usual, things were fuzzy.

One of us died. I don't know if it was me or the other driver but I could see death . . . although death seemed to shift in and out.

It was terrifying.

And there was something else. Something about the other driver. I could not figure it out. I had never been able to figure it out. I shut my eyes and went through every inch of the premonition. What was the mystery here? What was I not getting?

I didn't want to die. But I'm sure she didn't, either.

I could only see my hands on the steering wheel. They were shadowed here and there, and it was only quick flashes, but my hands looked like my hands about now. Not older, no more age spots, no more wrinkles or lines.

Would the event in this premonition happen soon?

And if it did, what could I do to save myself . . . and save her?

Jules sent us, by e-mail, three different invitations for her wedding. "Which one do you like most?" she asked my mother and aunts and me.

One of them had a photo of her and Mack, together, on his motorcycle. Orange and yellow flames were Photoshopped behind them. They were in full leathers, but Mack wore a black bow tie and Jules had a lacy white veil attached to her helmet. The text: "Come Celebrate With Us as We Take the Ultimate Ride!"

"Ooo!" my mother said. "I like that one."

A second photo was of Jules and Mack in jeans and matching black leather vests, black knitted hats, and black sunglasses. They were flexing their biceps, Jules in front of Mack, showing off their matching tattoos of each other's face. The text: "We Have the Tattoos, Now We're Getting Hitched."

"Their inner-twined souls are coming through keenly here," Aunt Camellia said. "You can feel the love."

The third photo was of Jules and Mack, both naked, from the back, standing on a beach during sunset, their motorcycles nearby. They were holding hands, my sister's long blonde hair flying in the wind, Mack looking huge next to her. The text, scrawling across their rear ends: "Don't Be a Beach Bum, Come to Our Wedding!"

"This one," Aunt Iris said, tapping it. "I think it's modern. We all need to embrace our individual bodies and stop being so critical, so shocked, by nakedness. Plus, the message is clear and I like clear and practical messages."

"Which one do you like, Evie?" my mother asked, as my aunts turned to me.

I studied all three. "I like all of them, but I think I'd go with the tattoos of each other's faces. They're getting married, it's permanent, like the tattoos. Plus, they look tough, and inside we all know they are two of the mushiest people on the planet Earth, so it adds to that underlying humor."

We Skyped Jules, told her our thoughts, and she decided on the tattoo invitation. "Tattoo invitation it is. We're going to hire a woman to paint fake tattoos on anyone who wants one. Plus, the invitations to our friends will tell them to wear their leathers! What do you think?"

"I think it's going to be a tough wedding," I drawled. "Bunch of tough guys and gals."

She looked confused, then she laughed. "Oh! I get it, Evie! Because leather is tough."

"You got it."

"Mom, you're going to remember to wrap black leather ribbons around the vases of the flowers for the tables, right?"

"Yes, I got your message! We'll wrap the vases in black leather."

"Aunt Iris, did you get our motorcycle photo?"

"I did!" Aunt Iris said. "And I juxtaposed it against crazy-looking orchids bent this way and that. The orchids look like they're talking to each other. We'll have that picture in each floral centerpiece."

"Thank you!" Jules grinned. "And Aunt Camellia, you're still making the lotions as the wedding gifts, right?"

"The lotion will be pink with a black label," Aunt Camellia said, "and it'll smell like roses. I'm going to call it Motorcycle Grease."

"I love it!" Jules gushed. "Wait 'til I show you my wedding dress! My wedding dress designer—her name's June and she's on the Oregon coast—is almost done. But don't ask about it! It's a surprise!"

"What's Mack going to wear?" Aunt Iris asked.

Jules was confused. "His leathers. Of course. Plus!" She put a finger up in the air. "A bow tie. Like in the invitation that lost."

I smiled at Jules, and she smiled back. "Hello, maid of honor sister-love! You look beautiful as always. When are you going to buy a motorcycle?"

"When my alpacas start to talk. When my butt gets smaller. When the goats stop escaping. When I start to want to run instead of only running when I have to. When my boobs get bigger. So your answer is: Never. I am never getting on a motorcycle." I had enough scary things going on in my life. I limit my life to safe pastimes only. A little blue house in the country by the ocean. A bookstore. Tea. Cake with thick icing. Reading at night on my porch. Caring for my animals. Having a nutritional slice of pie each night.

"I wanted you to ride in on a motorcycle down the aisle, gunning it, soooo loud. Growling."

"Oh, hell, no." Jules wasn't kidding.

"You could learn to ride for the wedding," Aunt Iris said. "I could help you. You would only need to know how to ride for twenty feet. Until you arrived at the gazebo."

"No."

"Maybe we could get her a fake motorcycle?" my mom asked. "Like a kid motorcycle?"

"No."

"Evie has enough going on without getting on a motorcycle," Aunt Camellia said.

"Yep," I said.

"Okay," Jules said. She brightened. "How about if Mack rides you in on a wheelie?"

"No. Double no. Hear me quiver with fear."

We talked about the wedding, the plans, and hung up, but not before Jules told us all she loved us. "Especially you, Evie!" She grinned.

"Especially you, Jules!" I said back.

Which is what we had said to each other our wholes lives, starting when we were little.

"I'm coming over to the island soon to help with the rest of the details!"

We waved and blew kisses.

"We can't wait to see you!" Aunt Camellia called out. "May blessings follow you always."

"Always remember we love you!" my mother said. "Be safe on your bike. Don't go too fast. Remember that a happy body eats vegetables."

"On a practical note, start making lists of everything you need to do for the wedding, and scratch them off when you're done," Aunt Iris said. "Don't let wedding details slip through the cracks, or you'll want to crack a week before the wedding like the other brides we're dealing with now. They're all crackpots."

Jules and I are different.

She is ebullient. Funny. Loud. Outgoing. Brave.

I am quiet. Reserved. Thinking all the time. Waiting in fear or trepidation for the next premonition or disaster.

Jules rides motorcycles too fast. She skydives. She hang glides. She likes to run, and will even run when a bear is not chasing her, which is about the only time I can imagine running and liking the ability to run.

I would get on a motorcycle only if there was a tsunami behind me and for no other reason. One is supposed to stay in one's seat on a plane, not jump out of it with a parachute. I would never hang glide for any reason.

Jules loves parties and social gatherings.

I don't love parties or social gatherings except on rare occasions.

Jules like wine and beer and hard liquor. She does not mind getting buzzed or drunk now and then. I will never get buzzed or drunk. I need to be completely in control of my mind as much as possible.

Jules travels whenever she gets the chance on her motorcycle, meeting new people, seeing new things.

I like my quiet life on the island, my beloved animals, my bookstore and my books, and probably will not leave it again, or leave only rarely. I protect my sanity as best I can.

And that is probably why we are so close. We are different, but we adore each other.

If for some inexplicable cosmic reason Jules is in the red car coming straight toward me in my premonition, trust me when I tell you that I will send my truck straight over that cliff before a hair on my sister's blonde head is harmed.

Chapter 11

～

Betsy Baturra
Multnomah County Jail
Portland, Oregon
1975

Jail, Betsy decided, is actually hell.

It's a hell wrapped in concrete, wire, and steel bars that has landed on Earth, dangerous and suffocating. She had a metal plank and a sinking, stained, skinny mattress for a bed. She had bars keeping her trapped like an animal; a toilet within her cell with no privacy; and a small, battered sink. She was told what to do and when to do it. The food was horrible, the lack of sunlight graying to life, the lack of freedom deadly to her mind and soul.

Betsy heard the crying at night, sometimes wailing when someone was having a particularly bad time. She heard the swearing and the shrieking fights, the yelling at each other and the heated arguing with the guards. She heard the orders being barked, and she saw prisoners, some of whom were mentally ill, or who had become mentally ill in prison, dragged out by guards for the slightest infractions.

Her roommate, Rainbow, whose real name was Margaret Cholo, was back. She had to go to isolation when she hit the guard with three fingers who finally came to check on Betsy when Betsy was dying from blood loss after giving birth. But

Rainbow was different now. She was scared. She muttered to herself one color after another, rocking back and forth.

Apricot.

Indigo.

Magenta.

Plum.

Sienna.

Violet.

Rainbow hid under her bed whenever she could. She wrapped her arms around herself and whimpered and shook in the corner.

Rainbow was dirty, her hair a wreck. She had refused to shower because she thought she would be dragged out of the shower and put in isolation again, only this time she would be "naked and white and in a beige cell alone with steel gray guards staring at me, touching me with yucky pink fingers."

Betsy tried to comfort Rainbow as best she could, their tears blending together.

The abject loneliness and the hopelessness was a gaping wound within Betsy. She could hardly eat, hardly sleep, her mind crumbling from losing Baby Rose and Johnny. She worried about Tilly, too, sweet Tilly, Johnny's little sister, who was now in foster care according to her attorney. There was no one to take care of her.

Betsy thought of her own mother, of her own father. They had never come to see her, and they never would, she knew that. She was gone to them, a humiliation, a curse from the devil. They had undoubtedly wrapped their arms around themselves in their fundamentalism and moved on. She wrapped her arms around herself, cold and alone.

When Betsy was younger, she got into trouble many times. Her father, Hansen, was a religious, hypocritical fundamentalist and her mother was weak, cowed and went along with everything he said. Now and then he would rage at her mother, insist that she obey, submit, behave. "Woman, do not break God's law! I am the head of the household. You are my helpmate. You are one of my ribs. You are steeped in the sins of Eve. Do not question me."

Her mother rarely questioned her father, but when he was in a bad mood, and he found her not obedient "enough," he would sometimes slap her, Mary's black hair flying out of her bun. "I am doing this for your own good! May Jesus forgive you for your insolence!"

Mary would tilt her head down in defeat and submission, her golden eyes closed.

When Betsy told them, when she was five, of her first premonitions, of someone getting hurt or drowning or, twice, ministers being arrested, and when those premonitions came true, her father had many consequences for her after he overcame his shocked anger. First, he called her a liar. Then, when the premonitions came through, he hit her with a Bible, he made her memorize long passages, he performed a séance on her, and he taped her mouth shut "so the devil inside of you will die."

He then told people at their small church, a church that did not like outsiders, to pray for his daughter, as she was "possessed" by demons and they had to "pull the demons out."

She was then, as a little girl, ostracized by the parents and the children of that church because no one wanted their children near a demonic little girl.

Betsy was scared of her premonitions but more scared of her father, who was a menacing, yelling figure who called her, a young child, "evil" and "possessed by the devil." That the devil possessed her made her wet her pants every time she thought of it.

Soon she knew not to tell her parents what she saw in the future, but when she was older she also knew she had to take action to save the people she loved. She let the air out of a tire on Miss Jane's car next door when she was seven. She knew how to do that because her mother's uncle showed her how to change a tire. "Your father is clueless and lazy, Betsy, so you're going to have to know how to do it," Uncle Jacko told her.

Betsy knew that Miss Jane was going to help her friend Dixon on his farm that day, based on the clothes she was wearing, the same clothes as in the premonition, and her arm was going to be ripped off by some sort of farm equipment. She could not have Miss Jane losing an arm. Miss Jane was only twenty-five and baked the best chocolate chip cookies, and she snuck them to Betsy through a hole in their fence. By letting out the air in Jane's tire, Betsy ensured that Jane couldn't go to the farm, and she avoided having her arm ripped off.

Miss Jane did not like her father. She sprayed him with her hose when he was yelling at Betsy one day in the front yard after church. Her father was telling Betsy that she was not "a good Christian. Not prayerful, not obedient, an embarrassment to the family!" He was soaked through from Miss Jane's hose. When Hansen charged her, his face mottled and red, Miss Jane sprayed him right in the head, then told him, "If you take one step onto my property, Hillbilly Hansen, I will shoot you."

Her father was livid, but he backed off and yanked Betsy inside, her feet dragging across the lawn. The next day Children's Services came out to talk to her dad and mom and to her. The lady was nice to her, but Betsy was petrified because her father whispered to her, "Don't say anything bad about me or you will go to hell and I will spank you there."

Betsy also knew that her dad would hit her with the Bible again or lock her in the closet in the basement and tell her to copy a book out of the Bible if she opened her mouth. While she was locked up, he would give her only bread and water, as if she were Paul in one of the jail cells in the Bible. She hated that because when she became super hungry her whole body shook and she became dizzy. She told the Children's Services lady that everything was "happy at home."

The next time Miss Jane saw her father, she called him "Mr. Monster Father" to his face. She was fearless! Betsy tried not to laugh, but Hansen heard her and she spent an afternoon in the closet.

Betsy knew exactly where three teenagers were lost when she was twelve because she saw one of them falling off the path and into a ravine. The three lost teenagers were on the news, and everyone was talking about them. "The news is grim, folks," a newscaster said. "The temperature is expected to drop below freezing tonight." Betsy knew what that meant: The boys would freeze to death.

When her father left for men's Bible study, she called her friend Collette, from school, and asked to speak to Collette's mother. Aurelia was a police officer. She told her everything, knowing what her father would do if he found out. But they were kids, too! Like her. They shouldn't freeze to death. Aurelia and a police lieutenant came to her home only a minute after her father arrived home. Her father tried to prevent her from speaking. "She is possessed," he told the police. "She knows nothing."

The lieutenant, whose nephew was one of the three lost teenagers, insisted that she be allowed to speak. Aurelia had to haul her father, screeching Bible verses, spittle flying, away from her. Hansen was doubly embarrassed that a woman was stronger than he was and that she was able to wrestle him to the floor, his head in a head lock. Betsy told the lieutenant what she saw, her body trembling, as she knew she was in so much trouble. As usual, her mother stood by, a weak mouse.

"I see a huge rock. Flat. Like how a rock would look if you sliced it in half, but it's on a mountain. It goes way up in the sky. There are pine trees and a river way below, and the river looks like a snake. All three of the boys are down by the river where there's an island in the middle of it."

"That sounds like the south side of Bald Peek," Aurelia said, her hand still on Hansen's head, squished into the carpet. "Off the Mahoney Trail."

Hansen screeched a prayer of punishment and penance.

Calls were made. A search in a whole new direction began. The kids were helicoptered out and at a hospital within the hour. Two of them were suffering from hypothermia. The one who had fallen had broken both legs. They probably would have died that night had they not been rescued. All three stayed in the hospital for days but would be as good as new soon.

Betsy was not as good as new. As soon as Aurelia and the lieutenant left, her father tore her pants down, leaned her over his lap, and hit her with his belt while her mother cowered.

Another time, when she was fifteen, Betsy pounded a rock into Mr. Zeiber's sliding glass door until it shattered, and she crawled in only a minute after he had a heart attack in the kitchen. In her premonition she had seen him struggling for air, arching his back, clutching his chest. She had taken particular note of his clothes, as she had learned to do: gray sweater with red trim on the cuffs, blue jeans with a hole on the left knee, black tennis shoes.

She called for an ambulance as Mr. Zeiber, only forty-five years old, gasped for breath on the floor, then she held his hand. Mr. Zeiber lived. Her parents were alerted to where their daughter was only when the police brought her home. The police explained that Betsy had told them that she had "heard" Mr. Zeiber's cries for help and that's why she broke the sliding glass door. Mr. Zeiber did not remember screaming, but he figured that he had and knew that Betsy had saved his life.

"Your daughter is a hero," the police said.

When the police left, Betsy's enraged father tossed her in the basement closet with the Bible, where she crumpled to the floor. He did not let her out for twelve hours, though she had saved a life. He gave her a can to pee in.

"Pray that God delivers you from the evil spirits within you. No one but God, our holy father, sees the future, except, perhaps, the devil, so you will stay here until the devil leaves you. And never leave the house without our permission again, Betsy! You are a cursed girl and I will save you from yourself!" To make her especially miserable, she was given only two pieces of bread and water, so her body shook and she became dizzy, as usual.

The men in the church performed an exorcism on Betsy at her father's request after that one. They told her to get naked on a table. She refused. She fought, she hit, she tried to run, she screamed. Finally they agreed she didn't have to get naked. Clearly two of the more creepy men were disappointed. When she was on the table Betsy sang songs by the Beatles until her dad put his hand over her mouth. She almost passed out from not being able to breathe. "Don't kill her, Hansen," one of the men said. "Let me examine her and I'll see if I can get the demons out."

Betsy never forgot that "examination." Her father stood by and watched, the men around her breathing heavily, her father the heaviest of all.

From the time she was young, though, she knew that sometimes she should say something, do something, to prevent something tragic from happening in the future, and sometimes she shouldn't.

She knew that Mr. Ralph, another neighbor, was going to die soon. He was going to fall out of his wheelchair and drown in his pool. But he was ninety-four years old and he had already told Betsy that he didn't want to live anymore. He had lost his wife, his brothers and sisters, and his best friend. He was extremely sick and coughed all the time. She didn't know if he rolled himself in or if it was an accident, but she did nothing to prevent it.

And she knew that her father was going to chop wood in the backyard and get distracted by Miss Jane in a bathing suit next door and bring the ax straight into his leg. The leg would gush blood and he would be in the hospital for a couple of weeks because of a bad infection that would almost kill him.

She didn't tell him what was going to happen, and she did nothing to prevent it. Those two weeks with her mother were the best ever.

No, she let the ax slide straight into her father's leg, and when he called out in agony, she pretended not to hear.

Later, he beat her for that, too.

It was bad enough to live in a household of control, reeking with religious fanaticism, and a fundamentalism that actively discouraged rational thought, facts, opinions, freedom, or joy, but it was worse knowing that your own mother, the person who should protect you above all else, would never stand up for you, Betsy thought. Her mother was weak, voiceless. She would not protect her daughter from her husband, no matter what happened to her.

And yet Betsy's mother, with black hair and golden eyes like Betsy's, had premonitions, too. She told Betsy she did. Her mother had, too, and her grandmother and great-grandmother. They were all Irish. "The second sight," she said. "We have it."

Yes, they had it. The difference was that Betsy tried to help others, while Mary couldn't, or wouldn't, help anyone, even her own daughter. Hansen knew—Mary had told him before they married—and he had been kind while they were chastely dating, until their wedding night. Then he had thundered at her for her wickedness, and things had gone downhill from there.

If Betsy had to choose, it was her mother's inaction that hurt her more than her father's belt, whipping through the air until it landed and split open her back.

Betsy thought she might well lose her mind in jail.

But as time went on, she thought that might be preferable to staying sane.

Chapter 12

⁓

"Serafina, with her shiny, multicolored rainbow tail, liked to help people."

"Like me, right?"

"Like you. One day, her brothers got into trouble with an evil merman who used to be king. He was a horrible king. He wouldn't allow the mermen and mermaids freedoms, so they had a mighty revolution under the sea and chased him out with golden swords and shields. King Koradome was not allowed in the Mermaid Village anymore. He lived miles away in an old black rock home."

"Then what happened?"

"Serafina's brothers swam over there one day to spy on him. They had heard he had magical powers and could turn people into fish and whales into people. It was said he could transform himself into a serpent or a snake."

"That's scary."

"The brothers spied on him from behind a line of rocks, but King Koradome knew they were there. He captured all of them in a cage and would not let them go. War was going to be declared between the good mermaids and mermen and King Koradome. Serafina was not supposed to go anywhere near her brothers in the cage, but she did anyhow because she loved

them so much. King Koradome, who was sneaky and danger-
ous, caught her and threw her in a separate cage."

"Oh no! Then what happened?"

"To get out of the cage, and to get her brothers out, Serafina
had to promise to give King Koradome something."

"What did she promise to give him?"

Chapter 13

~

"Let's talk about the pot you three are growing."

I stared at my mother and aunts across my blue sawhorse/butcher block kitchen table. I had bought pasta and French bread for us from Giannelli's in town and lit a bunch of vanilla-scented candles. In the center of the table I had my usual bouquet of roses, this time a mix of burgundy, red, white, yellow, and purple.

They'd come over in a rush, straight from the floral shop, kisses and hugs and "how-are-you"s, and hung up their hats. My mother had chosen a lime-green hat with white flowers for the day, rather demure for her. Aunt Iris was wearing a dark blue hat with tiny whales attached to the brim. Aunt Camellia was wearing a pink hat, tilted over one eye, with a pink net. We'd had dinner, then I'd made a pot of mint tea and served pink chiffon cookies.

They all froze for a moment after my statement. My mother and Aunt Camellia, sitting on the church pew, squirmed.

"More tea?" my mother said, holding my red teapot over my teacup. My teacup was full.

"A biscuit?" Aunt Camellia asked, holding up the plate of pink chiffon cookies, even though I already had three cookies on my plate. She likes to act British sometimes by calling cookies *biscuits*.

"Let's not be unpleasant," Aunt Iris said. "Or accusatory. Eat more salad. It helps with digestion and flatulence."

"Mom. Aunt Camellia. Aunt Iris." My white curtains with light yellow roses fluttered, as Sundance leaned against my leg. "You're growing pot in the greenhouse."

"The weather was so gorgeous today, a slight breeze, warm sun, not too warm," my mother said.

"The way the sun is glinting off the water tonight looks like sparkles. Sparkles bring out one's internal goodness, don't you think?" Aunt Camellia said.

"Let's have a conversation about when we all realized that we're feminists," Aunt Iris growled.

"We're going to talk about this," I said. Mars jumped up on a stack of books next to a wine barrel. The books fell down. He meowed in irritation, then took a leap onto the old library card catalogue. I sighed.

"Barnie's selling two of his pigs," my mother said.

"His pigs are delicious," Aunt Camellia said. "Tender. Soft."

"Should we buy the pigs?" my mother asked.

"Let's consider the economics," Aunt Iris said. "I'll make up a financial spreadsheet. Buying pigs versus buying the pork and bacon at the grocery store."

"I'm not going away," I said. I picked up a pink chiffon cookie despite myself. I'd have one. Or two. Not more than four. Venus jumped on my lap and purred. "This isn't funny. Pot is illegal, and you have a whole house full of it out there."

"No," my mother said, waving her hand dismissively. "Not a house full. It's a greenhouse."

"A house is a home when it's filled with love," Aunt Camellia said. "Who wants to watch a British love story tonight? I do. Would you like a biscuit, Evie?"

"A greenhouse is structurally different from a home," Aunt Iris said. "There are plumbing and electrical contrasts. The insulation and flooring are at opposite ends of the construction spectrum. Plus, we don't have that many plants. Let's not exaggerate, Evie. Be practical."

"But why are you growing pot?" I said. "You don't smoke pot."

"Oh, my, no," my mother said, but she glanced away. "I'm a lady."

"Never," Aunt Camellia said, but she found a sudden interest in my fluttering rose curtains. "I can't have pot interfering with my glow."

"Pot is an herb," Aunt Iris said. "Let me tell you about how Indians used herbs."

"You're kidding," I said. "This is how you're going to answer my question? You're all smoking pot now? In your seventies, you've decided to start?"

My mother sang a few notes of a love song. Aunt Camellia joined in. I knew the song. It was from a romance movie made in the fifties. Aunt Iris spread her arms out as if she were directing them.

"But there are a number of plants out there," I said. "You couldn't possibly smoke all that."

"We're florists," my mother said. "We like flowers."

"Marijuana is not a flower," I said. "It does not go in your bouquets, but nice try, Mom. Are you selling it? And, if so, to who?"

"It's *to whom*," Aunt Iris said. "It's important to be grammatically correct, Evie."

"I like grammar," Aunt Camellia said. "It helps a person get her innermost thoughts out correctly so she can clearly express her emotions."

"Me too," my mother said. "Especially semicolons. Most people don't know how to use them."

"I do," Aunt Iris said. "They're precise, that's why I like them."

"Who is buying pot from you?" I put my hand on Sundance's head. Surely he was behind me in this?

My mother sighed, so impatient. "People who are hurting."

Aunt Camellia tapped her blue rose teacup with a spoon. "People who are ill."

"Or dying," Aunt Iris said. "Isn't it better for all of us to die stoned than to die sober? It's a much gentler way to spend your dying time."

"I want to be high as a kite when I die," Aunt Camellia said, her face ecstatic at the thought. "High. As. A. Kite. Flying through the heavens, dipping into the clouds, rolling over rainbows."

"Sadie Almeter had cancer. She was in so much pain. We gave

her enough joints to smoke all day until she passed," Aunt Iris said. "She was ninety years old and said she wished she'd discovered it earlier. What did she call it, Camellia?"

"Magic sticks. She called it magic sticks. Even her grandchildren thanked us for helping to manage her pain. They smoked it with her when their parents weren't around."

My mother beamed. "It was a family moment. The third generation with the first, all stoned and happy. Now, don't you reprimand me, Evie! The grandchildren were in their forties. They were not children. They had children."

"Who else?" Sundance laid his head on my lap. I think he knew this conversation was pointless.

"Well, you know Pietre, the Frenchman, yummy Frenchman, who has that restaurant on San Lola Island?" My mother fluttered her hands. "We carry it across the ferry in my purse. I usually use the purple-flowered one, which matches my purple plumeria hat with the white feathers."

"I love that hat," Aunt Camellia said. "It's reflective of your passionate personality, your aura of commitment."

"It's purely medicinal, Evie," Aunt Iris said. "When Pietre was younger, his stepfather planted an ax in his back. He was also in a motorcycle accident in his twenties and his back aches badly now that he's older. He didn't want to take painkillers, he knew he could get addicted, so we bring him his pot."

"Then we have lunch at his restaurant. I had French onion soup the last time. With wine. It was scrumptious," my mother gushed.

"I had his famous croissants," Aunt Camellia said. "With butter. Everyone should eat butter."

"But we keep our businesses separate," Aunt Iris said. "At my insistence. We need to be logical. He pays for his marijuana and we pay for our meal, and we share a glass of wine on the back porch and watch the ferries come in."

"It's such a pleasant way to spend the day," Aunt Camellia said. "I feel rejuvenated after eating Pietre." She coughed. "I mean, eating *with* Pietre. I do not eat Pietre."

There was a silence. Aunt Iris muffled a laugh. My mother didn't bother to muffle hers.

"You're dating Pietre?" I asked.

"No, not exactly," Aunt Camellia said.

"You're seeing him."

"She sees *all* of him," Aunt Iris said.

"But we're not committed," Aunt Camellia said.

"Not dating then?" I asked.

"We're lovers," Aunt Camellia said. "Sometimes. I'm not dead yet. Why can't I have a lover?"

I shook my head. This was a little too much. "You can have all the lovers you want. But back to the pot. Who else are you selling to?"

"Do you remember Elsa Bryn?" Aunt Camellia said. "She had such severe anxiety she didn't leave her house for almost two years. Panic attacks, too. She's a cat hoarder. We brought her a little pot one day. She was a bit resistant at first, so your mother and I smoked it with her, out on her deck. You know she has that mansion overlooking the bay. She can see the whales frolicking about."

"She uses her binoculars to study birds. She's an expert birder," Aunt Iris said. "Encyclopedic knowledge. She used to go on birding expeditions before her anxiety overcame her."

"We helped her become herself again. We all lose ourselves sometimes," my mother said. "It's like who we used to be runs off into the sunset. Who Elsa was ran off after she experienced trauma. She was attacked in the city and beaten up, her purse stolen. Then they used her credit card to buy ten thousand dollars' worth of junk. She hid in her home, alone and lonely. Trapped. Can you imagine? Now she's out and about. Slightly stoned, but functioning."

"More mint tea?" Aunt Camellia asked. She tried to fill my already completely full cup, then said, "Whoops!" as it spilled across the table. "Have another biscuit."

"Please tell me you're not selling to kids," I said. "Please. You absolutely can't."

"Oh, my God!" My mother slammed her hands on the table, and my tea spilled. "Young woman! Do not insult us!"

Aunt Camellia reached over with her spoon and rapped my knuckles. Hard. "I'm going to pretend you didn't say that." She rapped them again, her face angry.

"Ouch!" Dang it.

"Evie Lindsay, how dare you?" Aunt Iris said, sitting up straight, brow furrowed. "I am insulted and offended. Surely you know us better than that? We would never sell to anyone under twenty-one. In fact, I don't think we have any customers under thirty. And they all need it. There are emotional and physical reasons for them needing our homegrown marijuana."

My aunts and my mother sat back and glared at me, arms crossed. Wow. I was in trouble.

But I was persistent. This was illegal. "Do you have a license?"

"A what?" my mother said.

"A license to sell medical marijuana?" I knew they didn't. I had a headache. I put my fingers to my temples. Jupiter jumped up on a stack of books and knocked it down. He meowed. I sighed. I had too many books or too many cats.

"You need flower power," my mother said. "For that headache. And what is a license to sell marijuana?"

"We have car licenses and that's all we need," Aunt Iris said.

"More cookies?" my mother snapped at me. She tossed cookies on my plate with anger, one at a time. I caught one before it flew off the table.

"We will accept your apology," Aunt Iris said, glowering. "I'm waiting, young woman."

"Please, Evie," Aunt Camellia said, leveling me with a disapproving look. She rapped my knuckles again. Twice. Ouch! Ouch! "We need healing here."

I sighed. I apologized. I apologized to my mother and aunts for suggesting that they might sell pot to minors. Even Sundance seemed to be looking at me with a reprimanding eye, that traitor.

We did not further discuss the legality of their selling pot at all. To anyone.

No, of course not.

They did, however, grudgingly accept my apology.

That night I put my feet up on my grandfather's old wooden sea chest. I stared up at the model airplanes my father had made as a kid, then at my pink rose wallpaper that somehow always relaxes me. Sundance climbed on my lap and put his head on my shoulder. He was carrying his friend Lizard in his mouth.

My aunts and my mother are growing and selling pot.

They are all in their seventies. They have white hair. They lead Christmas sing-alongs in the town square. They include drunken sailor songs and insert words like *Santa* and *Elves* and *Rudolph* in certain places to make them more Christmassy. So even the young kids sing loudly with their parents about "Santa sluggin' it down over yonder with his Irish lasses . . . Rudolph and the gang, why they had too much whiskey, one fell over the boat . . . Mrs. Claus, Mrs. Claus, let down your petticoats . . ."

They drink too much sometimes and dance in public. They insist that everyone get a costume and walk in the Halloween parade.

But I never thought I would say that sentence: My aunts and my mother are growing and selling pot.

I never thought I would think it.

Mars knocked down another stack of books. He meowed, I sighed. The yellow rose curtains fluttered.

"Let's go to bed," I said. And three dogs, four cats, and a stuffed green lizard, and I trudged up the stairs.

On Sunday I took Sundance, Butch, and Cassidy on a walk downtown. They love to go downtown. There are lots of other dogs on leashes with their owners, and they love to say hello and chat. I wanted to check in at the bookstore to make sure everything was going well, so I looped their leashes around a lamppost while I went in and they socialized.

After I determined that the bookstore, shockingly enough, was functioning fine and dandy without me, I bought a two-scoop chocolate fudge/peppermint ice-cream cone for its nutritional value. Ice cream is made of milk, and milk is one of the four food groups. The ice-cream parlor is owned by my friend Samson and his husband, Terri. Samson and I went to school together, and we used to play dress-up with my mom's and aunts' clothes, so he always gives me an extra helping.

"My sister and I heard you're magic."

I peered down at two girls. One was brown haired, one curly strawberry blonde. The girls' names were Kimberly and Kaitlyn, and they were eight and six years old. I was holding three leashes. My dogs were trying to make a run for it, so I had to hold on tight. In my other hand I was trying not to drop my healthy ice-cream lunch.

"I'm not magic." I was magical enough to know what they were talking about, though.

"Yes, you are." The older one, Kimberly, said it as if she knew better than me.

"Yeah," Kaitlyn said. "You're like a magic witch."

"I'm not a witch, because I don't have a black pointed hat."

Now, that threw the sisters for a second. Witches did have black pointed hats, everyone knew that.

"Maybe you're hiding your witch's hat," Kimberly said, eyeing me carefully. "Your mom and your aunties always wear flowered hats. Do they have witches' hats underneath their hats?"

"No, they aren't witches. Girls, think about it. I don't ride on a broomstick. So I can't be a witch."

The older one tapped her temple with her pointer finger as she thought. "Wait! I got it. You're a modern witch. You new witches don't do that old stuff anymore."

"You ride in your magic truck that flies at night. That one!" Kaitlyn pointed accusingly at my blue truck.

"My truck is too heavy to get in the sky. Plus, it's too old. It's tired."

Their brows furrowed. This was getting confusing.

"Anyhow!" Kimberly said. "We want you to tell us if we're going to get a doggie or not, so are we?"

I was friends with their mother, Pammy. I had known Pammy since I was twelve and she moved to the island when her mother, an actress, had an affair with a married actor in Hollywood. The married actor's wife, the daughter of a studio head, had her blacklisted, hence the move to the island to disappear and put the scandal behind her. She now owns the yarn shop.

I have never met a more allergic person than Pammy. She is allergic to cats, dogs, dust, pollen, grasses, milk, and nuts. She is glucose intolerant.

"No, you're not going to get a dog."

"What?!" They were mad. Kimberly crossed her arms and frowned. Kaitlyn put her hands on her hips, leaned forward, and glared at me, her blonde curls almost covering her eyes.

"You're not going to get a dog," I said. "But don't tell anyone I looked into your future and saw no dog. It's a secret."

"Never? No dog?" As if on cue, they both scrunched their noses at me.

"Not when you're children. I see you having dogs when you're adults. Four each." I didn't see a darn thing, but it seemed to appease them.

"I'm mad!" Kimberly said with a huff.

"I'm super mad!" Kaitlyn said with a puff.

"I'm screaming mad!" Kimberly said, then laughed.

Kaitlyn giggled. "That's funny! Screaming mad!" Kaitlyn screamed. I covered my ears. Then I had to use my tongue to right the scoop of peppermint ice cream because it almost fell off. I could feel ice cream on my face and in my left eyelashes. I wiped both with my sleeves, my dogs prancing about.

Their mother arrived, looking flustered.

"Hi, Evie," she said, giving me a hug.

"Hi, Pammy."

She pulled away from the dogs. They appeared a little offended by her poor manners. I suddenly felt like eating microwave popcorn. Extra butter. That would be so good. Ice cream and buttery popcorn are perfect together. A lot of people don't know that.

Pammy sneezed, then coughed. "I'm sorry. I'm allergic to dogs."

"I know, Pammy. I know."

We chatted for a while about everything, about nothing. I liked Pammy a lot.

She sniffled, blew her nose. "Bye, Evie. You're coming to Melissa's shower, right? Saturday?"

"Yes, we'll be there." Melissa was a classmate of ours. She had invited me, my mother, and my aunts to a bridal shower. She had promised "lots of wine. My new mother-in-law, the old jackhammer herself, will be there. I'll need to be drunk. Get drunk with me."

The girls turned around to glare at me, but smiles broke through.

Kimberly whispered, "I'm still mad about the doggy."

"Me too," Kaitlyn said.

I didn't take offense. They were simply blaming the messenger who had denied them doggies.

"I've had worse glares than that," I said.

They both started giggling.

"But you are a witch," Kimberly said. "I know that."

"A nice witch," Kaitlyn said.

Pammy, honking loudly, blew her nose.

I was right about the dogs, that was for sure.

"You're scaring me."

"How on earth can I be scaring you? I'm simply trying to help you find books that are not violent. The books that you've always read are all gruesomely violent." It was Monday, and the bookstore was full. Probably because I put a sign on the door about the Dark Chocolate Honeycomb cake we were selling, which is like eating heaven. "Be sweet! Come on in and eat!" I also had my tea specials up: Rose Hip and Passion Flower.

"But I like reading about violence."

"You should open your mind to something new." This woman! Geez!

"Why?"

"So that you can learn about other people and their lives. You can read a memoir and see life through someone else. You can read a biography and learn about someone who changed the world. You can read fiction or fantasy or science fiction and be swept away to a whole new time and place."

"I don't like being swept away."

"You don't?"

"No. I like to read about true life crimes."

"So I can't show you any other books?" I was exasperated.

"I'll make you a deal, Evie. You can show me other books once you show me the new crime books you have in."

"I'm feeling frustrated," I said to her.

"Many crimes are committed when people have pent-up frustration and rage. They often hate themselves. Or they are sociopaths or psychopaths. That's who I like to read about."

"And that's what you want to continue to read? Forevermore? Tell me you're kidding."

"I've never met a bookstore owner like you. It's strange. But I like it."

My hands flew up as in, "I give up." "I'm not strange. Well, I'm not *that* strange." Yes I am. But choosing a variety of books is important!

"You talk to people in a scary way sometimes, telling them to read this or that."

"I don't think you're scared."

"I'm not. I just felt like saying that. I like being scared when I read."

I looked down at the customer. Beatrice Winters. She had white hair wrapped in a bun. She was a nun for twenty years. Then she fell in love with a priest. They left their orders, and they've been married for thirty years. She was a kindergarten teacher for twenty years after her nun years. She was about five feet tall.

"Okay. Let's go find you more blood and gore and violence."

"And no more admonitions or reprimands, young lady," she reprimanded me. "I can read whatever I damn well please."

"I know you can. I'm trying to broaden your literary horizons because you are so stubborn."

"The only thing I want to broaden is my ass. My husband says my ass is skinny like a plucked chicken's."

She is petite. Mrs. Winters picked out three true crime books. I brought her a piece of Dulce de Leche cake with vanilla buttercream and cut myself a slice, and we ate it together at a table overlooking the bay. We both commented on the whales in the distance, a tail here, a fountain of water there.

She gave me a hug on the way out. "That was fun. I enjoy a civilized argument." She turned away, then back. "And tell your mother and aunts that I am looking forward to visiting them at their greenhouse shortly."

I groaned. "I didn't hear that."

"Yes, you did, dear."

There has not been a time in my life when I did not love books.

My parents were readers, too. We would sit, altogether, or my mom and Jules and me if my dad was deployed, and we would read. Often we would read in their bed. We would eat popcorn, or have a slice of pie, or we would all pile in and have Spaghetti and Books Night.

Books were my escape. I loved the stories. But I had an ulterior motive for reading: Books blocked the premonitions out. I loved being taken away to new worlds, where premonitions did not exist. As a child, as a teenager, the anxiety and depression, and the fear and dread, were so hard to battle. But books at least gave me a respite.

I read almost everything. Almost all genres. I read before I sleep. I read when I wake up. I read when I take a break at the bookstore. I read on Sunday afternoons. I read on Friday nights. I listen to audio books. My life is filled with words.

I understand people who are addicted to books. I have found that many people use books to escape life. To battle one problem, one challenge or another. Books keep the tears at bay. They also bring on the laughs, the wonder, the education.

Yes, I love books. I love stories. Always have, always will.

And I want other people to love books, too. Hence, I do get a teeny bit uptight with customers in my bookstore now and then. . . .

I met Emily Medegna when I was eleven. My parents, Jules, and I had moved to San Orcanita Island and into Rose Bloom Cottage about two weeks prior.

I remember a lot of hushed conversations in our Washington, DC, home right before we moved to the island. I remember my parents arguing, which they rarely did. The arguments, behind closed doors, always ended up with the two of them hugging, kissing, saying sorry, tears. There was a ringing tension in our house, though. Newspapers were put down when I walked in the room, the TV turned off when I got too close during the news.

"Is something wrong?" I asked my mother. She kissed me, hugged me, and said, a little too brightly, "Nothing at all, sweetheart. Let's go out for ice cream."

"Is something wrong?" I asked my father. He smiled, a tight smile, too tight, and said, "No, love, nothing at all. Hey. Do you want to go bowling this weekend?"

"What were you and Daddy fighting about in the bedroom?" I asked my mother another day.

"Oh, no, dear. We weren't fighting. We were having a discussion." She smiled, her voice too bright. "We were talking about Dad's next move, what he wants to do with his career."

"What were you and Mom fighting about in the backyard?" I asked my father. His smile was too tight once again.

"Nothing, honey. We were talking about . . . about . . . where we want to take you girls on vacation this year."

"What's going on?" I asked both of them at another dinner when they wouldn't talk. Our dinners were always noisy, chatty, filled with my dad's humor and my mother's laughter and Jules's funny stories and my conversations about how I wanted another cat.

"Nothing, Evie," my father said, then his voice broke a tiny bit. "We sure love you two."

"All is well," my mother said. "You are the light of our lives, girls. Have we told you that, Jules and Evie?"

But Jules had noticed, too, and we started listening at my parents' bedroom door. We couldn't understand most of the words, but we did understand the heated tone, the whispers, our mother crying, our father upset.

"I don't understand what they're mad about," Jules said.

"Me either," I said. "But I think Dad is crying."

"Yep. He is." So she started crying, too. And I did. What could be so bad that our dad would cry? He never cried. He was in the military!

But one day, after school, in November, our parents said to us, "Jules and Evie, we're going to move."

"What?" we both said, shocked and angry, at the same time.

"We're moving," my father said.

"Why? Where?" we said.

"We're moving to San Orcanita Island," my mother said.

"But I don't want to move," I said. "I like my friends. Bjourna just got two puppies!"

"And I like the house," Jules said. "I like hearing the army jets and playing Army Lady!"

"I'm sorry, girls," my mother said. "I know you'll miss the house and your friends, but we're going to move."

We cried, we fussed, and then our parents started talking about the island, which we had visited at least once a year for family vacations. Aunt Iris and Aunt Camille and their husband/current boyfriend would come to visit, too. All of us together.

We loved the island. We loved running through Grandma Lucy's intricate garden rooms, into the meadow, around our pond, and down to the beach where we could see the other islands and, sometimes, whales. We spied on coyotes and deer and raccoons, and we made dandelion crowns. We had even met some of the local kids during our vacations, and they'd come over to play.

Jules and I thought about it.

"I'll go if you get me a dog," Jules said. "A fluffy dog. A big one. Big, big dog."

"I'll go if you promise me I can have three cats," I said. "Not one. Not two. Three kitties."

Well, that did it. Our parents nodded. Bring on the pets, shut down the whining about the move.

We moved to the island within the week. Things at home were still tense between my parents, but the move seemed to lighten things some. I still saw them hiding newspapers. They would also turn off the TV quickly if Jules or I walked into the living room and the news was on, but we saw them holding hands again, which made Jules and I feel better.

We sold or gave away our furniture before we moved, as Rose Bloom Cottage already had furniture. We didn't have much stuff anyhow; military families know how to travel light. My grandfather was no longer at the cottage. He had fallen in love with a tourist named Yvonne with bright red hair. Yvonne was a teacher. He had moved to Arizona. We loved funny, friendly Yvonne.

So Rose Bloom Cottage was ours to stay in.

I met Emily my first day of school. I sat right by her in class.

Emily had brown curls, blue eyes like cornflowers, and a huge smile with a dimple in her left cheek. I met her mom, Patsy, after school the first day. She had brown curls, blue eyes like cornflowers, and a huge smile, too. Emily was an only child to a single mother.

Emily liked cats, and when she met Cupcake and Turtle and Sir Eats A Lot, she liked them, too. She liked our dog, Mr. Whale. My mother, as a self-trained floral designer, and Emily's mother, who was a potter, were friends, too. Both artists, my mom simply worked with flowers.

Then I had a premonition and I forgot about it and something terrible happened and I have never, ever forgiven myself.

"What do you think of your maid of honor dress?"

I was on Skype with Jules. She held up my dress.

Wow.

Whew.

Unique.

Daring, sort of scary.

Breathe deeply.

Okay!

She was smiling, so sunny, so hopeful, her blonde hair swinging, Mack's tattooed face staring right at me from her arm.

"I love it!" I said, with as much gush and mush as I could, as my insides quivered. I was going to wear *that*?

"I am soooo glad, Evie! You're going to look spectacular in it! It's perfect for that perfect figure of yours. I had the same woman make your maid of honor dress who made my wedding dress. They're different, but they belong together, like you and I belong together, as sisters, as best friend sisters! As love-sisters. I'm so excited, Evie!" She burst into tears.

"Jules, don't cry, please. You'll make me cry. You know when I cry I get carried away." I started to cry. I don't like seeing Jules cry even when she's happy. She started to sob in front of the computer. I started to sob. Her nose got red. I had to blow my nose. Her makeup was smearing down her face. I grabbed tissue and wiped at my cheeks. She made funny sounds, choking on her happy tears. I made a gaspy sound, too, that sounded like a frog choking.

"I'm so happy," she squeaked out. "Mack and I were in the hot tub last night. He's an intelligent man. He knows so much about creativity in the bedroom, well, in this case the hot tub, and he made sure I wasn't getting too hot, and I didn't make too much noise because of the neighbors, and then we talked about how we can't wait to be Mr. Mack and Mrs. Jules!" She honked her nose into a tissue. "I'm getting married and you're my maid of honor and Mom and the aunts will be there and Dad will be there from heaven and Mack's family will be there and all our friends are coming on their motorcycles in leathers!"

I burst into a fresh round of tears, so she did, too.

"Look at your dress!" she semi-shouted, shaking it. "Look at it!"

We both sobbed again.

The nonfiction book club met on Monday night. They read a book about Everest and invited me to join them, as usual. I had read the book. I will never climb Everest. I don't want to be anywhere near Everest. The scenes during the snowstorm scared me even when I was at home in the bath reading the book. I was so freaked out, I had a piece of apple pie. Apples are fruits. Therefore the pie was healthy for me.

The chess club came in later in the week. I played one game. I won. I had a croissant. Croissants are pretty, which means they add vitamins and nutrients to my day.

A group of women came in for their weekly coffee and treat date. They invited me, as always, to come and chat, so I did. They bought coffee cake. I had a slice, too. Coffee beans are healthy, therefore the coffee cake probably boosted my immune system.

I chatted with customers from all over the world. I sold books. I sold my mother's bouquets. She had titled them, as usual. "This Bouquet Is for a Saucy Woman Who Takes No Crap" and "Love Monster" and "Tulip Titillation."

I sold my aunt Iris's photographs of strange talking, laughing, sexy flowers and her cards. One that was selling especially well, which she'd had to reprint many times, was a purple flower that looked distinctly like a penis. Two red roses were clearly boobs.

I sold Aunt Camellia's lotions and potions. Her latest, which smelled like a blend of lemon and vanilla, was called You Light Me Up, Baby. It was selling well, too.

I was surrounded by books, my forever friends, who have encouraged me since I was a little girl to escape from my premonitions between their pages, to dream, to travel to places in my head, to learn, to see through others' eyes, and to imagine.

Book nerds get this.

They will understand me when I say that I love owning a book-store.

A pretty, red-haired lady in her fifties came in the next morning. My bookstore was full of tourists and people from town. We were having a rare rainy summer day, which was excellent for me. We were selling salted caramel chocolate cake, and we had two popular tea specials: Jasmine and Peppermint.

We were busy at the café, and we were busy at the cash register. I loved days like this *and* I couldn't wait to go home. There are few things better than reading on a rainy day while drinking coffee and eating pie, which is what I wanted to do.

The woman was striking, with light blue eyes and a lopsided smile that showed a lot of teeth. She was wearing jeans, a pink Windbreaker, and pink tennis shoes. I felt the oddest sensation when we started chatting about books, then I felt a premonition slide on through. . . . She was going to meet a man. I saw the man, slowly, coming into view in my mind. They were going to fall in love. They would be together for a long time . . . until they died. They would be old then. . . . I saw them with white hair, wrinkled.

I kept chatting with her; she wanted nonfiction. I suggested a few . . . and then I saw a man in the science fiction section. He was about fifty, too. Windblown hair. Looked as if he'd spent a lifetime outside. He was taller than her, trim . . . yes, it was him. She would meet *him*.

Was I supposed to help? Was it supposed to happen today?

Well, I thought, *why not?*

I couldn't miss this chance. Maybe I was the catalyst. Maybe I was the fixer-upper. Maybe I was Cupid! Evie Cupid, that's me.

I chatted with her; she found her book. I chatted with him; he found three, and they both ended up at the register at the same time because of sneaky finagling by me. The gentleman let her go first; they smiled at each other. And I saw it, their gazes held for a smidgen longer than normal. It was interest.

I rang her up and said to them both, "Well, one of you likes nonfiction and one of you likes science fiction." It was an inane comment. A nothing comment. But it opened the door to conversation. Book lovers are all alike. They are always so interested in what other people are reading, and why.

I finished her purchase while they were still talking about the nonfiction books she had chosen, then they moved on to his science fiction books. She had never read science fiction, but she would be willing to try. What was that book about? Oh, he was happy to tell her. But tell me about your interest in the Vietnam War. Why that time period?

And I lied and said, "I have to get rid of this cake. It was made yesterday. Let me give you two a free slice." All our cakes are fresh.

Oh, no, they couldn't, the man said. "I'll pay for it. Would you care to join me?" He looked at the smiling woman.

And she said, "I would be delighted. But let me pay."

"No, please," he said firmly. He was a gentleman.

"Nonsense," I said. "I refuse." I cut two thick slices of the salted caramel chocolate cake, added forks and napkins, and handed it over.

They were surprised and delighted. Free cake! They would remember this. They would remember the rainy, windy day they met on San Orcanita Island at Evie's Books, Cake, and Tea. They thanked me profusely, and he invited her over to sit by the windows overlooking the rainy bay.

They were there for three hours. I brought them ice water. Then free Jasmine tea.

When they left, still chatting, she turned and waved and mouthed "Thank you" to me.

When they were at the door, the gentleman turned his head and winked at me. "Thank you," he mouthed.

"You're welcome," I said, in turn, to each of them.

I love happy premonitions.

I saw Marco at Lupita's Mexican Restaurant, out on the patio with a group of men from the island. One is our doctor. Two are fishermen. One is a builder. They were laughing, being guys, talking, drinking beer.

I didn't want him to see me, so I scurried around the corner.

I paused and leaned against the wall of the hardware store. Marco was so hot. I liked his jawline. I liked his hands. I liked his shoulders. I liked his eyes the best. Dark and rimmed with black, with flecks of gold. I liked *him*. It's important, I think, to deeply like someone whom you're madly attracted to. There can always be lust for someone, but liking someone is the most important.

I brushed away a few tears, then my throat clenched as I remembered, once again, what would happen to Marco if we were together.

My heart about split in two. If a physician had an X-ray machine, he would see two half hearts right there, I was sure of it.

Nothing could help me and this cataclysmic romantic situation at all, except for, maybe, fettuccine alfredo.

I'd still hurt, but at least I'd get pasta.

Chapter 14

❧

Betsy Baturra
Multnomah County Jail
Portland, Oregon
1976

Six months after her baby was taken out of her arms, Betsy was cuffed at the wrists and ankles and led out of jail in her orange jumpsuit. In a specially equipped van that was made to haul prisoners back and forth to the courtroom, she sat shackled, two armed guards with her, their faces stony.

When she arrived at the courtroom, she went to a holding area and changed into the clothes her attorney brought her: blue blouse, black skirt, and a blue suit jacket. She had on flat black shoes. She knew the clothes were supposed to make her look conservative, serious, slightly frumpy, and innocent.

She was not the femme fatale the press said she was.

She was not the greedy girlfriend.

She was not the master manipulator.

She was not a cold-blooded murderer.

She was a young woman, defending the life of her boyfriend.

Betsy was numb. She was devastated. After the birth of her sweet Rose, her milk had come in and her breasts became rock hard and infected. She had shown the doctor, a male doctor, and he'd shrugged at her, gave her some pills, told her it would "get better on its own especially since your baby is gone," and that was that. The infection hadn't gone away. She caught a cold, and it went straight to her chest, caused pneumonia, and gave her a hacking cough. She was sick, weak, and depressed. She couldn't eat, and when she passed out in the lunch line it was back to the infirmary.

The doctor, a woman this time, was appalled at the infection in her breasts, and she took care of it as it should have been taken care of in the first place. Betsy's fever was at 103. She had no desire to fight anymore, even for her own life, but the medicine overruled her wish to die.

The ride to court from jail was bumpy and made Betsy nauseated. She knew that she and Johnny would be tried together. That was unusual, but the prosecutor wanted it that way. They were eighteen, Johnny still in high school, but they would be treated like any other adults.

The press was clogging the entrance of the courthouse. Her case, Johnny's case, had captured the eyes of the public. Peter, born Pyotr, Kandinsky had been murdered by his son and the son's girlfriend! Betsy knew what the press was saying: MURDER FOR MONEY . . . PAMPERED SON PLUS GREEDY GIRLFRIEND EQUALS A MURDER . . . YOUNG WOMAN LURES BOYFRIEND INTO KILLING HIS OWN FATHER . . . BEAUTY, LIES, DEATH: HOW TWO LOVERS PLANNED THE MURDER OF THE DECADE.

Not only was the case making national headlines because of the two young lovers, but both of the young lovers said they had murdered the father.

Betsy had told the police that she had stabbed Peter.

Johnny, to Betsy's utter shock, said he did it. She told the police Johnny was lying, she did it. Johnny said that Betsy was lying, he had killed his father.

Both of their fingerprints were on the knife, but the knife had come from Johnny's kitchen so his prints were expected.

The only other person in the room who could tell what truly happened was Tilly, Johnny's younger sister, who was seven years old at the time and had not spoken since the stabbing. Not one word. She was, as the press reported breathlessly, "almost in a trance . . . mentally comatose . . . lost her memory . . . not speaking. . . . Poor thing! Traumatized by watching her brother's girlfriend stab her father . . . or was it her brother who stabbed her father?"

The courtroom was noisy and chaotic. The rows were crammed with journalists and spectators who had managed to get in. No one could resist it: Betsy was young and beautiful. Johnny was young and handsome. And there was a dead dad.

Betsy should have been scared to death, but she wasn't. All was lost. She knew it. Her baby, Rose, was gone. Even her own attorney said that she could get twenty years, maybe life. Maybe the death penalty. It looked premeditated. But none of that mattered. She wanted Rose and could not have her, or her beloved Johnny. Her depression was black and oppressive, sucking out all hope of light. She felt done with life and living. The only thing that kept her from killing herself in jail was her premonition, the one that showed her driving and crashing amidst fir trees and orange poppies.

Betsy was manhandled out of the van, two deputies beside her in bulletproof vests, more in front and behind. She could hardly walk, a few shuffles at a time. She had taken a shower the night before because the woman in the cell next to her, Devina—a woman who was addicted to heroin five years ago and bought and sold the drug to feed her habit—insisted she do so. The heroin addict had attended an Ivy League school. She'd crushed her knee skiing and become addicted to the pain medicine, which then morphed into the heroin addiction.

"Shower. Please, Betsy. You look . . ." Devina paused, shook her head.

"I don't care how I look."

"You should," Devina said. "It'll help you. You look like a ghost."

Rainbow said, "Aquamarine. Carnation pink. Orange. You are many colors, Betsy. Let's bring out the bright ones. Gold. Silver."

So Betsy had showered and washed her thick black hair for the first time in a week.

Her eyes caught Johnny's and held. She teared up, and so did he. They had exchanged letters the entire time they'd been in jail awaiting trial. They still loved each other. They had cried over the baby they knew they would probably never see again, their tears staining their letters. They had been realistic, but they had been clinging to hope, too. They had been deadly pessimistic, and they had been determined to get out one day to see their daughter.

I love you, they wrote. I love you so much.

The judge hammered his gavel. The trial began.

Johnny and Betsy met at a café in downtown Portland where Betsy worked as a waitress. Johnny went there after school, after sports practice, for chocolate milkshakes, then started coming each day to visit Betsy.

They started talking, light chat, then they progressed, slowly, to opening their hearts. Betsy saw in him someone like herself: Lost. They dated, they fell in love. Johnny did not want to work in his father's company, or with his father. He hated his father. His father was part owner of a used car dealership that regularly ripped people off.

He wanted to be a farmer. He had been, every summer, to his grandma's farm, and he loved it. It had been sold by his father when she died. Even his grandma couldn't stand his father, who had tried to steal her money. Johnny wanted to sell fruits and vegetables, and specialty items, too, like cheeses and wine. He hoped to have a vineyard one day.

Farming sounded perfect to Betsy. She could be outside. She could have animals. She could hide from her parents and be away from people. The more people she was around, the more premonitions she had. It was fraught, it was exhausting. She wanted to help people, but it was tearing her down, wearing her down.

Betsy and Johnny had their first kiss at a picnic. Second kiss hiking. Third kiss by a waterfall. Their romance was slow, steady, awash in friendship and kindness. Betsy talked about her parents for the first time, their fanaticism, the violence of her father.

She told him about the beatings with a brush, sticks, a

wooden spoon, and her father's belt. She told him about all the times her father hit her with the Bible, all the verses she had to memorize, how her mother stood back and didn't help her when her father berated her, told her that she was the devil. How she'd crawled out her window in the middle of the night and left home after graduating early from high school, determined to be independent even though she wasn't yet eighteen.

Betsy told Johnny about the time, only a few weeks ago, when her parents found her at her apartment, the one she lived in now. The building was filled with students because it was near a university. She was working and going to college classes. She was still in her blue waitress uniform, splattered with ketchup and mustard, when she walked down the hallway and saw her parents by her front door. Music pounded out of a couple of the other apartments, doors open, students milling around.

"What are you doing here?" she said to her father as his face filled with a purple, throbbing rage. He hid behind his religion. He quoted the Bible; he had it memorized. But it was an act. There was no true love there, or compassion, or faith, only a desire to control her and her mother—a squat man using religion to manipulate and abuse.

"Don't talk to me like that, young woman," he hissed. "You sinful, disobedient, slutty wretch," his voice rose sanctimoniously, "Betsy, you will come home now and repent."

"No," she said, tilting her chin up. She was always tired from working and going to school, but she was proud of herself. She had escaped her parents, and she was living a whole new life. She still had nightmares about her father: He would chase her through her dreams, he would catch her and smack her across the face, and her mother would stand there and whimper and wring her hands but do nothing to stop the beating. She would wake up panting, sweating, angry, pained, then so incredibly relieved she wasn't living with him anymore.

"I'm not going home with you."

"Yes, you are." Her father's hands were clenched at his sides. She knew he was trying not to grab her, shove her against a wall, and tell her to "begin reciting Luke. . . . Name the books of the Bible. . . . Tell me the story of the woman by the well, you devil whore. . . ."

Her mother told her to "obey her father" in her spindly, frail voice, her eyes filling with tears. "Please, Betsy. Come home. We'll pray about this together. Right, Hansen?"

"Shut up, Mary," her father said to her mother, and her mother's head dropped. It made Betsy sick. It made her furious.

"You will never defend me, will you, Mom?" Tears rushed to Betsy's eyes, every tear a hundred cries she had never let herself have. Every tear a sign of the continuous betrayal of her mother. "You let him hurt me. You never tried to protect me."

"Betsy," she said, barely above a whisper, wringing her hands, her gold eyes anguished, the same eyes as her daughter. "Come with us. We've been so worried about you."

"I am safer here than with him, and you know it, Mom. You know what he's done to me. You know how he's hurt me. Why do you want me to live with that again?"

Her mother's expression showed all her guilt, her fear, her fearful selfishness, her powerlessness.

"You are an ungrateful, Godless woman who has embraced the blackness of this world," her father's voice boomed. "You will burn for this, but not until I have put you back on God's righteous path."

"I said I am not coming home. I will never live with you and Mom again. Why don't you try being nice to Mom? Then you'll have at least one woman who won't leave you."

Her father's face became even darker, his fat fists clenched and unclenched, his eyes narrowed. How dare she say no to him! How dare she defy him! How dare she disrespect him! She was only a girl. His daughter. He owned her. "You are a disgrace—"

She turned and walked back down the hallway. She would enter her apartment later, after they left. Tears spilled out of her eyes. When she had lived with them, she endured. But after leaving, after coming here, to college, to her job, where people were nice to her, gentle, funny, she was able to start seeing her life with her parents for what it was: Abusive. Lonely. Freezing cold.

Her father thundered up behind her, whipped her around, and smacked her in the face, her head twisting about before she crumpled onto the floor. Before she could struggle up and cover her head with her arms, two young men who lived down the hall shouted and intervened. They shoved Hansen away from her and slammed him up against the wall, his bald head crashing into the plaster. He was stunned, dropping heavily to the floor like a sack of potatoes.

One of the young men, who was studying biology in hopes of going to medical school, said, "How do you like being hit, dick?" He hauled Hansen back up and punched him in the face. "How do you like it now?" The bio student hit him again, Hansen's head snapping back, and dropped him.

The other young man, who was studying to become a nuclear physicist, said, "You sucker punched a woman!" His face was outraged, sickened. "What the hell is wrong with you?" The physics student hauled him up and shoved him back into the wall, Hansen's head again slamming into it.

Her father, on the ground, his head wobbling, stared up at the furious young men standing protectively in front of his daughter and was shocked. What had happened? How dare they hit him! His mouth opened and closed, opened and closed, like a gaping fish. His wife was peering down at him. What was in her eyes? Was it . . . triumph? Was it vindictiveness? Joy?

"Get out of here," Betsy said quietly, but the rage was evident. "Go. I never, ever want to see either of you again. I'm not taking this anymore. If you don't leave right now, I will call the police." She couldn't believe she'd said that. Even though her face was aching, her neck already knotting up, she was proud of herself.

Her father, trying to recover, trying to stand up, his stiff cheap suit rumpled, croaked out, "You are a girl and we will make you come home with us! Call the police and I will tell them the truth about your rebellious, slutty nature, your lies and your crimes. God will strike you down. He will punish you for your disobedience to your father."

To which one of the young men said, "No, dude. He's going

to strike you down because you hit your own daughter, and I'll bet you've been hitting her for a long time. That's called abuse, asshole. Didn't you know that?"

And the other young man said, "I was raised a Christian, and this isn't the way a father treats his daughter. My dad never treated me and my sisters like this. Anyone tell you that you're supposed to act with love if you think you're a Christian?"

Her father cursed them then, his "faith" completely leaving him as he used the f-word, her mother huddled against the wall.

The kid who was going to medical school said, "I don't like the f-word," and punched her father in the gut. He doubled over.

"Get out," Betsy said again. She could feel her face swelling. "Get out."

They left, her father hobbling, her mother crying. Her mother turned to hug Betsy, but Betsy held up her hands as in "Stop."

"You never helped me, Mom. If you wanted to live with a man like him, fine. But you never should have let me live with him." Something sharp and pained flashed in her mother's eyes, and Betsy knew what her mother knew: She was a terrible mother. She should have left her husband to protect her daughter. "You have premonitions, Mom. You chose to cower. You chose not to act, not to help people. You chose not to help me."

That her mother *knew* what she should have done, and didn't, made Betsy more angry, and sadder than before. She had been repeatedly abused by her father, and even now her mother chose her father over her. Hard to know who she hated more.

Her father turned, unsteady on his feet with his head all messed up. "Mary!" he boomed, spittle and blood flying out of his mouth. "Come! Now!"

Her mother shot one last look at Betsy, shame in her eyes, defeat in her body, grief on her face, and left to go to her father.

Betsy hugged the two boys who protected her, and they later became friends with both her and Johnny.

She told Johnny about how she had gotten herself declared an emancipated minor, though her father shouted and railed in court against it. His uncontrolled temper tantrum, his citing of the Bible and his "legal control" over her, his "God-given role as the man, the leader of this family, all in it shall follow my rules," had the judge signing the emancipation papers lightning quit.

The judge said, "I can see why you can't live with this anymore, Betsy. Are there more children at home? No? Good. Or I would have Children's Services on you, Hansen, in a heartbeat. You should not have children in the home. You are free to live your life, Betsy, as you see fit. Sit down, Hansen! I said sit the hell down! Now! Bailiff, remove him from the courtroom immediately. You are in contempt!"

So Betsy told Johnny the truth about her childhood, and Johnny told her the truth about his own father: He hated him.

Peter, Johnny's father, came in to the café one time when she was working, when Johnny was there having a burger.

Peter was wearing a pin-striped suit, which she thought was tacky. He was also wearing gold rings and a gold bracelet, which she thought were gaudy and probably fake. His dark hair was slicked back with grease, which made him look like he belonged to the mob. He hadn't smiled at her, but his black, raisin-like eyes had traveled grossly down the length of her body, stopping at her breasts and hips. She felt dirty. She felt evaluated and judged.

There are men who want to, who must, control women. When they can't control them, they become dangerous and violent. They think women are good for serving them and sex. Nothing more. Inside, they hate women.

Peter was exactly like her own father. He was a shady used car salesman. Her father pretended to be a man of God. What were the chances that two people would meet up, fall in love, and have the same type of father lurking and looming in their backgrounds? But maybe that was part of it: They saw the fear and pain in each other's eyes and reached out a hand.

But Betsy couldn't have known the truth about what Peter had done then.

There was something that Johnny didn't tell her about his father. Not for a while. He hadn't realized the truth until recently.

He had blocked it out. It hurt him to even speak of it. It brought rage bubbling to the surface like hot lava, next to the insidious fear that rose up whenever he was around Peter.

Johnny was scared of his father. He had every right to be.

Seated together, in court, Johnny's and Betsy's eyes locked and their desperate love was the same as it had always been.

"I love you," she mouthed to Johnny.

"I love you, too," he mouthed back.

They were young, they were in love, they were soul mates, they were supposed to be together.

The law thought differently.

Chapter 15

I deliberately stayed out of my mother and aunts' "medical" marijuana business, but I did remind them yet again, like a parrot, that it was illegal. They pooh-poohed.

"What will they do? Lock us up?" my mother said.

For some reason my aunts and mother thought this notion was hilarious, and they bent over cackling, their matching blue-flowered garden hats tipping back and forth. We were wandering through their mother's garden, cutting flowers for Hat Night. Hat Night is on the first Tuesday of the month when they each make the most "beaudacious" hat they can.

They put the photos of each hat on their website—Flowers, Lotions, and Potions—and the site gets a zillion hits, as usual, from all over the globe as people vote for their favorite. They post a goofy, funny photo of the three of them, taken by me, wearing each other's hats, so as not to "improperly influence the voting."

"Yes, they might lock you up," I said.

"Why so prim and proper?" my mother asked, then sighed, her white bell-shaped hair swinging.

"Why so fearful and afflicted by doom? I think you'll get in touch with your inner self if you smoke a joint, sweetheart," Aunt Camellia said, linking an arm around my waist. "It'll release your worries into the universe."

"Why so strict and rigid?" Aunt Iris asked. "You have to let go a little, Evie. Get wild and crazy. Do something off the wall. Derange yourself."

"Derange myself?"

"Yes, do something so out of the ordinary that you feel deranged," Aunt Iris said. "In a fun yet sensible manner."

"I am already half-deranged," I said. "My brain is a churning gray mass in my head with inexplicable tendencies to see the future. You think that's not deranged enough? By the way, when did you all start smoking pot?"

"We hardly ever do, dearie," Aunt Camellia said. "In fact, I think I've done it less than five or six or seven times." She paused. "Or eight."

My mother and Aunt Iris nodded.

"But it was fun," my mother said. "We did it before we led our friends in drunken sailor songs at Milton's birthday party last week."

I rolled my eyes. That was a noisy party. I left early. "It won't be fun if Chief Allroy comes on your property with a warrant, looks in that greenhouse, and then you're in trouble."

"Chief Allroy?" my mother squealed as if I'd made a joke, then burst into laughter, her hands flying in the air, both filled with bouquets of sunflowers.

"Chief Bick Allroy? You think he's coming on our property to arrest us? Let me envision that!" My aunt Camellia bent over as she laughed, pink Anne Boleyn roses on her knees. She then crossed her legs, and my mother saw her, whooped, and crossed her legs as they cackled.

"Hang on," Aunt Iris said, shaking her hydrangeas at me. "I have an image of Chief Allroy coming here with his handcuffs." Her laughter boomed. "Handcuffs!"

This image was, apparently, also hilarious.

"He'll get a warrant, come on your property, go into your greenhouse," I drawled, knowing that the harder they laughed, the more problems they'd have in the bladder department. "He'll read you your rights, tell you to get an attorney—"

"Stop, Evie, stop. You know I don't have a strong bladder!" my mother howled.

"Me either!" Aunt Iris gasped. "Evie, quick. Say something serious! Oh, do it, now! Something about politics, mathematics, scientific explorations, and discoveries."

I was not amused by their cackling. "Chief Allroy will put your hands behind your back," I drawled.

They shrieked again, then waddled their screeching selves back toward Rose Bloom Cottage's toilets.

"He's coming to get you now!" I shouted after them.

I don't know why this was so funny to them, but they howled.

"He's going to turn on the sirens when you're in the back of his police car!"

They could barely stand it.

"And then you'll go to town and be put in a holding cell in jail!"

More fun!

"I squirted!" my mother howled.

"Need fresh panties!" Aunt Camellia said.

"Dang getting old and my wrinkled bladder!" Aunt Iris said as her blue hat tumbled off her head.

Watching my aunts and mother waddle on into the house from the greenhouse, I thought of Jules and myself.

We could end up like them. We would be one sister short, but still.

It made me happy thinking of growing old with Jules. It brought me peace.

But we would not be growing pot in the greenhouse, that was for sure.

Aunt Camellia won for best hat later that week. She did create hat art. She started with a white straw hat, then piled on white roses, faux white birds, and white feathers sprayed with silver glitter. It was about two feet tall.

Aunt Iris used sunflowers, blue delphinium, and blue hydrangeas to make a mixed bouquet. She used a huge gold bow and plopped them on a dark blue hat that resembled a giant donut. She earned second place.

My mother made a bouquet of burgundy peonies, attached them to a purple felt hat that covered one eye, added burgundy netting that stuck out six inches on either side, and wrapped it with burgundy ribbons.

"Oh, pish. I hate losing," my mother said. "Let's drink some wine, ladies!"

Mr. Jamon came in for his weekly books.

"What are you thinking about today?" I asked him.

"I'm thinking I need a biography on Albert Einstein."

"Got it." I had one. He bought it.

"Also"—he leaned in close—"I need another romance. A love story."

I thought. "How about a book by Debbie Macomber?"

"Who's that?"

"She's a romance writer. Sweet romances. Happy endings."

"I'll take it. I still believe in love, you know." He winked.

Mr. Jamon came back in the next day. He garumphed.

"I'll take another book by Mrs. Macomber." He garumphed again, tapped his cane. "Maybe two more."

I have many of her books, so it took us a few minutes to figure out which would be best for Mr. Jamon. He was pleased with his choices. "An old man can still be romantic, Evie."

"Never said you couldn't."

He winked at me. "See you next Friday."

"Mr. Bob and Trixie Goat are here to visit you again," Tiala said, smiling.

"What?"

"Your goats. They came to visit you again. I thought you fixed that problem so they couldn't come to town anymore."

"They're out again?" I groaned and stepped out of Evie's Books, Cake, and Tea and spied my stubborn goats, Mr. Bob and Trixie, right up the street.

When they saw me, their ears perked up and they ran straight toward me with that lanky gait that goats have. The escapees were happy to see me, I could tell.

"I can't even believe this," I said. But I could.

How do Mr. Bob and Trixie get out of their pen? How do they know where I work? The only explanation is that I have come by here a few times with them on the way to Marco's and I've gotten out of the car to jet into the bookstore for a minute. But I have no idea how they know how to get to my bookstore. We are close to town, but not that close.

Their goat home is a mini-house. It has a blue roof and sides and an opening. It is very cute and welcoming. I make sure they have fresh hay. I make sure they also get carrots, sunflower seeds, and pumpkin seeds, which they love. When I am at home I often let them out to wander our property and peek in the pond and prance over my grandma Lucy's wooden bridge, because I know they won't leave and they like to visit Virginia Alpaca and Alpaca Joe. Plus, they are fascinated by Sundance and Butch and Cassidy, and the five of them will play around like best friends. So why leave home?

But there they were, heading down the street to my bookstore, with that odd gallop-skip. I put my hands on my hips as I watched, people laughing, moving out of the way, kids pointing. Their bells jangled.

They stopped right in front of me. Trixie Goat got on her hind legs to give me a hug. I hugged her because I don't want to hurt her feelings. Mr. Bob made a grunting sound.

"Get in the truck," I told them, pointing at the truck.

They turned to get in the truck.

"Tiala," I called. "I'll be right back."

She laughed. "Okay, goat lady."

I opened the front door of the cab and helped them in. Then I drove home, Mr. Bob's and Trixie's heads out the window, the wind running through their fur.

I swear they were smiling.

People waved at them as we drove by.

"You're naughty goats," I said.

They did not seem daunted.

Each day I walk from Rose Bloom Cottage to my own home through the flowers as they bloom during the spring, summer, and fall: Daisies. Tulips. Irises. Columbine. Lavender. Lilacs. Rows of marigolds. Jupiter's-beard. Foxgloves. Roses.

I find peace in the flowers. Who knew that my grandmother, a woman who was kind and filled with love and also filled with mental illness, would create something that I, two generations later, would wander through to calm my mind, soothe my nerves, and rest my almost ever-present anxiety as I await the next premonition?

There are painted Adirondack chairs all over. Purple. Blue. Green. Red. My mother says that chairs belong in gardens so that people can "find their own splendor amidst the petals." So I will often sit in one chair, then another, then a different one the following night, or sit in the gazebo.

I have never had a premonition while in the garden. It's as if the delicate colors, the petals themselves, block it out. I don't know how, or why, that would happen, but it does. How could our willow trees, or the roses that bloom all over the trellises and verandas, or the purple wisteria vine that winds up the gazebo, or the lily pads in the pond, or the secret garden room with the oak tree in the middle of it, stand in the way of premonitions that can hit me at any other time, in any way?

Maybe it's the tranquility. Maybe it's the quiet. Maybe it's being alone. Maybe it's my grandmother's loving spirit, still here, surrounding me like a protective hug.

At the end of the season, when the flowers are dying, I'll still sit in those Adirondack chairs or drink coffee on the bridge or lie on the yellow bench overlooking the meadow. Even in November, December, January, and February, somehow the garden protects me. It's as if the memory of the flowers, or maybe the bulbs that lie under the ground, the perennials that will pop up again, have filled the air with protection. But just in case, in the winter my mother always fills two huge barrels on my deck with purple pansies.

Lining the walkway between her house and mine, she'll plant more pansies. My mother, aunts, and I have also planted tons of crocuses. Purple. White. Yellow. Those are the first flowers up, and when I see those flowers, I always heave a sigh of relief.

They know me, my mother and aunts, and they know the sweet, inexplicable umbrella of safety that their garden offers me, via their mother, a woman of French and Greek descent, a woman of innate kindness who jumped off a cliff, her own demons chasing her into the air.

Marco came in a week later, on a Wednesday, to buy books.

"Hi, Marco." I smiled on automatic, so happy to see him. Then I was struck by the premonition I'd had of him, and me, and that cooled me way down. I shivered. I actually felt that shiver wind its way down my spine.

"Hi, Evie." He came to stand in front of me in his full masculine, healthy, manly way and smiled. "How are you?"

"I'm fine." I was so glad I'd washed my hair that morning. Plus, I'd put on my best jeans and a tighter blue shirt with white roses embroidered in lines down the front. It was a tad low cut, thank heavens. Maybe my lacy pink bra would show! "Can I help you find a book?"

"Yes. Please. I need a few books. I'm thinking history, a biography, and something funny."

"So let's start with history. Here's our history section." I turned. I hoped my butt didn't look too big, but it is what it is, my butt. Who am I to deprive myself of pie? Boring that would be. Plus, it's what I look forward to every night as I am alone, again, with my books: Pie. What is that saying? The more the cushion, the better the pushin'?

"What time period are you most interested in today?"

He liked World War II, but he also liked learning about the Depression era and how families and individuals survived.

We had a professional book conversation, which I loved because of my obsession with books and all things nerdy. I probably told him way more than he wanted to know. I could not seem to close my mouth and stop my stupid talking.

We then went over to biographies and he picked up one on Ernest Shackleton, the Antarctic explorer, after a long discussion we both enjoyed. At least I hope he enjoyed it. He was smiling at me. I probably droned on too long then, too. Then we headed to the humor section. I read a lot of humor because it helps me calm down.

We pulled a couple. He bought five books. I gave him a discount, but he refused. "Look, Evie, you bring your animals to me, I buy my books from you."

He asked about my animals and we chatted, and I insisted that he have a piece of marionberry pie, and I had one, too, and we ate in the café and drank blackberry tea. I hoped he would try to look down my low-cut embroidered shirt, but he didn't.

I told myself that this pie would not replace my evening pie, as pie is a fruit, therefore, nutritious, and I don't like to upset my nightly routines. Then he left and I went to my office overlooking the bay, knowing my employees could handle everything. I sank into my seat at my desk, pulled my arms over my head, and moaned.

I wanted that man, I did.

No, I told myself. You may not have him.

When I was ten years old I had a premonition about a morbidly obese woman on our street in the suburbs of DC who was always screaming at her husband and six kids. Three times I saw Gloria Yateman slap her kids across the face. I told my parents, and they called the police and Children's Services. The police and Children's Services did nothing, despite repeated calls from other neighbors/teachers who saw her hitting her kids, chasing them, wielding a belt like a lasso, and observing the obvious neglect when the kids were at school.

One time I saw Gloria try to run over her husband with their old clunky car. He was a beaten-down, exhausted man. I saw her slug him in the gut, and he bent over, not moving.

I knew the kids. The second oldest was named Coraline. She was in my class. She would come to school with bruises on her face. I heard her tell the teacher that she fell on the sidewalk or she crashed on her bike or she fell out of a wagon her brother was pulling.

They were all lies. The kids didn't have bikes. They didn't have wagons. They were all pale, unsmiling, scared, bruised kids. Especially Toby. He was in kindergarten and he still didn't speak. He had a dazed expression and clung to Coraline and her older brother, Rhett. Rhett was a super nice kid. One time someone was bullying Coraline, calling her "skin and bones" and "dumb dumb dumb!" and "retarded," and Rhett shoved him straight into the brick wall of the school and calmly told him he would beat his brains out if he picked on his sister again, and the bullying stopped. Rhett was a gentle but angry kid because of what was going on at home.

Their yard wasn't taken care of, and the gray paint was peeling off the house. I had been inside the house only one time, when Coraline said her mother wasn't home because she was shopping for new clothes. The house was a pit. There was stuff all over, in piles, you could hardly walk. Nowadays, we call that hoarding. Then, there was no label.

When we heard Gloria's car in the driveway, Coraline cried, "Oh no! Get out, Evie. Go out the back! Don't let our mom see you," and she and Rhett pushed me out a window and begged me to stay hidden as I left their property. I didn't leave, though. I watched through the back window. The mother came lumbering in, heavy, plodding, her hair all over like a porcupine's, drunk.

Gloria started swearing at her kids. She raised her hand to hit one of the younger ones, and Rhett caught her arm. She turned red as she swung her other arm through the air and cuffed Rhett as Coraline pushed the whimpering, frightened younger kids to the bedrooms.

Gloria saw all the kids running and she thundered after them, swearing and yelling, her body rolling from side to side. Rhett darted after her, tried to stop her, tried to distract her.

In the corner of the room, I saw a baby. Motionless. I hadn't seen him before. I didn't even know there was a baby. He was the loneliest baby I had ever seen. It was like he already knew that crying made things worse.

When Gloria came hobbling back in, dragging the fourth kid by the hair, still swearing, then tried to stuff rotten bread in his mouth for "complaining about being hungry, you ungrateful brat," I had a premonition: Gloria was going to die.

She was going to die wearing the same pink-flowered muumuu she had on that day. She might die later that day. It was going to be at night. She was driving her car, the car was swerving, as she drank straight out of a bottle. She was going to crash into a tree on a quiet, dark street out in the country. I saw her suffering. I saw her legs trapped. I saw her crying. I saw her bleeding. I saw the blood running down her face. I saw her yelling for help, trying to twist her bulk. I saw night turning into day, and she was still alive, but barely. Then I saw her close her eyes, giving up, her face scrunched in a mask of pain, sober at last, and take her last breath.

I did nothing to interfere in that premonition. A few nights later Gloria crashed her car wearing the pink-flowered muumuu and died.

There was no funeral. Coraline's dad, Buxton, had his wife cremated the next day. Buxton took a week off from work. He was a brainiac engineer doing something in the Defense Department and had been beaten up repeatedly by his wife.

Two days after her death, he had the kids take all of their mother's clothes out of her closets and dressers and bag them up for Goodwill. He had the kids go through all their things that didn't fit anymore, too, toys that no one wanted, furniture of no use, and they donated everything. They went through the house and bagged up all of the odd, useless things their mother collected and tossed the junk in a huge Dumpster he had brought in.

When the neighbors saw what was going on, we all went over to help. We joined members of Buxton's family he hadn't seen in years because Gloria wouldn't allow visitors. The Big Clean Out was "in lieu" of a funeral. There were about thirty people there.

Everyone went through the yard and tossed out old and broken furniture, piles of scrap wood, broken lawn mowers, a tumble-down shed, and other junk that Gloria hoarded. Buxton opened the garage, and they started tossing things out from there, too, including two useless cars that were hauled away and two decrepit trailers on the side of the house. Three giant bins were towed in and out over three days.

By the time we were all done, the house had been mostly cleared.

Buxton ordered pizza for all of us, and the kids' mouths dropped open. "Really?"

"Really." Buxton smiled, and you could tell the man hadn't had a lot of smiles in his life for a long time.

We had a neighborhood pizza party right there.

The improvements continued. The refrigerator and pantry lost the locks that their mother had fastened on them, and the shelves were filled with food. The kids bought clothes that fit. Buxton had the filthy carpets ripped out and replaced with wood floors. The windows were washed. The dishwasher hadn't worked for a year, so he had a new one installed. The new oven worked well, too. He had the house scraped and painted yellow, at my mother's suggestion, and a weekly housekeeper was hired.

All the kids, including the baby, started to smile and laugh, and they played outside now, with Buxton and with the other neighborhood kids.

What was wrong with Gloria? She was an alcoholic. She was a hoarder. Was there an underlying mental health or personality disorder there? Probably. But that doesn't make her easier to live with, and she made everyone around her miserable, scared, starving, and mentally ill themselves. That was what led me to do nothing. I had let Gloria die. I did not warn her. I did not warn her husband.

It has always stuck with me, but I don't regret it at all.

But that's the disaster of premonitions: You actually have to think, and analyze, to determine when, and how, you're going to help someone . . . or not.

Try figuring that one out when you're a kid. No wonder I'm screwed up.

Chapter 16

∽

"What did Serafina have to give King Koradome in order to get out of the cage and help her brothers get out, too?"

"Serafina would have to give up her colorful mermaid tail to King Koradome, scale by scale."

"Oh no!"

"Yes. King Koradome wanted to punish Serafina for having something so beautiful. He had always wanted her shiny, luminescent scales, so he cast a spell on her. She had to agree to the spell in order to get her brothers out of the cage.

"Every single time Serafina did something kind for someone else, a scale would fall off, swim through the sea, around the coral reefs and the sunken ships and the mountain ridges, and King Koradome would catch it in his greedy hand. He wanted to collect the scales one by one. He also wanted her family and her friends to watch her losing her special tail, then they would remember who was the most powerful merman of all."

"He's mean."

"Yes, and he knew that Serafina would not be able to stop doing nice things for people, helping them, no matter what it cost her."

"Was he right? Did Serafina stop helping people so she could keep her tail?"

Chapter 17

Chief Allroy was hiking and fell. He broke both legs. No one could find him at first. We all went out searching for him. Finally, right before the sun hid beneath the horizon, twenty-five-year-old Devonna Shepherd, who everyone says has the sight of an eagle, spotted him. He was way down a ravine, hardly moving. He did, however, raise a hand in hello, then passed back out.

He was helicoptered to Seattle. He was in bad shape but would make a full recovery eventually.

"Such a shame," my mother said that night at my house, where we were eating chocolate croissants that I'd bought from the bakery that makes all my delicious bookstore cakes.

"We'll have to bring him—"

"*Shhh!*" Aunt Camellia said, trying to be discreet as she nodded her head vigorously in my direction.

I rolled my eyes and put my purple rose teacup back down on my butcher block table. Sundance barked at Aunt Camellia as if he were in on the joke. Butch and Cassidy laid on my mother's and Aunt Iris's feet. Those dogs shifted their loyalties with my mother and aunts around. It was a tad annoying.

"What?" my mother said. "The pot will help with the pain."

"Those dang drug companies made those painkillers a whisper away from heroin," Aunt Iris said, so angry. She ran a hand through her short white hair. "A whisper! A millimeter! A feather! Profits before people. That's why all those good people got addicted. You want the chief to get addicted to something a hop and a scotch away from heroin? Neither do I. Pot is the practical answer."

"We can put it in his cookies," Aunt Camellia said, "and add a blessing." She spread her palms up and out, as if catching blessings.

"I can't even believe I'm hearing this," I said. Mars jumped on my lap. Venus jumped on a stack of books in the family room that were propped against my pink rose wallpaper wall. I knew he was going to knock them over. Yep. They tumbled down, and he hissed. "You're talking about making the police chief stoned."

My mother and aunts studied me curiously, then Aunt Iris said, looking straight at me, as if I weren't even there, "She's a little too Goody Two-shoes, isn't she?"

"I think she needs naked yoga," Aunt Camellia said. "Communing with grace from above will help her soul to relax, the stars a balm against her almost sanctimonious angst."

"It was her father," my mother said. "He always followed all the rules."

"I'm sitting right here, Mom, Aunts," I said. "Eating croissants with no pot in them."

"She does get snippy," Aunt Iris said.

I rolled my eyes. "What are you doing with the money, anyhow? You don't need it."

"We do need it!" my mother exclaimed.

"Why?"

"Antarctica!" the three of them said together. Then they laughed.

"What do you mean, Antarctica?" Sundance put his head in my lap. It didn't bother Mars. They're friends.

"We're going to Antarctica for a visit," my mother said. "And we're going to make special Antarctica hats. Warm ones!"

"I can't wait to see polar bears," Aunt Camellia said. "If I die and come back as an animal, I want to be a polar bear. Majestic, strong, wise. Also, they have sharp teeth, a warm white coat, and a strong bite."

A strong bite? Aunt Camellia wanted a strong bite? Did she have cannibalistic tendencies?

"I want to study the weather," Aunt Iris said. "The temperature during the day versus the night and how it shifts through the seasons. I'm interested in the ocean currents, the animals who live and survive in Antarctica, and what's underneath the layers of ice in terms of billions of years of history on that continent. I want to know who came first to explore Antarctica. Did they freeze to death and die? Who came next? I want to know about the effects of global warming. They better have presentations and videos to watch so I can learn something onboard."

. . . and there was the smart one whose mind freely, but sensibly, roams the planet.

"I want to be on a boat and make new friends and drink wine," my mother said. "We can share our love of flowers and hats with everyone. If it's a small group, hats for all! We'll add tiny penguins and polar bears and octopus!"

Hats and flowers and wine, that's my mom.

"So," my mother said, turning to her sisters, "back to the pot cookies for the chief. I'll create a scrumptious recipe, and we'll see how they taste."

Hats, flowers, wine, and *pot*. Unbelievable. "I can't believe this." This conversation was making me eat another chocolate croissant. Butch put his nose up to Mars's nose. Mars meowed. "You three are going to end up in orange jumpsuits."

"Then we'll make orange hats!" my mother announced.

"We'll wear orange panties!" Aunt Camellia said. "We'll embroider 'Jail Birdies' on the butts."

"We'll use the time in jail to study history," Aunt Iris said. "Look back. All the answers you need in life can be found in history."

They are in their seventies.

They are breaking the law.

They are going to make pot cookies for the chief of police.

Sundance barked. He thought this was funny, I could tell. Butch and Cassidy licked the aunts' hands.

Those dogs were irritating sometimes.

I picked up the stack of books that Venus knocked over, then studied my books.

Literary friends, all of them. I even had a library card catalog!

But it was getting a tad out of control. . . . I probably was a book hoarder.

"I have the food worked out for the wedding. I talked to Mom and Aunt Camellia and Aunt Iris about it last night," Jules said. With one hand I held my cell phone and with the other I pet Alpaca Joe and Virginia Alpaca. Alpaca Joe spit. "Don't do that, Alpaca Joe." He spit again.

The sky was cloudless, blue as blue can be, the ocean lapping at the edge of our property. Behind me were rows of bearded irises. The huge type. The type that look like they are the queens of all the flowers of the world. Sundance stood right by me, Lizard in his mouth, Butch and Cassidy barking as they ran around the property. Ghost was walking along the goats' fence. I don't know why. She likes to do that sometimes.

"What are we eating?" I asked.

"All American food: Barbeque!"

Barbeque. Yum. "I love barbeque."

"I can't stand any of those fluffy, silly, fancy meals that people serve at weddings. Everyone's starving after the ceremony. So we're having ribs! Corn on the cob. Potatoes with sour cream. French bread. Plus, hamburgers, too. So you can have ribs and burgers."

"Sounds delicious." Casual food for a casual, loving ceremony. Everyone would love it.

"And . . . we're getting kegs," Jules said. "Everyone likes beer so we're rollin' 'em in!"

"And wedding cake."

She laughed. "Oh, wait until you see the wedding cake! Plus, we're having pies. You can't have barbeque without apple pies. I know you love pie, Evie."

"I can't believe the date is sneaking up on us like this," I said.

"I know!" Jules said. Then she burst into tears. "I'm so happy to be marrying Mack. He is so thoughtful in bed. Last night he brought me a pink box and inside was a pink nightie with a motorcycle on the front. He also bought me black garters and black heels. He knows I love garters! He's a huggy, sexy bear."

"And he's smart." I was hoping we could talk about how Mack was out of bed. How was he out of bed, dear sister?

"Oh, I know! Mack is so smart at sex."

Nope. We couldn't.

"He knows when having sex twice in one night is all I can do. Hey! We're thinking of getting tattoos of handcuffs on each shoulder, to say that we're handcuffed to each other in marriage. Well"—she giggled—"in bed, too. One time I lost the key. Did I tell you that? I couldn't find the key to the handcuffs! But he's so strong. After an hour of searching he broke the bedpost. Then we had to buy a new bed!" She laughed again, then she burst into tears. "I can't wait to marry Mack and become Mrs. Jules!"

I teared up, too. I can't help it. Jules cries, I cry.

"You're making me cry harder, Evie!"

I sniffled. I blinked hard. The tears ran.

"I'm so glad you're my love-sister!"

"Me too! Me too!" I blew my nose, and we burst into another round of wet silliness.

I was watching a whale in the distance from our cozy beach at sunset when the car crash premonition came to me again. I grew cold, like a corpse, then sweaty. It was the same as always, mountain to my right, cliff to my left. Narrow road. Twists and turns. Orange poppies. The sun in my eyes.

The red car came from around the curve, straight at me, and at the last minute I turned the wheel to the left so she would hit my passenger side. I didn't understand why I did that. Why did

I turn my truck *into* her car? She slammed into my side, and the
steering wheel was wrenched out of my hands. We seesawed on
the cliff for a millisecond, as if to give us a last peek at life, and
then we both went over the edge and down the cliff.

My head was filled with noise. Metal on metal. Glass breaking. An engine smashing against rock. The roof of my truck
folding in. The truck rolled and rolled before I was hit with a
blast of pain and then . . . darkness.

Someone died. That time it was probably me. Maybe. I wasn't
sure.

There was something in the premonition I didn't understand.
Something mysterious. Something I couldn't grasp. Why did I
turn my wheel left, smack in front of an oncoming car? Who
was the other person? What was hanging over that premonition, and why the fogginess, the lack of clarity? Why did the
premonition change? That never happened with other premonitions.

"Evie," Olec Lavender said to me in the science fiction section of my bookstore. "If you please, I need to know what you
see in my future."

"I see you buying a lot of books here." Olec is about thirty-
five. He has some recognizable OCD, but it doesn't get in the
way of his inventing stuff that he patents and sells for a fortune.
Only way I knew that he had a boatload of money was because
he was on the cover of a national newspaper a few years ago.
They called him Super Genius. I call him Slightly Nerdy, Somewhat Eccentric Olec. He lives in a tiny, old log cabin with only a
fireplace for heat but has tons of land and six dogs.

"I buy two a week, as you know, Evie." He twitched, then
adjusted his glasses. "Monday mornings you and I meet to share
information and thoughts on literature, the classics, contempo-
rary nonfiction and fiction, and any new science or history-
based books. Reading time is from seven until nine o'clock at
night. Nine o'clock until ten o'clock is for online Calculus Club.
Then a fruit snack before sleeping."

"Right. It's a solid reading schedule." And there was that tiny OCD. Who was I to judge? I had some of that myself. Plus, general anxiety and a battle with depression and fear.

"And what is in my future, based on your findings?"

"I can't see into the future." I moved over to the gardening section, which lines the yellow rose wallpaper wall, and he followed. We have a ton of gardeners on San Orcanita, and tourists love picking up gardening books featuring their lush gardens. My mother and aunts' garden is featured in several books. When they are included, of course they are wearing their gasp-inducing flowered hats.

"I believe that is incorrect information, Evie, and I am experiencing some befuddlement as to why you are downplaying your phenomenal gift. It is my understanding that you have premonitions." His face scrunched in some confusion.

"You're an engineer. You also have a doctorate in physics. Why would you believe that I could see the future?"

"I have a master's in chemistry and biology, too, but that is neither here nor there. I say that only because I want to present an accurate academic résumé." He twitched again. "But I have deliberately left room in my mind for the possibility of things unexplained. You are in my brain as a thing unexplained."

"I am not a thing."

"I didn't mean it like that." His forehead puckered above his thick glasses and he appeared worried. "I apologize. I misspoke. We have had a misunderstanding. May I continue, or has my offense brought on an insurmountable barrier and therefore it is impossible for us to continue our conversation?"

"We can still talk, Olec, don't worry." Sure we could. I liked Olec.

His shoulders sagged in relief. "Thank you for your graciousness. Here is my quandary: I have met a woman in Seattle."

"I'm happy to hear that." I smiled at him. "I hope she is brilliant enough for you."

"She is . . . I believe the correct word is *lovely*. Extremely friendly. She is talkative and complimentary of me. She is affectionate, although we have not had intercourse. Excuse me, perhaps that was too forward? Too much information, as the modern saying goes."

"It's okay, Olec. I've heard more personal stuff than that."

"Thank you for understanding." He twisted his hands together. "There is a concern: She does need money now and then."

"For what?" Ah, no. Bad news.

"Sick father in Texas. Sick grandma in Mexico. Another sick grandma in Louisiana. They couldn't afford health insurance and they fell on hard times, so she, being a generous and kind soul, stepped up for them."

"You mean, you stepped up for them by giving her money."

He squirmed. "We love each other."

"You love her? How long have you known her?"

"Three months. One week. Four days." Checked his watch. "Six hours. Twenty minutes. We met online. We talked on Facebook."

"And then you met her face-to-face in Seattle?"

"Yes. We have been together, face-to-face, two times. Once commencing at one o'clock on a Saturday, at a Russian restaurant with forty-two types of vodka. But there was a Thursday meeting also, in a coffee shop that sold twelve types of pastries. She says we are soul mates. I am still exploring that possibility."

Yeah. Sounds like they're "moncy mates," with the money going in one direction. "How much money have you given her?"

"So far? Precisely to this date? Twelve thousand one hundred sixty-four dollars."

I tried to keep my face expressionless. I wanted to slap him upside the head and knock some sense into him, but I also wanted to bang her face into a bookshelf for taking advantage of a brilliant but vulnerable man.

"What I need to know, Evie, is if we have a future together."

Olec was eager. He was sweet. He spent way too much time flapping around in his billions and billions of extrabrilliant brain cells and didn't have a clue about women or social dynamics.

"Let me think." I had zero premonitions on Olec. I stared into the air. I raised my eyebrows. I tried to drum up a faraway expression in my eyes. I frowned. I looked mad, then sad. "Yes. I see it. I do have a premonition about this situation. Now, don't tell anyone, do you promise?"

"I promise." His eyes were open wide, waiting for my miraculous wisdom.

"It doesn't work out. You keep dating her and she keeps taking your money. It's a request for money here and there at first, like with all the relatives you've helped, and she kisses you and gets you all steamed up and says all sorts of romantic things, but then it's more and more money. You believe her because you have a warm heart, Olec, and you marry her and you lose almost everything in the divorce, even your log cabin and all your land," I shook my head, so sad. "You lose half your dogs."

His face twisted in pain. "No. No, not the dogs!"

"And she leaves you and moves out of the country."

He gasped. "She is from Russia!"

"Does that make sense then, Olec, for her to have a sick father in Texas and a sick grandma in Mexico?"

"And a sick grandma in Louisiana." His shoulders sagged.

"Lotta sick family members."

"I knew it." He shook his head, balding, but in a cute way. "I knew it in my brain, but I let my heart do the talking and the believing."

"I'm sorry, Olec."

"Me too."

I gave him a hug.

"I will stop thinking with my heart."

He went on Facebook on his phone.

"What are you doing?"

"I'm telling her I don't want to speak with her any further because she is going to near-bankrupt me in the divorce and take my log cabin and half of the dogs, then I am blocking her."

"Decisive."

"I know you would never lie to me, Evie."

"Never."

And that is where ethics and morals and decision making comes in again, but I knew I did right by Olec.

* * *

A new chief came to our island. He was about five years older than me. He'd been an assistant chief in Seattle.

His name was Reginald Ashburn III. Not Reggie. Not Reg. Reginald. Don't forget the III.

"Fancy pancy," Gracie said.

"Too good for us," Mr. Jamon said, leaning on his cane.

"He's not an islander," Koo said. "How did he get the job?"

I had no idea. The islands have an assistant police chief, Mandy Lass. She's smart and tough and brave, and she should have been named as the temporary police chief. Chief Allroy himself had told me that she was "definitely my successor. She's smart as a whip and knows how to deescalate situations, which many don't. She's tough, too. Black belt and military training."

"She's a woman," my mother drawled. "That's why she didn't get the job as chief."

"Because of her femaleness she is judged harshly, seen as weak," Aunt Camellia said. "Weak like a flower. This was sexism. Discrimination. Mandy should have been chief."

"For God's sakes," Aunt Iris huffed. "Will misogyny never die?"

The new chief, quickly earning the nickname Reginald Ass Burn, did not fit in. He was rigid and unsmiling. He actually gave out jaywalking tickets in our tiny town. He walked into businesses and stood with his arms crossed over his chest. He was immediately way too hard on the teenagers, arresting them for drinking or being out past curfew. He gave out parking tickets and driving tickets for minor infractions by the dozens. He harangued people about their dogs in town, reminding them of the poop laws, which offended all dog owners. Did they look environmentally unconscious? Of course they would pick up the dog poo.

Chief Ass Burn looked at everyone as if we were potential criminals. He glared. He stared. He was one of those men who had to throw his weight around. He had to display his power.

"This isn't the middle of a prison," Jolla muttered, Bella Mae beside her holding Mr. Pitto, the aggrieved iguana. "We're islanders. Proud of it. And we don't need this outsider coming in and making us miserable."

"Not even Mr. Pitto likes him," Bella Mae said. She swung Mr. Pitto around in the air, poor thing, his little feet trying to run.

We learned later that the new chief was the brother-in-law of Chief Turner in Seattle.

For revenge, most everyone on San Orcanita Island wrote a letter to Chief Turner and mailed it over.

It said, "NEPOTISM SUCKS."

We signed our names.

Going to bed at night is like going to bed with a dog and cat zoo.

Butch the dog is close friends with Mars the cat. They play together all the time, wrestling and rolling and chasing each other. Butch and Mars curl up on the end of my king-sized bed, bought because I knew I'd end up sleeping with my dogs and cats. Sundance sleeps on the other side of me, on his own yellow pillow. Yes, I know. That's ridiculous that Sundance has his own pillow, but whatever. Dog lovers unite! He also has his pink blankie and his stuffed lizard, which I've had to sew up and restuff several times over the years. Cassidy sleeps with her head on Sundance's back.

Jupiter and Venus sleep on a thick blue blanket all swirled up together on the floor, but if they get cold they crawl in bed, too. Ghost sleeps in a cat bed on the dresser right near me. It seems like whenever I wake up, Ghost is awake, too. The cats go in and out of the bedroom at night, but the dogs are pretty much down for the count.

Every night, after the dogs and I take our last walk, saying good night to the alpacas, the lambs, the goats, and the horses, we head home. I say, "Okay, everybody, it's time for bed," and off we go. I go to bed and read, they come up on the bed and play and roll around, but when I'm done reading, and that can take a while, especially if I'm reading a scary thriller or a biography that is particular intriguing, it's time for quiet.

I shut out the light and say, "Good night, everyone," and they settle down. Listening to them snoring on my white comforter with the red and purple embroidered roses makes me laugh. I mean, who does this? Three dogs, four cats on a rose comforter? I am an odd, odd woman.

"Evie, are your mother and aunts home?"

"Yes, they all are."

Mrs. Gaddo's face lit up. She was wearing her best Sunday church outfit, as it was Sunday and she was trotting off to church. I was in town, quiet at this early hour, my insomnia a plague last night, to check on my bookstore and to grab a piece of Kick-Quick Cowboy Coffeecake and a mocha. It's always wise to start off the day with a healthy breakfast. I had Butch, Cassidy, and Sundance on their leashes beside me.

"Splendid. I need a tad bit of"—she leaned in and whispered—"the la la cigarette."

Oh my goodness. Even churchgoing Mrs. Gaddo? What was the world coming to? "Ah. I understand. Well. They're probably still sleeping."

"Fine. I'm off to God's home—church. You know I'm leading the choir, right? We sound like a choir of angels."

"I've heard it's a talented choir under your direction." No, I hadn't heard that. That was a lie. I heard that the choir sounded like frogs choking, but I liked Mrs. Gaddo.

"We lift our words up to the Lord in prayer and thankfulness."

They also lifted up torturous noise. I was being uncharitable, and I told myself to shut the heck up, so help me God.

"I'll come for my la la cigarette after church, then," she said, still smiling, her steel cross swinging on her neck.

"I'll tell them." Sundance jumped up on my legs. Even with only three legs, he's a fine jumper. He wanted a hug, so I hugged him. He licked my face.

She leaned in and whispered, "The Good Lord made marijuana so my hips wouldn't hurt, that he did. Blessings all to him!"

"Blessings to Jesus."

"Praise be to God!" She gave me a squeezy hug. "I'll be by

your bookstore later to buy some of your coconut chiffon cake. I heard you have that in? It tastes so delicious with the . . ." She wiggled an invisible joint with her fingers and winked at me. "And I'll need a juicy romance. You know my authors. Have any new ones? You do? Perfection. So, must go. God is waiting! And he doesn't judge my la la la!"

I would have to agree with her on that. I don't think God judges pot smokers. Surely He has much better things to do.

I did think of Chief Ass Burn. He might well sit in judgment of my mother and aunts, swinging his handcuffs.

This was not a safe situation.

I warned my mother and aunts that night. "Chief Ass Burn will most likely arrest you if he finds out what you're growing in the greenhouse."

They laughed. They were making new hats. They were sending them to a hospital on the mainland for a fund-raiser for kids. They were using faux flowers so the "hats will last until Kingdom Come and beyond that into eternity," Aunt Camellia said.

"You have to take this seriously," I begged.

They pshawed me and attached more faux daffodils, wisteria, and tulips, a tiny lizard (clearly, faux), a yellow parakeet, and three butterflies on wires so they wiggled about. It sounds silly, but the Dr. Seuss–like hats were a creative, moving, colorful sight to behold.

"We are healing others," my mother said. "Physically and mentally. We should call ourselves The Hat Healers."

"We are simply selling happy sticks," Aunt Camellia said. "Everyone likes to be happy."

"We have a side business, and we're going to Antarctica," Aunt Iris muttered. "It's purely, practically economically driven."

What I felt purely, practically? Alarm.

The next morning, early, before I went to work, I grabbed coffee and sat down at our cozy beach on a log and stared at the other islands across the white bubbles of the waves. The sun was coming up, a soft yellow, slashes of cotton candy pink and a deep orange spreading across a few puffy clouds. The birds were busy, a song here and there, the trees whispering in a slight wind.

Sundance sat right next to me on my left while Butch and Cassidy wrestled and ran. Mars and Ghost were exploring the trees. In the distance I could hear Shakespeare and Jane Austen whinnying.

I had woken up deeply sad.

This periodic morning sadness has happened to me my whole life, but always on my birthday. I remember when I turned four, I had woken up sad and cried my eyes out. My parents were so worried as they were having a birthday party for me and had bought me a pink princess dress.

Over the years I have tried different things to bring me out of that morning sadness, which I have nicknamed Sucky Sally Sadness to give it some humor and me some control.

I have told myself, "It's hormones. You're fine."

I have told myself, "Get up. The longer you stay in bed and wallow in self-pity, the worse it will get."

And, "Suck it up. Stop whining. There are billions of people on this planet far worse off than you."

I have made myself list ten things that I loved or that I was looking forward to while lying in bed, that sadness a weight like a blanket of rocks, suffocating all light and air.

"In the morning, our nightmares might still be with us," Aunt Camellia said, trying to help. "Turn it around and embrace your daydreams, your hopes."

"If you wake up sad, kid, get your buttocks up," Aunt Iris said. "Start moving. Get something done."

"Pull your red gardening boots on and head to the garden," my mother told me. "You know you find your peace there."

What causes that morning sadness? I don't know exactly. The truth is that I have often felt a lost aloneness, as if I didn't belong, as if I was in the wrong place. I love my parents, love Jules, love my aunts, but I have always felt different.

I thought, even as a child, that I felt alone because of the premonitions. That it was the premonitions that were making me feel isolated. No one else in my family had them, so that right there, plus the fear and stress they brought on, set me apart in a terrifying way.

And yet.

There was always something else there, too. Something I couldn't put my finger on. It was a loneliness, a tearful well, a hole that was unfillable, settled deep in my soul.

I never understood it, but I've come to terms with it.

I ignore it, put it aside as best I can, and try not to think about it, because there's nothing to do about it. There's no way to fix it, so to speak. That's the hard thing I've learned: Sometimes we have a problem, but it's not fixable. It *won't* be fixable.

It is there. Always.

Over the years I finally realized that I must accept the hole I sometimes feel within myself and not dwell in it. Why let it take any more time out of my day than it already does? Why try to figure it out? There is no answer.

I finished my coffee. I stood and put my toes in the ocean, as did Sundance, my faithful, furry friend. I listed ten things that I loved, including my family, the ocean, the islands, my animals, and Marco. I pulled myself together and went to work, because this is what we do when life falls apart: We buck up and we go to work and we take care of people and our responsibilities.

Why? Because we must.

And maybe that answer is, boringly, dully . . . perfect.

The new chief, Reginald Ass Burn, came to my bookstore on Monday, his stomach tightly pulled in by his bulletproof vest. His eyes were narrow and squinty like pinto beans, his face puffy like a smashed marshmallow.

"Hello. I am Chief Reginald Ashburn the third, and I understand that you are Evie Lindsay."

"Hello," I said. I put out my hand, and he shook it. He squeezed my hand too tight, held it too long, stared at me too intently. His eyes dropped up and down my body quickly, but enough so that he knew I would see it. He wanted to make me feel checked out. Evaluated. Inwardly I said a bad word that started with an F, slowly.

I hadn't wanted to prejudge him simply because other islanders said he was arrogant, sarcastic, sour, unsmiling, and petty with his raft of tickets. But here he was, and it looked like people were right.

"It's nice to meet you." I disentangled my hand from his sweaty clutch. "Can I help you find a book to read?"

"As you can see, I'm on duty, so I can't look now, young lady." He puffed out his chest.

It was the tone. Condescension. Superiority. He was correcting me by saying *As you can see, I'm on duty*, I have things to do, busy me, and yet. There he was. In my bookstore.

"Oh. Well, I won't disturb you when you're on duty and searching for criminals in my bookstore. Have a nice day." I turned away, but not before I saw a slightly surprised expression cross his face, followed by irritation at my sarcasm.

He stayed, standing in the middle of my yellow bookstore with a scowl on his face, in the midst of my white shelves, my nonfiction and fiction and biographies and mysteries, my beloved books. He walked to the café and examined it, unsmiling, as if he were expecting to find a criminal between the purple tables, then he walked out to the deck and checked out everyone there, too. Apparently there were no criminals or potential crimes taking place among the townspeople and tourists, the families and couples, and the grandparents, who you really have to keep an eye on. The whales and seagulls were behaving, so he had nothing further to do.

He headed back in and stopped at the cash register where I was working.

"You are the owner of this place?"

This place. It's a bookstore, you idiot. He already knew I was the owner. "Yes. This place is called Evie's Books, Cake, and Tea. I am Evie." Too bad I didn't get a premonition about him. I don't get premonitions for the vast majority of people I meet, but it would be nice to see him working at a cat litter factory instead of staying here.

He stood there, staring down at me, and I met his gaze. I didn't miss the way his eyes dropped for a second to my breasts yet again, the creep. He was gross. Skin crawly gross. It was a power thing with him, and it was likely he didn't like women, particularly women who didn't cater to him or who made him feel threatened in any teeny-tiny way.

"How long have you had this place? How long have you lived here on the island with your husband?" He looked at the third finger of my left hand.

"I feel like I'm being interviewed." I didn't smile.

"You're not being interviewed. I need to know about the shop owners, about the people who live here, as I'm here to protect you."

"We're a mellow lot. There will not be much protecting to do." I deliberately did not answer his question. "How is Chief Allroy doing?" I knew exactly how the chief was doing. He was staying with his daughter and son-in-law in Seattle. I had gone to school with his daughter, Packy, real name Patricia, and had talked to her this morning.

He garumphed. "He is making progress, but he will be out for a while to rehabilitate. His age being a factor."

I laughed. The chief was only sixty-five. Give me a break. "Chief Allroy is in excellent shape. He runs five miles a day. He sails his boat. He chops wood." I let my eyes drift to his gut, then back up. He saw it.

"I noticed you didn't answer my questions," he said.

"I noticed that I am not required to answer your questions," I said.

His face tightened. He didn't like that. He liked to be *obeyed*. "I've heard things about you."

"I've heard things about you, too."

He seemed surprised, displeased. Who was this woman talking back to him? Where was the fear? The respect? Where was the ego-stroking? I bet the women on the police force in Seattle couldn't stand him.

"If you'll excuse me?" I didn't wait for him to answer. I smiled at the couple behind him, waiting to pay. They had a stack of books. "Welcome!" I said, putting their books on the counter right in front of the fleshy chief, who was then forced to move his heaving gut.

I could feel his eyes on me as I smiled and chatted with the couple. He wasn't too bright, but he was bright enough to see that my demeanor changed when I wasn't talking to him.

And there was San Orcanita's new, temporary police chief: Angry. Passively aggressive. Jacked up on himself.

He was a threat to my mother and aunts, no doubt about it.

Chapter 18

~

Betsy Baturra
Multnomah County Courthouse
Portland, Oregon
1976

Betsy Baturra and Johnny Kandinsky's trial began. Betsy and Johnny at the defense table, their four attorneys crowded around. Their attorneys were competent. They actually cared. They all seemed exhausted, rather pale.

The prosecutor, Alfred Morningside, made his opening statement. He was a prissy man, in a pin-striped custom tailored suit, a white kerchief in his pocket, his fingernails buffed. He painted Peter, Johnny's father, to be a saint. He listed how Peter worked hard at his company where he sold used cars, how his wife had left him with two children for a lover and had had no contact with the family for over three years. "He was a dedicated family man, a single father, who loved his children, Johnny and Tilly.... " He droned on and on, sanctimonious, arrogant.

Alfred pontificated about how Johnny and Betsy were at Johnny's house and how Peter had been knifed in the chest "in cold blood," for nothing other than "the money that Johnny would inherit." Then Alfred, who had a second major in drama and loved how the courtroom had become his personal stage, said in a deep voice, "Betsy Baturra and Johnny Kandinsky planned and executed the murder of Peter Kandinsky."

Shaylee Jefferson, Betsy's attorney, stood to address the jury when Alfred was finally done droning on and on, loving all of the attention. Peter, born Pyotr, was not a saint, she said. He had made many enemies in Portland, he had been sued on multiple occasions by people to whom he sold a car that broke down the first day, if not right off the lot. He owed money to many people and had declared bankruptcy in Idaho, where he previously lived, and in Portland. He had been in an altercation at his car lot with a homeless man, whom he had beaten senseless but who had left the area, could not be found, so could not testify. Peter also was in a screaming match with a woman in the parking lot of a grocery store over a parking space and had rammed her car with his, totaling it.

He had been, at best, a neglectful father. He had beaten Johnny and Tilly. He had beaten his wife, Gabriella, though she had been too afraid to go to the police, according to Johnny.

Betsy grabbed a knife to defend Johnny, his father hitting Johnny in the face twice, Shaylee said. "She thought he was going to kill Johnny."

Johnny's attorney, Orlando Mendelbaum, said that Johnny would admit to killing his father with the knife in self-defense. "He thought he was going to die."

Yes, both Johnny and Betsy said they killed Peter Kandinsky with the knife from the kitchen.

Different stories, so which one would the jury believe? But would it matter? They were both charged with murder—who held the knife, well, that wasn't legally relevant if they both planned it together. . . .

The trial ground on. Experts came and went. Police officers, detectives, forensics, the state medical examiner, etc.

Johnny took the stand first and was questioned by Alfred, the prissy prosecutor. "Where did you meet Betsy Baturra . . . How long have you dated . . . Are you in love . . . What did you do together . . . When did your father meet her? Did your father like her? Why or why not? Did she like him?"

"My father didn't like Betsy because he doesn't like any women."

"What about your mother?"

"He hated my mother because she wanted to leave him. My mother did not run off with her lover. She did not have a lover. You lied about that. She wanted to take Tilly and me and move away from my father, back to Mexico. My father couldn't accept that. My mother was beautiful, and she was his possession." Then Johnny took a breath, his hands in fists, his jaw tight. "I believe my father killed my mother."

That brought the entire courtroom to a screeching halt. For a moment, no one moved, then it was chaos. Only Betsy wasn't surprised. Johnny had told her a few months after they started dating that he thought his father killed his mother two years ago, when they were in Idaho, that he hadn't been able to figure it out when he was fifteen, that he couldn't believe it, he was too scared to believe it, but he knew the truth now. What Betsy didn't know was that Johnny was going to bring it up at trial.

Alfred was stunned down to his perfectly folded white handkerchief. This had not been revealed to him! He had been told by one of Peter's partners in the used car business that Peter's wife had left the family, run off with her lover!

Even Betsy and Johnny's attorneys looked stunned. They had not heard that part.

The judge pounded his gavel.

"Move to strike!" the prosecuting attorney yelled, his dainty hands moving through the air like axes. He loved that he got to make a dramatic gesture! "Move to strike!"

"It's relevant to the case," Orlando stood and said. "Johnny and Betsy were defending themselves, obviously, from a man with a violent past—"

"You have no proof that your father killed your mother," the prosecutor breathed, his face red as he pointed at Johnny, making sure his perfect profile was to the press. Hopefully they'd take a photo! "None."

"How do you know?" Johnny said. *"How do you know?"*

Chaos again.

The jury was excused and then the judge told the attorneys to approach. Phrases like "not relevant" and "this never came up before" and "We have had no time to address this, research this . . . you can't allow this, it's new evidence, not vetted . . . Johnny's making it all up . . . playing the jury . . . this is a lie . . . it goes to the threat that Johnny felt in the house, that Betsy knew of . . . it goes to the character of the man who was killed . . . it's abuse . . . it's a pattern . . . it gives weight to his self-defense . . . Are you serious?"

The judge allowed Johnny to speak after the jury came back in. "My mother, Gabriella Cortez Kandinsky, was abused for years. My mother's family was from Mexico. They worked in the fields. Her father died when she was six. He got pneumonia and no hospital would admit him because he was illegal. They gave him cough syrup and sent him home.

"When my mother was nineteen, her mother died. She was attacked by the owner of a farm. He wasn't even arrested. My mother met my father shortly after that, picking berries on one of his neighbor's farms. She was soon pregnant. I have no idea if she was willing to have sex with my father or not. My mother told me later that my father told her that he would tell the authorities that she was illegal and he would allow her to be shipped back to Mexico without us if she didn't obey him. She would never see us again. I remember"—he choked on his words—"I remember her begging him not to do that, on her knees.

"My father wouldn't let my mother work, would hardly ever let her leave the house. He called her fat. He called her a whore all the time. He called her a Mexican slut. He would beat her face until it swelled. I have no memory of my father ever being kind to my mother, and then, one day, she disappears. I think he killed her. We left Idaho for Oregon the day after he told us she left with a lover. Like I already said, my mother had no lover."

The noise in the courtroom raised again to a deafening level, and the judge pounded his gavel.

"This is all a lie," Alfred yelled, making sure he looked authoritative. "It's all a lie. This is something concocted by Johnny, egged on by Betsy, to bolster their ridiculous self-defense theory. He's made this up. There is no evidence that Gabriella was killed by Peter Kandinsky. None. No police reports. No witness. No photos. No body. Nothing."

"Objection!" Orlando shouted.

The judge said, "I'll allow it."

The trial went on, Johnny brave and composed on the stand.

The prosecuting attorney was agitated. Angry. Who was this teenager to make a fool of him? He was Alfred Morningside! A style icon some said. A top-notch prosecutor, destined for amazing things. Plus, his shoes! Always buffed for court. "What happened after Betsy murdered your father?"

"Betsy did not murder my father." Johnny paused and stared right at the jury. "I did."

Betsy shook her head at him as her eyes welled with tears.

"No!" Alfred shouted at him, his pin-striped suit straining. "You didn't. Betsy did. You stood by and let it happen. You planned it together."

"No," Johnny said. "I killed him. My prints are on the knife."

The prosecutor seethed. "That's because you lived at the house. The knife came from the kitchen. Her prints are on the knife, too. Betsy herself even told the police that she did it." For effect the prosecutor turned and pointed a finger at Betsy. Oh, how he loved to point! "That she was the guilty one."

"I told the police I did it," Johnny said. "She lied to protect me, but I'm telling the truth."

Chaos again.

"Your Honor," the prosecutor said, sweating, his perfectly coiffed hair coming loose from his hair gel, "Johnny did not wield the knife, Betsy did. He's trying to put doubt in the jurors' minds. He's deliberately trying to turn all evidence over to cause confusion and a mistrial, which will serve his agenda. He's trying to get them both off! This is an attack on the court and our system of government and justice itself and the United States of America and our Constitution!" he pontificated, wielding his pointer finger in the air like a pinwheel.

The judge told him to sit down *now* and yelled for "order in the court!"

Amidst the raised voices and the astonishment from everyone in the courtroom, Johnny winked, ever so slightly, at his beloved Betsy. She saw it through the tears streaming from her eyes.

Betsy was on the stand the next day. She was grilled and drilled by the prosecutor.

"What happened the day that Peter Kaminsky was killed?" Alfred was wearing a different pin-striped suit and had a crisply ironed purple handkerchief in his pocket. He had practiced in front of his mirror again the night before to polish his image and was satisfied with his performance. Drama classes had truly helped him over the years. Maybe he should have been on the stage as a Broadway actor? But no. He liked to win, at all costs.

"I ran to Johnny's house after work." She twisted her hands in her lap, in the same blue suit as the day before.

"Why?" said the prosecutor, but he knew. He'd seen the police reports.

"Because I..." Betsy stopped, swallowed hard. She knew no one would believe her, but she had to say it. "Because I knew that Peter was going to kill Johnny."

"How did you know that?" He raised his ever-so-slightly plucked eyebrows at her.

"Because I had..." She blinked rapidly. "A premonition."

"A what?" The prosecutor pretended surprise, as if he couldn't believe that such a stupid thing had come out of her mouth.

Betsy had already told the police about the premonition the night that Peter died, the night she stabbed him. She was eighteen. She was scared and traumatized, so she simply told the truth. She didn't want to kill anyone, ever. She did it to save Johnny, she told them.

"A premonition?"

"Objection, Your Honor," Betsy's attorney, Shaylee, stood. "She doesn't mean a real premonition, she means that she had a bad *feeling*. Only that. She and Johnny shared everything. Johnny shared his fear of his father, the abuse, that they'd been fighting, so Betsy simply thought that things were going badly at Johnny's house, as we all get bad feelings sometimes."

"Overruled."

"What do you mean a premonition?" Alfred pressed on, as if Shaylee had not spoken and tried to diminish his argument. "You mean, you can see into the future?"

The whole court room held their breath.

Betsy was scared now. She knew she looked like a loon. Mentally unstable. A freak. "Yes. I knew that Peter was going to kill Johnny, that he was going to turn and grab a gun from the gun cabinet."

"So you killed him because you had a premonition Peter was going to shoot Johnny?" Up went those perfectly plucked eyebrows again, in disbelief.

"Yes." She squirmed. The police had already talked about it in front of the jury, reading from their reports about that night and their conversations with Betsy. They had read her her rights, but Betsy didn't understand what was at stake. Her own attorneys had been appalled when they heard what she'd said to the police and had gone out that night to a bar for a couple of straight shots.

"Johnny accused his father of killing his mother. They were fighting about that. Peter was threatening Johnny because he was afraid Johnny would go to the police, then he punched him in the face twice and Johnny fell back."

"Did you see the gun?"

"No."

"Peter Kandinsky never pulled out a gun?"

"No. But he was going to."

"So you stabbed him because you knew he was going to grab a gun because you can see the future like a gypsy? Are you magic?"

"No, I—"

"Objection!" Shaylee shouted.

"Do you have a crystal ball?"

"Objection!" Shaylee shouted again, louder.

Johnny stood up, agitated. "No, that's not what happened. I killed my father. My father had just punched me in the face, twice, as he had done many times before. I thought he was going to kill me. Betsy is innocent. She did nothing, it was me, I stabbed him."

The cacophony in the court room was deafening.

Johnny and Betsy's defense attorneys put up a vigorous fight.

They said it was self-defense, that Johnny thought his life was threatened, Betsy thought his life was threatened, the physical altercation between Johnny and Peter was enough proof, the past abuse another indicator of Johnny's well-founded fear of imminent death. But as there was no weapon pointed at Johnny and Betsy at the time that Peter was killed, no gun on the floor, no bullets, no gunpowder, no police reports of past abuse, no police reports of a murdered mother, it did not hold up well.

Alfred said, again, in closing, that Betsy and Johnny were after his father's money. He said Johnny had been traumatized by his mother's disappearance when she left to be with her lover, that he had tried to falsely blame his father for killing her so he could get away with murder in this very courtroom.

"He's lying to save himself, save Betsy. He's making up stories. He's trying to confuse you. He doesn't realize how smart you are, jury members, that you'll see through this evil charade." Alfred pointed at Johnny and Betsy once again. It would make him click his heels together if that photo were on the front cover of the paper tomorrow! He was having a superb hair day, too. "Don't be fools!"

Betsy was painted as the manipulative, sly, sneaky young woman who tried to make it look like self-defense when it clearly wasn't. Betsy's premonitions made everything worse. The jury believed her to be delusional, or a liar, or a delusional liar. No one could see the future. Ridiculous. What a pathetic excuse. Plus, they believed that it was Betsy who held the knife.

The only witness?

Tilly Kandinsky. Johnny's little sister. But she was only seven when it happened, and she was still not speaking. She was in foster care. She was traumatized. She was now an orphan.

The jury was out for five days.

In the end, they voted to convict Betsy and Johnny of first-degree murder.

When Betsy and Johnny were pulled out of the courtroom after the jury verdict, he shouted at her, "I love you, Betsy," and she said back, in a whisper, which is all she could say through her constricted throat. "I love you, too."

They were both moved from jail and transported to prison. Their nightmares began anew.

The first night in her new prison cell, battling fear and grief, listening to bars clanging, a woman wailing, and a guard yelling, Betsy had the same premonition that had plagued her her whole life.

She was on the same road. It was tight, narrow, curving. The sun behind her was slanting through the fir trees. The mountain was on the left, cliff on the right. Orange poppies were scattered here and there, like a floral blanket.

Betsy saw her hands clutching the steering wheel. She looked over the edge of the cliff, to make sure she wasn't too close, and then she saw the blue truck suddenly in front of her as it barreled around the curve. A woman was driving.

She drew in a breath, then turned the wheel hard to the right and drove her car straight off the cliff. The car bounced down, glass smashing, metal clashing, the noise a screeching, splitting cacophony. She saw herself banging around in the car, her body thrust into the airbag. She felt the heat. She saw the flames. Was she going to burn to death? Was the car going to explode?

Why did she turn her steering wheel and drive straight over the cliff? There was still ten feet at least between her and the oncoming blue truck.

Did she die?

It looked like it. Her head was out the window, hanging like a rag doll. She sensed someone coming down the cliff, rocks slipping. She heard a scream of alarm, then another scream from pain. Had the other woman fallen? Was she okay? Had she died?

Betsy shivered.

One of them dies, she thinks. She felt the black claw of death, but the death was murky, blurry, and deaths were never blurry in her other premonitions.

Was it her? Was it the other woman?

Who was the other woman?

She pulled herself into a ball on her prison cot. She was cold, utterly depressed, and worried about her baby Rose. Was she healthy? Were her new parents kind and patient with her?

But if the premonition was correct, if the accident happened, she is released from prison at some point in time in the future.

She held on to that faintest glimmer of hope yet again.

She did not sleep at all that night. Prison is never conducive toward sleep.

Plus, her new roommate jumped her and beat her face up.

In response to Johnny Kandinsky's claim that his father had murdered his mother in Idaho, before they moved to Oregon, the police in Idaho searched the Kandinskys' abandoned home up in the hills. They searched below the home in the crawl space, the barn, and an outbuilding. They saw no sign of a crime, no blood splatters, no body. They never moved beyond the immediate property to search the acreage that Peter Kandinsky owned.

No one had ever claimed that Gabriella Kandinsky was missing. Plus, she was an illegal Mexican. She shouldn't have been here in the first place, even if she did marry an American, right? She had never applied for citizenship. She had simply snuck into the country. In all likelihood she had moved back to Mexico with her lover and was working there. She went home, they said.

There was no body, no signs of violence.

And, again, she was *illegal. . . .*

Case closed.

Chapter 19

❧

I saw Marco in town talking to a couple of other men. Both of the men were kind, friendly people. One was Zeb Lowry, who used to be a corporate manager at a huge shoe company and burned out. The other was a businessman who flew in and out of Seattle to the island.

I ducked into my friend Callie's shop. She sold women's clothing. The shop is called Abracadabra Now You Will Be Pretty. It's an odd name for a shop, but Callie says she has a grandmother who's a witch and her mother thought her grandma might truly have witchly powers, so there it is. Abracadabra. Callie has bright red hair. She's thirty-five.

"Hiding from someone?" she called out, and I made a face at her. "Ahh." She sighed when she looked out the window. "I totally get it. I'm thinking about getting animals so I can go and visit him. I don't even like animals—they get all slobbery and dirty and they poop—but every time I see him I can't talk. It's like my tongue gets all swelled up and I can't blink and my bladder gets a little wiggly."

"Your bladder gets wiggly?" That was bizarre.

"Yes. I don't know why." She sighed again.

"When your husband is around, you don't get all wiggly if you see Marco, do you?"

"I try not to. But you know Ziggy. The man's blind."

"Only in one eye."

"He's dense." She shrugged. "All men are dense, aren't they?

It's like they've got wood in their brains. They see what they want to see and ignore the rest. They ignore facts they don't like or can't comprehend. When I look at Marco and my toes curl in, I think bedroom thoughts. Hey!" She snapped her fingers. "While you're hiding here, can you see my future?"

"I can't see the future."

She went on as if I hadn't spoken. "I want to know if Ziggy will ever have an affair."

Ziggy loved Callie. I knew Callie loved Ziggy. I pretended to think about it. "No. Never."

She clapped her hands. "Yes! I knew it." Her brow furrowed. "Will I?"

I pretended to think again. "No. Never."

"Hmm!" She looked proud of herself and irritated at the same time. "Okay. Fine. But darn it, too. I was hoping for a quick romance on a girls vacation or something. One seductive Frenchman for a week."

"No, sorry. It's not in your future."

"Can you tell me another future?"

"No, I have to stick with the accurate ones. No affairs, no fun."

I snuck out the back of Callie's, but I couldn't continue to avoid Marco when he came into my bookstore looking all handsome and studly in jeans and a black T-shirt about an hour later.

"Hi, Evie."

"Hi, Marco." *You literally take my breath away.*

"Can you help me find some more books? I read all the ones from last time."

"Wow. You're a fast reader."

"You chose great books for me."

"What do you want to do with me?" Oh no. Oh no. "I mean, what book type, genres, do you want to be with?" What book did he want to *be* with? Must I speak in a carnal fashion? "Read. What books do you want to read?" I am a lovesick fool.

He smiled, so gentle in that masculine face, scars here and there, and I smiled back and tried not to groan in a sexual way.

First we found him three books. Then I asked him if he wanted to have coffee and a slice of six-layer mocha fudge chocolate cake with me. I was surprised at myself for that invitation. He seemed surprised, too, but pleased, and we had cake out on the deck and watched the boats sitting in the sun. We talked more, endlessly, easily, from one subject to the next, from animals to movies to the island to fun things we liked to do, until he said, "I have to go. I've got two horses and a sheep coming in to see me."

"You can't be late for them. The horses will think you're rude and the sheep will think you're ill-mannered."

"I try not to be either."

He smiled and I smiled back, and I could feel that pull of him. I could feel the love I had for him. I could feel how irresistible he was.

It stabbed me in the heart, that it did.

I stared out the window from my upstairs office and watched Marco cross the street like the sappy love-fool that I am.

My relationships with men in the past have all been shallow. Initially, in college, I went for the "bad boys," but not for the usual reason: Bad boys are intriguing and sexy and rebellious.

I assumed they would be fine if I broke up with them. They'd simply move on to another young woman. I also thought they would give me emotional space. They would not demand much from me. They wouldn't want to get serious because they were "bad boys." One was in a rock band that today churns out hit after hit. We're still friends.

One was a motorcycle rider who wrote a book about his adventures that sold widely, then he became a college English lit professor with six kids. When I knew him he had long hair, a bandana, a bike, and no money. With six kids he probably still has no money.

But those two men, under the bad boy persona, had soft hearts, and we were all hurt when I broke it off before they could breach the wall around me. I can't be honest with a man about who I am. I can't tell them I have premonitions. They would think I was looney. I could prove it to them, but then they would *know* I was looney. Plus, my premonitions are a huge part of who I am, what I battle. If I can't share that, we don't have an honest relationship.

Besides, who would want to live with, or be married to, some-one who not only sees premonitions but tries to stop them, rescue people or not rescue people based on objective/subjective/playing God reasons? It's head-case city up in my brain, with moderate to high doses of depression and anxiety, with some of that depression and anxiety buried in the sand and flames of a faraway place.

I have a put-together front, a smile that says all is well, like many women, but beyond the smile, scrape it a bit, and you'd see a semi-wreck who tries hard not to give in to many mental health issues.

I would like to sleep with Marco. I would.

But how do I sleep with Marco, walk away, and not let the relationship grow into something else? Marco is super interest-ing. He's deep. And he's a thriving, sexy man who would not sleep with a woman who he knew would walk away. That's not who he is. He doesn't deserve that kind of meanness and disre-spect, either. No one does.

Marriage is out of the question, even if I allowed him to get to know the true me.

I don't want to have children. What if this premonition thing is genetic, starting with me? My mother doesn't have it, my aunts don't have it, Jules doesn't have it, but my grandma had mental health issues galore. Maybe she was having premoni-tions. She never mentioned it, never had any predictions, but maybe she had something and it was passed on to me in a dif-ferent form.

I will not risk passing along this terror to any other human being. I will not inflict this on someone else. I will not have my kid suffering as I have suffered.

The most insurmountable problem was this, though: I could not be with Marco, as it would be a threat to his life. My pre-monition had told me so.

Chief Reginald Ass Burn watched me climb into my truck after work on Wednesday. He was parked at the end of Chrysanthemum Way, between the bakery and library, and standing like a beached whale next to his police car. I saw him spying on me when I was chatting with Ernetta Oliver outside the bookstore, people playing in the waves of the bay behind us.

Ernetta is in her forties and from the South. She is a southern belle with steel in her spine (as in, she grew up in Louisiana near the coastal marshes and is not afraid of alligators), iron in her fists (bar fights, only occasionally), and a brain that earned her a doctorate in math. She has zero belief in my premonitions, which means we get along well because I know she will never bug me about any predictions about herself. She is a true book nerd, however, so we can talk forever.

Before we parted, Ernetta said to me, "Chief Reginald Ass Burn is watching you, that possum."

"I know he's watching me. He's creepy."

She glared at him. "What are you staring at?" she yelled at him across the road. For such a small woman, she has a booming voice. The southern accent added flair. People on the street turned to see what the commotion was about.

He did not respond.

"I said," Ernetta boomed again, "Chief Ass Burn, what are you staring at? Speak up! You got grits stuck in your throat? You got your tongue stuck in a swamp? Bless your heart, has your brain decomposed again?"

I could see his face twist in fury and humiliation.

"I'm fixin' to come on over there and ask you these questions face-to-face, Chief."

"I don't need you telling me what to do, Ernetta. Quiet down, or I'll give you a ticket for disturbing the peace." He settled his wide girth back in his car.

"I don't like being quiet," she shouted, her southern accent even stronger. "I like for people to hear my voice, especially men."

We chatted about what a swamp monster Chief Ass Burn is. "I'm going home to cut a pile of flowers for my mom and aunts. They're making bouquets titled 'Don't You Mess With My Womanhood,' and they need more flowers. I'll see you later, Ernetta."

"Don't let that chief intimidate you. I've seen him watching you before. We've all seen it. He likes you, but in a dangerous way. I think he hates you, too. You should be married to Marco. Now there's a man's man. Plus, he's hot. I'll be in tomorrow. I want to find books on genetics, mastering chess, and the migration pattern of South American butterflies."

I headed out of town in my truck, driving the speed limit. I ignored the chief's car following me. As soon as I rounded the corner, out of North Sound, and turned left down another road toward our property, then to Robbins Drive, he was right behind me. He waited a minute as I drove in dread, farther away from town, then flashed his lights, turned on his siren, and rushed up on my bumper.

"I could foresee that one all on my own," I muttered. "No premonition needed." We were alone, which made my spine start to tingle.

"Evie," he said to me after he waddled up alongside my truck.

"Yes?" I wasn't giving him anything. I glanced at his face, his stomach bulging against his uniform. He was staring down his nose at me. For one second his eyes dropped to my chest.

"Do you know why I pulled you over?"

"No."

"License and registration and insurance."

I didn't want to give them to him, but I did. He stared at my license for way too long. "Is there a problem?"

He didn't answer me, and I knew he enjoyed that. Enjoyed the power of choosing not to answer a direct question. He took his time memorizing, I suppose, every detail on my insurance card and registration. It is utterly fascinating information.

He gave the license and registration and insurance back to me. I deliberately made sure I did not touch his fingers. The chief was a stew of misogynistic crap.

"Why did you pull me over?"

"Well, Evie, it seems like you have a little problem with one of your taillights. It's out."

"Oh. I didn't know."

"Now you do." He tried to smile, but it came out lecherous.

"I'll fix it."

He nodded. "I think that'd be a smart idea. So, Evie. We haven't had much of a chance to talk. Tell me about yourself. How did you get the name Evie? Like Adam and Eve. Are you the temptress? Are you the woman who leads a man to evil? Are you a woman who brings sin to others?" He smirked, as if he was so self-satisfied with his cleverness. I could tell he'd been thinking about this speech.

"First off, all Eve did was eat an apple because she was hungry and it was hanging in front of her face. Apples are not sinful. Adam hardly tried to prevent it, did he? Then he tattled on Eve to God. What a man. He blamed Eve. Second, Eve didn't lead Adam to evil. That's ridiculous. Adam was already weak and disloyal to her, though he was her husband and should have protected and stood by her, even in front of God. But then, the Bible was written by men, and men are known to blame women and want to control them at the same time. Eve did not bring sin to the world. Men have been gloriously successful since the beginning of time at bringing sin and violence and other depravity in without any help from women at all. Maybe you need to read that Bible story again."

His smirk faded. He could tell I was mocking him. And he had been so clever!

"I'm a Christian man, and I do know that story, Evie, which is why I brought it up. I think it's you who has it wrong. Eve sinned. Adam did not. Eve led Adam to sin—"

"Are you going to write me a ticket?"

He stopped. His face flushed.

"If not, I need to go. I have plans for tonight and I'll be late."

His whole body tensed, chest up. "Got a date?" The three words seemed as if they were torn from his tight-lipped mouth.

"I'm not required to tell you my plans."

His eyes narrowed. He liked the power to ask questions and get them answered even when they weren't his business. "I will be giving you a ticket. A car must be in working, functional order at all times, and yours is not." He turned on his heel and waddled back to his car and heaved himself in. I knew I would have to wait for a while. This was all part of controlling the situation. He would make me wait. He wanted to make me late for my plans tonight.

I called my friend Bettina at the bakery and ordered a key lime pie. I love those. I think they calm my nerves. Hence, nutritionally speaking, they're good for me. We also talked about the other cakes and treats she would be delivering to the bookstore in the future. Next I called Sandy at the hardware store because I needed to add more support to one of my bookshelves—too many books, too much weight. She knew just the thing I needed!

I texted my mother and aunts in our group text and wrote, "Pulled over by Chief Ass Burn on Robbins Dr."

"I'm coming," Aunt Iris said.

"There's no need to," I texted back.

"I'm coming," Aunt Camellia said.

"Don't bother," I texted back.

I called Tiala at the bookstore to make sure all was well. The science club was meeting that night. She expected, as I did, that there could be heated discussions about current scientific breakthroughs and discoveries, but we knew that there would be nothing thrown, including punches or plates, as they are a dignified group.

Finally Chief Reginald Ass Burn tumbled himself and his gut out of his car. I was on the phone with my mother. When he was in front of my window I said to her, "I love you, too. I'll see you later," and hung up.

I could tell he thought I was speaking to my "date."

"I didn't know you were seeing anyone," he said.

I put my hand out for the ticket.

His jaw tightened and he gave me the ticket.

I looked at the amount. "You have got to be kidding." It was outrageous. "That's outrageous."

"No, it's the price for a car that is not in proper working order. If you would like to argue, we can go down to the station and discuss this."

That was a threat. "I'm not arguing. I'm telling you it's an outrageous amount. Chief Allroy would never do this to anyone on the island. He would pull them over, let them know about the problem, chat for a while, and that would be it."

"I am not Chief Allroy."

"We all know that."

"Look, Evie, don't get smart with me," he huffed. "I can have you out of your truck and into the back seat of my car in two minutes with handcuffs on, your rights read to you."

I stared at him. He was a dangerous man. He would like that. He would like to yank me out of my car, manhandle me, shove me up against the back door, press his body into mine, and rip my hands back and into handcuffs. There was no one out here to see what was going on, and he would love that. He would relish it. He would take his time, he would taunt me, degrade me, his hot breath on my face, his skin to mine. That image made my stomach churn as if someone were spinning it as hard as they could with a wooden spoon. I turned to look out my front windshield and said nothing else.

"Got anything else to say?"

I didn't move.

"What?"

I said nothing.

He loved this, I could tell. He loved to put women into a submissive position. He loved to shut them down.

"I can't hear you," he said. "Any more smart-aleck remarks? Any more back talk? You want to tell me what you think?"

"You're trying to bait me. I have nothing else to say."

I did not look at him, which I could tell made him even more angry, but I was seething now, too.

He seemed to relent slightly, probably because there were cars coming from both directions. "Go and get the taillight fixed, then bring me the ticket and I'll reduce it. Maybe if you're lucky, and nice to me, I'll get rid of it."

I wanted to hit him. He wanted me to come to him, to be put in a position of supplication, to be groveling for something. Then he could have more power over me. He wanted me to want something from him and to ask for it. He wanted to spend time reducing me to nothing, and if this was the way he had to do it, he would.

My phone rang again. I turned it over so he couldn't see it was my mother calling again. Ah. It was my aunts in their cars approaching quickly from both directions.

They stopped in front of and in back of me, brakes squealing.

"What's the problem?" Aunt Iris said, darting out of her car. She was so mad she didn't have a hat on, and neither did Aunt Camellia, her white curls flowing behind her.

"Evie here has a broken taillight," Chief Ass Burn said.

"So what? She'll get it fixed," Aunt Iris said.

I told them what the ticket cost.

"You gave her a ticket?" Aunt Iris said. "Chief Allroy never would have done that. He would have informed us of the problem and stayed to talk, a reasonable response to a minor problem."

Aunt Camellia said, "I didn't know we were going to get robbed by our new police chief. Was that in the monthly newsletter?"

Aunt Iris said, "Your job as the chief is not to shaft the islanders. Were you informed of that?"

Aunt Camellia said, "All I see is blackness around him. It's like this dark, clingy, slimy aura. I've never felt slime before, so this is a curious situation."

"All I see is a lawsuit if he threatens to run me down to the police station for a broken headlight again," I said.

It was three against one, and he argued with them, tried to be the tough guy, but finally backed off but not before he said, "Do not interfere in a police matter again, ladies."

He drove off in a wave of dust.

"That one is trouble," Aunt Camellia said. "I can feel the evil circling him."

"What a dick," Aunt Iris said.

I looked at the ticket. Hundreds of dollars. For a broken taillight.

Aunt Iris took a photo of it and texted it off to friends. By the end of the evening the whole town knew about my outrageous fine for a broken taillight.

The next day, before work, I fixed my broken taillight. I mailed a check for the full amount to the address on the ticket. I would not, no matter what it cost me, go to the chief and ask him to reduce the amount. Sounds ridiculous, but I would not be in his presence and feed his ego or put myself in a position to plead. It was worth paying more to get my power back.

I did, however, identify Chief Ass Burn's superior to complain about the amount of the ticket. I made a copy of the ticket and my check at the bookstore and mailed the whole thing in, along with my summation of what happened, down to every last word that the chief said to me.

My question to his superior was, "Is this how a normal traffic stop should occur for a broken taillight?"

"What is that?"

"It's a tube. Duh."

"Gee, thanks, Jules. I was absolutely baffled." I turned the small tube around in my hands, the packaging from a DNA company around it. "I thought you had handed me a miniature elephant. Or a barbeque. Who knew it was a tube?"

"Very funny. Spit in it. It's new gene technology. I don't think I said that right." She tapped her temple. "Maybe I should call it DNA Detective Work."

Jules pushed back her long blonde hair. She had arrived from Seattle last night and had spent the night at Rose Bloom Cottage. She was in a tank top, so her tattoos were on full display, including my pink rose. She was wearing a number of necklaces and fabric/silver/gold bracelets up her arm. She always looked cool. Jules couldn't not look cool. I, however, thought I looked cool enough if I could fit into my jeans and my flowing shirts were clean. "I don't get it. Spit in it?"

"Yep. Think of it as spitting for genes. We're going to send both tubes off to this lab and find out where our ancestors came from. Mom and the aunts have always said that Grandpa was Norwegian and English, mostly, they think, and their mom said she was French and Greek. Again, they think. Nothing's for sure."

"And Dad said he was Scottish and English. We're mutts," I said. "American mutts."

"But let's find out what kind of mutts. Mack and I want to see what our kids are going to be made of. He already sent his test off, so I'm late. We're late. Spit away, sister!"

"So we spit and we can find out where our ancestors are from?"

"Yep. You got it."

"Why do we both have to do it? We're sisters. Won't we be the same?"

"Nope. We won't. Only identical twins have the same genetics."

"Huh. But we're both from Mom and Dad."

"Right. But you get fifty percent of Dad's genes and fifty percent of Mom's genes. Same with me. You and I get different percentages from each parent. It's like all the genes get shaken up in a genetic bottle and they spill out differently when the swimming sperm meets the innocent egg."

"That would account for why you're tall and blonde and have dark brown eyes and I'm black haired and somehow have gold eyes and I'm short and squat like a turnip with two pumpkins for a behind."

"Uh, let's rephrase, book nerd, and get the vegetables out of your language. You have magnetic gold eyes that everyone loves. You are short but you are not squat, and you have a figure that curves and men love. Anyhow, you might have more of the Greek blood because of your black hair, and I might have more of the Norwegian blood because I'm blonde. But maybe not. I might have more Greek blood and ended up blonde because of the other genetic ingredients. You could be the Norwegian Viking. I can totally see you in one of those steel bustiers holding a sword on a ship."

"And you love scotch and men in kilts, so I could see you being more Scottish."

"And you love tea and cookies, Evie, so you're probably more English. As soon as we're married, Mack and I are going to stop using birth control so I can get knocked up with a baby Mack. We're planning on spending a lot of time bouncing in bed on our honeymoon so with his strong sperm and my open ovaries, whoa ho! Baby could soon be on the way."

We spat in the tubes, filled out the paperwork, boxed it up.

"Fun," I said. "Don't be surprised if we find out that you are from outer space."

"Or that your genes are absolutely undetectable because you are a foreign species."

"I think we already know I'm a foreign species."

She gave me a quick squeeze. "Maybe you're a witch. Now, that would explain everything."

"I do have witch DNA. I think that's already been scientifically established."

"I'm going to mail these off when I go to town today. I bought tubes for Mom and the aunts. It'll be interesting to see their genetic recipes, too."

"Maybe we'll have a surprise," I said. "Wouldn't that be fun to have a surprise? To be from somewhere we knew nothing of, like Zimbabwe or Ireland or Russia?"

"Oh, I would love it. Hidden family secrets and all that." She put the boxes in her bag, then looked at me across the table. "How are you doing?"

"I'm fine."

"No, tell me the truth." She leaned forward, fiddling with one of her many hoop earrings.

I glanced at her tattoo of Mack. "You better not ever get divorced, because that is a huge picture of Mack on your muscle."

"I will never divorce Mack." Her face scrunched up as if she was going to cry. "Never. I love him so much."

"Geez, Jules. I'm sorry. I am. It was a joke. A bad joke."

"It's okay," she squeaked out. "It's okay." She squeaked again and teared up, and I gave her a hug and blinked my eyes fast so I didn't cry. Okay, maybe a tear or two squeezed out. Jules is very emotional. I am, too, but I squish it inside and then all of a sudden it bursts like a firework. Jules will cry when she's sad or afraid or lonely, although she hasn't been lonely since Mack roared into her life on his motorcycle, but she gets the cries out. I try to restrain myself most of the time.

"I want to know, though, Evie. How are you?"

"I'm fine. The bookstore is going well. Selling books, cake, tea, Mom's political bouquets, Aunt Camellia's lotions and potions . . . did you know she named one lotion Titillate and Fornicate? And I'm still selling Aunt Iris's flower photographs and cards that you can't quite figure out and can't quite look away from that have a seductive and sexual overcast to them. Who knew flowers could look like that?"

"And your fortune telling?"

That's what she called my premonitions. She's called them that since we were kids. As a kid, that's how she could describe it, and it stuck. "They're not that bad lately." That was a lie. But why burden her?

She smiled. "I love you so much, Evie. You're not only my love-sister, you're my bestie best friend ever in the world."

"I love you, too, Jules." I gave her a hug. "I'm going to look so hot in my maid of honor dress."

She laughed. "Roarin' hot! Wait until Marco sees you!"

I almost blushed. Dang, I am too old to blush, but I almost did.

"You're blushing." She laughed again.

Then I cried about Marco and she knew, as my mother and aunts knew, why I was crying and what I'd seen in the future for us, so she cried, too, in sisterhood.

"I'm sorry, Evie," she sobbed. "So sorry."

"Me too."

Later that night my mother, aunts, Jules, and I went to one of only two bars in North Sound. My mother and aunts climbed up on the bar and warbled and sang karaoke. They sang Sister Sledge's "We Are Family" and Aretha Franklin's "Think."

Then Jules got up with the band and burned the place down. She plays guitar. And she sings. She and Mack have their own band and do well locally. I mean, how cool can a sister get? She rides motorcycles, she designs stuff for motorcycles, and she plays in a band and skydives!

I should hate her, I should.

But I can't, so I don't.

I cheered along with everyone else when she was on her knees, strumming away and singing at the top of her lungs.

The Book Babes were back. They bought coffee and southern pecan praline cake.

They had read a book about a woman who made fantastical wood chairs with wings and dragons, giant teacups and pink crows, Picasso-style angles and jellyfish shapes.

They decided to draw the chairs they would create if they were painters and carpenters and they described why they made the chair they did.

"My chair is six feet tall and in the shape of a winged, imperial goddess. Because I am a goddess in my head when I've had too much tequila. That's what I do when I'm drunk: I pretend I'm a goddess. I even put on a white net tutu and a white shiny bodysuit and wear my silver heels. What is wrong with me?"

"My chair is more like a couch. I need a nap. I have five teenagers. Can you say 'Hell on earth'? No one tells you what it's like to raise teenagers, because if that secret became general knowledge, the human species would die out. Also, did anyone else hear the rumor that my son was the one who painted a red bra on that horse statue in town?"

"My chair is black. Pure black. Because that's the kind of mood I'm in now. I hate menopause. I'm sweating at random times as if I've got a hose over my head. I have hot flashes at night that soak my sheets. Did I want to go swimming on my mattress? No, I didn't. I've gained twenty pounds in six months. I have chin hairs sprouting every day. What? I'm a man? I need a beard for what purpose? Black chair, black menopause."

"My chair is colorful because I am eighty-two years old and

that's all I want to see from here on out. Color. Red. Blue. Purple. I've had enough tough times in my life, and every day forward from here on out I want to have red, purple, yellow, and orange around me."

"My chair is pink with a lion roaring in the background. See the head? That's how I feel. I feel like roaring. I'm a woman, hear me roar. Remember that slogan? Hear me, I'm going to roar." And she did. That long, growly roar startled everyone in the bookstore. One woman dropped a pile of books, and another dropped her teacup full of lemongrass tea and it shattered, but the book club clapped enthusiastically.

One can see why so many women want to join this book club.

"Spit here," Jules told my mother and aunts. She held out the DNA tubes to each of them. We were at my house, at my kitchen table, a row of pink Dolly Parton roses in short glass vases running down the middle.

Sundance had his head on my lap, and Venus was in my lap. Butch and Cassidy were wrestling in the family room. They'd already knocked over a pile of books and almost knocked over my wine barrel coffee table.

I'd made pasta and salad. I'd bought bread. Aunt Camellia had baked a butterscotch pie. I had a slice of that pie before dinner, simply as an appetizer, and a slice for dessert. Can't get too thin!

"Spit? Spit?" Aunt Camellia said, hand dramatically to her chest. "A lady doesn't spit. Poor manners. Not done."

"What in the world?" Aunt Iris said. "Why would I spit in a tube? Does that sound sane?"

"It's for a DNA test," I said. I scraped my fork across my butterscotch pie plate. No need to waste this scrumptious pie. A lot of people don't know that butterscotch pie is good for them.

"A what?" my mother said, but she said it with a sharp tone that indicated she knew what it was but couldn't believe we were doing it. I stopped scraping my plate and studied her.

"You spit in this tube," Jules said, flipping her blonde hair back, "and I'll mail it back to the DNA company and then they'll tell you what you're made of, what countries our ancestors are from."

The silence was prickly.

"Where I'm from?" Aunt Camellia said, with an edgy tone. "I'm from here. We're from here, San Orcanita Island. Our parents are from here. I left for forty years and wandered, but that is all I need to know."

"Aunt Camellia, you're not one hundred percent American Indian," I said. I saw Mars out of the corner of my eye. He was trying to climb a stack of books. Yep. He brought them down. What a mess. "You said your dad was half Norwegian and half English. You said your mother was half French and half Greek. But if you spit in this tube, you'll know for sure. It's this new genetic test. Evie and I already did it."

"You what?" my mother snapped. I turned to her, as did Jules. She seemed alarmed.

"Jules and I already did it and sent off our kits."

"You already did a DNA test?" my mother asked. She leaned forward, intense.

"Yes," Jules said. She looked as confused by my mother's sharp reaction as I felt. "I mailed it off when I was in town the other day and sent Mack a love letter."

Aunt Camellia's face froze.

Aunt Iris dropped her glass to the table, and it spilled.

My mother lost all color in her face.

What? What was going on here? Why the silence? Why the stricken atmosphere?

"Here, Mom, spit away," Jules said. "It'll be cool. Like a genetic puzzle. We'll all come up related, linked up on the DNA website when we get our results back. It'll show that you're our mom and that you two are our aunts, because we share the same genetic stuff."

"The website can link us up?" my mother asked, her voice choked. "They can tell you who you're related to?"

"Yes, because we're family," I said, baffled by her response.

"When the DNA test is sent back to you," Jules said, "you

get to see your percentages. You three will have different per-centages of Norwegian, English, Greek, and French from your parents. Plus, there could be some slinky surprises in there, at least I hope. Wouldn't that be fun? You three don't get the same blend. Evie and I will get different percentages, too."

"I don't need my percentages," my mother said, her hands clasped together so tightly her knuckles were white.

"I don't, either," Aunt Camellia said. She shook slightly. "Percentages are for math, not family."

"We know who we are," Aunt Iris said. Her voice was rigid. "This is ridiculous. Insensible! There's no need for a test."

I shared a concerned glance with Jules. What the heck? Why the resistance?

"You said that you girls have already done it?" my mother asked, threading her fingers rhythmically in and out. "You mailed it back?"

"Yes, we did. Jules mailed it. Why? It's interesting. That's all it is. Tells us something about our ancestry. Maybe Jules and I will find out that we're part Chinese."

"And if we find out that Evie is part Italian, it'll account for why she likes spaghetti and lasagna so much. We're already pre-dicting she's part witch."

We turned to smile at our mother and aunts.

They were not smiling at us.

"No, thank you," my mother said. She collapsed back in her chair, her face drawn.

"I'm going to skip it," Aunt Iris said. "The government knows enough about me already. They're invasive. When they have my spit, what will they do with it? Steal the information? Sell it to the highest bidder? Use it to determine what I'm going to get sick with and die of so my insurance company can deny me cover-age? Tell me they can link me to a crime I haven't committed? No. I'm not giving my spit away. They say that you'll find out more about your ancestors, but they're storing your DNA so they can use it. Like Big Brother. 1984 here we come!"

"I say no, too," Aunt Camellia said. "We're a family. That's all we need to know. We share the same familial auras. We share the same genetic spirits. We share the same emotional tie to our combined love."

"Please?" Jules said. "We can all compare."

"No," my aunts and mother said altogether, with raised, fraught voices.

"Okay," I said, trying to turn down the heat. "It's okay."

"Sure," Jules said, softer.

"Girls," my mother said, pressing both hands to her pretty, white bell-shaped hair, "it's been lovely, but I'm tired." And with no hugs, no kiss on the cheek, no "I love you," she walked out. I swear she wobbled. My aunts made their excuses, thanked me for dinner, and hurried out after my mother. No hugs there, either.

"What the heck just happened?" Jules said, baffled.

"I have no idea," I said. My instincts were like strobe lights. Something was going on. It wasn't what they said, or their verbal rejections. It was what they didn't say.

Later that night I saw my aunts and mother in the gazebo, the stars peeking out between the clouds, the purple wisteria in shadow. The roses nearby, in neat rows, were still in the quiet. Their heads were close together, then my aunts put their arms around my mother. They stared toward the ocean in the distance, lights from the fishing boats twinkling.

I had another piece of butterscotch pie as I watched them. Sometimes butterscotch helps me think better. I think. Or something like that.

But it did nothing that night to help me figure out what in the world was going on.

They worried me.

Chapter 20

⁓

"King Koradome, the evil merman, was right. Serafina kept helping people. She held sailors up in the water who had fallen off ships. She rescued her sister from the jaws of a shark. She helped the older mermen and mermaids when they were sick. She was generous with the shells she found in the ocean and gave them away as gifts to mergirls and merboys who needed a smile. She rescued a mermaid with four mermaid children who had been caught in a fisherman's net."

"Did she lose her rainbow scales?"

"She did. Every time. The shiny, colorful scales flew off one by one, with each kind deed, through the sea to King Koradome in his black rock home. He laughed in victory when one reached his palm, and he put the scales in a tall glass jar. He liked to stare at them as they shimmered with light and layers of color. He liked knowing that her family, that Serafina, was suffering as they watched her lose her special tail. First it was one row of scales, then another and another."

"Did she lose all of her scales?"

Chapter 21

~

"I don't like memoirs."

"What?" I glared at the sulky young woman in front of me with pink- and purple-streaked dreadlocks. She had a serpent tattooed on her arm. A mean serpent. "How can you not like memoirs? It's a peek into someone's life, a part of their life that's tragic or interesting or funny. How do you not want to read about someone else?"

Her eyes widened, surprised at my semi-anger. But, come on. You don't like memoirs?

"I don't."

I wanted to shake her right there in my yellow bookstore by my yellow rose wallpaper. "You have got to be kidding me. How do you learn about how others cope with their lives or the adventures they've experienced or their crazy families if you don't read memoirs?"

"I . . . well . . . I don't know." She seemed confused now, as if she was actually considering my question.

"You have got to read a memoir." I marched over to the memoir section and pulled down three books. "Try these."

"But I don't like memoirs."

"Now you're repeating yourself. You're irritating my brain. What's your favorite genre?"

"I like books about vampires."

I sighed. I groaned. I slapped my forehead so my brain didn't fall out of my ears. "Look. Vampires are fine now and then, but you can't build a personal reading library on vampires!"

"What's a personal reading library?"

I groaned again. "Sit down." I pointed to the seats by the windows. "Sit. Open the book. Read it."

"I have to meet my mother soon."

"Text her. Tell her to come here when she's done doing whatever. You have got to expand your closed mind and read about other people in this world who don't bite necks and have long teeth."

The young woman sat down and sulkily opened a book while I crossed my arms and waited. I stood there for one minute.

She liked the memoir so much, she didn't even notice when I left. Because I felt bad about getting mad at her, I brought her a piece of peppermint cake and chamomile tea. Her mother walked in. "How come your daughter reads only about vampires? I mean, bite me. That's a very limited scope of reading."

"What? You blame me? I can't control her. She's weird. She likes vampires. Look at her hair. She always wears black. Did you see that snarky serpent? She snuck out and got two tattoos on her butt last weekend—one of a skull, the other of a skeleton. Yeah, she has a skull and a skeleton on her butt. She listens to music that sounds like the devil banging on drums. She's out of my control. What can I do?"

I pointed to her. "Your daughter is reading, wait for it"—she raised her eyebrows—"a memoir."

Her mother gasped. "Are you serious?"

"Yes."

The mother bought her daughter three memoirs. The mother winked at me when she left. "No more vampires for a few days." She mimicked chomping down on someone's neck, and I laughed.

Jules had to leave the island the next day. She came into town to hug me at the bookstore.

"Whew. Got a lot ready and done for the wedding, but Mom

and Aunt Iris and Aunt Camellia are all quiet and secretive. I can't figure it out. It's something about the DNA test. It's confusing." She ran a hand through that long blonde hair of hers, then started playing with her three necklaces. "They seemed almost angry about the whole thing. Or worried."

"It's both, I think. Mom won't talk to me about it. I don't get it."

"I don't, either."

"Maybe they do think it's a violation of their privacy."

"Maybe they're worried that who they think they are isn't who they are."

"We'll show them our results when we get them. Maybe they'll feel better then, find it interesting and not invasive. They'll try to figure out which part of our makeup is from Mom, which is from Dad, then maybe they'll do it."

"Maybe."

Maybe not.

Probably not. I didn't understand their vehemence, how adamantly they were against the test. I didn't understand my mother's inexplicable sadness.

That bugged me. I like to understand as much about life as possible, especially with my premonitions curse, and this one I did not understand.

Two days later, Chief Reginald Ass Burn lumbered into my bookstore, my haven, my slice of literary heaven, in his uniform, chest puffed up, face flushed around the edges. His scraping negativity was already invading my space. It's hard to have mean people around your books, infecting them.

"Evie, may I have a word with you?"

As soon as I saw him I had tried to sneak like a snake up the stairs to my office. Surely it was time for the chocolate chip cookies I brought for a snack?

"Yes?"

"Privately, please," he commanded. He dropped those slitty

eyes to my chest. I was wearing a black classic T-shirt with my favorite women's rock band and jeans that stopped mid-shin embroidered with white roses at the bottom.

"I'm very busy right now," I said. "What can I help you with?"

"I want to talk to you about your ticket. Alone."

"I don't want to talk to you alone. What about my ticket? I paid it. In full."

"I told you, hon, that you didn't need to do that. You only had to get your taillight fixed and come to me with your ticket when it was done and I would reduce it. I told you that you might have a lucky day." He smirked at me.

Oh, gross. So gross. First, calling me "hon" and then saying I might have a "lucky day." He was trying to insert a sick slice of sexuality. In my bookstore! A place of literary excellence. A place for books, for authors, for creativity and pie and cake and tea and coffee. A place for kids to learn to love books. A place for reading, the holy grail of life.

"First off, don't call me 'hon.'" My voice was like iron crushing nails. "You are not a member of my family, you are not my boyfriend or husband. I have a name. It's Evie. Or you can call me Ms. Lindsay. I am comfortable with that. Second, I don't need to have a 'lucky day' with you for a ticket. I don't appreciate the sexual connotation, as it makes me feel nauseated. I didn't want to have a conversation with you, as our last conversation was unpleasant for me, so I paid it in full so I could avoid you."

His eyes narrowed. He had lost. In a way. He had way overcharged me but had wanted to cut the amount down, as he knew it was unreasonable. He had wanted to appear magnanimous, the generous male savior. I had taken his control of that scenario away.

"I'll need to talk to you about that, Evie."

"We have nothing further to say about it. You gave me a ticket, I paid it. I wrote a letter of complaint to your boss, as I thought the fine was excessive, and I made a copy of the ticket and I wrote down everything you said to me, verbatim." I watched with pleasure as Chief Ass Burn's face lost color and became a fleshy white. "I fixed my taillight. If there's nothing else, I have to work now."

I turned away and bumped straight into Marco. At some point he'd come up behind me. He was standing still, his eyes locked on the chief.

"Is there a problem?" he asked, his body stiff, watchful. He was wearing a short-sleeved black T-shirt, and his tattoos showed. Who knew that tattoos could be so sexy? I studied the tattoos for a second on those muscles, then tried to refocus.

"I don't think it's your business, Marco," Chief Reginald Ass Burn said, but he was uncomfortable, I could tell. Men who have nothing to them always get uncomfortable around men who have something to them.

"Oh, it's his business," I said. I told Marco how much my ticket was for a broken taillight but that I'd paid it in full.

"I heard about your ticket, Evie." He kept his eyes on the chief. "I received the town text about it. It was overly punitive, Reginald. I've never heard of a ticket being so high for a broken taillight. Surely the state of Washington has an average ticket price for that sort of thing. You've gone well beyond reasonable."

Chief Ass Burn twitched, flushed. "I offered to reduce it. All Evie here had to do was get it fixed, then make an appointment to talk to me at the station, and I'd take care of it for her."

"He said I could have a lucky day with him," I told Marco, not moving my eyes away from the chief. "I'm sure the chief only meant that I would get lucky in terms of paying less."

Marco took a step closer to the chief. He was about six inches taller, built like a tank, and ticked off. He stepped in front of me. I think it was protectively reflexive. Romantic. Although, I told myself, I could slay my own dragons. Still! What a handsome tattooed prince I had!

" 'Lucky day' is an inappropriate term to use with a woman, especially since you are the island's temporary police chief."

"I don't need you telling me what's appropriate and what's not, Marco. You stay out of this."

"No," Marco said, his voice quiet but hard. "I won't."

"Is there anything else?" I asked the chief.

Chief Ass Burn glared at both of us, back and forth, then smirked, but he'd lost some of his confidence. "Not now. Maybe later."

He left the bookstore. My employees, Tiala, Ricki, and Brenz, had watched the whole thing. They were right behind me, and I hadn't even noticed. Also behind me were about six other people who lived in town, plus another three or four tourists.

"Chief Ass Burn is a piece of work," Mr. Jamon croaked out, leaning on his cane with one hand while the other hand held a torrid bodice-ripper book.

We all nodded.

Marco had hardly moved, watching the chief leave.

"Hi, Marco." My voice was shaky.

"Hi, Evie. I was looking for some new books."

"I happen to sell books."

He smiled. I smiled. He was a gentle, tough giant.

And a reader.

That was one of the most attractive things of all about my Marco. He was a book nerd.

Book nerds unite.

I thought about Chief Ass Burn later that night. He was a threat. He was a heavy, unattractive man with control issues. Probably a narcissist. Praise him or he hated you. He wanted to date me, but he hated me, too, because I had rejected him.

I was worried. Not for me but for my aunts and mom and their new business in the greenhouse.

Once again, I told them of my ratcheting-up concerns after work the next day. We cut flowers for their business, armfuls of roses, then stood near Alpaca Joe and Virginia Alpaca as they stared at the four of us as if they were part of the conversation. As Sundance was by my side, that furry friend, it felt like we were having a human–animal meeting. In the distance Mr. Bob and Trixie Goat stood on top of their blue home and studied us as if saying, "What in the world? Why weren't we invited?"

"We'll be fine, dear," my mother said. She seemed sad. "No one will tell."

"We have to carry on our mission for nurturing the people of this island. The marijuana helps them, soothes their minds and bodies when they're broken," Aunt Camellia said.

"We're going to Antarctica on pot," Aunt Iris said. "At least, partially. There is no way we can sell enough pot to pay for the whole thing. Seeing and studying icebergs, ocean currents, and penguins is expensive. I'm the chief financial officer, so I know."

They had a chief financial officer for their pot business? Geez. What was my mother, the chief executive? I groaned. Was there going to be a board of directors next? How had it come to this?

I argued, they shut me down. Alpaca Joe spit. Virginia Alpaca made a purring sort of sound. Sundance looked up at me like, "We tried," and the goats bleated. Wait. The bleating was too close to me. Somehow, some way, Mr. Bob and Trixie Goat had escaped again, and they skittered around the edge of the alpacas' fence and right up to us to join the conversation.

"How did you get out?" I semi-shouted. "I can't believe this."

I would have to chase them to get them back into their pen. They kicked up their heels and ran.

"Please stop selling pot," I said to my mother and aunts, before Sundance and I ran after the naughty goats. "Chief Ass Burn is a problem."

My mother smiled, that mysterious sadness still there, though. "No one will tell him."

Aunt Camellia said, winding her curls on top of her head, "I've already put multiple curses on him with my vengeful candle."

Aunt Iris said, "He knows he's not allowed on this property. But I think I'll make a sign and nail it to the big oak right at the turnoff on Robbins Drive."

I spent over two hours caring for and visiting with my animals after catching Mr. Bob and Trixie Goat. Butch and Cassidy ran around with their tongues out chasing squirrels, but Sundance stuck right by me. I do have a favorite, and it is Sundance, but I would never tell, or show, my other animals that. I reached down and pet his head. He licked my hand, then stood up for a one-armed hug.

Mr. Bob and Trixie Goat climbed on top of the roof of their little house and danced around as if they enjoyed hearing their own hooves tap. Shakespeare and Jane Austen chased each other and came right over for me to pet their heads. The cats circled my legs. The alpacas wandered around their home. I think Virginia Alpaca likes to play hard to get. It drives Alpaca Joe nuts. The lambs trotted out of their pen in a little line, as usual. So obedient.

"Hello, Padre, Momma, Jay Rae, Raptor, and The TMan."

No matter how much work they are, no matter how early I have to get up every day to take care of them, no matter how many times I'm at Marvelous Marco's paying vet bills, I love my animals. They have given me peace.

Aunt Iris made the sign. She nailed it to the big oak at the turnoff.

It said, "Chief Ass Burn: You Are Not Allowed on Our Property."

That'll do it, I thought, getting to be quite the cynic. He'll definitely stay off the property even when he finds out you three are selling pot out of the greenhouse.

I was beginning to feel sick about their "business venture."

Jules and I received e-mails that the DNA company had received our vials of spit.

"Pretty fun, huh?" Jules said when she called me that night. "We'll find out where those ancestors of ours are from."

"We're from witch country. Soon we'll know."

"I think I'll get a sexy witch outfit for me and a warlock outfit for Mack. That'd be fun. Not long before I'm Mrs. Motorcycle Rider! Mack is so brave. He's so confident. When I bring home new sex toys, he's always game to try them out."

"That's very courageous."

"I know!" She sniffled. "Anything I want to try, he wants to try. He doesn't make me feel silly or stupid for asking, he just smiles that smile at me when I tell him, well, when I ask him if he wants to play dress up or do role-play or try new games or toys, and he always says, 'Anything you want to do, Sugar Love Jules, we'll do, you're my apple pie.' And so we do."

A little too much detail, but okay! "He has an adventurous spirit like you."

"Yes, he does. He'll try anything in bed at all. Doesn't even mind my crazy ideas! He makes me feel sexy." She burst into tears. "I love him so much! I can't wait to get married with you as my maid of honor."

"Stop, stop!" I teared up and blew my nose.

I drove Torrance's books out to him again and passed by the battered yellow house that I didn't want to see. On my way back I pulled into the drive, turned off my car, and let the memories pour over me. There was an air of depression around the sagging, dilapidated house, although maybe that was me personifying it.

Emily Medegna and I were best friends for three years. She was also close to Jules, because whenever Emily came over, Jules was there, too. We also had a bunch of other girlfriends of all ages on the island, the sisters and cousins of our friends.

It was an island gang of girls, so to speak. We spied on boys. We went on hikes with our moms. We played in the ocean. We went out on other parents' sailboats. We played in the lake and jumped off the dock. We had picnics. When it rained we read books together and made tents with blankets. We did not play with dolls. We did not pretend we were princesses, hoping to be rescued. We played Island Warrior Women and we fought off bad guys and zombies and King Kong with homemade swords and pretend bombs.

We were tough! We were brave! We were the Island Girls Gang.

And one day, one of the members of the Island Girls Gang betrayed the other by forgetting to help. Forgetting to prevent. Forgetting to save.

There was a disastrous, tragic consequence that was all my fault.

I betrayed my friend and her family, and her life fell off a cliff for years. She left the island. Then she disappeared. My guilt has never left me. I manage it, I forget about it sometimes, but it's still there, lurking.

I laid my head on the steering wheel, guilt, remorse, and unbearable sadness whipping over me like a wave, drowning me.

I fought my depression that afternoon. I could feel it coming on like a black *thing*. I knew how to handle it. I left my bookstore and drove to a lake in the local state park and walked around it until my legs ached. I breathed. I ate bananas because for some reason bananas help me with my anxiety. I had chocolate milk in the bath and ate strawberries. I washed my sheets and cleaned up the house. Organizing helps me get my mind off my depression.

It was late when I went to bed. I read for two hours, slipping into fiction so I could slip out of my dark mind-set. Sundance stayed up with me for most of the night with an expression that said, "Can we go to sleep now? Are you okay?" Sundance was so in tune with me and my feelings. His head was on his pillow, his pink blankie beneath him, Lizard in his paws. Finally I could no longer keep my eyes open.

"Good night, everyone," I said to the dogs and cats. And I whispered, "Good night, Emily."

"What's it like, Evie?"

"What's what like, Sally?"

"To see the future."

"I don't see the future." The bookstore was busy today. Partly because we were selling six-layer Chocolate Cake Ecstasy.

"You ran over to my house yesterday, coming out of nowhere, and stood under my tree right as Ellen was falling. You don't expect me to believe that you can't see the future."

"I was on my way to your house to visit." I was not on my way to Sally's house to visit. I had a vision of that cat falling out of her tree. The cat is eighteen years old. It's half blind and totally deaf. I mean, lots of people think cats are "selectively deaf." That is not the case with this cat. She is totally deaf. And Sally loves her.

Sally is a widow. She's a former doctor from Seattle. Her husband died last year. She is seventy-four and has been pushing that cat in a cat stroller for years. In fact her husband made her a cat stroller before cat strollers were even a thing. That's how much she loves Ellen.

But the problem wasn't only the cat. I saw the cat falling from the tree and one of Beck Hornwith's dogs biting it. The cat died. I saw Sally weeping over her body, and I couldn't stand it. That's why I had to run, which I hate to do, to her house. Running should be outlawed.

"No, you weren't coming over to visit, but thanks for saving Ellen."

"You're welcome."

"But what's it like? Can you see anything about me?"

I held a book out. The book was about the national parks.

She put a hand to her throat. "Oh, my goodness! Why? I wonder why? I'll take it, Evie!"

One week later, Sally booked a trip with a traveling group to see four national parks.

I had zippo premonitions about Sally. She needed to get out of her grief and live a little.

She had a terrific time.

The car accident premonition arrived smack out of the blue again as I was driving to the bookstore the next morning. The tight, curving road in the mountain was the same, the sunlight filtering through, the orange poppies.

But this time, when the red car came into view, instead of crashing straight into me, the driver, a woman, turned the wheel to her right when we were still ten feet away from each other and sent her car flying off the side of the road and down the cliff.

I stopped and I ran out of my truck. I saw the woman's head hanging limply out the window, her short black hair still.

She looked dead, and I scrambled down the cliff and ran to her.

Then I lost my footing and started to fall. I screamed as I crashed down the cliff, rolling, flipping, landing hard.

One of us died. Probably. I felt a death, then it skittered away. I can't believe that this premonition does not give me more clarity. All my premonitions give me clarity. I see what's going to happen.

Why does this premonition change and shift? I have no idea why, and that makes me worry more than anything else.

Mr. Jamon came in on Friday. The store was jammed, the line to get treats at the café ten people long. It was the Toffee Crunch and Candied Pretzel cake we were selling. Bettina knew how to bake.

"Hello, Mr. Jamon."

"Hello, Evie," he croaked out. "I'll need another book by Mrs. Macomber and I need something that'll keep me thinking, using the ol' noggin all night."

I gave him a historical fiction book about slavery—"history with a magical twist"—and a current book about social issues, minimum wage, and staying broke in America. "Nonfiction. We can all learn from this."

He was quite pleased, especially with Mrs. Macomber's book. "She believes in love," he told me.

"Yes," I said. "She does."

Then he leaned in and whispered, "I'll take another bodice ripper, too."

Chapter 22

∽

Betsy Baturra
Women's Correctional Prison
Salem, Oregon
1976

Prison was a torture for many reasons. Betsy was trapped behind bars, like an animal. She was told what to do and when to do it. Some of the prisoners were mentally ill. Some were mentally ill and dangerous. Some weren't mentally ill but were dangerous. Some of the women were nice enough, or interesting, or even friendly, and others were to be avoided at all costs.

It was gray, it was depressing, it was hopeless. Betsy had been given a life sentence. She might get out early for good behavior. She might not.

She had lost Rose. The only reason she decided not to kill herself was because of her premonition: It looked like one day, in the future, she was out of prison. Either she died or the other woman in the truck died, but maybe she had weeks or months or years to live outside of prison before that. She could hope.

Her first roommate attacked her with a piece of wood that she had sharpened into a tiny knife. The blood soaked through her orange prison shirt and she was sent to the infirmary. The roommate was sent to isolation and then transferred to a mental hospital. Her second roommate was schizophrenic and mean.

She and Betsy had a physical fight, and Betsy won. She was small but strong, and her survival instinct kicked in.

But they both ended up in isolation.

That was where Betsy came into contact with a guard named, ironically, sickeningly, Duke.

Duke was in his midthirties and already balding. He had a heavy stomach that dripped over his belt. He had bad skin; bad teeth; and the deadened, soulless eyes of a panther.

The first time he saw Betsy, on duty in the isolation ward, he stopped making crude jokes to two other guards, who clearly couldn't stand Duke, to pant over Betsy.

"Whoa. Look at that beautiful bitch," Duke breathed.

"Hey," one of the other guards said. "Knock it off."

Duke didn't even bother to glare at him. He watched Betsy being led into an isolation ward and said to himself, "Yum. That one is mine."

And that's when Betsy's life in prison became even worse.

On a blustery night, Duke slid Betsy's dinner in through the tiny slat of her isolation cell designed to break people in half, to bring them to their knees, so that they obeyed forevermore. "Hello, sexy lady."

She didn't bother to hide her disgust. He saw it on her face, so he dumped her food on the floor. "That'll teach you to be more friendly to me."

The food dumping happened on the second night, too. Duke said, "Give me a pretty smile, darling," and leered at her. Betsy did not smile. He threw the food through the slit, angry, but enjoying the power struggle. She would be on her knees soon. He was practiced at this with the "captives."

The third night he said, "Betsy, I can make your life easier or harder. Understand? Now show me what's beneath that shirt." Betsy was demoralized, near deranged from isolation and grief and used an expletive that started with an F to tell him what she thought of that. He tossed the food in once again.

On the fourth night he opened up her door, furtive, quick,

knowing he wasn't supposed to be there and said, "Do you want to eat?"

She blinked at him. The less she spoke to that vile man, the better.

"I said, bitch, do you want to eat?"

"Yes."

He undid his pants. "You know what to do." He leered at her. He was proud of his size. He was big, longer and wider than other men, he believed. Like a stallion. He could drive women crazy with The Pistol. He hung well. He was blessed.

She screamed as loud as she could, and it echoed off the beige-yellow concrete walls. He clocked her, on instinct, right across those high cheekbones, barely missing those puffy lips. "Bitch. I will make you pay for that."

He shoved his little snake back in his pants, enraged at the screaming, and slammed the door.

"What's going on, Duke?" Coralee, another guard, asked. Coralee was twenty-eight and had a degree in criminology and wanted to go to law school. She couldn't stand Duke.

"I don't know. She's crazy." He was panting. His anger always made it hard to breathe. Black was edging his vision, his body ready to attack. "I put her food tray through the opening and she tossed it to the ground like she's done the other nights. I went in to talk to her, calm her down, pick up her food for her, and she swung her fist right at my face twice. She should be in the psych ward."

Through the tiny slat, Betsy said calmly, loudly, "He opened the door, called me a bitch, pulled down his pants, showed me his tiny pencil dick, and told me what to do with it if I wanted to eat."

"She's a liar," Duke said, agitated, his fat face scrunched up. "That didn't happen. I was trying to help her. I was going in to talk to her so she'd eat."

"He wanted me to eat him," Betsy said. She tried to keep her voice strong, but it cracked. She tried not to cry.

Coralee and the other guards didn't believe Duke. Betsy may have been a murderer, but they knew Duke, the warden's nephew, was a lying, scheming jerk.

"Get out, Duke," Coralee said. "Go to the warden's. I'll be there in ten minutes."

"You believe this liar? This murderer?"

Coralee peeked through the slat at Betsy, on the ground, her skinny arms wrapped around her skinny self, then at Duke. Duke was a craven, disrespectful, nasty liar. A man who was not half as smart as any woman here but believed himself to be twice as smart because that's what he wanted to believe. "Yes."

Betsy felt her face swelling up. She was dizzy. She was aching. She felt sick from the punch.

"We'll get you another tray," Coralee said, "but first you're going to the infirmary." One of the guards headed off to get the tray, following Duke, who was punching the air with his meaty fists and swearing. That Coralee could order him around, that infuriated him, too. Women should never be in charge of men. Stupid woman. Stupid whore.

He listened, seething, to Coralee telling the warden, his uncle, what happened to Betsy, the murderess in isolation. Duke called Coralee a liar and pretended to be outraged.

Coralee told him that his nephew wasn't fit to be working in the jail, that he was an egomaniac, a danger to the women prisoners, continued to insist on unlimited power, and had a problem with authority, especially with women. "I've worked with him for a year now. Look, sir, we're not responsible for our family members," she told the warden. "We've all got relatives who are loony or corrupt, but you are responsible for this prison and the people in it."

The warden told Coralee not to tell him how to do his job, and Coralee apologized.

The warden sighed. He knew his nephew had a brain filled with filth, but he loved his older sister. She was the sweetest woman he had ever met. It was Rosalind who had comforted him when their parents were screaming at each other when they were kids. So he didn't fire Duke. He told Duke, "Stop making problems for me here, and keep your damn hands to yourself or you're out of here."

That set Duke off, too. He had a miserable job. There had to be some perks. All these women. Some were butt ugly and fat and gross. Others weren't so bad. They even did things for him when he promised them perks. But Betsy was the most beautiful woman he'd seen in his life.

She was his.

And he would have her.

He would get his revenge on Coralee, too.

Betsy was given a job in the prison cafeteria as a short-order cook, so to speak. It wasn't the worst job. She liked to cook. It was the one thing she and her mother did together. Her mother had taught her how to make everything from scratch to save money: Bread. Pies. Cakes. Casseroles. Chicken dishes. Turkey dinners. It was all centered around Betsy's mother "performing her wifely duties in the kitchen," as her father always said, but it did give her time alone with her mother.

The food in prison was flat, but maybe she could make it better. She would try. She had nothing else to do. Plus, in some small way it reminded her of her and Johnny's plans. They were going to farm together. They would sell the food they grew on the farm. It would be organic. Their organic food would make people's lives better, healthier. They would have a farmhouse and acreage. They would have apple, pear, and cherry trees. They would have blueberries and potatoes and carrots and lettuce.

Every time she envisioned that farm, selling at farmer's markets or a small grocery store, she would feel a sense of hope, of light, but then her reality would crash in on her along with the bars in her cell and the group showers, and darkness would descend. Still, she hung on to that image, that future.

Her new cellmate was named Eartha. Eartha was twenty-two. She was in for attacking her stepfather. He had beaten up her mother one too many times. She had tried to kill him, but it hadn't worked. "I could not tolerate seeing my mother's face bashed in one more time," she said. "He always threatened to kill her if she left him, so I decided to take things into my own hands with a hammer when he was drunk and passed out."

Her defense attorney literally fell asleep at her trial, twice. The judge had to shout at him. In the end, she was found guilty of assault and was in for three years. "Hopefully we can stay roommates for that long," Eartha told her after a week. "You ain't crazy and you ain't mean, and you haven't tried to kill me yet, so we're good."

Betsy liked Eartha. She was almost six feet tall, smart, loud, opinionated, interesting, and funny. They were an unlikely best-friend pairing, with Betsy being small, quieter, reserved, and depressed. But perhaps because they were so different, they got along. It was the only thing about prison that Betsy liked. She even shared her future plans with Eartha.

"I like it," Eartha said. "I'll be your manager."

So Eartha and she made plans for their grocery store even though Eartha thought Betsy was dreaming. That girl was probably never getting out of prison.

Duke would not leave Betsy alone. He always tried to be near her whenever he could. He watched her. He stalked her. Betsy was elegant and petite, and she disdained Duke. Who was she, he thought with a burning rage, to reject him? Does she think she's better than him, the little murderess? Does she think she can treat him with such dismissiveness and rudeness and get away with it? This was his domain. *His.* Not hers. He was the guard. She was the prisoner. She should be subservient to him.

He would try to talk to her when she was in her cell. He would try to touch her when she walked by in a line with the other prisoners. She would yell at him, "Get your paws off of me, you animal." He would try to rub up against her any time he could, which wasn't often, as there were other people around and he knew where all the cameras were, but he was always there, waiting to rub.

Duke tried, for a short time, to sneak behind her while she was doing dishes in the cafeteria. As soon as she saw him coming, his beady eyes locked on her, she would get a bowl ready. When he stepped up behind her, she would pretend to be surprised, turn, and toss a bowl full of soapy, dirty, preferably hot water on him. The first time she did it, he ripped the bowl out of her hands and threw it. It shattered on the floor. He then turned her around and put her hands behind her back and cuffed her, shoving himself up behind her.

"Get off of me!" she screamed, gasping for breath as his weight pressed in on her. "Get him off of me." Other prisoners turned to help, but it was no use. He was a guard and no one was allowed to touch a guard. Plus, Mrs. Grisham, their boss, was out that day—her daughter had given birth to twins—so there was no one to ask for help from.

"You attacked a guard," Duke panted, so excited, thrilled!

"No, I didn't. I defended myself because I didn't want your sweaty, fat hands on me again. Quit trying to touch me, Duke!"

He dragged her off, her arms almost being pulled out of their sockets, to isolation. He would teach her a lesson as soon as he could. When Coralee came in for her shift, she complained to the warden about Betsy being there again. She knew what was going on. "He came up behind Betsy, again, and attacked her," she told the warden. "Then Duke blamed her for it."

"He said she turned, unprovoked, and threw scalding hot water on him in order to make an escape," the warden said. He couldn't look Coralee in the eye.

"You have got to be kidding," Coralee told him. She was getting more bold in her speech. She figured she'd make a competent lawyer. "You can't possibly believe that. You know your creepy nephew is obsessed with her."

The warden sighed. If it wasn't for his sweet sister, he would have fired Duke long ago. He sighed again. He should have been a grocer. Or a plumber.

Coralee made dang sure that Duke didn't "visit" Betsy on her shift or on any of the other shifts. No one crossed Coralee, so when Duke tried to sneak down there when Coralee was off shift, he was refused by other guards.

Betsy only had to spend two days in isolation, because the warden intervened. If hot water had truly been thrown, she would have been in there far longer than that.

When she was released she was confused and exhausted,

which is what isolation does. Plus, it makes you feel like you're losing your mind as the walls close in ever closer. When Betsy was headed to the cafeteria a week later, Duke grabbed her and dragged her out to a supply closet and shut the door. He knew that supply closet, and the short hallway on either side of it, didn't have a camera on it.

He didn't realize that Betsy would fight as hard as she did, especially after he smacked her so she would obey and shut up. In the end, his testicles were smashed by her raised knee so hard, and with such force, that he fell to the ground. She stumbled out of the closet, her prison shirt ripped. Mrs. Grisham, back from helping with her daughter's twins—they were so adorable— saw Betsy, her face bruised and swelling, and complained to the warden.

But there was an ol' boys network in the prison, and the warden was his uncle, so no one did anything to punish Duke, but Mrs. Grisham told him to "stay the hell out of my kitchen, you piece of crap, Duke."

Betsy cried in her cold, bare cell that night, Eartha's arm around her. "I'm gonna kill that son of a gun for you, Betsy," Eartha said.

"Please don't," she sobbed. "I don't want you in here any longer than you need to be."

Betsy hated prison. Everyone did. It was dangerous. It was devoid of all elements of a normal human life. Freedoms. Choice. A job. Family and friends. Weather. Walking. The beach.

But Betsy found two surprising things.

For many women there, they'd made one mistake. One. Usually in conjunction with a toxic relationship with a man and/or with drugs. There wasn't much that separated most of the women in prison from the women outside of prison. Once sober, once they were out of the way of bad influences, they were like everyone else.

About thirty percent, Betsy figured, were mentally ill. She couldn't understand why they were there in the first place. Prison was enough to make anyone lose their mind. It was worse for those who had already lost it. The vast majority of the women in prison had been poor all their lives. Many were minorities and clearly had had grossly inadequate defense attorneys representing them. They were sentenced for things that Betsy knew a wealthy white woman would not go to jail for. Or their sentences were way too long, overly punitive.

Now many of the women, they deserved to be there. They were sick and dangerous and had no morals or empathy and they were a danger to society. She avoided the monstrous ones as best she could.

The monotony in prison killed her spirit. The fear killed her soul. The loss of Rose killed her heart. The abuse from Duke disgusted her, scared her, repelled her.

Betsy longed for Johnny. She lived for his letters. She wished she could see a premonition about the two of them, together, happy in the future, out of prison, but she saw nothing.

She thought of Rose every day and prayed that she would have a happy, safe life. She worried about Tilly constantly. Now and then she would get a picture in an envelope, drawn by Tilly, but no words. She knew that Tilly was in foster care, traumatized by what she'd seen. Betsy hadn't even known Tilly was in the room when she'd killed Peter. Tilly was now a child with no parents, no brother. Alone.

She felt responsible. Her guilt made her ill. If she was ever out of jail, she would make it up to Tilly. She had no idea how, but she would. Tilly deserved it.

Betsy was hit with the car-crashing premonition again after a particularly bad day where Duke was staring at her, eyes narrowed, his hand near his crotch and making a swishing motion. Eartha yelled at him to "get your long tongue back in your marshy mouth, get your short dick under control, and stop staring at Betsy with your piggy eyes. She don't want you, Duke, she never will. You're like pond scum to her. Pond. Scum."

Eartha was hauled off by Duke to isolation. Later, Duke came back and baited Betsy, calling her names, telling her he was going to keep Eartha in isolation for weeks unless Betsy "started being nice," but she didn't respond. She turned her back in her cell and wouldn't speak. She felt awful about Eartha.

That night she had the premonition again, but this time there was a twist at the end.

She was on the same road. She was driving the red car. The sun was behind her, glinting through the trees. There were orange poppies. The road was narrow and she turned around the curve, cliff on her right, mountain on the left. She was distracted by the cliff, then turned her eyes back to the road and the blue truck. Before she could react, the truck turned and drove straight off the cliff.

"Oh, my God!" she screamed. She stopped, her car dovetailing. She called 911 and started tripping down the cliff. The woman's truck was upside down, the windows were shattered, the airbags blown. The engine had steam rising from it.

The woman was halfway out of her truck, through the shattered window, limp and not moving.

Then the truck exploded.

She wanted to cry. She wanted to scream.

She did neither.

She vowed to change the ending.

Chapter 23

～

"Evie," Chief Ass Burn said to me outside the grocery store. He was not in his uniform. He was wearing a blue shirt that fit snugly, like a diaper, around his sagging gut. "I think we've gotten off on the wrong foot."

I was carrying a bag full of healthy foods including: Truffles. My friend Nicky makes them. He used to be a sous-chef in Los Angeles. He quit so he could live a life. Now he makes truffles from his home in Doe Bay. And I might have had a fresh peach pie in my bag, too, that my friend Kat Metts made for the store. But I had bananas, too, to combat my anxiety. I would run later to burn off the truffles. I laughed out loud at my own funny joke! Running equals torture. In my right hand I carried a root beer float. They were giving them away. If it's free, I'm going to eat it.

I saw his eyes slip to my chest, then hips, for a second. He disgusts me. "Is there something on my shirt?"

His eyes flew to mine.

"You looked at my chest, and I thought maybe there was something on my shirt. You've done it before."

"No, nothing's on your shirt." He smiled, and it was a mix of being caught and triumph. He had gotten to me, and he liked knowing he could irritate me.

"Stop looking at my chest," I told him.

"I'm not. Do not accuse me of something I haven't done." He smirked.

"Look, Chief Ass Burn, we got off on the wrong foot because you are arrogant and rude and like to throw your weight around"—I dropped my eyes to his bowling ball gut—"but the truth is that I don't want to talk to you at all, so we need to avoid each other."

I turned and left, and he grabbed my arm and said, "Now, slow down, little lady, we're gonna talk this out."

I felt his sweaty, clingy fingers, and this roar of disgust and anger came over me. Who was he to touch me, to restrain me? I didn't give him permission. He could touch me because he's a man and he wants to? He's entitled to that? He can hold me back because he sometimes wore a uniform? He can force a conversation because he wants the conversation to take place, regardless of what I want?

"Let go of me," I semi-shouted, yanking my arm from his claws. I turned and accidentally on purpose flung my entire root beer float on his shirt, too darn bad. "Don't ever touch me again."

Maeve Biller, twenty-nine years old and an artist, shook her head. "Nice, Evie. I saw the chief grab you, and you fought back. You aren't allowed to grab women, do you know that, Chief Ass Burn?"

"Well done," Mrs. Liu said, her white curls bouncing about in her ponytail. "When I was younger, we used hatpins to get rid of frisky men, but the root beer float worked, too. Are they still giving them away?"

And Bo Proudfoot, a geologist and author, glared at the chief and said, "What the hell's wrong with you? You can't put your hands on a woman like that."

"I want to speak to Evie," he huffed, wiping his shirt and glaring at me. "Privately."

"I don't want to speak to you." I walked past him but not before I heard him say, "You're gonna regret that, Evie."

"I heard that!" Maeve Biller said. "That was a threat! Why is it that men who grab women then feel like they can threaten the woman when she protests? Why is it that when men get angry at women who rebuff them they feel like they can take revenge or retaliate? Why do you think that is, Chief Ass Burn? What gives you the right to threaten Evie just because she doesn't want your hands on her?"

"I heard it, too," Mrs. Liu croaked out. "You told Evie she was going to regret emptying her root beer float on you when you grabbed her without her permission. You deserved it. If I had a hatpin, I would have used it on your crotch. Poke, poke!"

"I heard it," Bo Proudfoot said. "And I am reporting you."

"Don't come near me again," I said. I stood still and strong and furious. "I will protect myself if you ever try to touch me again."

The chief took off, a disgusted look on his face for them and hatred in his eyes for me. That's how narcissistic men look at women they can't control or who don't bow down to them: with hate.

And they want revenge.

You've popped their ego. You haven't stroked it. And now you're in trouble.

Or my mother and aunts were in trouble.

I headed home, took care of the animals, and went to bed early with three books: Romance. Nonfiction. Science fiction.

I brought up a slice of peach pie. I wondered if Marco liked peach pie.

Marco called me that night, Sundance lying beside me on his pillow with his pink blankie and Lizard, the other dogs and cats still running around the house and in and out of the dog/cat door. "Are you okay?"

"Oh, sure." I ran a finger around the edges of one of the embroidered purple roses on my comforter. For some reason, doing that helps me to relax.

"I heard about what the chief did."

"I'm fine. I told him not to touch me. He'll back off."

"What a dick. I'm sorry, Evie."

"It's okay. I'm fine. How are you?"

He wouldn't let me change the subject, asking questions, swearing at the chief. I finally got him to take a breath.

"I'm fine, Evie, but I am ticked off at the chief. I'm working, taking care of animals, including one dog who ate a five-year-old's birthday cake and got sick and another who leaped over the back fence to be with his girlfriend and in the process broke his leg."

"Anything for love," I said.

"Yes." He laughed. "I think he was making a grand gesture."

We chatted and laughed, and before I knew it we'd been talking for three hours.

"All right, Evie. I've kept you too long."

"It was nice to talk to you."

"Highlight of my day," he said, soft and warm. "No, probably the highlight of my year."

We laughed.

I missed him. I wanted him. I loved that guy.

When we hung up, I choked up.

The next day, Marco put his "sorry" into action.

He went to talk to the chief. They met up in front of the hardware store. I heard about it later. Marco told the chief to stay away from me. That I didn't want to talk, or interact, with the chief, that he was not to touch me.

Chief Ass Burn laughed and said, "She's not your girlfriend, Marco. As I understand, she's turned you down. Small island. Once she gets to know me . . ."

"She has gotten to know you," Marco said. "And she doesn't like you. You're harassing her."

"I'm not harassing her at all, but nice try. You step over that line one more time and I'll arrest you for threatening me."

"Do it," Marco said. "I dare you."

"You're not going to win, Marco. I will."

"Evie is not someone to win."

I'm told that the chief backed down. Marco is well over six feet, has tattoos, and is former military. The chief wasn't that stupid.

I talked yet again to my mother and aunts and told them to stop selling pot. "Chief Allroy is not here. Chief Ass Burn is and he's out for me, and he will transfer the anger he has for me to you. You need to shut it down."

"I am not afraid," my mother said. She was making a daisy chain from fake daisies for a new hat.

"My soul says I'm at peace," Aunt Camellia said. She was trying to knit. She was terrible at it but smiled at whatever she was making anyhow. It poked out in circles on two sides and looked like a small bottom. I tilted my head. Was she making underwear for a misshapen bottom?

"If he comes on our property, I will run him over," Aunt Iris said. "We can bury the body in the pond. Or under the rocks under momma's bridge. More pie, Evie? I know chocolate cream is your favorite."

I did have another slice of chocolate cream pie, but only because high-quality chocolate is healthy for you. Everyone knows that.

"I'm compiling my honeymoon wardrobe," Jules said. We were on Skype about midnight on Thursday. I was in bed with Sundance, Mars, and Ghost. "What do you think?"

I stared at what she held up for her "honeymoon wardrobe." It was all lingerie, by Lace, Satin, and Baubles in Portland. Fluffy. Sexy. Silky. Made for love and passion. "Are you planning on going out at all?"

"What?" She pulled a red lacy nightgown over her blue tank top and shorts to show me. "Look at this one!"

"It's very pretty, but all you have is lingerie. I know Mack has a surprise destination honeymoon for you. But you'll probably be going out, too. So you are planning on bringing real clothes, right? Dresses? Jeans? Shorts?"

She giggled. "I don't know. I'll have an outfit for the plane ride, and I can wear the same one back. Oh, wait! He says we're going someplace hot, so I also brought my bikinis!" She held three up.

I had tried! "Looks like you're set."

"I think so!" She laughed, flipped her hair back. Her tattoos were on glorious display. I saw my pink rose, the bouquet for our mom and aunts, our father's orca. "I can't wait to see you again, Evie. You're the best sister in the world." She dropped the bikinis and the lingerie and gazed at me through the computer screen. Her eyes filled up. My eyes filled up. She sniffled. I sniffled. She made a choking sound, and I felt my throat closing up. I blew my nose. She blew hers. Then we both gave in and cried.

"I'm getting married!"

"I know! I'm so happy for you, Jules." My voice broke. "I know that Mack will be the best husband. He'll always be there for you. You'll laugh and ride motorcycles and be cool cats together." I help up Ghost and Mars so she could see them as tears rolled down my cheeks. Sundance barked at her. I knew he was trying to make her feel better.

"I love you so much, Evie! Hi, Sundance! Hi, Mars and Ghost!"

"I love you, too, Jules!"

"Mack is so smart." She blew her nose again. "The other night in bed he knew exactly what position I wanted to be in before I even asked!"

Now that is one smart man. Sundance barked again.

We laughed.

I had to bring Mars, Jupiter, Venus, and Ghost to see Marco. Thank the Lord it was time for their annual exams and shots so I could gaze upon his gorgeousness. I am meticulous about my animals' health. A healthy animal is a happy animal. But a healthy glimpse of Marco would make me a happy animal, too.

I made an appointment, sitting on my leather couch at home that afternoon, but Marco had no time for a week. My cats leaped onto my lap. One of them jumped off a pile of books leaned up against my pink rose wallpaper and knocked them to the ground.

"He's jammed," Gayle told me. "I've got you in for Tuesday, last appointment for the day because . . . uh . . . huh . . . because you work late!" she said victoriously. Aw, Gayle. What a pal. "I may see you tonight, Evie. I'm coming to your mom and aunts' house for Sailor Singing Tunes."

"I'll look forward to seeing you." I would stay for a while and sing along, then leave. I can handle social stuff for a while, then I get overwhelmed.

"I've got my sailor hat!" Gayle said.

There. I had something to look forward to. Drunken sailor songs.

I pet my cats as they crowded onto my lap and then started to fall asleep one by one. I can't get anything done with a pile of cats on my lap, so I pretended to sigh and think of all the things I should be doing like cleaning my house, which is so boring. Or trying to get in shape, which is so painful. I picked up a book and happily began to read as they slept.

Then I daydreamed about making love to my love, Marco.

That night the singing sailors all converged for dinner on the deck at Rose Bloom Cottage, the red and pink roses pouring over the outdoor trellis. The women all wore sailor gear or sailor hats, with flowers my mother and aunts added. They were loud, funny, and sang on full blast.

When I watch my mother and aunts I don't fear getting older. After all, if one is allowed to get older or old, you are lucky, indeed.

Plus, my mother and aunts feel grateful to be in their seventies. They have been through the beauties of life. They have been through the hardships of life. They have lost and loved. They have worked hard all their lives. They know what they value the most: Family. Us. Friends. The island. Helping other people.

They laugh, they drink, they grow flowers and run a shop and hang with their friends. They do nice things for people all the time and bring joy to others and to this whole town with their wild shenanigans.

They are gifts. They are living life.

I admire them. I respect them. I love them, funny hats and all.

The sailor songs, which my Aunt Camellia printed out, had a lot of salty language and swear words. They were hilarious. I needed songs to lift my heart, and it was lifted on the sometimes poorly but enthusiastically sung musical notes in Rose Bloom Cottage, a sailor hat with daisies and delphinium on my head.

Sundance howled, joining in. What a cool friend he is to all of us.

Chapter 24

❧

"Serafina kept doing kind things for others. She told her parents that she couldn't be who she wanted to be if she stopped, so she didn't. One row of rainbow-colored scales was soon gone, then another, then another, from her waist to the end of her tail. She grew greener and greener, but she found that she liked having a shiny green tail."

"Like her whole family."

"Like her family. Serafina knew she could cry about losing her scales, but what would that do? It wouldn't bring the scales back. Plus, every time she played with her brothers in the waves, or they swam out to sun themselves on a tiny island in the middle of the ocean, or rode on the backs of whales altogether, she knew it was worth it. She never could have been happy without her brothers, if they had been locked in King Koradome's cage."

"What happened when she had no more scales left?"

"Well that's where this story gets interesting."

Chapter 25

"I love you so much, Evie."

"I love you, too, Mom." It was Sunday afternoon, and we were walking the property, greeting the animals. Alpaca Joe was standing close to Virginia Alpaca, as if afraid to let her out of his sight. He's a little too possessive. We said hello and Virginia Alpaca stuck her nose out to be pet. I hugged her. Alpaca Joe spit.

Sundance walked right beside me, wobbling a bit as usual, while Butch and Cassidy ran around ahead of us. I saw Ghost in the distance, right by the yellow-orange rose garden, and I saw Mars and Jupiter underneath the iris leaves. I think Jupiter had a mouse, but I didn't look too carefully.

We said hello to Shakespeare and Jane Austen, who whinnied. I gave them each an apple. The lambs filed in as a line of five to see us, and the goats stood on the roof of their little blue house. "Stay in your pen today, Mr. Bob and Trixie Goat," I called out. I picked up Ghost and gave her a hug after she wound herself around my legs. I love my animals.

My mother was wearing a plain old blue hat today, which was highly unusual. Where was the fluff and frill, her ribbons and flowers? Her mind was elsewhere. She was deep in thought, worried, distracted.

"Mom?"

She turned to me, and I stared. Were there tears in her eyes?

"What's wrong?"

"Nothing. I was . . ." She cleared her throat, took off her hat,

and ran a hand through her neat, bell-shaped hair. "I was thinking about how wonderful it was when I held you in my arms the
first time when you were a baby. You were pink and sweet, so
tiny."

"Probably screaming."

"Yes. You were screaming. You screamed for days. Weeks."
She stopped, as if she'd said too much.

"I didn't know that. Sorry about that. Hope I didn't blow
your ears out. I didn't know I was that loud for that long."

She nodded, her face drawn. "You had a lot to say."

"Mom, what's wrong?"

"Time goes by so quickly."

I put my arm around her. She was pale, her happy energy not
there today. We headed out to the pond, then sat down on the
red bench, the lily pads floating, so soft, a blue heron taking off
in flight, his wings graceful, strong.

"Maybe I'm feeling sentimental, emotional, because Jules is
getting married. You own your own bookstore, you've turned a
run down carriage house into a home. You're both so smart and
strong and driven, and I love you two. You are my heart, you
and your sister, as you both were your father's heart, too."

I ached for my dad, a pain in my chest. The pain for a
beloved parent never leaves, I think; the grief sneaks up on you
sometimes, bringing an aloneness that only that parent can fill. I
took a deep breath as she wiped tears from her cheeks. "Mom,
what is it? There's something else. Are you sick? Is Aunt Camellia or Aunt Iris sick?"

"No, no. We're three healthy, old rebels who sometimes
drink too much wine."

"But you're upset." I was so worried. What was this all
about? There was something wrong. There had been something
wrong for weeks.

She smiled at me, too brightly. "Love for you two makes
me cry."

That wasn't it. She always told us she loved us and she didn't
cry about it. I pried a bit, and she diverted my questions,
changed the subject, I tried again, and she sashayed away con-

versationally speaking, and we started talking about the flowers she was going to plant for her fall bouquets inside the greenhouse. The blue heron came back, gliding over the pond.

I studied her. She was staring at the heron but not seeing it.

"Mom, please. What's wrong?"

"Nothing, dear. Nothing at all."

She lied.

My worry ratcheted up another ten notches.

Finally, my glorious cat appointment with Marco rolled around. I washed my hair and blew it out into a clean black wave. I put on red lacy underwear and a red lacy push-up bra. Marco would see neither, but I needed confidence. I pulled on a red shirt with ruffles down the front and unbuttoned one button too many. I laid on my bed to squeeze myself into my light blue jeans. I needed to go running or work out. I laughed as I sucked in to button them. Nah. That would hurt. I slipped in my earrings with three red roses hanging in a row.

As usual, I'd scheduled myself for the last appointment of the day. I told Gayle after Marco arrived on the island and I started bringing him my animals that I always needed the last appointment of the day because I worked late. I tried not to laugh when I said that. Gayle tried not to laugh, too. She is anything but dim.

"Of course you do, dear," she said, so calmly. "I'll always schedule you to be the last person here. I'll have to leave, to go home to . . . uh . . . uh . . . to talk to my cats, which will leave you and Marco alone, dear Evie. You and Marco alone. All by yourselves."

That day, after the shots were given to my cats, to their utmost outrage, shrieking and meowing, Gayle said with a smile, "See you tomorrow, Marco. Bye, Evie. Tell your mother and aunts I said toodles."

Marco was polite, friendly, after the cats' appointment was finished. They were irritated, but they'd get over it.

"Want to watch the sunset?" he asked.

Yes. No. I did! I couldn't. I shouldn't. I should leave. "Yes, I'd love that."

Marco had an area in his clinic for cats to play, and we left the little devils to their own devices. Ghost glared at me one more time for making her get her shots, then she bounded off while Mars wrapped himself around my leg, insecure and shy. Funny how animals have people characteristics.

We walked toward his house, the sun on its way down to sleep.

"Do you want wine?"

If I drank wine I'd probably end up wrapping myself around Marco like a drunken, naked nymph. "No, thanks."

"Want to watch the sunset from the deck or the beach?"

How about your bedroom? Can we lie on the bed? "Let's walk to your beach."

We chatted as we walked down a dirt trail, over a couple of rocks, to the sandy beach. We sat side by side on a log, watching the sun head down. There is nothing more peaceful than watching a sunset on the island. The sun's rays reflect on the water, the waves roll, the trees sway so gently, like a greeting to each other, the spray from whales shooting into the sky on lucky days, the other emerald green islands a postcard in the distance.

I closed my eyes and breathed. It is only here, on San Orcanita Island, that I get this peace. It's why I don't want to leave the island again, or as little as possible. I can be alone in nature yet have the people I love best, my mom and aunts, Jules, Marco, and my animals all right around me.

We sat in silence and watched that magical, moving painting. I teared up because I am a sap.

"You okay?" Marco asked.

"Yes. Sunsets make me cry."

"I understand. I try to watch as many sunsets as I can," Marco said.

"I do, too. Each one is like the last gift of the day." I turned to him and could see the emotion in his face. "I've had a lot of practice staring at sunsets to calm my brain down."

"Same here. There are a lot of nightmares that I battle with pretty regularly. Some are worse than others."

"Do they keep you up at night?"

"Yes."

"Do you sleep much?"

"No." He turned to me. "Do you?"

"I have insomnia. I read until I sleep."

"And you have premonitions."

There it was. What we hadn't talked about, but I'd known he knew. "Yes."

"All the time?"

"I have them sometimes."

"Do you want to talk about it?"

"Do you really want to hear about it? You'll think I'm out of my mind. Flat-out crazy."

"I have never thought that about you, and I won't when you tell me."

I told him, watching his face carefully so I could determine if and when he thought I was a lying loon, a delusional daisy. I told him when it started as a child and the premonitions I had then, through my teen years, and a few recent ones. I made sure I told him about a few premonitions that came through that could also be proven by others. For example, the little girl who was almost hit by the white truck.

"I heard about that one."

"Do you believe me, Marco?" Please believe me. "I don't want you to think I'm lying. I don't want you to laugh at me."

"Yes. I don't know why you have premonitions. If you were to ask me before I met you if I thought anyone could have premonitions, I would have said no. But I do believe you, Evie, and I would never laugh at you."

I wanted to sink into him, to hold him. "Thank you. It's a curse. I wish I didn't have them. I never wanted them. I try to control them as best I can, to shut them down."

"You said your premonitions eased up when you moved back to the island."

"Yes." I told him about moving suddenly to the island as a

child, the whispering my parents were doing then, their arguments. "I think they wanted to get me to the island in hopes that the quiet would quiet the premonitions down, and they were right. I have fewer premonitions here. When I go to Seattle or the mainland, they ramp right up. It's like getting hit with a Mack truck, only the Mack truck is carrying visions of the future for many people. The ocean is calming. The beach in front of my home is calming. The stars, the deer, the elk, all of my animals, especially Sundance, are calming."

He asked a few more questions, gently.

"I have no idea why I have premonitions about one person and not the other. I have no idea why I might have several in a week, then none for weeks or even, now and then, none for months. It happens out of the blue, and I can see someone's future, clear as if I'm watching it on TV." Except for that one recurring deathly crash premonition. . . .

"It sounds"—he paused—"awful."

"It is awful. I've struggled with it my whole life. After college I thought I was losing my mind. I worked for a chain bookstore, saved my money, then took a trip camping. A long trip. Months. My mind was breaking down and I needed to get away. A few times, when things were relentlessly bad, when I hit the skids, I haven't wanted to live."

He dropped his head into his hands.

"Marco."

He shoved his hands across his face and I could tell he was brushing away tears. "I'm sorry, Evie, I am."

"Don't be. There are billions of people on this planet struggling with far harder things."

He reached out a hand, and I took it automatically. His hand was warm and strong, and mine was lost in it. I was turned on from the second I saw Marco today. Every second with him heightened it. I was a mass of desire and lust.

I sensed his tension, too. I felt the vibes between us. How do you describe the sparks between people? He was looking at me, and I took a deep breath and we leaned in at the same time. Soon I was having the best kiss of my life, multiplied by a hundred. I was utterly lost in Marco, one arm around that broad back, one hand on his muscled thigh, and then he swung me up and over and onto his lap. He kissed so well. All of his attention into it, into me. I pressed myself against him, and he pulled me close.

Don't pant, I told myself, but soon I was whisked away and could no longer think. I unbuttoned his shirt quick as a lick, then put both hands on that broad, warm chest, exactly as I'd wanted to do since the first time I saw him. He was strong and muscled and smelled like a delicious cupcake and the island winds and Marco himself. Before I knew it my shirt was off and my red bra was somewhere else and we were half naked.

That kiss went on and on and I couldn't think, didn't want to think, until his hands were on the button of my too-tight jeans.

"Oh no. Oh no."

"What?" he said, still kissing me, wild and free and yummy.

I dragged myself off of him, feet in the sand, panting like I didn't want to pant, half naked in that sunset.

"What is it? What's wrong?" he asked. He stood up and towered over me. I wanted to grab him, hold him, tell him that nothing was wrong, and I wanted to straddle him on the sand.

"This is not a smart idea." I crossed my arms over my boobs.

"Why? Why not?"

"I'm not dating."

"You've told me that before. So let's not date." He took a step closer to me, pulled me in again, his shirt all the way unbuttoned because of my lust. "We will remain friends who hang out together."

"Marco, I'm standing in front of you half naked. That does not seem to indicate we can remain friends. Plus, I'm a mess. You don't want to date me."

"I like messes."

"I have problems, issues. Premonitions that freak me out."

"I have problems and issues. I do not have premonitions. I do have nightmares and scary flashbacks that take me straight back to Iraq and battles and blood and fighting and people dying and screaming. So if you are a mess who wants a mess, I'm the mess."

"I'm sorry, Marco. I truly am, but I can't. I can't do relationships. I can't have relationships. It doesn't work. They don't work for people who are wrecks."

"We can be wrecks together." His voice was low and deep, persuasive.

"No, I can't." My voice cracked, pain filling me from head to foot.

He sighed, pulled me in for a hug, his head resting on mine.

"Evie. Can we not try? Take it slow? Take it easy?"

I shook my head. I wanted to cry. Cry because I was rejecting Marco. I love Marco. I always will. "No, I'm sorry." And I turned, and I stumbled away, tears smearing my vision.

"Evie . . ."

I started jogging back to the clinic. It was when I was jogging, my boobs bouncing, that I realized I did not have my red lace bra or my red ruffled shirt. This was unfortunate, but I was not going to run back for them. I grabbed the cats out of the clinic, two in each hand as they meowed about the indignities of it, and put them in the truck.

I looked back at him when I was in my truck, trembling, wanting him so bad, at the same time wanting to have a meltdown. I had one cat on my shoulder, one in my lap, and two in the passenger seat. They had their paws on the window staring back at Marco as if they missed him already and their hearts were breaking, like mine.

I am doing this for your own good, Marco, so you will live.

On my way home, three minutes after I left Marco's, I saw the police lights, red and blue and flashing, behind me. A second later the siren pierced through the night. Chief Ass Burn was behind me. He must have been waiting for me, right by Marco's house. My stomach started to churn. How sick is that? I have a police chief stalking me.

I said a very bad word. Then another one. I wiped the hot tears off my face and told myself to buck up.

I was topless with cats meowing all over me. I searched frantically for something to put on, and I finally found it inside one of the cat kennels. Mars's favorite cat blanket. It's pink with white mice. I wrapped it around myself like a halter top, and in the nick of time I tucked it in under my armpits.

Chief Ass Burn rapped on my window, and I pushed the button to bring it down.

"Why did you pull me over?"

"You were swaying in your lane."

"No, I wasn't." I sure as heck wasn't.

"Step out of the car."

"You have got to be kidding."

"No, I'm not. I'm issuing you a Breathalyzer, Evie, to make sure you're not drunk."

"I'm not drunk. I haven't had anything to drink."

"Get out, Evie, or I'll arrest you for not obeying my orders." He smirked at me. Oh, how he loved this. Loved the power.

I climbed out of the truck, making sure the cats didn't escape. In the distance I saw headlights through the darkness. How embarrassing. I was being tested for being drunk in this small town. It would be all over by tomorrow.

"State your name." He eyed my naked shoulders, then his eyes dropped to my boobs.

"My name is Chief Ass Burn," I said. I let my eyes fall to his shoulders, then his beefy chest, then lower, all the while keeping a disgusted expression on my face. "I like to ogle women's breasts and make them feel judged and disgusted."

He flushed. "One more small-aleck answer, missy, and I will have you at the police station, overnight."

"Gross. Alone with you?"

"Name, Evie."

"You already know my name."

A truck stopped in back of Chief Ass Burn's police car. Whew. It was Marco.

"What's the problem, Reginald," Marco said, his voice hard. Suspicious.

"This isn't any of your business, Marco. And it's Chief Ashburn to you."

"I think it is my business, Reginald. Why did you pull Evie over?"

Marco stood protectively right by me, his shoulder in front of mine.

"Move out of the way, Marco, or I will arrest you."

"You're harassing, Evie. You're stalking her. You were waiting for her right outside my house. As soon as I saw her leave, I saw you follow her."

"I'm asking Evie questions, Marco, to make sure she's not drunk driving. Step aside!"

"She's been with me. She didn't drink anything."

Chief Ass Burn's mouth tightened, he flushed, then swallowed hard. "Move out of the way, Marco, before I arrest you for infringing upon my investigation and interfering with a possible arrest of an inebriated driver." He pointed at Marco, hating him.

"I'll answer the questions, Marco." I put my hand on his arm. He was so angry with Chief Ass Burn I thought we were going to have a fight. Marco was trained in the military. He was in top shape. He would whip Chief Ass Burn in two seconds, but it was Marco who would go to jail for years if he assaulted a police officer. I squeezed his arm, pressing myself closer to get his attention. "Please, Marco."

Finally, Marco stepped back about six inches.

I answered all of the chief's questions, including telling him the alphabet frontwards and backwards, counting by ten to two hundred, naming fifty states in a song when he asked me to name five, and I walked in a straight line in my cat's mouse blankie. Chief Ass Burn was more and more disgruntled that I was passing the tests and he couldn't take me back to the police station to be alone with him.

Marco stood right by me and fumed. At one point he said,

"Why don't you ask her to speak in French to ascertain she isn't drunk?" and "Maybe if you had her count to a million you could get a better idea as to her inebriation. See if she can remember all the words to 'Phantom.' "

Two cars pulled over. Three islanders crossed the street to see what was going on.

The chief finally gave me a Breathalyzer test. He tried to stand close to me, but I said, "I am not comfortable with you standing so close. I can smell the onions on your breath and your body odor."

"Step back," Marco said, glaring at Chief Ass Burn.

The three people, all longtime friends, crowded around Chief Ass Burn, Marco, and me.

I blew into the Breathalyzer. The chief was clearly disappointed.

"What did I blow?"

"I'm not required to tell you."

"Actually," Elizabeth Bellagiio said, who was a judge, "you are. What did she blow?"

"The test shows no alcohol," Chief Ass Burn muttered reluctantly, with disappointment and embarrassment.

"Then she's not drunk and she's allowed to leave," Marco said. He turned me toward my truck.

"That's correct," the judge said. "Unless there is another problem, Chief?"

"Yes. She was swaying in her lane, so I'm issuing her a ticket."

"I was not swaying in my lane." I had been upset, that was true. But my eyes had never left the road.

Marco said, "I'm reporting you again for false charges and for stalking Evie."

It was Marco and me and the judge and the two other friends, all in line facing the chief, glaring.

"Go ahead, Marco. Be my guest." He smirked at me. "If you want your ticket reduced, come and see me, Evie. You might get lucky."

I grabbed Marco's arm as he lost it with the chief, as did Mel

Stanton, a brawny fisherman who got in Marco's face and said, "Man, calm down. Don't do it." The judge, standing right in front of him, said, "Back off, Marco. You won't win with your fists here."

"Stop stalking me," I said to the chief. Marco's jaw was so tight I thought he might break his teeth.

"I'm not stalking you. I'm enforcing the law, Evie," the chief said, smirking again. "And you will follow it. See you soon."

We watched the chief drive away. I was so mad I wanted to spit nails. I glanced at the amount of the ticket. It was another fortune. If you received a certain amount of tickets in one year, couldn't they take your license? Couldn't they cancel your insurance? I would not be able to drive my truck.

"Give that to me," Marco said, and took it, seething.

"I like that pink halter shirt, Evie," the judge said. "Is that a new style?"

"It's such a soft material," Maci LaFolette said. "Plus, the white mice are cute."

"Thank you." I felt the anger drain out of me. I didn't look at Marco. If I did, I would have laughed. Probably half hysterically, but I would have laughed.

After everyone left, Marco said, "I thought you might need this."

He handed me my red lacy bra and red ruffled shirt.

"I'll follow you home, Evie," he said, so gentle.

I nodded my head, then turned around and gave him a hug, because the truth was that the chief was creeping me out and Marco was my hero.

He followed me home down Robbins Drive and turned off at my driveway.

The cats missed him immediately.

Late that night I sat outside on my front porch and watched my mother and aunts' flowers swaying in a slight wind, the darkness casting shadows. I tried to calm my anger. Sundance sat right beside me on the step, and Mars lay sleeping in my lap.

I had a vase of Judi Dench apricot roses nearby, and their scent was sweet and pure.

Flowers are so delicate, intricate. They are natural wonders and miracles. How come daffodils look like the sun? Why are irises so elegant, a blend of colors that seem magically hand-painted? And peonies. Are they three flowers squished into one? So full, so perfumy.

I wiped away a few tears. Sundance edged closer to me.

"Oh no!" Mr. Bob and Trixie Goat ran over to me, their bells clanging in the night. I swear they were smiling. I laughed. "How did you escape again?"

That's why I keep animals. I love them and they make me laugh, even when I'm crying.

Later, Marco sent me a copy of my ticket. He had paid it. But he attached a letter that he had sent to Chief Ass Burn's superior, detailing the traffic stop and the exorbitant cost of the ticket and what Chief Ass Burn had said to me.

Wow. The man could write.

I thanked him by giving him five books I knew he'd love. I brought them to his clinic.

"Thank you, Marco." I had given him a check for the ticket. He had ripped it up.

"My pleasure, but you didn't need to give me these books. It was the least I could do. I'm sorry it happened."

"I'll be glad when Chief Allroy is back."

"Me too."

I wanted to hug him, but I didn't. I smiled, turned away. I knew he was watching me get into my truck and drive away from his idyllic home on the island with, undoubtedly, a bouncy and comfy bed where I would not get to bounce or be comfy.

"You're not selling pot out of Flowers, Lotions, and Potions, are you?" I set my fork down on my table. I had invited my mother and aunts for dinner at my place. I had candles down the center of the table, interspersed with Mister Lincoln red roses in three glass vases.

I'd made chicken parmigiana and lemon pie. No. That's a lie. I bought chicken parmigiana from the new Italian restaurant and a lemon pie from Bettina. I had a small piece of lemon pie before dinner to cleanse my palate.

"No, heavens no!" My mother's tone was outraged, as if I had asked her if she stole horses from neighboring farms.

"Goodness gracious golly! How could you think that?" Aunt Camellia said, all high-and-mighty. "Marijuana? In Flowers, Lotions, and Potions? Never." She shook her finger at me. "Don't even suggest it, young woman."

"We are businesswomen," Aunt Iris said, her brow furrowed at me. "We make decisions that positively affect our profit line and elevate the level of the company. We do not sell products that do not enhance this goal."

"We can't have people coming to the counter and saying, 'One tulip bouquet, one joint,'" my mother said. "Or 'Roses and mowie wowie, please!'"

"Oh, my gosh," I moaned, knowing my question was perfectly legitimate. "I'm not intimidated."

I had seen a number of people following my mother and aunts to the greenhouse. Chatting, laughing, gossiping. They would come out with a small bag of marijuana, wrapped in a pink ribbon. Yes, pink. And the pink ribbon always held a flower, a black-eyed Susan, white daisy, lupine, dahlia, or snapdragons, depending on what they had in the greenhouse and outside. They were selling *pretty* pot.

"Nothing wrong with making pot lovely," my mother said when I talked to her and my aunts about it.

"Flowers add love to life," Aunt Camellia said, clasping her hands together in joy. "Romance. A taste of floral heaven."

"Packaging is important from a practical, marketing perspective," Aunt Iris said. "We are a business."

"I'm so excited about our Antarctica trip!" my mother said, clapping her hands after one more reprimanding glance in my direction.

"You're not going to follow my advice, are you?" I said. Dang it. I had neatly piled up about twenty-five books against the light blue armoire into which my grandma Lucy used to climb and sing songs, and Venus jumped up on it and knocked it over.

"More lemon pie, honey?" my mother said, holding her hand out for my plate.

"Advice can be given but not acted upon if the receiver does not intellectually or spiritually agree," Aunt Camellia said.

"If we want your advice on our Antarctica business, we'll ask for it, young lady," Aunt Iris said. Then she squeezed my hand to take the sting out of her words.

I stared at them with some suspicion as they dug into their lemon pie with an overload of enthusiasm.

They had the munchies, didn't they?

Chapter 26

❧

Betsy Baturra
Women's Correctional Prison
Salem, Oregon
1978

After performing dish-cleaning duty in the kitchen one night, Duke lay in wait for Betsy. Duke had been able to switch shifts without much notice. There was a new guy handling the schedules and he didn't know all the dynamics yet. He didn't know that Duke had many enemies and he was not supposed to be near Betsy. He didn't know that Coralee was doing her best to keep Duke away from her.

Duke excused one of the guards and said he would take Betsy back to her cell. The guard was new and young, and he knew Duke was the warden's nephew.

Betsy began to shake as Duke took her elbow. "No, Duke, Carson is supposed to take me back. Carson, you take me back."

"I-I . . ." Carson stuttered. "I'll do it, Mr. Duke. I'm supposed to do it. I've . . . I've been assigned."

Duke told Carson to stop "being a pussy. Shove off, Carson, or I'll report you."

Carson said, "It's my job," and Duke slammed him into a wall. Carson sunk to the ground.

"See?" Duke laughed, bending down and putting his face smack up to Carson's. "You are a pussy."

When they rounded that one blind corner, right by the supply closet, where Duke knew the cameras didn't reach, he quickly opened the door. Betsy's hands had not yet been cuffed by Carson, and Duke hadn't noticed in his hurry to steal her away. He shoved her up against the metal shelves, her face crashing into an edge, then pulled on her orange pants, yanking them to her knees, as she fought through the dizziness.

Duke kept one sweaty hand pressed into her back, her face and chest smashed into the shelves. Through the ringing in her ears she heard him unzipping his zipper, undoing his belt, and pulling his pants down. He was panting. He was groaning. He said, his breath hot and putrid on her neck, "And now you're going to get what you've been wanting, Betsy. Begging for." He put his hand around her neck. "If you make a sound, I will snap your neck."

For a second, she didn't move, couldn't move, couldn't breathe, her head splitting, but then he moved his hand to take down her underwear, and suddenly she could breathe again.

She was disgusted. She was sick with fear. She was about to be raped by a repulsive, gross, violent man. All of her fury over losing Rose and Johnny, being constantly watched and harassed by Duke, being locked up, it all roared out. It roared out through the fog of depression that she lived in behind the cold, scary bars. It rose from the deepest part of her soul, this animalistic, teeth-baring, rollicking rage.

Betsy, her orange prison pants down around her ankles, a raw scream emanating from her throat, picked up a container of cleaning powder and swung it at Duke's head with both hands, as hard as she could. The container bashed his cheek, and cleaning powder sprayed his face, burning his eyes. He let out a guttural yell of outrage and swore from the pain, temporarily blinded.

She then picked up a broom and rammed the handle right into his naked groin. He yelled and bent over, breathless. She yanked up her pants and kicked him as hard as she could in the head with another scream of fury, and he went down, stumbling to the floor, his eyes squeezed shut against the stinging powder, one hand on his balls. For good measure, she kicked him in his huge gut, which blew his air straight out, his face red and strained.

She bent over his writhing form and told him about the premonition she'd had. "You're going to hit a deer, Duke. It's going to come straight through the window of your truck. Your truck will hit a tree. You will never walk again."

Duke felt a cold rush of fear flood his insides. He wanted to kick her, shut her up, hold her down and finish the plan, but he couldn't move. She kicked him in the head again and screamed as she opened the door to the supply closet.

Guards rushed in, hearing the screams.

"She attacked me," Duke said, rolling on the floor, swearing, his face covered in cleaning powder. "Betsy attacked me." He struggled to get up, still holding his balls, no one helping him. "That woman is a psych patient. She shouldn't even be here. She's a danger." He tried to roll over, to stand up, but he forgot his pants and underwear were around his ankles. He tripped and fell, straight down, naked butt up.

No one helped him up. He swore again, rolled over, then bent to pull up his pants over his rapidly swelling groin, hardly able to see because of the cleaning powder in his eyes. "I need water for my eyes! Water! Water!" He stumbled out. "Get me water!"

"I didn't attack him," Betsy said, scared now, defeated, because she knew she would be in isolation by that night, probably for months. She wrapped her arms around her skinny waist and stared at all the guards, begging Coralee with her eyes to believe her.

"Duke made Carson leave so he could take me to my cell. He shoved Carson, and Carson hit the floor. Go talk to Carson. Duke knows there's a blind corner here that the cameras don't reach. He pulled me in and shoved me against the shelf." Betsy didn't know it, but her eye was black and swelling rapidly. She also had a swelling cut across her cheek that was bleeding down her neck. She was pale.

"I defended myself because he was going to rape me. That's why his pants were down around his ankles."

"I believe you, Betsy," Coralee said gently. She'd seen it all in the few years she'd been here. She couldn't wait to get out and go to law school. She'd seen sick, dangerous inmates, and she'd seen sick, dangerous guards. "This will never happen to you again. I'm sorry."

Betsy bent her head, leaned against the shelves, and passed out, her head a mass of pain. Coralee and two other guards caught her and brought her to the infirmary, where for once she had a kind nurse and a kind doctor. They let her stay two extra days to rest.

She was not sent to isolation.

Duke was fired from the jail by his uncle. Duke about lost his mind, he was so mad. He shoved everything off of his uncle's desk before he left. He would immediately tell his mother and she would give his uncle a piece of her mind! Wouldn't she?

Life was so stupid unfair. Betsy caused him to get fired. She teased him. Flirted with him. She wanted him, and he fell for it. He hated Coralee, too. He would get back at her. He knew where Coralee lived. Coralee thought she was better than him. She was a woman. They could never be better than him. He would pay her a visit. He had paid many women "visits" over the years, starting in high school, when they rejected him.

He went to the doctor because of his still-swollen groin. The doctor said there might be "permanent damage." The doctor, a woman, did not seem to believe Duke's story about how a woman inmate "went wild" on him. His eyes burned for two days, turned red, and his vision blurred. His head pounded where Betsy had kicked him, and his gut was all bruised up. It even hurt to drink beer.

He would get his revenge on Betsy if she ever got out of jail, he thought, getting super drunk that night, then passing out on the patio of his apartment.

Three days later, after hitting the deer, crushed against his steering wheel and unable to move or feel his legs, he remembered what Betsy had said.

Duke never walked again. He never attacked anyone again. He was alone and bitter the rest of his life.

Chapter 27

∽

Tilly Kandinsky
Portland, Oregon
1975–1985

Tilly, Johnny's younger sister, stopped speaking on the night her father was killed. She had been a frightened, quiet child ever since her mother left, cowering from her raging father, but that night she completely shut down.

Tilly hid behind the couch during Johnny's argument with her father, but she saw everything, she heard everything. She saw the knife, she saw the blood, she saw her father collapse. When the police tried to talk to her, she moaned and rocked back and forth and cried. She could not explain what happened, her eyes staring into the air at a faraway place.

She buried the trauma, the murder, the screaming, the gush of blood.

Tilly was sent into the foster care system, where she was almost catatonic for the first year. Eventually, lost in the system, she had the usual and expected horrific things happen to her: Abuse. Neglect. No love or care. Shipped from one house to another, one school to another, where she disappeared to other people and to herself. A few of her teachers tried to help, tried to get her to talk, but she wouldn't. Mostly, though, she was ignored. Dismissed. Case workers were in and out who barely remembered her name. In fact, at one stretch she didn't see a case worker for almost two years.

She was put into a mental health institution because she was fourteen and still hardly talking, so she must be crazy. The mental health institution did more to harm her than help. Tilly roomed with psychotic teens. Dangerous teens. Suicidal or homicidal teens. And some who were like her: traumatized. Many were from foster care. Some were poor. Others were middle class or from prominent and wealthy families.

Tilly rarely saw a psychiatrist, and when she did, all he did was stare at her chest. Another one hardly looked at her and spent ten minutes with her filling out paperwork and calling her mother about a bad date she'd had the night before. The man was such a jerk, the psychiatrist whined to mommy. Didn't even pay for dinner!

Finally, at sixteen, she was moved to a new foster care home. She was the only child. The couple was in their sixties, patient, and wanted to help kids. It was the first time she felt love since her mother and Johnny.

Tilly also saw a therapist named Kate. Kate was compassionate, smart, and experienced with working with traumatized kids. She tried to get Tilly to open up. Once a week Tilly went to her appointment, and they played cards together. Eventually Tilly said yes or no, then spoke in short sentences. With the kind steadiness of her new foster parents behind her, she started to talk more. She started to remember what happened that night, bits and pieces sliding in and out of her mind, one vision after another.

Tilly remembered her father yelling at Johnny and Johnny yelling back. They were fighting about her mother, who had left when she was five years old. There was something else she was trying to remember. It nagged at her brain. It was right there, almost there, a whisper, a hidden secret . . . something happened that night before her mother left . . . what had she seen? What did she know? What was trying to come through from the prickly shadows of her scared and damaged mind? It had something to do with her mother . . . something Johnny said.

Her therapist told her that her memory was coming back and not to push it but to embrace it. To be brave. Tilly tried not to push it, but whatever it was scared her, like a threatening monster of hate. The monster was trying to tell her things that made her shake. Not only about the night her father died, but about a night that happened two years before that.

Tilly eventually realized that she needed to remember everything for Johnny. For Betsy.

So she allowed her memories to crawl back in, inch by inch, so they wouldn't kill her, which was one more brave thing that Tilly Kandinsky had to do in a life filled with fear and other utterly terrifying events.

Chapter 28

∽

I entertained myself with daydreams of Marco and me. Why did I do that to myself? It hurt. It made me feel lonely and lost and hopeless.

I did it anyhow. I daydreamed of us dating and in bed and taking care of all our animals and reading on his deck as the sun slid down into the ocean and being in bed together and hiking around the island and going to the cool lake and hugging through the night in bed.

I daydreamed when I worked, and rode Shakespeare and Jane Austen, and chased the goats who escaped again, and tossed a ball to Sundance, Butch, and Cassidy. I daydreamed about Marco when I was with my mother and aunts at their house and we were making hats.

"Are you all right, dear?" my mother asked when we were at Rose Bloom Cottage on a warm evening, the ocean frothing at the edge of our property, a greeting of sorts, the clouds puffy. We were making hats for a fund-raiser for the community center. My mother had piled her white hat high with faux roses in pink, white, and red. It was definitely a Dr. Seuss kind of hat. She had strung red buttons together and wrapped them around the roses like a ribbon. At the top of the pile of roses she had placed a tiny red, sequined hat. "A hat on a hat," she'd told me, smiling.

"I believe that something is off with your spirit," Aunt Camellia said. Her hat was the widest hat she'd ever made. It was burgundy, floppy, netting over the front. There was a magical garden all over it, complete with daisies, irises, and tulips, a willow tree, a small barn, and a tiny light blue house. "I have recreated our garden."

"Everything going well with the bookstore?" Aunt Iris asked. Her hat was blue felt, and simple, until she glued silver sequins all over the brim, then attached a giant two-foot-long peacock she'd bought online. "For some reason, peacocks remind me of how important correct money management is."

"I'm fine."

They glanced at each other, worrying.

"Don't worry," I told them.

"It's what I do best," my mother said. "Worry about you."

"She's quite talented at worrying about you," Aunt Camellia said. "As you know, dear. It's in her genes, she cannot remove it. It's part of who she is, as your mother."

"It's going to cause you to get an ulcer, Poppy," Aunt Iris said. "You have to stop."

"Mothers worry," my mother said. "We can't stop."

"I love you three," I said. My hat was something you would see a woman wearing to the Kentucky Derby. Red. Enormous brim. I was adding twenty purple ribbons to the back that would hang down about three feet. To the front I pinned felt flowers in yellow and white, with pink centers.

"I love you, too, darling daughter," my mother said. "You and your sister and my sisters."

"I love you, too, my fairy sprite," Aunt Camellia said, attaching a plastic butterfly that wiggled on a spring.

"I've always loved you," Aunt Iris said, pressing down on the sequins. "No need to get mushy about it."

It was a sweet moment.

Until a cloud came over my mother's face, dark as a thundering night.

After school one day, when I was fourteen years old, I had a premonition. I hadn't told my friend Emily I had premonitions because my parents said I shouldn't tell anyone on the island.

Jules was sworn to secrecy, too. They did know that sometimes I took action with the premonitions in order to prevent them from happening, and they helped me sometimes, too, to save someone, but we all tried to work as quietly and as anonymously as possible.

My father, being in the military, was especially helpful on our "reconnaissance missions," or our "spy sorties," or our "Victorious Adventures." He named them so that I wouldn't be so afraid of what I'd seen and would view helping people as an adventure, not a scary burden.

I had a premonition about Emily's mother, Patsy. I saw her with a man I didn't recognize. He was tall with a reddish beard. In my premonition, they had a terrible fight and he shook her, then pushed her, and her head hit the wood floors in her kitchen with a bounce. The blood spilled into a dark puddle, and she died.

The boyfriend stood over her, panting, furious, then scared. He started to shake her, calling her name, begging her to "Wake up, Patsy! Oh, my God. Oh, my God! Patsy!" He started to cry.

I was petrified. Sure enough, Emily told me that her mother had started dating a man she didn't like. I met the man, who had a reddish beard, and I didn't like him, either. I told my parents my premonition, and I swear their faces went white.

They invited Emily; Patsy; and the boyfriend, Gavin, over for dinner at Rose Bloom Cottage. After they left, my parents talked and I eavesdropped.

"I can see it, Poppy," my father said to my mother when they thought I was in my bedroom. "He's controlling. He's too intense. He watches Patsy all the time. In the military we get rid of that kind of guy."

"I didn't like him at all," my mother said. "There's a simmering anger there. He's so possessive and suspicious."

My parents sat down to decide what to do. Both of them soon told Patsy, gently, that they didn't like Gavin, didn't trust him, were concerned. She was offended and hurt and did not break up with him.

So that strategy didn't work.

Then, when Patsy had a bruise on her face, my mother called the police chief, who arrested Gavin. But Patsy didn't want to press charges, she said she fell against her car, and she let Gavin back in the house.

So that didn't work, either.

My father went to talk to Gavin, who used to work in construction but now seemed to laze about their house, now and then doing odd jobs around the island. He told Gavin he knew he was beating Patsy and it had to stop. He told Gavin he would regret hurting Patsy. Gavin was scared of my father, who was tall and had a steely gaze, but it didn't stop him.

The bruises kept coming.

My father bought Patsy a gun. They later learned that Gavin found it, though Patsy had hidden it in the back of her underwear drawer, which showed that Gavin was going through her things. Gavin was "hellfire furious at you," she told my father, weeping. "He says he's going to beat you up."

My father laughed.

Finally, desperate, I told Patsy what I had seen for her future when I was at her house after school playing warrior princesses with Emily, even though my parents told me I should never tell anyone on the island about my premonitions.

"Miss Patsy," I said in a whisper, even though Gavin wasn't home, "Gavin is going to kill you. You're going to get in a fight and he's going to push you hard and you're going to crack your head open on your kitchen floor and die."

She looked alarmed, shocked, then she said, "Stop it, Evie. You're like your parents. I get it. You don't like Gavin. But I love him, he loves me. He's got a temper, but he can be kind and he treats me like a princess. I can change him. Love can change him. He'll change, you'll see. He had a hard childhood." She knitted her hands together. The hands that made such unique, colorful art. Her pottery sold right off the shelves at Island Pottery, my mother told me, "as soon as she can make it, it's gone. Patsy has such talent."

"You aren't a princess," I whispered to Patsy, so scared.

"He's going to kill you unless you tell him to get out of your house, and then Emily is not going to have a mom."

"I can't believe you're talking like this, Evie. Like you can see the future when you can't."

Patsy looked at me with fear, her eyes blinking rapidly. She didn't believe what I was saying, for the most part, but inside she knew what I was saying could be true. It *could* happen. Gavin was violent. Patsy was young. She'd had Emily when she was nineteen, and she was still naively hopeful, blaming herself. "I provoke him. I make him angry. But we make up. He doesn't hit me very hard and he's always sorry. Plus, this"—she waved at the bruise on her face—"doesn't happen often."

"It happens a lot, Mom," Emily said. "He hits you and hurts you and you cry. You think I don't hear you crying, but I do. It's scary. He's scary." Emily burst into tears.

Patsy opened and shut her mouth.

"I hear it when you two are in your bedroom. I can hear you crying when he's saying bad words to you. That's why I pound on the door. To make him stop. I don't like him, Mom. I don't want him here."

Patsy was shocked, but defeated, too, and infinitely sad. Gavin was a master manipulator, and Patsy had been alone and lonely and vulnerable for a long time. Sometimes he could be endearing, engaging, charismatic, and sensitive. Gavin had money. He bought her new clothes. They were conservative clothes, high necked because he said he didn't like Patsy "looking like a sexy, dumb hippy" in her island clothes, but Patsy wore them anyhow. She went from embroidered, flowing, modern clothes, with necklaces and tight jeans, to high-necked sweaters in gray and white.

But she had a man! She had a boyfriend! Gavin would provide. He'd already told her that he would put Emily through college. She was not able to see the facts, though: The man hardly worked. How could he put anyone through college?

"How do you know he's going to kill her?" Emily asked me, her voice weak and scared. "How?"

"Sometimes I can see the future." I whispered the words, not wanting to tell my secret, but I had to tell them because Patsy was so nice and I didn't want Emily to have no mother. "But don't tell anyone. Please. It's a secret."

"No one can see the future," Patsy said, but her voice wavered. "Don't lie, Evie. That's wrong. I'm going to talk to your mother about this."

"Go ahead. She already knows. That's why my parents keep trying to get you to break up with Gavin." Her face went white. "Miss Patsy, he's going to kill you. You have to break up with him. That's what I'm trying to tell you. You can come and live with us until the chief can get rid of him and get him off the island. My dad is in the army and he has guns."

But Patsy wasn't ready to kick Gavin out. She loved him! He was always so sorry after he lost his temper. He was getting better.

"Leave him," my father told her.

"Leave him," my mother told her. "Come and live with us. Let my husband handle Gavin."

I remembered what Patsy was wearing in my premonition when she was killed, and every day after school when she picked Emily up, I looked at her clothes. Nope. She wasn't wearing the brown sweater, beige slacks, and a pumpkin scarf. I even told Emily, "When your mom is wearing the brown sweater and beige slacks and her scarf with pumpkins on it, bring her to our house. Hide her. That's the day she's going to get killed."

"Okay, Evie." She took a deep breath. "I'm scared."

The school's Halloween dance was coming up, and Emily and I and Jules and her friend Sunflower were going to be characters from *The Wizard of Oz*. My mom made our costumes. I was the wicked witch, Jules was the straw man, Sunflower was the good witch, and Emily was Dorothy.

We were all so excited that when I saw Miss Patsy in the car waiting to pick up Emily after school, I forgot to check her clothes. So did Emily. Emily and I decided that she should come to my house right after school. Her mom said yes, and we ran off while Patsy drove off to her bloody death, her life spilling out of her on her kitchen floor.

If I hadn't been so excited about Halloween, I would have noticed what Patsy was wearing. I would have told my parents, and they would have helped me figure out what to do. Maybe they would have raced to get Patsy, or invented an errand, or my dad would have taken Gavin off for a beer or down to our boat.

We could have prevented it.

But I was young and having fun, and I forgot, and Emily, my best friend, and her mother, Miss Patsy, a beautiful young woman, who was trapped, paid the price.

"I'm coming over to the island soon!" Jules said. "I'm packing up all my wedding stuff in the truck. I've been painting motorcycles night and day because these orders keep coming in, and I'm almost done. Last night I painted a mermaid. The owner wanted her to have purple hair. So pretty. Anyhow, I'm going to take time off to relax before the wedding and the honeymoon because we'll be in bed all the time, and I don't want to be sleepy!"

I smiled at Jules through Skype. She was packing as we talked. "Look at our gifts for the wedding guests!"

Oh. My. They were black cloth headbands with JULES AND MACK FOREVER in white along the front. You tied them in the back and the ends hung down through your hair. Very stylish and motorcycle-ish.

"They're cool and radical and perfect," I said. "Everyone will love them."

"It's a way to unite everyone, pull us all together on the day when Mack and I commit to our passion and come together forever and ever as one body."

"I can't wait to put mine on. Finally, I will be cool, look cool. Your wedding is going to be a bash."

"Oh, Evie," Jules choked out, her fingers laced together, tears coming forth. "You're always so supportive of me. Everything I do. You're so encouraging. You told me to start my motorcycle painting business, and now I have six people working for me. And you told me to give Mack a chance and I did, and now look. He's my soul mate. My love mate. My bed mate. We don't even fight. If we have a disagreement he says, 'Let's go to bed and think about it,' and then we make love and we forget what the little argument was about. He goes to work and takes care of all those sick kids and they love him and I do my business and then he comes home and we have a quickie before dinner and then we talk and I tell him my problems and worries and he hugs me in bed and lets me lie on top of him until I feel better. And all because you said, 'Give Mack a chance.' You've always wanted me to be happy and yet you have to deal with fortune-telling and it's made your life so hard, yet you want me to be happy . . ." She stopped, overcome. She blew her nose. She snuffled.

"You're making me cry again, Jules. Please don't." I wiped my tears.

"Okay, okay! But I love you, love-sister!" Her voice pitched up, chin trembling. "Wait. Evie." She wiped her tears away. "I know I've asked you this already, but have you had any premonitions about us?"

"No, I haven't." And that was true. Premonitions work in odd ways. "But I feel your happiness. I feel his happiness. I feel your love together."

"Oh! Oh! Oh!" She put her head down, hands to face, overcome.

"Don't do it, Jules, don't do it! You're making me cry more!" My voice broke. Dang it! She makes me cry too much! We both burst into a fresh round of sloppy, noisy tears.

"I can't believe you're getting married!" I sobbed.

"Me either." She put a hand to Skype, and I touched her fingertips to mine.

It's so exhausting being this emotional.

On a sunny morning, blue and sweet, Mr. Jamon told me he wanted a book "set in Africa. I've never been there, I obviously won't go now, so I need to learn about it. I've only read about twenty books on Africa—I checked my book list on my computer—so my education is lacking on that continent. What do you have?"

I gave him my two favorites.

"And one more romance."

We went to the romance section. He chose another bodice ripper set in the 1800s. He winked at me. "Getting to know my feminine side in 1850."

I laughed.

"We all need love, don't we?"

"We sure do, Mr. Jamon."

"I'm an old man who still believes in romance!"

It is hard to catch goats.

Goats are quick and they are tricky. They don't like to be caught, they don't want to be caught, they want to be independent and free.

I finally grabbed Mr. Bob and threw a rope around his neck. If he were human, he would be a rebel. Leather coat and a cigarette hanging out of his mouth, his jaw unshaved.

"Stop it, Mr. Bob, right now!" I told him. He bucked about and struggled. I had to grab him so I could check his left back hoof. He seemed to be limping. "Stop fighting. Dang it, Mr. Bob!" He pulled on the rope and it shouldn't have caught me off balance, but it did. I tripped over my boots and landed in mud, the "leash" slipping right from my hand.

He wriggled out of the loop around his neck and took off, bucking his back legs at me. When he was ten yards away, he glanced back at me as if to say, "Ha. Ha. I have outrun you again, peasant. Bring me more food."

Trixie trotted up and sniffed me. She is a gentle sort, but she has a temper. She ran over and bucked Mr. Bob in the head. Mr. Bob ran away, and she came back to check on me. We are bonded in woman power. I know she's a feminist.

Sundance growled, then ran after Mr. Bob, who skittered away and then jumped on the roof of his blue house. Sundance barked at him, my dear friend.

I pulled myself up and out of the sludge and wiped myself off. I looked over at the sheep in the next section. They were gazing innocently back at me as in, "We had nothing to do with this. We are innocent."

Shakespeare and Jane Austen looked at me, chewing their hay. "That goat is annoying," I could almost hear them saying. "Such a pest."

Mars, Jupiter, Venus, and Ghost watched from various areas, two sitting on the fence.

I had a feeling they were all laughing at me in a kind and loving way, as if I had deliberately entertained them.

"Fine, you rebellious and difficult goat!"

Mr. Bob threw his hooves in the air on top of the roof to show me who was boss, and I ducked between the slats in the white fence and headed home, through rows of hydrangeas, columbines, and purple and yellow daisies. I needed a shower. I was now dirty and sweaty because of a naughty goat.

Sundance ran up beside me and licked my hand. What a pal.

Chapter 29

⤙⤐

Tilly Kandinsky
Portland, Oregon
1985

When Tilly was seventeen years old, she was able to put all the drifting, terrorizing pieces of her life together like a puzzle, and she remembered the night her father was killed.

She flinched as she remembered her father punching Johnny in the face, screaming at him . . . She saw Betsy bursting through the front door, her face not surprised at all, as if she knew what she would see . . . then Betsy turned toward the kitchen and ran back out with a butcher knife in her hands and stabbed her father after he hit Johnny again, Johnny's head snapping back.

Tilly remembered, too, what her brother and father were fighting about, and what Johnny accused her father of doing. Was Johnny right?

Tilly's mother left when she was five. That's when they all of a sudden moved away to Oregon from Idaho. But as her mind cleared, Tilly began to wonder if her father was telling the truth about her mother leaving her. Her mother had loved her. She had told Tilly she loved her every day. She hugged her all the time, made her Mickey Mouse waffles on Sunday and her lunches for school every day. She tucked notes into her lunch sack. She took her for ice cream and to the movies, even if her mother had bruises on her face or she walked with a limp after what her father had done to her.

Tilly's father told her that her mother had left them when she got up one night to give her a hug because she'd had a nightmare. Her father was all dirty, mud dripping off of him, standing in the family room in his black gardening boots.

"Your mother left us," he said, panting, his face red and sweaty. "She doesn't love us anymore."

"What? Yes, she does," she protested, already tearing up. "She loves me."

"No, she doesn't, Tilly. She had a boyfriend and she moved out, and we're moving, too. Start packing."

"I don't want to go without Mommy! I'm not leaving without Mommy!"

Her father slapped her across the face, sending her sprawling into a wall, and told her, "Shut up and quit crying, you stupid baby."

Then Johnny came out of his bedroom. He was fifteen years old. Her father told him that they were moving, that their mother had left them. "No she didn't," he said. "She didn't leave us, she wouldn't do that."

Their father roared and grabbed Johnny by the throat and shoved him against the same wall and told him to shut up, too, or he would "beat the hell out of him." Tilly screamed. "Let him go! Let him go! Daddy! Stop, he can't breathe!"

They moved the next morning and left Idaho. Tilly remembered that her father told a neighbor, an elderly man they passed on the way out of town, that the "whole family is moving," which was strange because he had told her that her mother had left them. Maybe he was embarrassed that his wife had left him, she thought, initially. . . .

And now, with Kate, her patient therapist, Tilly finally allowed herself to think about her loving mother, how Gabriella never would have left them . . . and what the dirt on her father's boots meant.

Tilly had never read Johnny and Betsy's trial transcripts, but she read them now. That was the last piece of the puzzle. The therapist said, "What are you going to do now?"

Tilly told her.

The therapist nodded at her. "I was hoping you would say that."

Tilly was working hard in high school, dreaming of going to college, and she had a job at an ice-cream parlor.

With money from that job, and three hundred dollars from her foster parents, she flew to her old home in Idaho. After she landed, she took a bus and then hitchhiked. Their old home, out in the country, off a dirt road, no neighbors around, stood tilting. Abandoned. A lazy raccoon and an alarmed possum darted out when she stepped into the entry.

The house was dark, shabby, rickety. Yet the curtains with the embroidered Mexican flowers her mom had sewn were still there. She would wash them and use them herself. She picked up some of her mother's other things that had not been stolen: two flowered aprons; one tablecloth with red tulips, and one with a Mexican village; several mugs and her favorite teapot painted with a Mexican family. She took a few of her mother's colorful Mexican-style shirts and skirts that still hung in the closet like ghosts.

Tilly, her hands shaking, found her mother's faux pearl alarm clock under the bed, two red-framed photos of cats they had owned before her father had killed them, and her mother's colorful silk scarves, one of which her father wound tightly around her mother's neck one rainy night. She decided to leave that one at the house.

She found a black garbage bag for her mother's treasures, then grabbed two dolls she hadn't had time to take when they left. She looked through a collection of children's books her mother had bought her. Some were too moldy to keep, but she managed to salvage five.

Tilly lifted a floorboard under her mother's nightstand and pulled out a purple sock. Her mother's money was still there:

$800. She remembered her mother hiding money from her father, probably so she and Tilly and Johnny could one day escape.

Tilly sat on her parents' bed frame and cried like she hadn't cried in years. After she pulled herself together, she brought the bag outside, took a deep breath, and went searching for what she didn't want to find but knew she needed to find.

She crawled under the house. It was moldy and smelled like a sewage. The house had tilted, so one part was open to more daylight than the other. She saw nothing there. She headed to their crumbling red barn. She climbed up to the hayloft and peeked around, then she explored their weathered outbuilding and saw nothing except tools and her father's old lawnmower.

Tilly knew that the house, barn, and outbuilding had been searched by the police after Johnny accused their father of killing their mother during his trial. When she read the trial transcripts, her brother had never mentioned a door in the ground. Why would he? He didn't know about it. She had remembered the door only recently, when she'd started thinking more and more about how her mother disappeared. The door that skipped through her mind was ominous, dirty, so scary she blocked it out for years.

But Tilly remembered one time, before her mother died, when she had followed her father. She held her pink teddy bear in one arm and a bag of popcorn in another. Her mother had made her the popcorn, her face bruised, her hand clutching her stomach, before she went to bed. It was the middle of the afternoon, but her mother said she was tired.

Tilly was bored and Johnny was at school. Her father zoomed up their driveway in his black truck, then drove into the back part of their property, up the hill, down the hill, and behind a rim of trees near the stream. Her father had warned her never to go over there, ever, but she went anyhow. She would be a detective! She had read a book about a girl detective.

Tilly ran and skipped and jumped, up the hill, down the hill, and hid behind the rim of trees near the stream until she could see her father. He seemed to disappear near the rim of trees, to the right of a large rock. She scampered closer and saw him with a long package in his arms, wrapped in black plastic. Then he disappeared below the ground!

What happened? She heard a door shut, but there were no doors in the ground. She was deeply frightened all of a sudden. Her father had a temper. He hit her mother, he hit Johnny. He hit her sometimes, too. She didn't know where he had gone, but now she wanted to get away. She felt something scary, something threatening, so she ran back to the house and never told Johnny or her mother what she had seen. If her father found out, he would beat her with a belt again, she just knew it.

That afternoon, Tilly took a deep breath and headed out toward the back part of their property, up the hill, down the hill, and behind the rim of trees toward the stream. She didn't know where to look at first. She knew now that her father may have had a hiding place back here. She was so young when she'd seen him with the black package, but what she saw wasn't right. Was there a cellar all the way out here? Had he dug a hole? Then she saw it. The rock she'd remembered as a child. Her father had disappeared to the right of the rock. She got on her hands and knees and moved nettles and dirt for over an hour until her hands finally hit wood.

She brushed the dirt and rotting debris away until she uncovered a door in the ground, with a handle and a padlock. She could not remove the padlock, but she could remove, by stomping on it, the rotting wood around it. At first, when the door finally gave way, she saw nothing but a moldy ladder. Below that, a black pit. There were ropes and chains on the walls. There was dirt on the floor.

Tilly peered into the gloom. A rush of cool air that smelled of rot and mold and something else wrapped itself around her. She coughed, covered her face with her elbow, and sat back until the smell dissipated. Shaking, knowing she would see what she didn't want to see, she gripped the ladder hooked to the side of the wall.

She wanted to run. She wanted to call the police. She wanted to get out of there, the sense of evil cloying. But more than that, she wanted to know. She climbed down the ladder, a step at a time. When she reached the bottom, the stench unbelievable, as if the devil had rotted, she took a deep breath, told herself to be brave, once again, and looked around.

Instantly, she wanted to scream.

Tilly swallowed down the bile in her throat. Inside the carved-out dirt room, in the place where her father told her never, ever to go, were the bodies.

She recognized one of her mother's favorite dresses on a skeleton.

There were other skeletons. They wore dresses, too.

Tilly fought nausea and dizziness. She couldn't breathe. She scrambled back up the ladder, collapsed on the ground, and wretched.

Momma, she cried, her head tilted toward the sky when she let out a tortured cry. Oh, Momma.

The police came to Tilly and Johnny's former home in the country. She could hardly speak. It was as if she had regressed to when she was a child after her father was killed. She met the police at the end of the dirt road. They drove her back up to her home, then to the back part of their property, up the hill, down the hill, and behind a rim of trees toward the stream. She showed them the door in the ground, to the right of the rock, the door into hell, her whole body trembling, swaying. The police helped her, gently told her everything would be okay. But they hadn't seen what she had seen. How could they know? Nothing would be okay.

She pointed to the ladder. One of the policemen climbed down. She heard him gagging. Then he swore and yelled back up, "We got a crime scene."

The press had a field day after the discovery of five women's bodies in a secret dirt cave underground near Johnny and Tilly Kandinsky's childhood home in Idaho.

Evidence was collected at the Idaho house and at the home in which they'd previously lived in Portland. Two more women were buried underneath the crawl space of that home. It did not take long to pin the murders of the women on Peter Kandinsky.

"Will my brother, Johnny, and his girlfriend, Betsy, be released from jail?" Tilly asked in front of news reporters and cameramen, her voice wobbling, her body shaking. "You see, this is who my father was. He was a serial killer. Betsy killed him to protect Johnny. If she hadn't killed my father, my father would have killed Johnny, maybe Betsy, and more women after that if he wasn't caught. Betsy ended up protecting all of the women whom my father would have killed in the future."

And, finally, "I remember that night. I'll tell you what happened." And she told herself to be brave one more time, to fight for Johnny and Betsy, and she told the press what happened, including that she saw her father turning toward the gun cabinet. "He was going to shoot Johnny. I know that for sure."

The prosecutor's office fought against a new trial for Johnny and Betsy. They didn't want to be seen as having been derelict in their duties, incompetent! They didn't want to admit they had been wrong, that the barely eighteen-year-old Betsy and Johnny had not deserved time in jail. Their reputations had to be protected! Their egos had to remain uncriticized! One of them was running for governor, and he could not have a bad high-profile case like this on his hands.

Tilly was seven years old back then. She was a silly girl. She couldn't remember anything correctly, could she? Why open up the case again because of an emotional, unstable teenager's new testimony? Johnny and Betsy had killed the father in cold blood, and that was that. And for God's sakes, the murdered women in the dirt cave could not be brought up in a new trial. That was irrelevant, unnecessary, it lent no new evidence to the case!

The judge, though, saw it radically differently. Judge Callie Tsoko scheduled a new trial for Johnny and Betsy, though separate, and the information about the murdered women could be brought in by the defense. She did not allow any foot dragging by the prosecutors. This time, with so much attention on the case, Johnny and Betsy received a gang of top-notch attorneys and their assistants. The lead attorneys were women, and they loved a fight.

The jury believed Tilly during Johnny's new murder trial. They understood that she had been seven when she saw her father killed. They understood that she was traumatized and didn't speak for years. They did not like it when the prosecuting attorney asserted that, since Tilly had spent time in a mental health center, she was crazy or imagining things or delusional.

The girl's mother had been murdered, her father was abusive to her family, she saw her brother, or his girlfriend—there was some confusion there—kill the father in self-defense, so of course the poor thing would be traumatized! It didn't mean she was delusional!

They also didn't like it when the prosecutor intoned with dripping condescension that Tilly, who looked young and fragile, was lying to get her brother out of jail. They believed her when she said that Peter turned toward the gun cabinet to get the gun to shoot Johnny, for sure, and probably Betsy. He'd killed women before, why not now?

The jury didn't like the prosecutor. He was an arrogant prig. He was a snob. One juror privately called him The Weasel. They would definitely not vote for him for governor in the future. The trial dragged on, the old case reopened, people testified, detectives and police, forensics, etc.

Johnny and Betsy both testified. After the jury heard questioning by the prosecutor, they noted that Johnny didn't remember his father turning toward the gun cabinet, but he'd been hit in the face, twice, so how could he remember that? And Betsy hadn't seen it, either, but she was trying to protect Johnny from the serial killer! The prosecutor tried to make it seem like a big deal, about the gun cabinet, as if Tilly was lying, but the jury wasn't buying his snobby smack.

The jury was dismissed to deliberate. Didn't take long, thank heavens. They'd had enough of this circus, the photographers, the press. And they were sure of their decision.

They found Johnny not guilty. Easy-peasy. Clearly it was self-defense.

The judge released him.

She apologized for the time he had already served. "You are free to go, Mr. Kandinsky. Good luck."

Johnny, who had also suffered in prison, who had been beaten up more times than he could count, who had lifted weights and learned how to box and had become huge and muscled simply so he could defend himself, hung his head, his hands to his face. He tried not to cry, but it didn't work and he sobbed. He prayed for Betsy, his love for her had only grown over the years. Oh, how he prayed.

Betsy's trial was held directly after Johnny's trial with an old judge named Seymour Mansfield. The jury heard from detectives and the police who had been on the case before. They heard from forensics. They heard from Tilly, and what she remembered.

The dead body of Johnny's mother and the other women helped, in the sense that the jury knew that Peter was one sick son of a gun.

But still.

The prosecutor, a woman named Zoe Benedict was a competitive, cold, manipulative woman and tried to make mincemeat of Betsy when she took the stand. That Betsy had had a "premonition" of Peter killing Johnny was excellent cannon fodder for Zoe.

"Tell us about your premonitions," Zoe asked, believing that the jury would think that Betsy was crazy, probably violent. Definitely mentally ill.

"Objection," Betsy's attorney said.

"Overruled," the judge said. "Let's hear them."

"Recess, please," Betsy's attorney shouted.

"No," Betsy said. "No recess. I'll tell the truth."

"No recess granted," the judge said. "Let's hear about the premonitions."

"I have premonitions, now and then, about people." Betsy closed her eyes, then opened them and spoke to the prosecutor. "You're going to go home early today and your teenage daughter is going to be in bed with her boyfriend. In about a month she's going to realize she's pregnant."

The prosecutor laughed but looked stunned. "My daughter is only fifteen. She's in school today, then she has soccer practice. But nice try. Can we get back to the case?"

Betsy stared back at her, unblinking, then turned to the judge. "Your wife is planning a surprise party for you. It's tonight."

The judge's mouth opened. "She is?"

"Yes. Your brother is flying in."

"My brother is?" His face broke out in a smile, briefly, then he told himself to stop it, to show no emotion, be professional. A judge couldn't believe in premonitions!

"And to this juror," she turned to a woman, about seventy. Smartly dressed. "You should say yes to the proposal you get tonight. He's a good man and you'll be happy." She didn't tell the woman that her soon-to-be husband would die in two years. It wouldn't help. The man had an incurable cancer. They had to enjoy the time they had left. Fear and treatments would do no good.

The woman smiled. She believed in premonitions. Why, her sister had them now and then, too. They were Irish, so it made sense. The woman nodded.

"And to this juror," Betsy said, nodding to a man with dreadlocks, "You know that fishing trip you and your brother have planned for next weekend?" The man's eyes flared open. "Your brother is going to call tonight to cancel. His wife is pregnant. You'll go to their house to celebrate."

"Objection!" Zoe the mean prosecutor finally sputtered, still reeling from the lies Betsy had said about her daughter. "Objection, objection!"

"Objection overruled," the judge said, still thinking how fun it would be to see his brother. "You were the one who brought this up."

"But I object now!" the prissy prosecutor said, quaking in her $600 shoes.

"Too bad," he said. "Sit down."

"And to this juror." Betsy pointed at a young woman. "Your

brother is going to get in a car accident tonight. He'll be okay. But go to the hospital." She paused, then stared hard at her. "Mend things with your brother. Don't let anything get between you two again." The juror cried.

The prosecutor stood again, her designer suit straining as she breathed hard, already wanting to hit Betsy for lying about her daughter. She had seen her daughter ... she had talked with her daughter ... she had spent time with her daughter ... well, she couldn't remember when they'd last talked, or spent time together, but she'd been busy with this trial! And when she did have time, she needed to get her hair and nails done and go to the spa. Appearances brought on promotions and pictures of herself in the newspaper.

But her daughter, Cassandra, she was not having sex with a boy. She liked playing the violin! She was a child. She envisioned her in kindergarten. She envisioned her on Saturday morning. She still liked to wear those fluffy, blue, footed pajamas. She was not having sex!

Prosecutor Zoe thought that Betsy talking about her premonitions would make her look like a lunatic, but it didn't, she could tell. The jurors were eating it up. She was so angry she wanted to slam her fists into the table.

"That's all I know," Betsy said. She had never, in her whole life, had premonitions about a group of people. They always came to her one at a time, one person at a time. The only reason, she figured, that she had had multiple premonitions at once was because she was so stressed, so scared, and so broken. She had no strength left. That allowed the premonitions to break in altogether, as fractured pieces into her fractured mind. That had to be why. She turned to the judge. "Have fun tonight."

It was silent in that courtroom.

"You want the jury here, Betsy," Zoe said, trying to collect herself, trying to control her temper, "these smart men and women, to believe that you knew what was going to happen that day when you killed Peter Kandinsky? That you envisioned it, it came to you like a bolt of lightning to your head and you knew it would happen?" She made a scoffing sound in her throat.

She would demolish this stupid woman for what she said about her daughter in open court.

"Yes. I saw it after I got off work as a waitress. It was clear as day. I ran to his house and I heard them arguing about Johnny's mother, with Johnny accusing his father of killing her. Peter was raving, I've never seen anyone that angry. He hit Johnny in the face, twice. Johnny would be dead had I not done what I did. Peter was going to shoot him. Johnny's head was going to be split open like a cracked melon."

"How did you know?"

"Because I knew that Peter was going to turn to the gun cabinet."

"So you saw Johnny's father going for the gun in the gun cabinet?" she sneered at Betsy.

"No, I saw it in my premonition."

"In your crystal ball?"

"There is no crystal ball."

"You never saw him turn, that day, in *real* life, for the gun?"

"No."

"Then there was no threat to your life," the prosecutor snapped. "Peter Kandinsky did not have a gun."

"There was a threat to Johnny's life," Betsy said. "He was going to be shot and killed by his father because Peter was incensed that Johnny was accusing him of killing Gabriella, Johnny's mother. Peter was afraid that Johnny would go to the police and he would go to jail, so he was going to kill his own son."

"Without a gun?" The prosecutor tried to look puzzled. "So you stabbed him. You defended Johnny from a gun that was still in the gun cabinet when the police arrived."

Betsy's attorney said, with a semi-shout, "Fifteen minutes with my client, please."

"Granted." The judge hit the gavel. He was already looking forward to his party.

The next day, the seventy-year-old woman told her new friends on the jury that she had received a proposal, to her surprise, the night before and she had said yes. The jury clapped for her. Love comes to all ages!

The juror with the dreadlocks was thrilled! The fishing trip was canceled, but that's because his brother and his wife were four months pregnant. They had not announced it until now because they had already had three miscarriages. Every time, the family grieved. This time his brother and his wife didn't say anything until they were past the danger point. His brother was going to name their child after him. The man with the dreadlocks cried, he was so happy.

The young juror with the brother in the car accident hadn't slept. She'd been up all night with her brother at the hospital. They had made up. They had talked and laughed and cried. "I can't believe it. My brother and I haven't talked for a year, and now we're best friends again." She cried, too.

The prosecutor, Zoe, looked ill. Yes, her teenage daughter, her sweetheart, her baby, had been having sex for at least six months with her boyfriend. They were going to make her take a pregnancy test tonight.

And the judge. Well, the party had been a ton of fun. Even his law school buddies had flown in for it. That Margie! What a wife! She was the best thing that had ever happened to him. Best decision he ever made was to propose to her. She knew how to keep a secret. His brother was staying for a week! He would call in sick as soon as this stupid trial was over.

The jury, stunned about the premonitions, had listened to Tilly tell her story about how her father had turned toward the gun cabinet to get the gun to kill Johnny and probably Betsy, other witnesses, blah blah blah, then closing arguments.

They went into deliberations.

Their thoughts? It was clearly self-defense. Peter was going for the gun. Tilly had said so. That Betsy hadn't actually *seen* Peter going for the gun cabinet was a nagging, irritating detail, but eh. Johnny hadn't seen it because he'd been punched in the face twice and was too dizzy to see it. Probably. Yes, that was it. They were mostly *sure* of it.

They decided to, legally speaking, disregard that teeny tiny detail. They couldn't quite find Betsy innocent because of the premonitions—that wasn't scientific enough, it wasn't credible evidence, it wasn't, well, admissible, so to speak. Can't use that as a reason to let her out of prison, could they?

But wasn't it *remarkable* what Betsy knew about them? . . . They again talked about the proposal, the car crash, the new baby. The judge looked tired but happy. Must have had fun at the party. And the prosecutor, well, she looked exhausted and worried. Teenagers can be so much work and so much trouble.

Also, the jury knew that Peter was a serial killer. The prosecutor had fought like a hellfire dragon not to have that brought up, but the judge overruled her. It was relevant. It showed Peter's character and what he was capable of. Peter deserved to be killed. Too bad he wasn't killed sooner, that psychopath.

Johnny and Tilly had been beaten repeatedly by their father. A father should protect his children, not hurt them, so if there were some lingering questions about the knife and Betsy running in, well, whatever. A child abuser should die, like a psychopath should!

The jury filed in. They sat down. Yes, judge, they had their verdict.

Everyone sat forward in their seats. The courtroom was packed. Zoe was exhausted and worried. She, her husband, and their daughter had finally talked after she finished yelling at her. Her daughter was always lonely, always alone, she told her parents. Her boyfriend was the only one who paid her attention. He was kind to her, funny. "You and Dad always work. Why did you even have me? You don't want me."

Zoe was crushed, as was her husband. They were lousy parents. Was their sweet daughter pregnant?

"What say you?" the judge asked.

"Not guilty," the jury forewoman intoned, then smiled at Betsy.

The courtroom exploded. Clapping, cheering, the press calling the results in to their respective newspapers.

"You are free to go," the judge said to Betsy. He was befuddled by the whole premonition thing. He didn't believe in premonitions. He didn't believe in magic. He didn't believe in curses. He didn't believe in God. So what the hell happened with this woman? How did Betsy know about the party? He went home early that day, he was so tired from being up late with his brother.

Betsy cried. Johnny walked around the defense table, pulled her up and hugged her close as the cameras clicked, news reporters shouted out questions, and everyone else in the court room clapped and cheered.

"Ready to be farmers?" he asked her, overwhelmed, grateful.

Sobbing, she said yes.

Tilly joined them, wrapping her arms around her brother and his brother's girlfriend, who she always thought of as a sister. They were a family. The three of them. Forever.

Tilly had found the transcripts of the first trial interesting.

Neither Johnny nor Betsy had seen Peter turn toward the gun cabinet. That had been an enormous legal problem for both of them, Tilly knew. If they hadn't seen him turn to get a gun, there wasn't much of a self-defense defense.

Tilly hadn't seen her apoplectic, raving father turn toward the gun cabinet, either.

But she believed Betsy's premonition. She believed that her father *would have* turned toward the gun cabinet had Betsy not stabbed him with the knife first.

Tilly loved Betsy and Johnny.

She wanted her family back. She wanted to live on a farm.

She chose love . . . and a tiny lie.

For the next two months Johnny, Tilly, and Betsy lived together in a small two-bedroom apartment near Tilly's high school on the east side of Portland. Johnny had received the money for rent from an organization that helped out ex-convicts.

There was laughter and barrels of tears in that apartment, small but warm and clean, and certainly much better than jail. They cried for the years lost when they weren't together, for what Johnny and Betsy had endured in jail, for what Tilly had gone through in a lonely foster care/mental health institution existence until her final kind and loving foster parents.

All of them were traumatized by their experiences, but one had to survive, and they started talking the second night about what to do to make money.

Johnny got a job at a lumber supply shop in two days. The business was fading rapidly. The widowed, childless owner was seventy-five years old and had Parkinson's, but this was his baby, his business. Johnny told Marvin the truth. Marvin knew about the case and he took Johnny on anyhow. Johnny worked sixty hours a week. The business started to turn around.

Betsy was hired at a big-box store after she sent out a hundred applications and was rejected for all. It was the only place that would hire her. Betsy worked full-time. She eventually went from pulling in carts and custodial work, including cleaning the bathrooms, to checker, to assistant shift manager, to the manager on shift, to assistant manager, to the manager of the whole store.

Within three months, Betsy and Johnny were married. It was just the two of them in front of a minister, a friend of Marvin's, plus Tilly and Marvin. Their honeymoon was to the beach for a weekend. They splurged by going out to dinner and eating clam chowder. Betsy did not change her last name. If their daughter was ever allowed to access the adoption paperwork in the future, if the laws changed, she wanted Rose to be able to find her.

They saved every penny. After Tilly graduated, they moved to the country, thirty minutes away from their jobs but worth it. The three of them craved peace and nature. The owner of their rental home was an elderly friend of Marvin's. He was going to live with his daughter in Fresno, but he needed someone to care for his six beloved horses, his three dogs, and his chickens and to keep an eye on his property. His home was white, two-story, rambling, and built a hundred years ago. The rent was cheap.

Johnny, Betsy, and Tilly moved in, pampered the animals, fixed things that were broken or worn down or rusty, cleaned the windows, scrubbed the rest of it, painted walls, and planted a huge garden. They all found gardening therapeutic, and it helped to cut down on the food bill. As they planned, years ago, they started selling their vegetables at the farmers' market on Saturdays along with apples, blackberries, and blueberries that were already growing on the property.

Johnny made a wooden stall and a sign that said ROSE'S MARKET. They worked their day jobs during the week, the market on Saturday, and were together on Sunday. They saved every penny so they could hire an attorney and get their Rose back—or at least get visitation. They wanted to know she was okay. They wanted her to know they loved her. They longed to hug her.

When Johnny and Betsy had enough money saved from their jobs and Rose's Market, they talked to an attorney named Frieda Yann and told their story. Frieda was already familiar with it. They had been falsely imprisoned. It was self-defense. They had been declared innocent. They deserved to have their daughter back. Frieda could whip almost any other attorney's butt and eagerly took the case. Under the hatchet she held in one hand, a legal brief in the other, she did have a compassionate side. But she had an ulterior motive, too: She knew this would be an epic legal case, egged on by Frieda.

The state fought back. They had taken baby Rose, as Johnny and Betsy were in prison and could not parent. It would be disruptive to the child's life to return the girl to them. It would tear her from the people she believed were her parents. The girl doesn't even know she was adopted. It was tragic, the state said, but the child must remain where she is for her own sake.

The press loved the story: Johnny Kandinsky and Betsy Baturra, the woman who had premonitions, had spent ten years in jail and lost their daughter. Now they were married and they wanted their love child back! Both were photogenic, articulate, likable.

The arguments raged on TV, in talk shows, in newspapers. Should Baby Rose go back to her biological parents? Yes, said some. They had been declared innocent. They never should have served time. Rose is their daughter. Wouldn't you want *your* daughter back?

No, said others. Too disruptive to the girl. It would ruin her life to be ripped from the arms of the only parents she knows.

What about visitation? Surely Johnny and Betsy deserved visitation with their daughter. Yes, said some. No, said others.

On and on.

The judge paid no mind to the circus outside his courtroom doors. He had six kids. He couldn't imagine losing any of them, but he ruled for keeping Rose with her adoptive parents. "This is a tragedy for everyone," he intoned.

Betsy sobbed, broken. Johnny felt sick, his face stricken with grief. Tilly shook.

Frieda, metaphorical hatchet up and raised, asked for the records to be unsealed so Johnny and Betsy could visit Rose.

No.

Frieda, wanting to kick some butt, asked if the birth records could be unsealed when Rose was eighteen. She would be an adult then, able to make her own decisions.

No.

Johnny and Betsy lost. The records were sealed forever, as the law required then. Rose would stay where she was.

Johnny and Betsy cried in court. The judge was sympathetic. Even the opposing attorney for the state was sympathetic. Frieda the hatchet swinger was sympathetic but super pissed off. She hated losing.

Johnny and Betsy went home to their one-hundred-year-old rambling farmhouse in the country that day and cried again. They cried with Tilly. They cried in their garden, they cried as they lay in bed, their arms empty, their hearts battered. All through the long, dark years of imprisonment, where Johnny and Betsy were both beaten down by the fear and isolation, the abuse and deprivations, they had clung to the hope that they would see each other again, see Tilly, and see Rose.

They had lost Rose again, and they went down a long black tunnel for months. It was as if she'd been taken from them all over again, and the grief clawed at every ounce of happiness.

The longing to see her never went away. The love never went

away. They clung to hope that one day something would change and they would see her. They clung to a future they wanted, even when it seemed impossible. They clung to each other, their love unending, even when their tears mixed for the daughter who was out there . . . somewhere.

Betsy and Johnny took a leap three years later and opened a small grocery store about fifteen minutes from their home. The building had been a saloon eighty years ago, then a saddle and boot store, then farming equipment. It had been unoccupied for ten years.

Betsy quit her job as the manager of the big-box store and she, Johnny, and Tilly cleaned and scrubbed, painted, replaced the electricity and the plumbing, and opened up Rose's Market with red-and-white-striped awnings, fresh fruits and vegetables, cheeses, wines, breads and cakes, and the best meat they could find. They grew rows and rows of roses on their property— burgundy, white, yellow, pink, purple—and sold bouquets in honor of their Rose.

What they didn't provide from their own large gardens, they bought locally. They named the deli Marvin's Deli. When Marvin saw the scrolling sign, in red, his favorite color, he leaned on his cane and cried.

They named the fruits and vegetables section Tilly's Garden. Tilly chuckled when she saw it when she came home from a break from college. "Well, I do like getting my hands dirty." Tilly studied business and Spanish. "But I hate kale. Do we have to sell kale?" Yes, they did. "We're not rabbits!" After Tilly graduated, she worked for Rose's Market full-time.

Betsy found Eartha, released from prison years ago, and hired her.

"I'm happy to be back with my best jailbird friend," Eartha said. "My momma taught me how to bake pies. How about I be your pie maker?"

"Bake your pies," Betsy told her.

Betsy also found Rainbow. She was out of jail and living in a homeless shelter. She had been on the streets off and on when her mental illness became too much to handle and she lost whatever minimum wage job she'd been able to grab. There was a small room above the grocery store, with a kitchenette and bathroom. Rainbow lived there. She rested, recovered, went with Betsy to see a doctor for the appropriate medications, and eventually worked as a cashier. Rent was free.

Betsy organized cooking classes at Rose's Market. Customers could come and learn how to make crock pot dishes and homemade pizza and pasta primavera. They had cake-decorating classes. Eartha taught her pie classes. Every Thursday night everything was 10 percent off. The crowds came. It was only 10 percent, but it was fun for people. They liked the price break. They liked the cake samples and cookie samples and bread, cheese, and fruit samples.

At Rose's Market you could decorate Christmas and Valentine cookies with your kids and you could paint Easter eggs. Santa came, and so did the Easter bunny.

Rose's Market specialized in cheese and wine, honey and breads, desserts and fresh fruits and vegetables. Their motto: Peace. Love. Delicious Food.

Johnny and Betsy bought the home from the owner who was still living with his daughter in Fresno and decided not to return. He had seven grandchildren! There were a lot of soccer games and ballet recitals! They needed him. Betsy and Johnny continued to pamper his animals, sending him photos regularly so he could still see them.

They opened a second store, again named Rose's Market. Tilly ran the second store.

Johnny kept his job as the manager of the lumber yard, as Marvin could not work much anymore, and he would not let Marvin down. Johnny, Betsy, and Tilly moved Marvin into their own home, nicely remodeled by then, and took care of him the last year of his life, as he had no one else. A nurse came in to help during the day.

When Marvin died he left everything he had to Betsy and Johnny. Betsy and Johnny thought that Marvin had no other assets. The business had been failing when Johnny arrived on the scene. It now made an impressive profit, thanks to Johnny, but they had no idea of Marvin's net worth. Marvin had an old house he'd lived in for sixty years, never remodeled. He also had fifty acres, free and clear. Johnny hadn't known that Marvin owned all of that land around his home. It was near to neighborhoods, and builders wanted to buy it.

Plus, Marvin had half a million in the bank, and $50,000 literally in a mattress in his guest room. Betsy and Johnny found out about that stash when they read the letter Marvin wrote to them, telling them he loved them as his own children. They grieved for Martin, a decent, kind man who had given Johnny a chance and paid him fairly from the start. They used part of the money to start a scholarship fund for their employees and their children.

They opened a third and fourth store. Then a fifth.

All of the markets were called Rose's Market. All of the fruits and vegetable sections were called Tilly's Garden. And all of the delis were called Marvin's Deli.

He would have liked that.

At thirty-eight unexpectedly, miraculously, Betsy became pregnant. Johnny and Betsy had tried for years, after they had established themselves, to get pregnant, but they couldn't. The doctors had run test after test, but they couldn't find anything wrong. They resigned themselves to a childless life.

The pregnancy was a joy, yet it was filled with grief, too. It triggered their feelings of deep loss, their searing grief at losing Rose, but Kayla was a smiling, easy baby, and she soothed their tired souls, added love to their battered hearts, and peace to their lives. Aunt Tilly was thrilled.

One day, they told each other, the sisters would meet.

They hoped, they prayed.

Chapter 30

❧

"Serafina only had three more scales left, all the colors of roses: red, pink, and yellow."

"I love roses."

"I know you do. You've always been your mom's and my rose, you know that, don't you?"

"Yes, you silly. You say I'm your rose kid."

"You are."

"Tell me what happened to Serafina."

"She rescued a dolphin who had been pushed up onto the sand. She had to wait until nighttime so no one would see her. She used her tail to push herself onto the beach, then grabbed his tail and pulled him back in."

"She lost another scale."

"Yes. She lost the bright yellow one. Then she was down to two scales, rose red and a soft pink. A three-year-old merchild became lost in the ocean, and Serafina was the one to rescue her. A teenager who was snorkeling panicked in the water, and she pulled him to shallow water. No one believed him when he said a mermaid rescued him."

"All the scales were gone then and she had a green tail, right? Like the other mermaids."

"Yes. Her last scale floated through the ocean's wave to King Koradome. Then something magical happened."

Chapter 31

～

I was reading the newspaper on my phone while my mother made me my favorite soup, chicken curry with coconut milk, in my kitchen. The sliding glass doors were open, and the breezes from the ocean floated in, warm and salty. I could smell the faintest scent of the sweet roses I'd planted around my home. Sundance sat right at my feet, as usual.

Sometimes my mom and I will cook dinner together, just the two of us, and then watch a movie. Whoever is not cooking will read the paper out loud and we'll talk about politics and social issues and celebrity gossip and new books that are reviewed.

I had bought two miniature pecan pies for the movie. Pecans are nuts. Nuts are protein. Therefore, pecan pie is healthy. I think everyone knows that.

"Hey, listen to this," I said to my mom from my kitchen table as she ladled our soup into bowls. The goats had escaped again and were staring as us through my sliding glass doors, waiting eagerly for me to see them and run them down, as usual. I pretended I didn't see them because I hate running.

"This article is about two people, a couple—a boyfriend and girlfriend. They were teenagers when they killed the boyfriend's father. The girlfriend said she did it, the boyfriend said he did it. The girlfriend was pregnant. Her name was Betsy."

I looked up as a thundering crash filled the kitchen. My mother had dropped two empty soup bowls.

"Mom, oh, my goodness. Are you okay?" I dropped my phone and went straight for her. "You're in sandals. Come this way so you don't get glass in your feet." I stuck my hands out and grabbed hers, guiding her over the glass. "Sit down. I'll clean it up. Mom? Mom?" She had a faraway look in her eye. "Momma? Are you okay?" I handed her some water. "Here, drink this." She sat down heavily, as if her legs had given out, and I cleaned up the mess. I kept an eye on her.

"Let's have the soup, dear," she told me, her voice constricted. "Perhaps I need to eat."

"Okay." I ladled up the soup, turned off the stove, grabbed the spinach salad and our French bread out of the oven, and sat down.

"Mom," I said quietly, carefully, "Are you sick? What's wrong?"

"I'm fine."

"Mom, please, I know something's wrong."

She put her hand on my arm, but her hand shook as if there were a live wire in it, and I covered it with my own. "I'm fine, sweetheart. Read the rest of the article. It will . . . I want . . . I think . . . it will distract me from this." She waved a hand in the air.

"Are you sure? Okay." I picked up my phone. My concern for my mother was sky-high. There was something wrong and she wouldn't tell me. I was trying not to force it out of her, but I was close to it.

I read to her the case about Johnny Kandinsky and Betsy Baturra. "Do you remember that case?"

"Yes, I do. Quite well." She was pale.

"Mom, please eat," I said. "You—"

"Let's hear the rest of the article." Her voice was firm. I don't argue with my mother when she uses that firm voice.

I read the rest of the article to my mother: The couple was released from prison because Tilly Kandinsky remembered what happened the day of the murder, and blew open the investigation of her father, a serial killer.

"How odd," I said. "Betsy predicted things during the trial

that would happen to the judge and the jurors, and they did, which helped her case in saying she had premonitions about Peter Kandinsky and how she had foreseen he was going to kill Johnny." I stopped reading. Wow. There was someone else out there who had premonitions, just like me. She wasn't a fraud, she wasn't trying to steal people's money. "They tried to get their daughter back after they were released. They went to court. They had attorneys. But the courts said no. Even though their convictions were overturned, the courts said their daughter, named Rose, could not be returned to them. They found in favor of the adopted parents and that it would be too traumatic to make the girl move."

My mother sat very still.

"It was a difficult case," my mother said.

I looked at her, and I could feel my brow furrowing. "A difficult case? How so?"

"Well, the woman, Betsy, said she had premonitions, and I didn't believe her."

"But you believe me."

"I know, dear, but she was trying to use it as her defense. No one believed her, that's why she was in jail. They thought she was delusional, and a liar."

"I'm sure people think that about me, too. Anyhow, this article is about them and where they are now. Johnny and Betsy bought land and started farming, then they opened a grocery store called Rose's Market, my favorite market. They now have a chain of grocery stores up and down the West Coast. I love their cheeses and wines and homemade breads. I love their fruit. So it says here that they are hoping that their daughter contacts them through this new DNA test, like Jules and I did. They were interviewed by a newspaper and several TV stations."

My mother made a choking sound. "They've taken a DNA test?"

"Here, Mom. Have water." I handed her the glass. "Do you want some wine? You seem so stressed." She looked stressed. Her face was pinched, mouth a rigid line.

"I'm fine, honey." My mother choked again. "I'm fine. I'm fine."

Why the repetition? My mother did not repeat herself.

"Yes, they took a DNA test."

"What else does the article say?"

"They said they're hoping their daughter takes a DNA test, too. They said their daughter was born in Portland in 1975. They named her Rose. Baby Rose."

My mother made another choking sound.

"Sure you're all right, Mom?" I stood up and put my arms around her. "Are you upset? I know you have several weddings coming up. Are you stressed about the work? I can help you."

"Yes, yes. That's it. I'm stressed, dear." Her hands were shaking. "About the flowers. The tulips. Daffodils. Peonies. Chrysanthemums. Marigolds. My, the peonies. Roses. Many roses. Thank you, dear, we might have you help with the hats. Let's have our soup, shall we? Yes. We'll have the soup. The soup I made for you and me. The soup."

Was she having a stroke?

"Eat, Evie. Eat."

"Mom—"

"That's enough, Evie." Her tone said she was done with this conversation. "I'm fine. Everything is fine."

Clearly, I thought, as I put down my soup spoon and watched her, almost vibrating with stress, everything was not fine.

My brain was frazzled. I was worried about my mother. I wanted Marco but couldn't have him. I had driven by Emily's house and felt guilty. I was worried about Chief Ass Burn and what he would do to my mother and aunts if he found out about their side business.

I knew I'd probably have a premonition. The more together I am, the more rested, the fewer premonitions I have. If I'm upset, I'll go down a premonition rabbit hole. I'll wake up nervous and anxious, and I'll start wondering when the next premonition will hit. Then it'll hit. It's like worrying about having a panic attack and then you make yourself have a panic attack.

It didn't take long for a premonition to creep in.

A young man wandered in looking for a book on bike rides on our island. He had a lopsided smile with a lot of teeth and black hair in a ponytail. He was with two young women. They were all in biking clothes. They were chatting, enjoying my yellow bookstore, trying to choose which desserts they wanted to buy.

I saw it then, a clear flash. The young man was going to end up with a broken neck. I saw him in a ditch, unconscious, one of the young women screaming, racing down to help him, the other biking away for help.

I closed my eyes for a second and studied the premonition. Yes, today he was in the same clothes as he was in the premonition, which meant that it would happen today, probably. It could happen the next day, if he wore the same clothes. That's another torturous part of premonitions. I can look at what people are wearing during my premonition, but they might be wearing those same clothes another day, too.

But I couldn't take a chance. As they studied the raspberry tortes, the giant chocolate chip cookies, and the chocolate peanut butter cheesecake, I took in every piece of his clothing, down to his socks and shoes. He probably thought I was checking him out. Whatever.

I smiled at them. "Biking, huh?" Yes, they were biking. They rode up from the ferry, they loved the island, so many places to bike to!

"What kind of bike are you riding?" I stared right at the young man so I would be sure to get his answer.

He cheerfully told me the type of bike he had, and I was familiar with the brand. "What do you ride?"

I told him the type of bike I had, that it was blue.

"I went with blue, too. My mother's favorite color is blue, so I thought, what the heck? Honor mom, right?"

"Always," I said. We chatted more, then I said to Tiala, "Could you help these three find the book by Genesis Ringold? She's a local, she's been all over all the islands, hiking and riding her bike, and she knows the best places."

"Yes, no problem," Tiala said, and the three followed her. I noticed one of the women stopped at the mystery shelves and the other stopped at nonfiction best sellers.

I went out to my deck overlooking the bay and closed my eyes. I made myself repicture the accident in the ditch. His socks didn't match. They were both white. But one had a brand name written across the top and the other had a different brand name. Obviously this wasn't foolproof; he could wear mismatched socks again, but today his socks were the same mismatched pair as in my premonition.

I got my little knife out of my purse in my office, went outside the bookstore, and slashed the tires of his blue bike—blue for his loving mom—as subtly as I could. I am skilled at slash and dash. It was one strike against the front tire on the way to the mailbox, one slash against the back on the way in with the mail.

The young man was going to be hit by a truck and land in a ditch, which would snap his neck, but with my interference he would need to get new tires. That would allow plenty of time for the truck to be on its way and change the premonition.

I went right back into the bookstore and rang them up. They each bought another book in addition to the one on bike rides and trails on the island.

I didn't like seeing the look of despair and anger on his face when he saw his mangled tires, but it was better than having a mangled neck, and I was able to send him to Harry Charles, who I knew would give him a good deal.

I gave them all chocolate chip cookies and a cup of Kenyan coffee before they left. It was the least I could do for saving his life.

Jules and I both received emails from the DNA company on Saturday afternoon.

"Don't open it!" she yelled at me over the phone when I called to tell her. She was on the last ferry tonight from Anacortes and headed to Rose Bloom Cottage. "We'll do it together."

"This will be fun," I said. "How do you think they'll categorize 'Witch Ancestry'?"

At ten that night, Jules at my house, both of us in matching heart pajamas, we set our computers side by side.

"Here we go. This is where we find out that you're part Italian," she said to me. "It'll explain that black hair."

"And this is where we find out that you're actually Chinese, Jules. That'll account for your blonde hair."

We eagerly opened our e-mails, read the information, then looked at the pie graphs and studied the percentages.

"Wow," I said, stunned as I examined my graph. "I can't believe this. This isn't what we were told by Mom and Dad and Grandpa. I'm 22 percent Iberian Peninsula. Twenty percent Russian. Thirty-eight percent Irish and 12 percent Welsh. And unknown. Eight percent. They can't trace it yet? It's a mixture? What does yours say?" I turned to Jules.

"There's got to be something wrong," Jules said.

"Why?"

"Look at my graph."

I scooted over. "What? This can't be right. There's a mistake."

Jules's chart showed English, Scottish, German, and Norwegian, for a total of 83 percent, and 10 percent total of Bantu, Mali, and Senegal, plus 7 percent unknown.

"This doesn't make sense," I said. "We should have exactly the same genetic background as sisters. Our percentages would be different—you'd be 10 percent of one country, like Scottish, because of Dad, and I'd be 15 percent—but we're not..." I peered back and forth at the computer screens, as Jules was, comparing and contrasting. "This can't be right, Jules. We don't share any of the same countries at all. Not one."

"They probably got the spit mixed up with someone else's," Jules said.

"Right. There was a spit mistake."

"This is a mess," she said. "I can believe the English, Scottish, and Norwegian in our DNA. We were told that by Mom and Dad and Grandpa. And having German in us is believable, too. But what in the world with the Bantu and Mali and Senegal?

And what about Grandma? She said she was French and Greek, but neither one of us has French or Greek in us...."

What the heck? "I have no idea...."

"This has to be wrong. Here," Jules said. "Let's go online and check out who we're related to. Maybe somehow we're related to the same people, you and me, and they got that part right. And the part about where we're from, that's where the mistake is. Yours is wrong or mine is wrong or they're both wrong."

"Yes, let's try it." It didn't make sense, but . . .

We went online to the ancestry website. We figured since we were getting our genetic information, we could meet long-lost cousins, so we had bought the whole enchilada. We logged in. We went to the place where relatives could be found and messaged. . . .

"Look at this!" Jules said. "We have second cousins on here, third cousins. One's in Galveston. Two are in Norway, one in England. A German . . . Huh. I don't get this. This is confusing. There are two second cousins in Mali. One in Senegal. And . . . these are their photos."

The cousins in Mali and Senegal were black.

"I don't get this," Jules said. "But they're both pretty."

We studied the people on our screens, back and forth, back and forth. There was something very, very wrong again. None of Jules's relatives matched mine. Not one. My relatives were in Portland, Oregon, three of them. They were in Mexico and Russia, and several in Ireland and one in Wales. They were in Texas and California . . .

"Okay. They've screwed this up," Jules said. "We need to call the DNA company and tell them about this. Geez. This is irritating. Mack and I need to know what recipe our kids are going to be. What ingredients."

I studied my screen, totally confused.

There were two people on my family tree—Betsy Baturra and Johnny Kandinsky—who were married. It said that these people were my parents. There was also another woman . . . Tilly Kandinsky. It said it was highly likely she was my aunt.

But this couldn't be right. Betsy and Johnny were not my parents. Poppy and Henry Lindsay were my parents.

Tilly Kandinsky was not my aunt. Aunt Camellia and Aunt Iris were my aunts.

Where had I heard those names before? Johnny and Betsy. Johnny and Betsy. I racked my brain. *Tilly.*

"Oh, my God," Jules said, looking at my screen. "This isn't right. Those are not your parents. This DNA company has royally screwed up."

"I'm looking them up on Facebook." I found the woman's name and her page. My breath stuck in my throat, my heart pounded. "That woman, Betsy, looks exactly like me." Looking at Betsy was like looking at me in twenty years. She had thick black hair, like mine, although she had a few streaks of white. I have gold eyes. She had gold eyes. My eyes tilt. Hers tilted. We had the same mouth, same high cheekbones.

Jules was breathing rather heavily beside me as we stared at the photo of Betsy.

"We're not listed as sisters," Jules said. "And that . . . that woman . . . who is listed as your mother . . ."

I stared at the screen with Jules, her cheek almost touching mine.

Yes, something was very wrong.

"You look like her," Jules breathed. "It's like looking at you in twenty years."

"She owns Rose's Market." I touched the screen with a trembling finger.

"That's my favorite market," Jules mused quietly. "Great wine. I don't understand what's going on."

"She has a daughter," I said. We stared at the girl's photo. Her name was Kayla. Black hair. Gold eyes.

"She looks so much like you did when you were a teenager," Jules breathed.

I was starting to understand, even as my brain pushed back, unable to accept. I remembered where I'd read those names before.

It all came to me in a rush. Like a tsunami. Like a hurricane. Like a thunderstorm.

Betsy and Johnny were the young couple who were jailed for murder.

They had to give up their baby. The baby was born in Portland, like me, in 1975.

Tilly, Johnny's sister, remembered what happened that night after years of not remembering anything, after years of not speaking. . . . Dead women in a dirt cave under the ground in Idaho, dead women in a crawl space under the basement in Portland. . . . Betsy and Johnny found innocent in their next trials.

They fought in court to get their baby back. They lost.

They had named her Rose.

Oh. My. God.

"Evie, I want to apologize to you."

"Thank you." I turned away from creepy, obsessive Chief Ass Burn and started walking back to my bookstore as dignified as I could while holding a thrashing Ghost in her cat carrier and a pile of books in my other arm. Ghost was hissing and meowing. I think she sensed Chief Ass Burn's basic disgustingness.

"And I bet you want to apologize to me." He hurried around and stood in front of me, stomach out. North Sound wasn't crowded this morning, but there were people milling about, fishermen in the bay, bikers riding through on their way to the lake.

I laughed at him. After what I learned last night, I really didn't want to be dealing with this shark, so it made me, paradoxically, laugh loudly. "You have to be kidding."

"You owe me an apology. I apologized, now you apologize and we'll call a truce."

"What would I need to apologize for?"

He flushed with anger, his sneaky pig eyes narrowing. "Undermining my authority with the other islanders. Not obeying me when I told you to bring your ticket in to me when your taillight was fixed so I could reduce it. Telling Marco to defy me. Back talk from you when I had to run a Breathalyzer on you because you were swaying in your lane. Not bringing that ticket to me so I could reduce it. Reporting on me to my superior. Calling me Chief Ass Burn when that is not my name. You are unfriendly and rude and disobedient . . ." He paused and coughed. "Disobedient to the law."

"Disobedient?" I wanted to choke. "I do not have to obey you. I don't have to be friendly to you. I can say whatever I want because we have something here called free speech."

"And there you go again, Evie," he said, taking a step closer, his stomach coming straight at me.

I put Ghost, who was cat-screeching now, right between us. She hissed at Chief Ass Burn. "Don't try to intimidate me, because I don't intimidate. Now step back." I said "step back" loudly.

His mouth tightened, then inexplicably he smiled. Which was so creepy it made my whole body tense up.

"You want the truth, Evie? I think we could be friends, if you lose some of your attitude and stop trying to challenge me. When are you free for dinner? We'll go to dinner, talk this out, come to an agreement. You haven't even taken the opportunity to get to know me."

"I like my attitude and I'm not changing it. You feel challenged because you would feel challenged by any woman who doesn't praise you or stroke your ego. I am never going to dinner with you, and I don't want to get to know you any better." I turned and walked around him toward my pretty bookstore.

"Evie, stop!" he ordered in his police chief's voice.

I kept walking.

"It's Marco, isn't it?"

I didn't stop.

"Well, if you want to date a man who has a thing for animals, go ahead. If you want a real man, then there's me."

He makes me sick. I turned around and he was smirking, chest out. "You, Chief Ass Burn, are nowhere near the man that Marco is." A rush of anger charged through my body. Chief Ass Burn would not leave me alone. He was making this idyllic life, this serene island, which had always been a haven for me, ugly. Plus, he'd criticized Marco, and I was flaming mad. "Marco has integrity. He is a highly intelligent military veteran. He is brave and compassionate. He heals animals all day, every day. He treats people with respect and with kindness. You two are entirely, completely different. Don't you ever criticize Marco again. I don't want to hear it, and no one on this island wants to hear it. In any comparison between the two of you, you will lose out."

He was almost purple with fury. "You're a—"

"What?" I taunted him as Ghost hissed again. "Say it. I would like to be able to write it down in the documentation that I'm keeping about your behavior on this island and how you treat people. So complete your sentence."

"You're threatening a police officer."

I laughed. "Then arrest me. My first call will be to my attorney because it is illegal to lock a woman up because she won't go to dinner with you. My second call will be to your superior, who is already getting complaints left and right about you. So. Do you want to arrest me because I hurt your massive ego by telling you that you are nowhere near the man that Marco is?"

"I'll arrest you for telling people the future like a gypsy and lying to them," he huffed, but I saw the malice behind his eyes, the desire for revenge. Narcissists always have to get revenge. They do not forget, they do not forgive. If you do not treat them like you think they're God, they will attack. "You're ripping them off. You're running a scam and you're preying on vulnerable people and leading them astray."

"You're a fool, Chief Ass Burn. I never charge people, I never take money, I never take anything. But go ahead. Find one person on this island who wants to file charges against me for being a gypsy. I dare you."

I walked away, his eyes burning a hole in my back, Ghost almost apoplectic.

He would do everything he could to get back at me. He was a vile snake.

"Mom," I said, "Aunt Camellia. Aunt Iris." I fiddled with my teacup at Rose Bloom Cottage. I was shocked. I was angry, hurt, confused. I felt betrayed.

Beside me, Jules was shocked, too, and quiet.

I'd spent much of last night at the beach, staring into the darkness, the gentle lapping of the waves the only noise I needed, as my brain was a hive of noise and chaos. Under the moon's white-gold tunnel, I'd walked through my grandma's garden, past the gazebo, the pond with the lily pads and the bridge. I sat on her colorful benches and saw two deer and hid in the secret garden room where a six-foot statue of a fairy watched over the perfectly trimmed boxwood and maple trees.

I could not find peace.

My reality of my own life was not mine. My truth was not my truth.

I had called the DNA company. I had talked to a very nice woman there. She explained how the tests were done, how the tubes were handled, how "many people find surprises in their DNA." DNA did not lie. There were no mistakes.

"Jules and I received our information back from the DNA company."

My mother dropped her delicate purple rose teacup. It clattered to her saucer and broke. I stood right up to help her, as did Jules and Sundance. My mother didn't move as we picked up the shards of china and wiped up the tea. She stared straight ahead, stricken. Aunt Camellia and Aunt Iris, always helpful, did nothing to help us, either. They had frozen, exactly as our mother had, their faces worried. Resigned. Guilty. And, overall, pained.

We sat back down again, at the table where my grandpa used to pluck feathers out of chickens, Sundance at my feet. I tried to get my emotions under control. It is not every day you find out you are not related to your parents and you are not related to your sister when you thought you were. In fact, there is a whole other family out there who says you belong to them. "When I first received the DNA information I thought there was a mistake." I took a deep breath. "There was no mistake."

I stopped as my mother's eyes filled.

"Mom? Please, Mom."

She leaned back in her chair, her body crumpling, her eyes shutting, as Aunt Camellia put her arm around her.

"DNA doesn't talk about love," Aunt Camellia said, her voice wavering. "And that's what we have here."

I felt a bit faint.

"Too much information can, statistically speaking, cause problems," Aunt Iris said, but it was weak.

Beside me, Jules twitched.

"Mom, Jules and I, according to this DNA site, are not sisters. We're not related at all."

My mother opened her eyes, then started to cry, her face in her hands. My mother so rarely cries.

"You are not my biological mother and Dad is not my biological father, are you?"

Her shoulders shook.

"Oh, Mom." I didn't know what to do. I was so angry at her, but I loved her, too. I didn't want to see her cry like this.

"Remember our bonds, our family bonds," Aunt Camellia said.

"Family is family," Aunt Iris said.

"Mom," Jules said. "Are we both adopted?"

"No," my mother sobbed. "No. Just my beloved Evie."

I sat back, my mind numb. Jules sat back, too. We didn't think that Jules had been adopted, but we knew there was a possibility. She looked like my mother and aunts—blonde hair, although their hair was now white, dark brown eyes. Jules resembled them in photos when they were her age.

"I'm Baby Rose, aren't I?"

My mother gasped, as did my aunts.

"Yes, darling," my mother finally choked out, "You are Baby Rose."

I was Baby Rose. My biological mother and father had been jailed for murder. One of them, probably my mother, had killed Johnny's father. It was a huge trial. Their baby, me, had been taken from them after Betsy gave birth in jail.

"Evie," my mother said, tears all over her face. "I couldn't get pregnant. We didn't know what was wrong, and the doctor didn't either. I was nearing forty and we'd been trying for years. We went to an adoption agency. It was run by the state. We applied. We were interviewed multiple times. Finally we qualified. We were so happy. We heard about a baby being born, a girl, and we wanted you." She stopped, ran her hands over her face. "We said yes."

I nodded, feeling my heart squeeze. Sundance put his head in my lap, sensing my distress.

"Your father and I decided not to tell anyone that you were adopted except for Aunt Camellia and Aunt Iris and your grandfather. Your dad's parents were gone by then. We were moving from one base to another, we had been abroad, so it was easy to present you as our daughter, born in Portland, to everyone when we moved again to another military base."

"Why, Mom? Why didn't you tell me?" But I knew why. I wanted to see what she would say. What she would admit to, what she wouldn't.

"I always wanted you to feel like ours. So did Dad. We saw no harm in that. Remember, back then there was no DNA, people weren't linking up to family members they never met. We thought you would always believe you were ours, as in our hearts, you always were, you always are."

"And?" I prodded.

"And your parents were in jail for murder," she whispered, stricken.

"You didn't want me to start asking questions about them."

"I didn't want any taint on you from your biological parents. Two parents who had committed a murder? Who had killed the man who would have been your grandfather? Wasn't that too much of a burden for a child to bear? Why have that history around you? And your biological mother, not only was she in jail but we were told that she was crazy, that she believed she could see the future. We didn't believe that, so we thought she was a fraud or mentally ill."

"And then I started seeing the future, having premonitions, and she didn't seem so crazy anymore, did she?"

"No, honey, she didn't." My mother knitted her fingers together, back and forth.

"Tell me what happened when I was a baby."

"We went to the jail to pick you up the night you were born. It was snowy, icy. Your mother should have been transported to the hospital, but she wasn't because of the weather, I think. Maybe she hid that she was in labor so she could have you to herself as long as possible, or maybe the labor was too fast. I don't know. We were told when you were born. We were told it would be less than an hour or so before we could hold you, take you home, but it took longer. Over two hours. We don't know why it took that long."

"When did you put together that my mother was the one who killed my biological father's father?"

"It was all over the newspaper at that time. Two teenagers killing one of the fathers? It was a major news story. Betsy Baturra . . ." She stopped, then said, "Your bio mother said that she killed her boyfriend's father, Peter Kandinsky, but his son, Johnny, your bio father, said that he did it. Both of their fingerprints were on the knife. But the evidence pointed to your mother. Then it came out that she was pregnant."

"And you went to the jail not knowing whose baby you were getting but you guessed?"

"We wondered. Then a guard there told us who you were. He had been in the room when Betsy delivered. He looked ill, and your father asked if we could help him, and the man, the boy, he was so young, told us who was having a baby. I doubt he meant to tell us, but we went to help him because it looked like he was going to pass out. I'm sure he didn't even realize that we were the adoptive parents."

"But your names are on my birth certificate."

"We put our names down. Not hers. Not your biological father's, as we were legally allowed to do. We were your parents."

"Did you worry that I would turn out like my mother? That I would be violent, like my mom, or have a mental health issue?"

"No, I didn't. We loved you from the start, and I knew your

dad and I would raise you with a lot of love. If you had a mental health issue, which we knew you might, given your mother, we would help you as best as we could."

"And when I had the premonitions when I was a little girl?"

"Initially we were devastated. You were like your mother. In fact at her second trial, after she'd been in jail for ten years, she made premonitions about the judge and the jurors that came true."

"But by then you had to believe my mother's testimony, that she had foreseen Johnny being shot by his father."

Her face grew so sad, it looked like it was sagging in on itself. "Yes. We came to believe that Betsy was telling the truth at her trial. We came to believe that she stabbed Johnny's father because she knew he was going to shoot Johnny. But what could we do? Come out and say that you, Betsy's biological daughter, also had premonitions and they were correct every time? That would have catapulted you into disaster. It would not be admissible in any new trial, that was for sure. And if the press found out, they would hound us, hound you. Forever your name would be associated with hers and, equally as bad, you would be labeled as an oddity. The daughter of a murderer who has premonitions—like her mother."

"I get it, Mom."

"But there we were." She started to cry again. "Betsy and Johnny were locked up, in cages, in jail, suffering, without their daughter while we happily, lovingly raised you."

"What did you think when they both received new trials? After Tilly remembered what happened and the bodies were found?"

"Tilly was seventeen then and entirely credible, as you know from reading the article. When Johnny's and Betsy's sentences were overturned and they were released, we were relieved for them, but we were also so frightened. We knew they would probably come after you. Why wouldn't they? They had been locked away and shouldn't have been, and you were their daughter. They worked hard and saved their money, then they hired top-notch attorneys and the whole case exploded again. It was front page news. Your parents' argument was that they had been found not guilty and they should now be able to raise you. Millions of people agreed with them, and if they didn't agree that Betsy and Johnny should get full custody, they did agree that they should get visitation.

"That's why we moved you up here to the island when you were eleven. The news was too much. It was all around us. We wanted peace for you, privacy. Your dad and I were scared to death. We wanted to shelter you. What if someone found out who you were? It would be a media circus."

"Were you contacted by the adoption agency? By the state? By Johnny and Betsy's attorney?"

"We hired an attorney. He handled everything for us anonymously. Back then, and because of the circumstances of your mom being a convicted murderer, the adoption records were sealed. Your parents sued to get the information, but the court denied them. Your bio parents fought and lost."

"So they wanted me." I tried to breathe, feeling my bio parents' pain. Sundance, sensing this, licked my hand.

"Very much. And we were scared to death they would win, that they would get custody of you, or visitation."

"But Mom. Why didn't you tell me later, when I was a teenager?"

"Because you're *our* daughter, not theirs." She reached for my hand. Her hand was freezing cold. "I didn't want to bring this mess, this stress, into your life. When would I tell you? When you were in kindergarten? Honey, your parents are murderers. What's a murderer? Let me explain it to you. . . .

"Or should we have told you when they were trying to get you back as the trial ground on? Bring that fear into your life that you would be taken from us and sent to live with another family you had never met? How would you have felt? You would have been petrified. Or as a teen, should I have told you? When you were battling premonitions and depression and anxiety that was almost crippling you?"

I was angry at her. I was angry with my father. I was angry

with my aunts. "Mom, everyone has a right to the truth of their own reality. I understand why you didn't tell me as a kid. Given the circumstances, I may have done what you did. Even when I was a teenager, I understand why you didn't tell me. That kind of history could mess up a teenager's mind, especially mine because I was a wreck, but as an adult, even at eighteen, don't you think I should have been given the truth about who I am?"

My mother sat back. "I don't know."

"You don't know?"

"No. For all the reasons I told you. How are you better knowing what you know now?"

"I'm not better, Mom, but I want the truth. Why can't you see that?"

"The truth is that I am your mother, your father was your father."

"I know that, Mom." I saw the tears in her eyes, but I also saw guilt, and doubt, and the fear that she would lose me now. "I wish you had told me as a young adult."

"Your father and I, we debated endlessly, but we didn't want to tear your world apart. I had lied to you, too. Your father had lied to you. Both by omission. I felt awful. But how do you walk back from such a monumental lie?"

"But it wasn't about you and how you would feel walking back from a lie, Mom. It was about me. It would have helped me to know Betsy, to know that having premonitions was genetic, to talk to her and reach out to her for help and advice. It would have helped me to know Johnny, to meet Tilly, to later know I had another sister."

"And then what, Evie?"

"What do you mean?"

"Then you go to that family, you're furious at me, at your dad, and we lose you. You stop talking to us. Then we've lost our daughter."

"Mom." I was shocked. "Why would you think you would lose me?"

"Because you share the same blood with them. Betsy gave

birth to you. You both see the future. Those are enormous bonds. You could have chosen to live with her, to call her Mom forever."

"You will always be my mother. Always. I love you so much, but I am livid with you, and with you, Aunt Camellia and Aunt Iris, for not telling me."

Aunt Camellia burst into tears.

Aunt Iris's chin trembled and she dropped her face to her hands.

"Mom," Jules said. "I think you should have told Evie."

My mother dropped into another round of choking tears. "I know. Maybe you're right. I don't know. Maybe. I'm sorry. I am. I did what I thought was best."

"You all knew this secret about me," I said, my voice cracking with pain. "You've all known how lonely I've often felt, how alone. There was something missing, and I couldn't explain it, couldn't fix it, couldn't deal with it. I thought that it was me, that something was wrong with me. I thought it was my premonitions that were setting me apart, but it wasn't. I had been taken from my biological parents, and somehow, some way, even though I was a baby, I felt it. That separation is what caused the inexplicable hole I have felt, I have battled, my whole life."

My mother shook her head back and forth, not in the negative, but as if she was emotionally crushed, jerking this way and that.

"Knowing I was adopted could have helped me in so many ways."

"I know," she said, crying. "I know. I'm sorry. I see what you're saying now. I didn't handle it right. Evie, please. I love you so much. Please forgive me. Please."

Jules reached over and held my hand. Her hand was shaking in mine.

"Mom, my bio parents, Betsy and Johnny, they were found to be innocent of murder. It was self-defense. They lost me for all these years, and they clearly wanted me back. I understand why you didn't want to hand me over as a child, but when I was eighteen, or a young adult, you could have told me. When I read that article about them, what struck me was how desperately they wanted to find me. That's why they did the interviews, the talk show. The DNA test. To find me."

My mother hiccupped and sobbed again.

"They weren't bad people, Mom. They did not willingly give me up."

I did not have children, so I could not fully understand the heartache a parent would feel for a child who was gone. But I could imagine part of it. My bio parents had lived for decades without their own child. Their own daughter.

I had had enough. "That wasn't right, Mom. If not for me, then for them. They were teenagers when all this happened. They went to prison. You should have told me so I could have made my own decision. My decision would have been to find them, knowing their story. I'm thirty-seven years old. They have not known for decades if I was alive or dead, healthy or sick, happy or not. Wouldn't you want to know if it were your daughter? If it were me or Jules?"

"Yes. Yes, I would have wanted to know." My mother was trembling and her sisters had their arms around her. They were three white-haired women in their seventies, and they were all crushed. I could see that. I was crushed, too. I was crushed for them and for me and for Betsy and Johnny. "Aunt Camellia and Aunt Iris. Wouldn't you want to know your niece? I'm sure my aunt Tilly would like to know me."

"Yes," they said, their voices weak. "Yes, we would."

"One more question," I said.

"Anything," my mother said.

"Did you know that Johnny and Betsy named me Rose?"

"No, we didn't. Not until their trial ten years after we adopted you."

I have loved roses all my life. They calm me down. I had them painted or embroidered on my clothes. In vases at my table. My pink and yellow rose wallpaper at home and in the bookstore.

Surrounding my home. Growing up my trellis. I thought it was because my mother and aunts and grandma loved roses. It was deeper than that.

I couldn't talk about this anymore. I was having trouble getting deep breaths. I do not like when I can't get deep breaths. It reminds me of anxiety, and I hate having anxiety. I stood up and said, "I love you," to all of them and walked home through the moonlight, through rows of roses, which now had a deeper meaning for me than before. I stopped to smell several, trying to calm down.

I heard my mother call my name, her voice broken. I heard my aunts call my name, their voices filled with pain. My sister did not call my name. She knew I needed to be alone.

Sundance walked beside me.

Once again I headed to our beach. I felt like I could hardly walk, as if I were moving through a wave of lies and deceit. Butch and Cassidy came running, bursting out of the cat/dog door at my house. Ghost tumbled on over, as did Mars.

I sat on a log and cried and cried. For me, for Johnny and Betsy, who had had their baby ripped out of their lives, and for Tilly. I cried for the terrible things that had happened to both of them in jail and, for Tilly, in foster care, traumatized and not speaking, that had been detailed in online articles that I'd read for hours.

I cried because my life had been cracked open and filled with lies. I cried because my father wasn't even here to comfort me and I wanted his comfort, even though I was mad at him, too. I cried because of Marco and how much I loved him, and wanted him, and I cried because I felt bad for this happening right before Jules's wedding.

When I was cold, I called to Butch and Cassidy and went home. The goats hopped around and I said hello but didn't bother chasing them back to their blue home, which was clearly a disappointment to them. I took a bath and didn't even eat my pie that night. I climbed the stairs to the loft, my body feeling as if it had been beaten up, the dogs and cats following behind me. I was so screwed up I couldn't even read. I turned out the light.

Sundance plopped his head right next to mine and licked my tears. "You're my best furry friend," I said to him, whispering, in case Butch and Cassidy heard. Jupiter and Ghost appeared and found their favorite sleeping spaces.

My hot tears dropped into Sundance's fur.

It had been a long day at the bookstore. Lots of tourists, and we'd sold a fair amount of books. They loved the desserts, the white chocolate cranberry cake and bourbon caramel spiced pie, and our tea specials: Sweet Cinnamon Milk and London Fog.

I sold Aunt Iris's sensual photographs of flowers; Aunt Camellia's lotions, including new ones she had named Bedside Body Art and Love Potion Pink; and my mother's bouquets, two labeled "A Woman Must Find Her Power and Wield It" and "Love and Romance Are on My To-Do List."

The History Nerd Book Club had their monthly meeting, and they had proceeded to analyze the siege of Leningrad during World War II down to the finest detail. There were maps drawn and military analysis and a review of what the people there had to do to survive. There were some raised voices, which alarmed customers enough to hurry on over and join the near-raucous historical discussion. A professor of Russian history happened to be there and gave a wonderful fifteen-minute lecture that everyone found mesmerizing, in particular the cannibalism that some people in Leningrad resorted to.

After they left, Mrs. Lennert hustled in and told me her problem.

"Look, Evie, I need to know."

"I can't see into the future, Mrs. Lennert."

Mrs. Lennert scoffed, then leaned over the counter and rapped in her ex-teacher's voice, "You listen here, young woman, I have known you since you moved here as a little girl and your mother put your hair in braids and you ran around holding a fake pink gun to shoot zombies."

"Mrs. Lennert."

"Dear." She put her hand on mine. "I have never asked you before."

"Yes, you have. Many times."

"But this time I need to know."

"I don't see anything, Mrs. Lennert. Nothing."

She was displeased. "I am going right down to your mother and aunts for a little flower power and I'm going to speak to them about you."

It was as if I were still a child and she was reprimanding me, even though she was the one buying pot. I sighed. This is the problem of living in a small town on a small emerald island where your mother and aunts live. "You are welcome to do that. Tell them I said hi."

She patted her white hair. She knew her threat wouldn't work with me. "All I want to know is if Seymour will ask me to marry him or sleep with me and take off. What's the problem? Why so stubborn?"

"I'm sorry. I don't do fortune telling."

"*Humpf.* You're being obstinate and unhelpful."

"I'm sorry." Mrs. Lennert is seventy years old. Shouldn't she know by now if a man is going to sleep with her and take off? On the other hand, her paramour, Seymour, is seventy-five. He had a cane and a hearing aid. If he does take off, at least he won't be taking off rapidly.

"Mrs. Lennert, you need to ask yourself how you feel about Seymour and then you need to ask him if he's going to sleep with you and leave you."

She furrowed her brow. "I would rather lean on the accuracy of your premonitions."

The accuracy of my premonitions? Well, they were accurate. Except for the one with the fiery car accident when I die. Probably. Maybe. Could be. "I did get three more autobiographies in. Would you like to see them?"

"Only if they're autobiographies about powerful, strong women who know their minds. You know I can't stand reading a book if I think the woman is shallow or weak, following a man around like a silly puppy dog and letting him make decisions about her own life."

I did not laugh at the irony. "No weak or shallow women, I promise."

That night I crawled into bed with my cats and dogs and three books.

I am a Crazy Cat Lady.

And a Crazy Dog Lady.

Is there such a thing as a Crazy Alpaca Lady?

At least Marco understood being crazy about animals.

I wondered if Betsy, Johnny, Kayla, and Tilly liked animals. Would they think I was a crazy animal lover?

My mom and aunts and I were not talking. It hurt all of us, but I needed time.

Time to deal with their lies, filled with love though they were.

When I received a message on my ancestry account the next morning I choked on my coffee and had to spit it out.

Dear Evie,

My name is Betsy Baturra. I am your biological mother. I would love to meet you, to talk to you, but I will respect your privacy if that is what you would like. Your father, Johnny Kandinsky, and I have been together since we were seventeen. We have been married for twenty-seven years. We have a sixteen-year-old daughter, Kayla, your sister, and you have an aunt Tilly. They, too, would love to meet you, but we will all respect your wishes.

Our story is complicated. You may have looked us up online. Please know that the online portrait is not always true.

What is true is that Johnny and I have always loved you. We were devastated to lose you. Every day of our lives we have prayed for your health and happiness.

I am sure that you have read that I have premonitions. I have had no premonitions about you, or your future, but I am wondering if you have the same gift. My mother had it, as did my grandmother, and her mother before her. It is the Irish second sight.

Please call me at the numbers below, or e-mail me, or Johnny, if you would like. I have also enclosed our address. We would be happy to come to you, too, at any time, including today.

Yours sincerely and with all my love,
Your mother, Betsy

I sat back, stunned.
Shocked.
There she was. Betsy Baturra.
Mom.

I showed the letter to Jules.
"What are you going to do?" she asked.
We were sitting at my kitchen table that night, yellow Julia Child roses on the table. Jules was showing me the photos of the motorcycles she had recently custom painted, and we were sampling two pieces of pie—marionberry from a farmer friend named LaRenti and lemon custard by a man who had recently moved here named TeeRee—that I was going to sell in the bookstore. Obviously, the pie eating was purely for professional reasons.

"I'm going to write back to her. Soon. But not yet. I have to think this through. Do I want to meet her? When?" I looked at my dad's airplanes hanging from the ceiling. Why did you have to lie, Dad? "Do I want new parents and a sister in my life all the time? Part of the time? Will they like me? Will I like them?"

"Yep, wait it out and think about it," she said, slinging an arm around my shoulders. "This marionberry pie is heaven. Have a bite." She held out her fork. "Open up, sister-love."

"Delicious."

*   *   *

I saw Marco on his boat. I was sitting in the gazebo reading a book with Sundance. I knelt down like a spy and peeped out. He was with three other men. They were laughing and talking. I thought my heart would stop beating, collapse, and be sucked into the rest of my body.

He was so dang handsome, the wind brushing his hair back, his arms muscled, his smile wide.

I loved that man, I did.

But Marco loved his boat. That was a problem. A deathly problem.

My premonition of Marco's death was stark and horrifying, I didn't even like to think about it. Thinking about that premonition before I went to sleep had always given me nightmares.

Together with Sundance we were out on his boat at the tail end of dusk. The boat started taking on water in a freak storm, thunder and lightning, the works. We were not near the islands, not near home, I don't know where we were, but night soon caved in, the inky blackness all around us, like a suffocating black blanket.

The boat started to sink, why was not clear to me. Marco had a life raft on board and he inflated it, pushed me into it, then tossed Sundance to me, which knocked me over. The boat suddenly lurched to the side and Marco fell over. He cracked his head on the rail as he went. I grabbed the oars of the lifeboat and went around the tilting boat to get him, screaming his name, my screams lost in a blast of thunder.

I couldn't see him, I couldn't find him. I was nearing hysteria. Sundance was barking. The boat went down, the suction pulling on the raft, and I paddled back, still screaming his name, but he was gone. The rain pounded down, the lighting highlighting that I was alone, in a raft, on the ocean, Marco under the water, dying if not dead.

In the distance, I could see two boats, speeding straight for me. Marco had sent out a Mayday signal. I took off my life jacket and dove off the raft as soon as the suction stopped, searching for Marco. I came up for air, the waves slamming against me, but no Marco. He had had a life jacket on, too. Where was he? Why wasn't he bobbing to the surface? Was he stuck, pinned somehow? I dove down again and again, telling myself to be calm, to find Marco. The two boats arrived, and the people hauled me out of the water with a life ring, then grabbed the lifeboat with Sundance barking in it.

Marco was gone.

In my premonition I see myself on my knees, keening, sobbing, shaking in the dark on the rescue boat, my despair endless. I want to jump in the water and be with him, drown myself, go where he has gone.

And that was why I could not be with Marco.

It was his destiny to die on his boat if I was with him.

My problem with the premonition is that I could not exactly remember what either of us was wearing. It was dark. It was raining. We were wet. I couldn't tell. Also, I think I was so terrified when that particular premonition hit, like a rock to my face, that our clothing didn't penetrate.

Boating was part of Marco's life. He loved it. He would want, he would need, someone who loved it, too. If I am not with Marco, if I am never on his boat with him, he will live. Now one could say that we could make a rule that we will never sail together, but it's not good enough. It's one mistake, it's letting down our guard one time, and he dies.

Plus, I'm screwed up. Hair-raising premonitions. People I have to save with, sometimes, only a few minutes to do so. A high dose of anxiety and depression that comes and goes that I have to fight. Sometimes that depression is based in sand and burning flames in a place far away. I also don't want to leave the island again, which would be restricting for anyone. Who wants to live with a semi-hermit? I have deliberately let some people die without warning them what's coming for them. He may well have a moral issue with that. I have an endless need to be alone to get my brain sorted out and my rampaging emotions evened out. I'm a book hoarder.

I could kill him, *and* I could make him miserable as his wife. I'm a real prize.

No, Marco is better off without me. That is not said as an irritating martyr. It's said as truth.

Thinking about a life without Marco, or worse, thinking about life without Marco when he gets married and has children . . . well, that dumps me in an emotional gutter.

But it is what it needs to be.

I know that.

Chapter 32

〜

Betsy Baturra
Portland, Oregon
2012

Betsy saw the car crash premonition again when she was driving to the original Rose's Market for a meeting.

The cliff was on her right, mountain on her left, the one-lane road curving. The sun behind her shone through the fir trees, the orange poppies almost glowing. She looked over the cliff, not liking how steep it was.

The other driver, in the blue truck, coming straight toward her on that one-lane road, swerved as she slammed on her brakes. Betsy swerved, too, away from the truck, but it was too late. The truck dove tailed and their head-on collision was a dead-on hit.

At first they wobbled together, like a teeter-totter at the edge of the cliff, then they both, at the same time, together, crashed over the side.

Betsy knew they were rolling as her car collapsed around her, the sides smashing in, the roof bending, her body thrown around under the seat belt, her head slamming into the airbag.

She thought they were taking more air for a second before her car rolled one more time. The crush of metal was louder than it had ever been, as if she were in a can that had been squished by a giant foot.

One of them died, she thought. Maybe both of them. There was an air of death amidst the cacophony of noise, the flames, the black smoke, and the shattering of glass.

But it was also unclear . . .

She gritted her teeth and went to the meeting at Rose's Market.

When she left the meeting she thought of Rose, actually she thought of Evie Lindsay, her daughter. The daughter who had taken a DNA test. She had learned all she could about Evie and her bookstore. They looked almost identical, and the resemblance to Kayla was uncanny.

She prayed and prayed that Evie/Rose would answer the message she wrote to her.

"Please, Rose, please," she whispered, her voice sounding raw and desperate even to her. "Evie, please."

Chapter 33

On Halloween night Gavin killed my best friend's mother, Miss Patsy.

Two neighbors out walking their dogs heard Patsy screaming and came running. They heard Gavin yelling, "Wake up, Patsy! Oh, my God. Oh, my God! Patsy!"

The neighbors ran to the house. One of them was a retired police officer, and one was a retired firefighter and paramedic.

They rushed to the kitchen as Gavin was rushing out, grabbing his keys and wallet, his face red, stained with tears. The retired police officer stood his ground and yelled at Gavin not to move, but he did not have a gun, and Gavin was panicked so he shoved him aside and took off in his truck. The police officer and the firefighter bent over Patsy, who was bleeding profusely, and tried to help.

They called 911 and said they needed a helicopter to take Patsy to the hospital. They did CPR in Patsy's home, and they continued until the life flight crew took over.

Patsy was wearing her brown sweater, the scarf with pumpkins on it, and her beige slacks. She died.

Gavin sped off in his boat, out of his mind, but was immediately plucked up out in the ocean by the coast guard. He would get a sentence of life in prison. He had two other convictions for assaults against a former wife and former girlfriend and a multitude of antistalking orders.

My sweet friend Emily was so shocked that her mother had

been killed, she stopped crying altogether the next day, her eyes vacant, her face gray.

Emily and her grandma, Patsy's mother, who sobbed through the memorial service, packed up with help from all of us, and they moved to Texas, where her grandma was a teacher. We wrote letters for years. Emily later became involved in drugs and alcohol. It was obvious why—she was numbing the pain of her loss. No father—he had abandoned her before she was even born—and her mother murdered. Her grandma died, I knew that, when she was twenty-one, and Emily was on her own. I haven't heard from her in years.

Patsy's death was my fault.

All my fault.

I saw that beating coming, I saw death leaning over her, and I saw what Patsy was wearing, I could have done something to save my best friend's mother. I should have noticed her clothes that day, but I was too excited about the Halloween dance. I have never been able to get rid of that guilt. The guilt led to depression. Yes, I know I was only fourteen years old. Yes, I know that Gavin was responsible.

But the worst thing about having premonitions is that when you can prevent something bad from happening to someone, and you mess that up, you live with that guilt, as irrational as it sounds, for the rest of your life. I failed Emily and I failed Miss Patsy.

And because of my failure, Patsy could not mother Emily, and Emily got into drugs and disappeared. I didn't even know if she was alive.

I drove by Emily's house when I delivered books to Torrance, who was almost healed from his surgery. I stopped, backed up, then pulled into the driveway, the willow tree blowing in the wind.

I have always missed Emily, and I hoped that her life was happy and healthy. She deserved it. Her mother had deserved it, too.

Marco came over to my house on Sunday evening.

He had called first, asked if he could come over to talk, and

I'd said yes. I couldn't resist seeing him. I was miserable. My own loneliness was like a living, breathing tangle of pain.

"Thanks, Evie." He sat at my table. I had made him hot chocolate and put a huge dollop of whipped cream on it, plus a stick of chocolate. And I'd given him a slice of peach pie. I was trying not to cry. Trying hard.

"Wow." He actually smiled. "Now that's dessert. Thank you."

"There are peaches in the pie, which puts it in the fruit group," I said, my voice cracking a tad because he is warm and loving and always looks at me as if I mean something to him. As if I'm important. He looks at me gently. And with lust. It's a potent and near irresistible combination. "And the hot chocolate has milk in it, which puts it in the milk group."

He nodded at me.

"It's my best excuse." Sundance tried to get in my lap, but I gently pushed him down. Ghost climbed up on the table, and I gently put her on the floor. I hoped the goats would not try to come in. I sniffled, tried to hide it by saying, "I think my cats are making me sneeze."

"You don't need an excuse to eat peach pie. Eat what you want."

His face was so handsome, but he seemed tired. Stressed. For once in my life I couldn't eat peach pie. That was a dang shame, but I was too miserable. I'd actually lost fifteen pounds. My butt was smaller, my boobs were smaller, and I felt weak and drained. I didn't even have the energy to get something nice on. I was wearing a zippered pink sweatshirt and jeans. I did make time to put on Aunt Camellia's lotion called Rose Hips and Bust.

"Evie, I've asked you out many times and you've said no."

"I know."

"I need to ask you something."

I knew what he was talking about. "Yes. I've had a premonition about you. About us."

I saw the worry in his eyes, but also courage. "Was it a good premonition or a bad one?"

"It was a bad one." My eyes flooded. "You die in it, Marco. You drown."

He was silent for long seconds, his hands clasped together, not eating the pie. "Well, that's not good."

"No, it's not. You see, Marco..." I rushed forward so I could calm him down, reduce his worry, about how and when he died. "I'm with you. We're on your boat. There's a storm. It's nighttime. You pitch over into the water. The boat goes down, the suction almost taking me down in the life raft. I'm trying to find you, but you're gone. I'm screaming, I dive in and out of the water, but the night is so dark, the waves so bad, I can't find you. Sundance is barking, I'm crying. It's the worst premonition I've ever had." Including the premonition where I might or might not die in a calamitous car crash.

He stared at me, then said, his face clearing, "Then we need to stay off my boat. It's that simple."

"We can't. It's one mistake on our part, one boat ride, one time thinking that it's okay and it's not. I've even tried to see the clothes we were wearing, but I can't. It's too dark, the storm is too heavy. The whole thing petrified me." I drew my hands across my face, my breathing somewhat gaspy, like I was drowning.

"But we can make sure we're never on a boat together."

"It will kill you, Marco. I can't risk it."

"We can. We will. We will not be on a boat together. Ever."

"Marco, that's not the only reason I can't be with you, even if you want to be with me."

"I want to be with you."

"I'm a mess."

"You aren't."

"Yes. But there's more."

"What is it?"

"I have to be alone a lot. If I'm not, I feel like my brain is breaking down. I feel like it's going to explode. You see me when the animals are sick or hurt. I put on who I want to be for you. It's not like I'm lying to you about who I am, but I'm only allowing you to see part of me, not all of me, certainly not the tearful, deeply scarred person that I am, that I hide from every-one else. I can function at work, then I come home, take care of my animals, talk to my animals as if they're human, like Sun-dance." Sundance heard me say his name and tried to get on my lap again, but I didn't let him. "I hide in my books for hours so I don't have premonitions. I have insomnia. Sometimes I fight depression and anxiety. It's not pretty, it's not easy."

"Look, Evie. I was in a war. You want a mess? I'm a mess. I have flashbacks and nightmares from my time in the army. You know this. I have regrets. I hate myself for what I did over there sometimes. Sometimes I believe that everything we did over there in Iraq was wrong. When bodies are strewn all over the ground, dead, the mothers are crying on both sides. Other times I believe we did the right thing. We wanted to get rid of a dan-gerous man. But the politicians, usually old and white who have often never served, start the wars but don't fight them. We do. My buddies did. My memories haunt me. I have to willfully pull myself together, pull myself out of Iraq and what I saw, the in-juries, the deaths, and blood, and what I did when I was follow-ing orders, or giving my men orders. War screws people up.

"I'm screwed up. I have let you see the part of me that I want you to see, too. But I haven't let you see all of me, not the part of me that is still struggling, years later, with the war. We're both wrecks who are trying hard to be normal. To feel normal."

"I can't do it, Marco." I felt this well of unbearable sadness. "I'm sorry."

"Why, though, Evie? Why can't you try? Do you not like me? Do you not see any possibility of a future? We talk, we laugh, we're alike in some ways, not in others, which makes it interest-ing. You're the smartest woman I know. You're witty, and you don't let anyone walk on you, I've seen it with the chief. But you're kind. Everything you do for people on the island, not only bringing them books and helping your mom and aunts make hats for fund-raisers but for saving the people that you do. You love books, you love your animals, you love your fam-ily so intensely. You're so loyal. And yet you've got this whole other mysterious part to you, this huge, deep inner life that I find compelling and interesting. I love how you live your life. I love your laugh and your curiosity and your sarcasm. Please try. Try us."

Why? Why couldn't I do this? Because I am a flawed, bizarre human being. "I feel scared even thinking about us, Marco. I don't think I'm meant to be with any man. I don't even want to leave the island, that's how isolated I am. I don't have the confidence to be with you. I don't have the courage to open myself up like that. And I cannot guarantee that I won't fail you and get on a boat and you'll die. I love you. I do. I started falling in love with you that first day I met you in my bookstore. It was instant. It was a miracle. But I also knew we wouldn't be together."

He dropped his head in his hands.

Maybe I shouldn't have told him I loved him. Maybe it hurt him more. It hurt me more to admit it. It certainly was not time to tell him that I had a whole other family. Why add more bizarreness to an already bizarre situation?

I put my hand on his head, then to his shoulders. He didn't look up when I muffled a cry and walked out my door and off to talk to Shakespeare and Jane Austen about my busted-up heart and my stupid personality, and my lack of bravery.

I saw him leave shortly afterward as I stood in the shadow of the willow tree, Sundance by my side.

I lay on the ground and stared into the tree, utterly miserable.

I woke up the next morning feeling as if my life had shifted and fallen over a cliff. There were no more pretenses between Marco and me.

It would be my move to make. He would not do so again. He would respect my decision. He was all man, a true gentleman. He would give me space.

I missed him already as if I'd lost a leg and an arm.

I didn't want any of my animals to get sick.

But I wondered if I could get one of the goats to pretend to be sick so I could see him again.

Or maybe Sundance. I could give Sundance some of my underwear again and we could go and see Marco . . . I glanced down at Sundance. He stuck his head up, then cocked it to the left as in, "What are you thinking?"

I petted his head. "If you feel even the slightest bit sick, let me know, okay?"

He wobbled his head.

"I'm going to write to her," I told Jules when she came up to visit again from Seattle to prepare the final details for her wedding. "She's my biological mother. I want to talk to her. I want to talk to my dad. And my sister and aunt."

Jules nodded and swung an arm around me as we sat on the bench in the gazebo, the sun setting, deer in the field. "I think you should."

"I'm not talking about it with Mom and the aunts."

"Yep. Let that one be."

I felt hot tears flood my eyes because of my continual sanity problems. "I think I need some pie when we go back."

"Let me slice it," Jules said. "It's the apple pie, right? Let's eat popcorn, too, extra butter."

"Might as well have ice cream with it, too."

"Mix the flavors."

"It's healthy," I sniffed. My mind was swirling. I had a new mother, father, aunt, and sister. Marco was gone. My mother had lied, and so had my aunts and father. I needed healthy food to cope. "Popcorn is made out of corn, which is a vegetable. Apple pie has apples in it. Ice cream is in the milk group." My voice pitched up with emotions. "Might as well watch a romance movie while we eat."

"Agreed. Stop crying, you're going to make me cry, Evie."

"I love you, Jules."

She sniffed.

"Don't cry, Jules."

"I can't help it. There has been a lot of stuff going on here! A lotta stuff!" Her mouth trembled.

"I know, I know!"

"And I'm getting married to Mack!"

ALL ABOUT EVIE   337

We both burst into tears, hugging each other close.

"Mack is so patient and understanding. He knew I needed another woo-woo last night and I didn't even need to ask for it!"

She snuffled.

I laughed through my tears.

"Why are you laughing, Evie?"

She was genuinely perplexed. "Because sometimes people laugh and cry at the same time and that's what I want to do."

"Okay!" She laughed. "I'll do it, too!"

What do you say to a woman who gave birth to you?

A woman who clearly wanted you in her life, who fought to have you in her life, in court.

I had no children. I had planned on never giving birth to kids because I didn't know if this premonition problem was hereditary. Now I knew. It solidified things for me even more. I would not wish this premonition monster on anyone. However, it was not beyond my imagination to understand how traumatizing it would be to lose a child and how hopeful she and Johnny would be, waiting for my reply.

I took a deep breath the next morning. Okay. I was ready.

Dear Betsy,

Thank you for your letter. There is so much to say, I don't know what to say.

I would like to meet you, Johnny, Kayla, and Tilly.

When is convenient for you?

Sincerely,

Evie

"You haven't read a book in five years?" I stared aghast at the woman in front of me. She was in her early thirties.

"I have six kids. I've been knocked up for years." She pushed brown curls off her face. Her hair was long and messy. "My husband has the kids back at our campsite. I'm supposed to be shopping for groceries. One is two years old and has such volcanic temper tantrums he passes out. Neat trick. Two of them are twins. They're four. They're awful. It's like watching a crime family develop as they deliberately plug the toilets.

"One is six, and she insists on dressing like a frog and hops around every day. She won't answer unless I call her Froggy Frieda. The eight-year-old is mouthy. She's going to be a wild-ass teenager and give me white hair. The ten-year-old wanders off like he's some freakin' explorer and I have to find him. He brings a magnifying glass and a toy bow and arrow with him. Who does he think he is, a hunting scientist? My husband keeps wanting to have sex with me. I don't want to have any more sex. Look what happens when we do. Now do you see why I haven't read?"

I calmed down. Whew. She had an excuse for not reading. This was not the usual circumstance of choosing not to read because you have nothing in the way of a curious brain.

"Okay. You have a decent excuse, so I won't be mad at you. What do you want to read?"

"I want to read a book where there's a woman doing something exciting with her life. No kids, for God's sakes. No husband. That would ruin the whole book for me. I do not want to read about what I'm already living. My husband has gas right now. We're in a tent. Do you know what it's like to sleep with a gassy husband and six kids in a tent? I'm miserable. I hate being in a sleeping bag. It makes me feel sweaty and trapped. We're here for seven days because my husband wanted the kids to experience the outdoors. I'm experiencing hell. How would you like to change a kid's diaper in a tent in the middle of the night with a flashlight in your mouth? It's a mess. It's unsanitary. It's disgusting.

"I want to read about a woman who's traveling and working a cool job and has lovers. A lot of lovers. She has to have high heels and she can take men down and out when they irritate her.

I'm feeling vengeful. I want a kick-ass woman. For God's sakes, no camping or any outdoorsy crap. Do you have a book like that?"

"I do." I led her over to the series I knew she would love. "Here. Sit down and give me your phone."

She handed me her phone. I leaned against my yellow rose wallpaper and called her husband and introduced myself. "Hey, so everything is fine, but your wife is having car trouble. . . . I don't know, a clanking sound . . . and I'm taking her to the auto shop here on the island that I go to. It's going to be about a four-hour wait because Sherman has three cars ahead of hers. Yeah. Sorry about that. Oh, no, no! No! You don't need to get a taxi to come get her. Not at all. She's talking to the mechanic and asked me to call you."

Her mouth hung open.

"I bought you four hours of time, girlfriend. Get reading, and I'll bring you some chai tea latte and a slice of toffee crunch cake with chocolate icing."

She was so grateful she teared up, the poor thing.

I checked that night for a letter from Betsy.
She had written right back, minutes after I'd written to her.

Dear Evie,
I write this with tears. I am so grateful to you for writing to me, as is Johnny. He, too, is in tears. How about if we come to you? We can come at any time. We can come tomorrow, but perhaps that's too soon? If you are free this weekend, we would be happy to see you.
Love, your mother, Betsy, and your father, Johnny.

Dear Betsy and Johnny,
Yes, I am free. I live on San Orcanita Island off the coast of Washington. Thank you for coming. I don't leave the island often. It is beautiful here, you will love it.
Evie

In three minutes I received a message back . . .

Dear Evie,

Thank you so much for letting us come to see you. We will arrive this weekend, on Friday. Please let us know if we can take you out to dinner. Please bring anyone you would like to bring.

Love,
Your mother, Betsy, and father, Johnny

That night I rode Shakespeare on a trail around the island to think.

I was going to meet Betsy, Johnny, Tilly, and Kayla.

It was hard to fathom.

Impossible.

Yet . . . exciting. She had premonitions. I had premonitions.

I was not alone with this strange affliction.

Would the hole in my soul heal? Had I always known that I was not with my biological mother? Had I subconsciously always felt that loss?

I pulled on Shakespeare's reins and we watched the sunset, lavender and burgundy, gold and yellow, orange and white.

Sunsets, especially on the island, always give me hope.

A family walked into Books, Cake, and Tea.

The woman had brown curls. She had a beaming smile. She was pretty. Her husband was tall and slender, somewhat gangly, glasses. He looked like a stereotypical image of an engineer: super smart. She was pushing a stroller with a baby in it and holding the hand of a girl who looked about two. Her husband was holding a boy who looked to be four and holding the hand of another boy who was clearly a twin. There was a girl about six, too, with brown curls.

It was the six-year-old girl who caught and held my eyes the most. She had blue eyes like cornflowers. A big smile. A dimple in her left cheek. She was skinny . . .

I looked up again at the mother, who was coming toward me, smiling, laughing, her arms out.

"Evie!" she called out. "My favorite member of the Island Girls Gang."

I put a hand on the counter near the register. It couldn't be. It was.

"Emily?" I squeaked out.

"Yep! Here to play Warrior Women with you again!"

She hugged me tight and we laughed. She kissed my cheek. "I've missed you."

"I've missed you, too. So much." I was so glad to see her, but then my guilt hit, my utter anguish about what I'd not done for her. How could she hug me? How could she be glad to see me? How come she didn't hate me? Why would she even come in the bookstore to see me?

"This is my family," she said to me, then turned toward them, "And this is Evie, my best friend."

Emily's husband, Eric, took the kids back to their cabin on the lake while Emily and I had coffee and red velvet cake with cream cheese icing out on the deck. They had bought a pile of books. They let the kids pick three each, and I gave each of them one as a gift.

"So you're here on vacation?" I asked. The gulls called out in the distance, two sailboats meandered by, and a couple had a picnic on a rowboat.

"Yes. But"—she grinned at me—"I think we're going to move here."

"You are?" I was cheered by that but dismayed, selfishly. How could I live with the guilt of what I'd done to her if I saw her all the time?

"Don't you want me to move here?"

She'd seen it. That flash on my face. "Yes, of course I do. Where do you live now?"

"We're in Silicon Valley. Smart One"—that's what she called her husband—"developed a few apps and now we're looking to get out of the traffic and noise and crowds, and Smart One needs a break. He'll invent another app or two, but he says he wants to do it without being bumper-to-bumper. So we're at the cabin and looking for homes."

"I can't believe it. Oh, my gosh. I would love to have you back here."

We chatted a bit longer, then Emily said, "I know I told you that when I was a teenager I got into drugs. And alcohol."

"You told me some, not much. You asked if I did drugs, told me you did."

"I did. I was aching for my mom. I think all my grief, and that trauma of losing her, of Gavin killing her . . . it came out in my teens. I was so lonely. My grandma . . ." She paused. "She was kind and loving to me. She put me in an expensive rehab three times. She understood, though. She understood why I did drugs. She was hurting, too. She'd lost her daughter. My mother was her only child, and I was her only grandchild. Anyhow, she became sick, terminally sick, and I finally got my head together. I went to outpatient rehab meetings and I took care of her. I took her to all her appointments, her treatments, her surgeries, but there wasn't any hope, right from the start. She was eighty-six. She died when I was twenty-one. I lived in her house and I was so lost, so alone."

"I'm so sorry, Emily."

"I planned her memorial service and funeral. Four hundred people showed up. She'd been a teacher at the high school for thirty-five years. She taught English, and she lived in the same house that whole time. Her students would pop by and see her. She was well liked in our neighborhood. She volunteered at the library and the homeless shelter. After the funeral, after everyone came to our house to talk about her, I drove back to the cemetery and stood over her grave. There were so many flowers everywhere. She was buried right next to my mom.

"I stood there, right in front of both of them, and I told them that I would never touch drugs or alcohol again. Even though I was grieving for my grandma, which had triggered grief for my mom, I didn't. I haven't. My grandma left her house to me and her money. She had a lot, actually, because my granddad had worked for forty years for the railroad. I went to rehab, and this time I committed to it and dealt with losing my mom. I got my GED, then I went to college and became a teacher, and I met Eric at the beach one day in California, where I'd moved to get away from all my memories, and that was it. Eric is the kindest, most generous person I've ever met. His background is messy, too, but we decided we would give our kids a safe and happy life."

"And now you have five beautiful kids."

She grinned. "And..." She leaned in. "I've got a bun in the oven again."

We laughed and clicked our coffee mugs together. "But tell me, Evie. I can see something in you, something's troubling you about my moving here. Don't deny it. What's going on?"

"Oh!" I hesitated. "I feel so guilty, Emily," I whispered, gutted. "Ever since your mom was killed, this guilt has stalked me. I forgot to check what she was wearing the night she was killed. It was my fault. I let my excitement about the Halloween dance get to me and your mom died because I wasn't watching carefully enough."

"Evie, you were a kid. We were kids. You told us about that premonition. I should have noticed her clothes, too, but I didn't. My mom obviously didn't even notice and you told her what outfit she would be wearing. She didn't believe you could see the future anyhow. I finally don't feel guilty anymore. It was entirely Gavin's fault. If you had interfered with that premonition that night, he would have killed her another night. He beat her up all the time. She'd told him several times to get out, she didn't want him there anymore, and each time he'd flip out. He even threatened to kill me if she left him. Gavin would never willingly have allowed her to leave him. Never. He was going to kill her whether or not you interfered. I didn't tell you half the stuff that was going on even though you were my best friend. I was scared to death of him."

I thought about that. I hadn't known that he'd threatened to kill her on multiple occasions, that he'd threatened to kill Emily, too. But maybe Emily was right. I had seen one scenario. If I had interfered that time, what was the likelihood that Gavin would have tried again? It was high. Extremely high. The abuse would not have stopped and Patsy would have eventually left, or tried to leave, to protect Emily, and he would have come after her. I exhaled. Deeply. I think it was the first deep breath I'd taken around this issue ever. "I am so sorry, Emily, though. I am."

"You have nothing to be sorry for. You need to forgive yourself. You need to let it go. You need to not blame yourself for one more day, Warrior Friend. Zombie Fighter. Dragon Slayer Girl. This was not your fault, it was not your responsibility."

I smiled through overwhelming relief. "King Kong Wrestler. Space Alien Fighter. Queen of Lily Pads Island."

"Best friend," she said, hugging me. "I'm so sorry you suffered like this, Evie. I truly am."

"Best friend, I'm glad you're back."

"Me too, Evie. We'll be Zombie Fighters again in no time."

"May the power be with us! We'll just have to make sure we're Zombie Fighters around your kids' nap times."

"And I won't be a fast Zombie Fighter the huger I get." She patted her stomach.

I couldn't believe it. Within three days Eric and Emily found a home on the island overlooking the ocean, with land for "all the monsters to run around on," Emily said. "Also. We're getting chickens and goats." They had bought the land where her former home stood. They would demolish the house and planned to build a playground there for the town.

Her kids ran over to us on her new property, and I hugged all of them. Emily had introduced me as Aunt Evie.

"You were our mom's best friend when you were a kid!" Alexi said, her toothless smile so cute.

"My best friend still," Emily said, hugging me.

The kids hugged me again and I ended up tackled on the ground, giggles all around.

* * *

That night, after I had dinner with Emily and Eric and the kids, I went home, exhausted. Kids are tiring. I put on my red boots. Mr. Bob and Trixie Goat were out again, but I didn't have the energy to get mad. They skipped right over to me, all victorious and happy, and walked with me while I did my animal rounds, feeding and taking care of everybody.

I said hello to Virginia Alpaca and Alpaca Joe. Joe spit, his spit relentless, Virginia Alpaca let me pet her. I visited with the lambs, who followed the mother in a line to the fence so I could pet them. "Greetings, Padre, Momma, Jay Rae, Raptor, and The TMan."

I talked to Shakespeare and Jane Austen and gave them their hay. The cats twisted in and out between my legs, then sped off to find mice to catch, and Butch and Cassidy barked. Sundance, as usual, was right by my side. My best furry friend.

I sat on the beach with my arm around Sundance and thought about Miss Patsy and Emily.

Emily had gone through a dark, black, scary place for years when she lost her mother.

I had felt guilty for years.

She had let it go, so now I needed to let my guilt go, too.

I stared up at the night sky, a handful of stars glimmering, and said, "I love you, Miss Patsy. I am sorry."

I swear I saw a whale blow his spout in the distance.

I took that as a spiritual sign, as Aunt Camellia would have said, and laughed.

"Johnny, Betsy, Tilly, and Kayla are coming up Friday night to see me."

My mother, aunts, and I were sitting in the gazebo. They were drinking wine. I was drinking lemonade. It was dusk, the wisteria leaves floating in the wind above us.

"They must hate me," my mother said, her hand an unsteady mess as she pushed her hair behind her ears.

"They must hate us," Aunt Camellia said, her voice breaking. "There can be no emotional spectrum in which they wouldn't."

"We deserve it," Aunt Iris said. "It's clear when one takes a moment to rationally see this from their side."

All three of them seemed tired. Older. Sad to their bones. I felt bad about that.

"They won't hate you," I said. "They're not here to hate anyone. They want to meet me."

My mother straightened up from her hunched position. "I was wrong to deny them you, Evie." She hunched back down, as if too tired to sit up straight, which was so unlike my mother.

I didn't argue with her. My whole chest felt tight. I loved my mother and my aunts. I still felt betrayed. They had denied me the truth of my own life. I would rather hear the truth than live in a fuzzy haze of a reality that is not real. Plus, there were extenuating circumstances: My premonitions, which Betsy could have helped me with. My parents and aunts knew I struggled with depression, that I mysteriously felt lost and alone throughout my life, and they probably guessed why that was, but did nothing. Plus, Betsy and Johnny had been so young when they'd had me, then lost me. Was there no sympathy for them?

This whole thing had shaken my world like I was in the center of a snow globe. It had turned my relationships with my parents, though my father was long gone, and my aunts upside down.

"This is a hard situation," I said.

My mother and aunts were miserable. They seemed to have shrunk and aged since I'd found out about Johnny and Betsy. They were worn out, guilt-ridden. I knew all about guilt and I didn't want them to live with it.

"It's hard for them, for me, for you all." I took a deep breath. They loved me, I loved them. I knew that my aunts saw Jules and me as their own daughters. Forgiveness had to come into play here. "There's been enough pain. You know what would make this situation better?"

They all three sat up. "What, honey, tell me," my mother said. "I'll do anything."

"Me too," Aunt Camellia said, her face blotchy from tears. "I have been reaching out to the universe to bring peace to this situation, love. I, too, worry they will hate us. More than that, I worry every day that you hate me."

"Tell me what to do," growled Aunt Iris, although she was choking back emotion, too. "Be practical and spit it out."

"Make them hats."

That was an extremely popular suggestion.

Their faces brightened. Hope came from sadness, light came from darkness, joy came from guilt and regret. "We'll do it!" they said together.

"I love you all," I whispered. "I truly do."

"We love you, too," they said, together again, as if on cue.

We are an emotional bunch and had a long hug in the gazebo, the wisteria floating around us.

Sundance squished his way in and barked. He likes group hugs.

"Evie," Mr. Jamon croaked over the phone, then coughed. "Did you get the new romance I ordered?"

"Yes, it's here." I had it right under the cash register at the bookstore.

"I'll come get it."

"Hang on. You sound terrible. Are you sick?"

"Pneumonia. That's why I need that book."

"Mr. Jamon, don't you dare. I'm coming up."

"No, no. I can do it." He coughed like a fiend.

"Stay in bed, or I'll have my mother call and yell at you."

"Dang. You would do that to me? You play hardball. Lord knows I do not need your mother on my case. Okay. I'll see you when I see you. These romances are helping me see life through the eyes of a woman, and it's been a fascinating and enlightening experience. You know I still believe in love, Evie!"

I left the bookstore for Mr. Jamon's.

I'd never been to his house, which was odd, as the island was small, but I didn't want to simply wander up onto his property.

Mr. Jamon was somewhat of a hermit, too, quite private. He'd been that way for decades and did not invite many people up the mountain.

I'd been at the bookstore since six that morning and needed a break, needed time to think. It was a shiny, lovely day. My mind was on two things as I drove up that curving mountain road: Marco, and my aching, throbbing heart, and Johnny, Betsy, Kayla, and Tilly coming that night to take me to dinner.

I imagined making passionate love to Marco as I drove, then shoved it out of my mind when I arrived at Mr. Jamon's sprawling house at the top with panoramic views. He had made omelets with vegetables from his garden, despite the pneumonia. We had a nice chat. I made him take the medicine the doctor prescribed him even though he called it a "pharmaceutical rip-off! Mumbo jumbo medicine. The doctor's a quack."

He loved the romance books I brought him. "My feminine side was buried for decades, but I'm finding it now, Evie. I'm finding it, and Dorothy seems to like it!"

Dorothy was his new girlfriend, three years his junior.

"Watch out for Chief Ass Burn," he croaked out to me when I left. "I heard he's got a thing for you. He's a serpent. A bad one. I've told him to back off and stay away from you."

That was sweet. Chivalry was not dead.

"That one wouldn't know how to woo a woman. I know how now because of all my romances. I've got it down! Ask Dorothy!"

"I'll watch out. Thanks for the omelet."

"Drive carefully. Watch out for the curves as you're headed down the mountain. There are blind corners, so don't rush."

"I'll do that, Mr. Jamon. Take your meds tonight."

"You're as bossy as your mother and your aunts, the old battle-axes." He winked.

I laughed.

I kept my windows down for fresh air, the mountain road curving here and there, tight, one lane, my mind back on Marco, then on Johnny and Betsy and the dinner tonight. I was excited to see them. I was worried. I was a tad-bit anxious. I was feeling tearful already, and emotional, and all fizzled up inside. Like an almost-exploding can of pop that had not been opened yet.

Betsy. Johnny. Kayla. My aunt Tilly. All of them. New family. What would they be like? Would they like me? Would I like them? What role would they have in my life going forward? What did they want? What did I want?

Tonight we would meet at a restaurant in town.

I took the curve, mountain on my right, the cliff to my left. Orange poppies. So pretty. My mother and aunts love them, and not only because of my mother's name. They love the delicacy of that flower, how it grows without help, how it flows into the meadows here on the island, around ponds and lakes, like an orange shawl . . . and yet those flowers had haunted me my whole life because . . . because . . .

"Oh, God," I whispered, shocked, scared. "Oh no. Not now, please, not now."

I took the turn, and there it was.

My premonition. My oldest premonition. The one in which one of us died.

Probably.

Chapter 34

❧

Betsy Baturra
San Orcanita Island
2012

Betsy glanced at the cliff below her to the right as she drove around the curve, her windows halfway down, the wind warm. San Orcanita Island was the most serene, peaceful place she'd ever been, but she knew it was because her daughter was here, her daughter Rose. She smiled, then she laughed, the notes dancing through the open window and out around the blue-green island. She could not wait for dinner tonight with her daughter. *Her daughter!*

She and Johnny, Tilly, and Kayla had come to the island on an early ferry and had breakfast in town. They took a drive to the bucolic blue lake at the campground and hiked the two-mile loop. Then Johnny wanted to go back to their bed-and-breakfast "for a nap, to rest my bones." Kayla and Tilly wanted to shop in town. Betsy had wanted to take a drive, to explore this exquisite place where her Rose lived. She drove up the mountain, away from the lake, the road curving, the view of the ocean sparkling, the sailboats white dots between the other green islands.

She saw the orange poppies growing on the side of the road. She had always loved poppies, but they had haunted her all these years because she knew they were in the premonition that she'd had her whole life, knowing that it meant death. Probably.

Her hands suddenly gripped the steering wheel. She felt as if she was choking.

"Oh no," she said out loud, realizing what was happening. "Oh, God, no. Not now, please."

The blue truck appeared around the curve, the road so tight, too tight for both of them.

Betsy saw the flash of black hair. She had seen a photo of her daughter when she saw her name on the ancestry website and had eagerly looked her up, landing on the Books, Cake, and Tea website. She had been stunned by the likeness. Betsy was looking at herself decades ago.

So now she knew. It was Rose in the truck, her beloved daughter. She was in the premonition she had had all her life, starting from when she was a child, where one of them dies, or both of them, probably, maybe. Betsy made an instant decision, her heart clenching, her eyes filling with tears. She saw Johnny's face. She saw Kayla, still in high school. She saw Tilly. But she would not lose this child, her oldest, her firstborn. Her love. The child who had never, not for a day, left her heart. Her Rose.

Betsy didn't hesitate. She turned the wheel of her car hard to the right and headed straight over the cliff. She had sensed death in this shifting, changing premonition; it had been fuzzy, but she would not let Rose die. She was her mother, after all. A mother would die for her child in an instant. Now was her instant.

My eyes locked on the other driver coming right toward me in the red car. I saw a flash of black hair. I saw eyes like mine. It was Betsy. It was my biological mother. Shock paralyzed me for a second as my truck continued to plow down the road. One of us would die, probably, or both of us. It was foggy, but death hung heavy over this day.

But Betsy had a daughter, Kayla. She was only a teenager. I had no children, and her daughter needed her. She should live, not me. Betsy had also spent ten torturous years in prison. She had endured enough pain and loss in her life. It was my turn.

I turned the wheel of my truck left, toward the cliff. I would go. Betsy would live.

But . . . what in the world? Her red car turned right as I turned left . . .

Chapter 35

 ~

"All of Serafina's shiny rainbow scales were now in the glass jar owned by King Koradome. He laughed and laughed when the last scale, a red one, appeared through the waves. 'Now,' he said, 'I am the owner of the most beautiful scales in the world. They are all mine, forever mine.' Then he cackled evilly, which made all the fish and dolphins around him swim off, as they could recognize danger when they heard it."

"Was Serafina sad?"

"A little. But she had saved a fisherman in a storm, which is why she lost her last scale, so she knew she'd done the right thing. Afterwards she and her sisters and brothers went to explore a cave together and they made pearl necklaces so she felt better."

"What did King Koradome do with all of her scales except stare at them and do the evil laugh thing?"

"Well, a magical thing happened then."

"What?"

"King Koradome didn't know the whole story. He used his own magic to take Serafina's scales away every time she did something kind for someone else, but he wasn't a smart merman. He didn't know that the rainbow-colored scales would dissolve into dust when they were all together again until they were returned to the owner."

"So Serafina's scales all became dust in the jar?"

"Yes. As soon as the red one was dropped in. But one of her

brothers knew of the deep magic and he had been watching the king. When King Koradome saw the dust in the jar, he became enraged and he tossed the jar so fast and so hard, it sped by an octopus and lodged in purple-and-orange coral. When the king wasn't looking, the brother swam over and grabbed the jar of dust and gave it back to Serafina.

"As soon as Serafina touched the scales, they turned back to their original colors: Deep purple. Lemon yellow. Dusty pink. Burgundy and azure blue and lavender. But Serafina knew that she shouldn't be the only one with such beauty anymore. She placed the scales in her mother's garden. They shimmered and shone, and mermen and mermaids came from all over the world to see the magical garden. The garden brought smiles to their faces, wonder, joy."

"But was it hard for her to give up her rainbow tail forever?"

"A little. But she knew that when she became an old, old mermaid, she could look back on her life and know that she had made so many people happy. It was definitely worth it."

"So when I save people or help people, I make them happy, right, Daddy?"

"Yes, Evie. When you are old you will be able to look back on your life, as I hope you do now, and know that you saved people's lives, you made their lives better, even if they'll never know what you did for them."

"It's hard with all these premonitions."

"I know."

"Hey! I need a magic mermaid tail!"

"Your magic mermaid tail is in your heart, Evie."

"It is?"

"Yes, but you won't ever lose it. Your helpful heart is yours forever, and I love you."

"I love you, too, Daddy."

My dad died in the sands of the Middle East when I was twenty-one years old. Those sands have haunted me.

It was the worst thing that had ever happened to me, Jules, and my mother. My parents were in love, they told me, from the first time they met when my mother was traveling through Europe with her sisters, all with backpacks on their backs. My father was with a couple of army buddies and they met in a bar. At the end of the backpacking trip, my mother stayed to be with my father in Germany on his army base.

Cue up the whirlwind courtship and marriage.

I don't know when my father went from being in Special Forces in the army to working for the U.S. government in undercover operations. Not even my mother knew exactly when things changed. It wasn't something he was allowed to talk about. He still "deployed," but sometimes he would leave on a dime. Twice a helicopter actually came to get him. He had a bachelor's degree in criminology and a master's in international relations from an Ivy League school. He was smart and quick. He was gentle and compassionate. He was driven and focused and brave. He was a family man.

He was shot to death, set on fire by rebels, then dumped in a ditch where he was found by U.S. military forces out searching for him. The rebels who attacked him were hunted down and killed by the army, their cement compound destroyed and leveled until it was a smoking, lifeless ruin.

It did not bring my father back. The grief was all-consuming. The rage at what they did to him was all-consuming. My mother, Jules, and I each cried an ocean of tears, often standing in the ocean at our beach, those tears literally reaching the waves. The horror of what had happened to my father, the vision, was unbearable.

A few days after he died, I told Jules and my mother the story about the brave mermaid who lost her scales because of kind acts toward others. Jules told us a story that our dad had told her about a magical unicorn who helped everyone see color in their lives, like our mother's flowers, instead of gray and black.

My mother told us our father would always be with us in our hearts, in the stories he told, in the hugs he gave us, in the songs he sang, in the laughter we shared. "He'll be with you in how you live your lives, girls. He'll be with you in the lessons he taught you, the morals he gave you, the generosity and kindness that he showed you. He's here on the wind, he's standing in the ocean with us, he's in our flower garden, and at Rose Bloom Cottage. We can remember him reading books with us, drinking tea, and baking cakes. Love never dies, it's always with us, he's with us."

Our tears continued to fall in the ocean, our arms wrapped around one another.

I loved my father with all that I am. He was honorable and good. I have never stopped missing him.

Chapter 36

∽

My head was buried in a pillow and I didn't want to move, my back aching. Where was I? Why was I rocking back and forth? Was I on a boat? I should not be on a boat. . . .

Then I remembered. My brain cleared as if it had been covered by mist and clouds. I remembered the one-lane road, the curve, the mountain and the cliff, the orange poppies. I remembered how I turned my wheel so I would not crash into Betsy. I remembered my premonition. I was now *in* my premonition. I shuddered as my stomach dropped.

I must be dead. Surely I am dead. I must be on my way to heaven, although I thought that when I went to heaven that I would not physically hurt. Surely heaven takes away pain? My neck hurt, my back hurt, my body hurt.

My world tilted again, then back. Like a teeter-totter. I have never liked teeter-totters.

Ugh. I didn't think I would feel any nausea in heaven, either. I thought heaven would be warm and light and a ton of fun. Where were the angels? Where were the golden gates? Where was the harpist?

I tilted again.

Maybe I'm not dead yet, I thought, my head still buried in a pillow. Why was my head in a pillow? I was so confused. Maybe I'm in that in-between zone. That would make sense, for me to be cursed like that. Stuck between life and death. For someone who was plagued with premonitions, who was odd and different, this made sense in an ironic, punishing sort of way.

I breathed once, then twice as I tilted back and forth again, then I heard it, someone shouting my name. But not my real name. My other name, Rose. The name no one called me.

"Rose!"

Then "Evie! Evie!"

But it was muffled. The names were blended and softened. I sunk back into my pillow because my world tilted again and I was getting dizzy. Ugh. Stop moving, world!

"Rose! Rose!"

I slowly stuck my head up, the pain buzzing around as if it were loose in my head, a small painful marble pinging here and there.

Over my pillow, which I realized was not my pillow but my airbag, I looked into trees. In fact, I was looking into the middle of a tree trunk. My truck tilted again, up and down, like a ride at a carnival, and I realized something extremely scary: I was in my truck and I was halfway over a cliff. The tree was blocking me from going all the way down.

I had not flown straight off the road and into the air and over the cliff when I turned the wheel of my truck to avoid hitting Betsy. I was still on the road. Barely.

"Rose!" I heard that voice again, a woman's voice, scared but demanding, insistent, and I turned my head.

Betsy. There was Betsy in her car. My biological mother. The one who went to jail for ten years with Johnny.

I wanted to wave cheerily at her, but I was afraid to move. If I tilted the car forward, I'd go right over the cliff. It was then that I realized one more important fact, and it explained why Betsy was in her car and I was in mine but she seemed so close: Her car was imbedded into the side of my truck. I could see her. I could almost reach her, her window on the driver side halfway down.

"Don't move, Rose!" she yelled at me, her voice pitched up in fear. "Wait until we stop moving. Don't move!"

I closed my eyes in terror. We were so close. Finally we had met, finally she was here and I knew the truth, but our cars were smashed together. We were in my premonition. My probably-death premonition. I wondered if she'd had this premonition her whole life, too.

I looked into her eyes. Those gold eyes were the same as mine, and within that gold I saw her kindness, her goodness, and her panic. I knew what had happened. She had turned her car to save me. I had turned my truck to save her. We had crashed to-gether, sacrificing ourselves, but at the same time causing an ac-cident, temporarily saving us both.

My truck and her car finally balanced out. We were still a teeter-totter, but we were in the middle. We were mildly stabi-lized.

"Get out, Rose!" she yelled. "Get out now!"

I instinctively turned to grab the door handle, to escape this metal coffin, then stopped. What was keeping me from falling over was her car, smashed into mine. If I got out, my weight could shift this whole thing, these two hunks of metal sand-wiched together. My truck and her car would tilt without my weight balancing things out, and the car and truck and Betsy would go tumbling over the cliff. I knew what happened then. I could almost feel the burning of the flames and smell the black smoke from my previous premonitions.

I took a deep breath, sadness filling my chest. I did not want to die. But I could not live with her death on my head. I had been ruined with guilt from Patsy. I could not take on guilt from Betsy. I shook my head. "No. You go," I shouted back to her through our open widows. "You have a daughter."

"No." She was resolute, her chin set.

Her car and my truck started to sway again, up and down, like a carnival ride before you take the big dip down, although there would be no fun thrill or cotton candy at the end. The end would end with tangled metal and an explosion.

"I will not go before you. When we stop moving the next time, get out of your truck, Rose. Get out."

"We'll go together," I shouted at her.

"No," she said, her eyes flashing with anger, which I knew buried her fear. "You first."

"No," I said, tears coming to my eyes. "Together."

"Please, Rose," she said. "Go first. I am begging you."

"I won't," I cried, my tears starting. "I will not."

I saw the expression of defeat on her face. She knew we didn't have much time, and she knew I was not budging. The vehicles ever so slightly balanced out again in our midair teeter-totter.

"We'll do it together, at the same time," she called out. "Ready?"

"Yes. Are you?"

She nodded, and slowly, carefully, her eyes never leaving mine, she reached for the handle of her car door. Both of us getting out of the vehicles at the same time would shift the weight, but we could do it as gently as possible.

I opened my door, then looked down, and my brain felt as if it had been electrocuted by fear. There was nothing but air below my foot. My back wheels were on the street, the hood of my truck scraping the tree, and the rest was held by Betsy's car. I felt sick. I would have to put my right foot on the inside of my truck and stretch my left foot out to stand on the street. My breath caught, but I told myself to buck up. No one likes a wimp. You can do this. You can do it.

I glanced back at Betsy as we tilted back again, fear eating rational thought. She was ready. She was waiting. There was no way she could know, from her position, that my door was not over the street.

"Now!" I yelled at her as my truck started tilting again. This was it. It was get out or die. I saw her move to get out, her body jerking toward her door, then I moved. I grabbed the steering wheel with my right hand for leverage, put my right foot on the floor, and reached my left foot out toward the road. I pushed with my left hand against the window frame. I shoved myself out of the truck and onto the road, stumbling several steps in my rush and landing on my chest. I scrambled as far away from the cliff as fast as I could as I heard metal scraping on metal, reverberating off the mountain.

I turned my head to find Betsy, ignoring a blast of pain shoot through my body like a sword.

Where was Betsy?

Where was Betsy?

On firm footing now, I ran to the passenger side of her car. I saw her inside, struggling with the door as both vehicles eerily tilted back and forth, back and forth.

I pulled the handle from the outside. It wouldn't open. The door had been jammed in the accident. She could not exit the passenger door or she would step right off the cliff. The truck and car lurched forward.

"Open the window all the way!" I screamed, terrified.

"I tried, I tried! It's stuck. Get back, Rose! Stand back!"

"No! Come through the window!"

I reached my arms in to grab her, and she started scrambling through the window, hardly fitting, the window halfway down. The vehicles screeched against each other again, a grinding, echoing, deathly noise.

I had my hands under her arms, her hands gripping my arms, and I pulled as hard as I could while she kicked free. The cars made a final grinding, banging noise, and I yanked her out as they both tumbled over the cliff. Betsy landed straight on top of me and I fell to my back, my head slamming against the pavement. Her car and my truck bounced their way down the cliff, the noise deafening, then landed with a thud before one of them, or both of them, exploded, crackling flames and black smoke flying up.

She levered herself over me. "Rose, are you okay? Are you all right?" Her golden eyes, like mine, were wide, her face panicked.

"I'm fine, hurt only a bit." That wasn't true. My head felt like it had split open. My neck felt like there were spears sticking through it. "How are you?"

For long seconds she didn't say anything, then she smiled and her tears fell on my face. "Rose," she breathed. "Except for this accident, this is the best day of my life. The very best day! I get to see my daughter again." Then she cried and we both sat up, and she hugged me close and I hugged her back. Hugging Betsy was as normal to me as breathing . . . or reading.

"I have always loved you, Rose. Always." Her mouth trembled. "And thank you for saving my life."

The flames and the billowing black smoke were seen from town and from Mr. Jamon's house. Mr. Jamon came down gripping his cane, in his robe with his inhaler, gasping for breath but endearingly worried about me. He'd called 911 for the police and an ambulance.

Chief Ass Burn did not come. No one asked why. No one knew where he was.

I later found that interesting, but we were all better off without him there.

Betsy and I went to the hospital and were treated in different rooms. We were banged up and bruised. My head hurt, my neck hurt, my back hurt. Nothing that wouldn't heal.

I saw Marco running by the hospital's window, his face creased with alarm and worry. When he rushed in, he came straight toward me. My mother and aunts scampered out of the way, smiling. I could tell they were trying hard not to giggle. Marco hugged me close.

I hugged him back, my heart thudding like a darn fool.

My mother and aunts clapped. They had been so upset when they got the call about my accident, they forgot to put on hats.

"He's here," my mother said with a high note of victory. "He's here!"

"Love has conquered once again," Aunt Camellia said, clasping her hands together. "It was in their auras."

"About time they got things straightened out," Aunt Iris said. "Best to be efficient, even with love."

I was so happy to see Marco, I cried all over his shirt.

Then I held his hand and I told him what happened and who had been in the other car.

He was rather shocked. I knew exactly how he felt. I hugged him again, I couldn't help it.

*   *   *

I met my father, Johnny, at the hospital, a tall and barrel-chested man. He said, his voice low and gravelly, "Rose, I am your father, Johnny. I can never thank you enough for saving Betsy's life. You risked your own to save her." He choked up. Grabbed my hand. "Thank you so much for letting us come and see you. We are so grateful. How are you?"

He tried to keep from crying, but I saw those tears. His face was lined from the stress of his life, the time in prison had taken a toll. Losing me, he told me later, had been far, far worse than prison, but his smile was full of love.

He had the look of a boxer, which I learned he practiced all the time in prison to strengthen himself for when he was jumped or attacked.

I met my younger sister, Kayla, in the hospital, too. She looks exactly like I did when I was her age. Thick black hair, gold eyes, same build, same height, same worry.

"Can we talk later, you and me?" she asked. "These premonitions are driving me out of my mind. I'm so glad I have a sister now to talk to."

Tilly was reserved but thoughtful, caring. She hugged me tight. "I've wanted to do that for decades," she told me.

That night, we all had dinner together at Rose Bloom Cottage instead of going to a restaurant. I had invited Marco, but he had declined. "This is your night, Evie. You need this time with them."

My mother and aunts had made them extraordinary but elegant hats. Betsy's, Kayla's, and Tilly's were light pink/light red/light yellow wrapped with faux roses "so they can keep them forever and remember this day when they found their Rose." They added ribbons, netting, and glitter spray. Johnny's was a black mobster type of hat with a white band around the top and a pink rose.

"Sexy," Betsy told him. We laughed.

We had dinner and we had dessert, a Baked Alaska, which my aunt Iris set on fire and said, "I think I would have been a talented arsonist." The flames glowed off the crystals in our chandelier.

"I am sorry," my mother said to Betsy and Johnny, wiping her tears. She explained to them why she didn't tell me I was adopted as a child and then as an adult. Betsy and Johnny were very gracious. They did not argue with her, and they did not question her decision.

"We understand, Poppy," Johnny said. "We want to thank you, and you, Iris and Camellia, for raising and taking such loving care of Ro—" He stopped. "Of Evie. You were obviously wonderful to her. Look how she's turned out." He turned to smile at me, and that boxer's face teared up again. Betsy reached out a hand to him and he took it, as she blinked away more tears.

My aunts, even tough Iris, teared up, too.

"Evie is smart," my mother said, "and has dealt with her premonitions as best she can, helping others, saving others. Why, a few days ago she actually climbed up on the roof of a house and fixed several shingles because she saw the owner, an older man, trying to fix it himself and breaking a hip on the way down."

I had done that. It wasn't fun, because I hate heights as much as I hate running.

"She has a soul that shines like the sun," Aunt Camellia said, hands to heart.

"She's had a heckuva time," Aunt Iris said, nodding at Betsy. "Maybe you can help her get her head on straight with the premonition problem. Form a plan. Analyze what's been done in the past to help in the future."

Betsy and Johnny had hired an attorney and gone to court to get me back. My parents had hired an attorney to prevent it. My parents had not told me I was adopted, neither had my aunts, thereby preventing Johnny and Betsy, innocent kids when I was taken from them, from being in my life. But, I thought, as I watched Johnny, Betsy, and Tilly, they were not there to be angry. They were not there to attack my mother or aunts.

They were there for love.

They were there for me.

They wanted peace.

My mother and aunts had filled three scrapbooks with photos of me as a baby, toddler, kindergartener, teenager, and beyond. There were even about twenty photos they'd taken of me in the last year. They wrapped them up and presented them to my new family.

Betsy hugged those photograph books close to herself, as if she would not let them go, ever, tears streaming down her face, Johnny's arms wrapped around her.

Johnny, Betsy, Kayla, Tilly, and I hiked around the bucolic blue lake at the campground on Saturday. I later introduced them to all my animals. The goats escaped again, and they agreed my goats were naughty. They loved Sundance and marveled at how well he could run on three legs. Butch and Cassidy were happy to have new friends, the lambs lined up, and Shakespeare and Jane Austen said a gracious hello. The cats were shy. We went out for Mexican food that night in town. We rode the ferry to Lopozzo Island for ice cream together. We laughed, we talked, we hugged. I felt comfortable with all of them immediately. I felt as if I could be myself. I felt that mysterious hole closing in my heart.

Betsy and I had time to talk alone, sitting on our beach, and we talked about her time in jail, the trials, the grocery stores, her eternal hope that she would meet me one day. We talked about our premonitions, what it was like to live with them. Everything I had felt, she felt.

To me, seeing into the future, seeing people get mangled and hurt and run over and crushed and killed and sick is a living nightmare. Trying to intervene, or choosing not to intervene, is relentlessly exhausting.

"You've saved people, Evie," Betsy said, her hand in mine, as natural as if we'd been holding hands our whole lives. "Never forget that."

That was true.

"When I'm working at the market and all of the sudden I get a vision of what may happen to a customer on her way home, a car crash, perhaps, and I have to drop everything, leave a meeting, and go and help, it's tough. But that one person, she's okay.

She's saved. To them it's worth it, isn't it? So to us, it has to be, too."

It is definitely worth it to them.

"The images are sometimes so bad, I feel kicked in the face," Betsy said. "But that kick in the face makes me do something. It makes me reach out to others. I accept that for some reason the women in our line can choose to save. My mother said no to it and wasted her life. I said yes, you say yes, Kayla says yes. Is there an option to say no? Yes, there is. But then you would be someone you are not, honey. You would be someone you wouldn't like or respect."

Betsy hugged me, and I hugged her back.

She felt like home. She felt like Mom.

I had two moms, two dads, two sisters, and three aunts. I was a lucky gal.

I talked alone with Johnny, too. We talked about how he had lost his mother to a violent man and how my best friend, Emily, had lost her mother to a violent man.

"A man should be strong but gentle, protective and caring to his wife and kids," he said. "I don't understand these men who act otherwise. It's not how a true man acts."

I told him about the guilt I had felt about Patsy, and he told me about the searing guilt he had felt about his mother, about not being able to protect her. "I know, though, that Patsy and my mother would not want us to feel that way. I think we honor them by being loving in our lives to others."

I sat and thought about that and had to agree with him. I ended up telling him how I felt about Marco, and the sailboat drowning premonition, how messed up I was, and how my premonitions and not wanting to leave the island would be difficult for anyone to live with.

"Evie," he said. "I love your mother with all my heart, with all that I am. Not seeing her for ten years nearly killed me. She is much like you, not only in terms of her premonitions but in the other things that she deals with, the depression and anxiety, although both have lifted completely since you found each other. My point is that I want Betsy in my life no matter what. I can't live right without her. I am not Johnny without Betsy. We have gone through the hardest ravages of life, but still, we're together. We laugh. We talk. We are of one heart. Do you believe yourself to be of one heart with Marco?"

"Yes."

"You love him beyond yourself?

"Yes."

"And he loves you?"

"Yes."

"Then why are you preventing your two hearts from being together as one? Marco knows you. He embraces you as you are, as I have always embraced your mother. That's the important thing: He loves you as Evie."

Who knew my father, a prisoner for ten years, who still boxed and had an intimidating face when he wasn't smiling, could be so romantically poetic? So right?

"Takes a lot of courage to take that leap, Evie."

"I don't know if I have it."

"I think you do. You have shown courage throughout your life. Let me ask you another question, if I may?"

"Please."

"If you had died in that car accident with Betsy..." He stopped, took a deep breath and rubbed his face with both hands, clearly shaken at the thought, before he started again. "Would you regret not being with Marco?"

Whoa. Put that way! "Yes."

"Do you have your answer, then?"

I blinked, I thought, I nodded. "I think I do."

"We've sure missed you."

"I missed you all, too. I always felt you. Right here." I tapped my heart.

Intimidating boxer-man became all teary-eyed. "I want nothing but the best for you, Rose. We have loved you forever."

* * *

When Johnny, Betsy, Tilly, and Kayla left on Sunday, and I stood waving at the ferry, we were all in tears, and yet I knew I would see them again. And again, forever.

They were family, after all.

I later learned why Chief Ass Burn did not come up the mountain to check out the explosion.

He had "accidentally" locked himself in his shed.

At least, that's what people told him when he finally busted down the back wall of his shed with an ax.

That was the story . . . no one would have locked him in his shed on purpose. Oh no. That wasn't the island way . . . probably . . .

Because Johnny and Betsy had included the media in their search for me, they did one more interview. "We have found our daughter through a DNA test. . . . She is beautiful and generous. . . . We are grateful to her and her family for including us in their family."

They did not reveal my name or where I lived. They protected my privacy. They told me they would be doing no future interviews, though the interest was high.

"We will always protect you, Evie," my father said. "Always."

I bought another pickup truck, since mine had exploded.

A woman who rescued horses was selling hers. It was five years old and black, double cab, a real monster of a vehicle.

"Trust me," she said in her red cowboy hat and boots, "you will feel like a ball-busting woman driving Esmerelda here. She doesn't let anyone get in her way."

I laughed and bought Esmerelda.

She growled at me when I turned the key in the engine.

On Thursday at dusk, Sundance became ill.

I called Marco's clinic, then called his cell phone, as it was listed as the emergency number. He called me back.

"Bring him in, Evie."

I was almost hyperventilating while driving with Sundance's limp head on my lap, his tail wagging slowly, up and down. He was failing, I could tell. He needed medicine or an operation or something. He wasn't going to die. He couldn't die. He couldn't leave me.

"Hang on, Sundance," I said, crying, petting his head. "We'll get you fixed up. Hang on, honey."

I felt Sundance's breathing change as I pulled into Marco's driveway, then into the clinic's parking lot. He lifted his golden head, and I put my head down on his and he licked my face, but it was weak, his breathing labored, his body floppy. He could hardly move.

Marco opened the door on the passenger side. "How is he?"

"Not well." My voice broke, cracked.

"Let me have him, Evie," he said, so gentle.

Marco picked Sundance up and carried him into the clinic, his body limp.

He laid him on a table, listened to his heart, examined his eyes, put his hands on his body. He shook his head. "I'm sorry, Evie."

"Oh no. Oh no. Oh no." I put my head to Sundance's and cried. Sundance licked me again. "Sundance, baby. I love you. Oh, Sundance!"

"Evie," Marco said. "I'm going to give him a painkiller, then let me carry him out to the beach. You can say goodbye there. Under the sunset. He would like that. Let's not let him die here."

I sobbed and nodded, and Marco, strong Marco, gave him the painkiller, then carried Sundance out to the beach. I sat down, leaned against a log, and he put that huge dog in my lap.

"I'll be at the house. I know you need time alone with him."

I nodded and cried into Sundance's golden fur as I held him like a baby. I stared into his eyes and he stared into mine, and his lips moved, like he was smiling at me. I had had him for seventeen years. He wagged his tail at me, and I kissed him. We watched the sun go down together as I cradled him, rocked him, the sky filled with scarlet and lavender tonight, the waves quieter, but maybe they seemed quieter because I was sobbing.

"Sundance," I whispered. "I love you, baby. I love you, I love you, I will miss you so much." I would miss him every day. He was my constant friend, my true friend. I thought of all the times we'd walked the island together, how he'd followed me through the rows of roses, peonies, sunflowers, and daffodils on our property, how he'd chase birds with such abandon, and how he'd been so excited when I came home from work every day, as if we'd been parted for years. I thought of the camping we'd done for months after my brain misfired and I flamed out, the places we'd seen, the waterfalls and rivers, the mountain ranges and sunny beaches.

I remembered the time he'd barked when a rattlesnake had gotten too close, and one time he'd lunged at a strange man who approached our tent, turning into a protective, fierce dog I hadn't seen before. I thought of the way he loved his pink blankie and his stuffed friend, Lizard, and how he had overcome losing one leg to run with the best of them.

I put my face next to his again and he weakly licked my cheek, a kiss of love, a kiss of goodbye, then he sighed, one last breath, his eyes on mine, and died in my arms.

I was inconsolable that night.

Marco gave me a hug, and I hugged him back. We wrapped Sundance in a soft blue blanket, and he put him next to me in the truck. I would bury him tomorrow in a special place that he loved under the willow tree overlooking the bay with his stuffed friend, Lizard, and his pink blankie.

The next morning I told my aunts and mother, and they cried, too.

Marco showed up as he'd told me he would, and he dug the grave. I placed Sundance in the grave with the pink blankie and Lizard, and Marco put the dirt on top of him.

My mother and aunts sang "Amazing Grace" as I cried and Marco held my hand.

We each told a Sundance story.

Butch and Cassidy were unusually quiet next to me. The goats escaped and stood right beside us. When Mr. Bob started kicking his feet up, Trixie head butted him. The lambs were lined up behind the mom, and Shakespeare and Jane Austen peered over the white fencing. Ghost curled around my legs, Mars, Venus, and Jupiter nearby. Virginia Alpaca and Alpaca Joe also watched us. Joe didn't even spit.

We each took turns putting dirt on Sundance's grave.

Sundance had literally saved my life when he started pulling on my pant leg when I wanted to jump off that cliff. He had given my life light and love from the start.

I went to bed without Sundance that night and cried because he wasn't on the pillow next to me with Lizard. He was not there in the morning for our check on the other animals, so I cried. I cried when I came home at lunch for a break and Sundance wasn't there jumping up and down with excitement at my return. I cried when Sundance wasn't there to walk over the bridge in my grandma's garden or to sit next to the lily pond with me. I went to the secret garden and stared up at the fairy, no Sundance.

I decided to drown myself in work and went in early the next day. I helped customers and I welcomed the Book Babe ladies, who told me, "We want to read a sexy book this time. What do you recommend?"

I pulled out a famous sexy book, and at first they said, "We can't read *that*." And then they changed their minds after I showed them a scene from the middle of the book. "Well," one huffed. "Maybe we could give it a shot."

I couldn't sleep the next night so I read a mystery until two in the morning. Then I stopped and told myself to face things. I thought about Sundance and became all upset again, I thought about Marco, too, and decided that I was a pathetic wretch of a self-pitying woman.

I loved Marco. I knew that. I missed him. How do you explain that deep, passionate love? To me, it's a heart-to-heart thing. Your hearts are reaching for each other. They match. They have found their heart partner, exactly as Johnny said.

I wiped away tears and then stopped. I felt my breath catch. I could hardly breathe.

I thought about the premonition in which Marco dies. When he falls off the boat in a storm after he cracks his head. I thought about the devastation, the loss, the hysteria. It was the worst premonition ever.

But Sundance was on the boat with us.

Sundance was dead.

The premonition would not occur. The drowning would not occur. We had passed it. We had passed the time of the storm and the sinking.

Oh. My. Goodness. Marco would not die on the boat.

I closed my eyes. I put my hands on my chest. I rocked back and forth with relief. With joy.

Could I be with Marco now?

He knew about the premonitions, the depression, the anxiety, saving people, my need to be alone. I could be my blender-twisted self with him.

"We can be a mess together, Evie," he had said.

I could do messy, couldn't I? I envisioned us together. Once I went out with him, I think we'd take the street down to marriage. The avenue that doesn't end. The cul-de-sac that keeps coming home.

I had almost died in an accident. Johnny had made me see how much I would regret not being courageous enough to be with Marco. He asked me if I loved Marco more than myself. Waaaay more. I loved Marco beyond love.

I would call Marco tomorrow and ask him to have dinner, pie, cake, and tea with me. I would be brave and put my favorite roses on the table. Then I would ask him if he wanted to spend the night.

That would be fun!

* * *

"Hi, Gayle, it's Evie, is Marco available?" It was early, and I'd hardly slept.

"He's gone, sugar," Gayle said.

"What do you mean he's gone?" My hand gripped the phone.

"He left for a vacation this morning."

"Oh. Where is he going?"

"Alaska."

"Alaska?"

"Yes. He's going to meet his brothers there. It's a fishing trip."

"Do you know what ferry he's taking?"

"The nine o'clock."

"Thank you."

I flew into Esmerelda like a mad woman and headed for the ferry landing.

This was reckless. I would look like a damn fool.

What did I care about being reckless, though? I had been a damn fool many times and I was still standing, wasn't I?

The town of North Sound was in my rearview mirror as I drove down country lanes, past farms and old homes and the bay and the blue-gray ocean and turned into the ferry parking lot. I could not believe my luck: A space opened up and I pulled in. I ran to the ferry, though I do so hate running—what a ridiculous sport that is—bought a ticket, and ran onboard three minutes before it was leaving for Anacortes.

Now all I had to do was find Marco.

I went through both decks, no Marco. The ferry wasn't crowded, so I should have been able to spot him right away. I turned around the outside deck . . . and I saw him.

Black hair. Sunglasses. Jeans and a sweatshirt. He was standing at the rail, staring out at the islands. He looked tired. His shoulders were slumped. He had lost weight.

I took a deep breath, then went to stand beside him.

"It's a beautiful day," I said.

"Evie." He put his glasses on his head, his eyes hurt, wary.

"Hi, Marco. I heard you're going to Alaska."

"Yes. With my brothers."

"Gayle told me. Marco." I closed my eyes, took a breath. I would get right to the point. "Sundance was on the boat with us when you . . . you drowned."

"I know."

He remembered. "And Sundance is . . ."

"I know."

"You were waiting for me to make that connection, weren't you?"

"Yes. And when you did, which I knew you would, I didn't want you to feel pushed into making a decision about me. About us."

"I think I made that decision."

"You have?"

"Yes."

"And what is it?"

"Marco, if you will still have me, I would love to be with you. I love you. Every single time I've seen you, talked to you, I love you even more."

He blinked rapidly, that black hair brushed by the wind, those shoulders broad, that face, tired but now hopeful, tough-guy but sweet, manly but filled with love.

"I am sorry for what I put you, and us, through. I am a messy human tornado."

"It's okay, Evie, it really is."

"It's not, but . . ."

He shook his head ruefully, smiled, a glorious smile, open and sexy. "Look, Evie. All I care about is right now. And our future. If you want to be together, that's what I want, too. It's what I've always wanted. It's why I moved to the island. It was you, Evie. It was all about Evie. When we talked at your bookstore, when we talked through the e-mails, when we talked on the phone when I was still in Oregon, I knew I'd found my soul mate. I love you. I will always love you."

I put my hands to my face, so relieved, then stepped in to hug him. He bent down and hugged me close, and we laughed. Our laughter sailed right around that white ferry boat, up into the blue sky, around the green islands, and back to us. He gave me a long kiss, sweet and passionate, and smokin' hot.

"You'll say yes, won't you?" he asked.

"I'll say yes, handsome. Indeed I will."

I insisted he go on his Alaskan fishing trip with his brothers.

"Go," I said. "I'll be waiting."

"Promise?"

"I promise."

And I did.

I told my mother and aunts that Marco and I were dating each other because we could. They had known about the boat-drowning premonition, but now there would be no disaster on the sailboat and I could not live without the guy.

We each picked out a special, crazy hat from the hat wall, then danced around their kitchen in Rose Bloom Cottage, under the chandelier their mother bought because she believed in fairies, next to the crystals that were hung for spiritual blessings and continued happy sex lives.

"You have outlasted the premonition and now you can dance toward your future, my dear daughter," my mother said.

"Your stars have aligned," Aunt Camellia said. "Your hemispheres have come together as one, the galaxy blessing you."

"I'll bet he's a tiger in bed," Aunt Iris said. "He'll make you roar."

I called Jules, and she squealed and said, "I'll make you your own custom motorcycle. It will say Evie and Marco, Love Muffins."

"Uh, no. No dangerous motorcycle."

She was disappointed. "I'll paint you a picture of one!"

"I'll take that."

I told Johnny, Betsy, Kayla, and Tilly, and they were thrilled for me.

"Two hearts into one for our Evie," Johnny said. "This is one of the greatest days of my life."

* * *

Chief Ass Burn parked outside my bookstore after work on Saturday afternoon.

"Hello, Evie."

"Hello." I did not stop to talk to him. I kept walking to Esmerelda. The woman with the red cowgirl hat had been right. She was a woman's truck, and I did feel like a ball-busting woman driving it.

He followed me. "I'd like to ask you something about your mother and aunts."

I felt cold, freezing cold, as if ice had entered my body. I turned to face him. "What about them?"

"Do you know what they do in their greenhouse?"

That ice was coming up my throat, filling it with more fear. I tried to hide it. "Yes. They grow plants and flowers."

He chuckled. "Is that it?"

"Yes. What's the problem?"

"Now I can't tell you what that is, little lady. I'm the chief and we keep all investigations under cover. Plus, sometimes we need search warrants."

I felt myself go cold. "I have no idea what you're talking about."

"I think you do. But maybe we could make a deal." His eyes traveled down my body.

"I think I'm going to throw up," I told him. "Because any deal with you makes me feel ill."

That comment fired his hatred straight up to the sky.

I called the assistant chief Mandy Lass, who should have been chief but wasn't because she did not have the "correct" plumbing in our male-dominated, misogynistic police hierarchy.

"What the heck is going on?"

"I can't tell you that the chief is getting a search warrant for your mom and aunts' greenhouse and that he'll probably get it soon. Like, within minutes. "

"Thanks." I hung up.

* * *

"Get rid of the pot," I shouted at my aunts and mother as soon as I got home, running into their kitchen. "Now." I told them about Chief Ass Burn.

"Oh, my goodness," my mother said. She put a hand on a hat wall to steady herself.

"Curse that fat man," Aunt Camellia said, "with intestinal bugs, bacterial diseases, and a dead possum."

I blinked at her. "Wow. Creative."

"We must take immediate action," Aunt Iris said. "I'll call Yank and Bobbi and tell him and his son to have tractor trouble on the road out of town toward us." She picked up her phone. "That'll give us a few minutes to get rid of the mowie wowie."

"That is a splendid idea," my mother said. "And I'll call Diana and tell her to set up a road block about a half mile down Robbins Drive in case he gets around the tractors."

"How will that help? He's the police chief!" I said. "He can go around a road block."

"She can use her lambs."

"Her lambs?" Diana had tons of lambs.

"Yes. They're obedient. She'll let them out on the street and park her car. They won't leave her, they love her. I'll give her a ring." She dialed Diana's number and, to my amazement, Diana agreed happily, and would pile her lambs into her trailer and get things going "lickety-split," I heard her call. "Ta la!"

"We need to burn the marijuana," Aunt Iris said.

"That's right," I said. "We need it out of the greenhouse and into the fire pit."

"We need to get rid of the evidence," my mother said.

"Let's move," I said.

"No, Evie," my mother said. "Not you. Only the three of us."

"You must protect your innocence," Aunt Camellia said. "You are angelic, and you cannot step into the problem we have brought unto ourselves, despite your loving warnings."

"Stay here," Aunt Iris said. "Do not get involved. We caused this, we will handle it."

"Give me a break," I said, and ran for the greenhouse, my mother and aunts running behind me, no Alice in Wonderland or Dr. Seuss hats on, no time.

The marijuana burned well, even though it took us several runs back and forth to get all the pot plants out and heave them onto the fire pit. We also had to get rid of the apparatus. I had no idea there was so much stuff in there. "Mom?!" I said, aghast. "Aunt Iris! Aunt Camellia!"

"Medicinal usage," my mother said, holding up a finger.

"Only for our adult friends who needed relief from the pain of the world, the pain from fraying, elderly, or sick bodies that needed a way forward into peace," Aunt Camellia said.

"Our financial goal is money toward our Antarctica trip," Aunt Iris said. "I want to study the migration of the animals. The severe weather patterns—"

"Not now!" I said.

We heard that the two tractors, all of a sudden breaking down, together, on the one street out of town, worked well for a while. Chief Ass Burn was purple with fury. He waited, he yelled, and finally he drove his police car up and then back down an embankment, sirens blaring at Yank and Bobbi. His police car became stuck and, gee whiz, no one helped. He finally gunned it and got out and back on the road.

But the lambs on Robbins Drive slowed him up, too, as they were bunched together, bleating. Diana stood in front of them, her truck and trailer parked at an angle, and would not let Chief Ass Burn by. "My trailer broke down. The engine doesn't work. Hey! Back up! Do not hurt my lambs, Chief Ass Burn, or I will take your big butt to jail! My lambs have every right to hang around outside until I can get the engine to work on my trailer again!"

There was no engine on the trailer, but it was all Diana could think of. The sirens scared the lambs, and they eventually parted enough for the chief to drive off-road, where he became stuck again momentarily.

The pot was burned to a crisp, and all the growing paraphernalia was hidden underneath the gazebo by my mother, my aunts, and me by the time he arrived. We even had time to sweep and hose the greenhouse down.

Chief Ass Burn spotted the fire pit, the smoke, and he knew. He didn't even need to go to the greenhouse. His face grew red and mottled.

"Chief Ass Burn," I called out. "You look like you need a book to read. Maybe a romance."

"I hope this will be a short visit so my temper is not triggered, Chief," my mother said.

"Time for you to take your negativity and poor karma and leave," Aunt Camellia said.

"You've got a warrant," Aunt Iris said. "You've executed the warrant. You have found nothing. You must leave. My attorney is on the way for obvious legal reasons." That was true. The family's attorney was on a ferry and she would be here soon.

Chief Ass Burn stalked off, but not before coming over to me. "You won't win, Evie. You'll regret this."

"She had nothing to do with anything," my mother said, her voice furious. "She lives in the carriage house and came home from work a few minutes ago."

"That's it. I'm not even going to pretend I believe in Zen or karma or auras," Aunt Camellia said. "Get out." She pointed at him, her voice raised to a yell, and Aunt Camellia never yells. "Get off of our property now."

"Don't you dare threaten my niece," Aunt Iris said. I had never heard her so angry, her voice hard and steely. "I will not tolerate it."

"I'm watching you, all of you," Chief Ass Burn said, then he glared at me one more time, turned on his heel, and left. Only he turned too quickly and smashed right to the ground. He swore.

"Bad words," I said. "Please don't swear. It offends my sensibilities."

"I'm going to miss that pot," Aunt Camellia said as the chief left our property with the sirens on and lights flashing.

"Oh, pish," my mother said. "You hardly ever even smoked it."

"I know. But it made me feel adventurous."

"Adventurous?" Aunt Iris said. "How about we go and plan that Antarctica expedition if you want adventure?"

"It's a porpoise, packed ice, and pot vacation!" my mother said. "What a blast."

That night my mother and aunts changed their mind about Antarctica.

They had done some thinking.

Jules's DNA test said that she had Bantu, Mali, and Senegalese in her blood.

They determined it wasn't from their father. His lineage, Norwegian and English, from family lore and letters, and DNA test, backed that up. It wasn't from Jules's and my father. His lineage, English and Scottish, from family lore and letters, and DNA test, backed that up, too.

So the Bantu/Mali/Senegalese most probably had to be from their mother's side. We thought about Grandma, Grandma who wore wings and believed in fairies, who created a magical garden that protected her, and who jumped off a cliff, arms outstretched. She said she was from France and Greece. There was no French or Greek by lore or letter or DNA test in Jules.

Grandma had olive skin.

Thick black hair.

Very dark eyes.

"She was passing, wasn't she?" Aunt Iris said

"I think she was," my mother said.

"Sad, in this country that she felt she had to pass to live a life," Aunt Camellia said. "That she knew it would be easier for her if she did."

"She was born in 1910 in Mississippi," my mother said. "I think we know why she lied."

"I may have lied, too," Aunt Iris said.

"Yes," we all agreed. We might have. And that was incredibly sad.

We sat in that for a while, thinking of Grandma Lucy, whom I had only known through my mother and aunts and her winding, lush, magnificent garden. She wasn't mentally well, but she was filled with love. Obviously one of her parents was white or part white, or both were part white . . . who knew what violence occurred throughout her ancestral line to make it so.

"We should go to Africa," Aunt Iris said. "Back to our roots. It makes the most sense. It's logical."

"You are so smart, Iris," Aunt Camellia said. "Your brain is a blessing."

"That is brilliant," my mother said.

And they put Antarctica and penguins and studying climate change and the history of Antarctica's land mass aside and began planning a trip to Africa and what hats they would bring.

The Book Babes were reading about a woman who created collages with paint, tiny tree branches, miniature trinkets, fabric, feather, sea glass, and other cool things.

They decided to make their own collages. Their tables were filled with canvasses, paints, fabrics, feathers, sequins, branches, buttons, beads, tiny treasures, et cetera, that they had all brought.

Their canvases were soon filled with color (except for the woman who was going through menopause who made her cool, modern portrait all in black). They invited me to make a collage, and I did. I made our garden. I used scraps of fabric in different colors and layered petals, leaves, and tree bark one on top of another. I added the ocean in the background, the bridge, the secret garden, the lily pond and my blue carriage house.

It was, we all decided, the best book club ever.

"We need to start having Art Night for Babes here, is that all right with you, Evie? Don't worry, we'll clean up!"

"It is if you let everyone join." They agreed. Art Night For Babes was popular instantly. I had twenty women the first night. I sold orange chiffon cake and rum cake and two tea specials: Mandarin Orange Spice and Lemon Nutmeg.

More people in, more books, cake, and tea sold!

Chief Ass Burn was removed from his post, his badge taken away.

Mandy Lass became the temporary chief.

Chief Allroy came back, soon retired, Mandy became our official police chief, and peace reigned again on San Orcanita Island.

When Marco came to my home after his Alaskan fishing trip, I greeted him exactly how a good fisherman's lady should greet her man: in red lingerie and heels.

He smiled and reeled me in.

We made my bed rock the waves that night.

I woke up wrapped around Marco, my head on his chest. He was still sleeping, the sun barely over the horizon. Butch and Cassidy were with us, as were two cats.

I smiled.

There were not many men who would allow dogs and cats to sleep in the same bed. But I knew that Marco let his four behemoth dogs sleep in his bedroom, so we were a dog/cat friendly couple.

"I love you, Evie," he had said, right before we went to sleep. "I will always love you."

"I will always love you, too, Marco," I told him, then I cried because I am a happy mess and he held me close, and even tough guy got teary-eyed, and then we laughed, in joy, at us.

Marco and me.

Us.

Chapter 37

⌣

The day of Jules and Mack's wedding was bright and warm and clear, like a colorful island postcard. White rays of sunlight shone on the ocean waves, the other islands green bits of paradise in the distance. The purple wisteria blooms had died back on the gazebo, but we filled it with yellow, pink, and purple roses and purple ribbons that floated on the wind.

Jules had been on the island for a week, and she, my mother, aunts, and I had been working nonstop to make sure all was ready.

Betsy, Johnny, Tilly, and Kayla came. They were thrilled to be invited. The four of them helped all day to get the lush, creative flower centerpieces made with the black leather ribbons and the tables set with white linens, silver flatware, and candles. They all hugged me again, tearful. We had been e-mailing and texting and calling, and I was getting to know them.

I heard a growling in the distance, and I knew what was coming: Mack and Jules's friends. From everywhere, all over the country, they were here, on their motorcycles all coming off the same ferry. We all went down to the driveway to greet them.

Dozens of bikers on bikes of all sizes, all of them dressed in their leathers, entered the property. My mother and aunts, in their fancy, ruffled, sparkling purple, yellow, and pink dresses and matching heels, and identical long double strands of real pearls, waved. They put their hands above the most fantastical hats ever made in this galaxy and wiggled their hips. The bikers waved back, smiled, laughed and gunned their bikes.

The wedding was soon to begin.

Upstairs in Rose Bloom Cottage in her pink childhood bedroom, Jules was a wreck.

My mother and aunts hurriedly came outside to get me, all a tizzy. I was telling the band where to set up and directing the caterers and bartenders, Marco helping like a wedding planning pro. A package arrived with stacks of boxes from Julia's Chocolates in central Oregon that we were placing on each table, as it's the best chocolate on the planet Earth. I was planning on getting changed into my maid of honor dress, but for now was whipping around in a flowered yellow sundress.

"Come," my mother panted, pulling on my arm, her towering hat askew. "You need to talk to your sister. She'll listen to you."

"Jules needs your sisterly spirit," Aunt Camellia said, her face creased in worry as she held onto her hat with both hands. "Your emotional strength as a woman."

"Get in there and fix this problem," Aunt Iris said, her hat off as she shook it at me. "Your sister is flipping out and we need a solution."

"But what's wrong?"

"You'll see."

They shoved me into Jules's childhood bedroom. She was in a pink fluffy robe stained with coffee and red wine. She was pacing, having a hard time breathing, her hand on her throat.

"What's wrong?"

"I'm getting married!"

"But you want to get married," I said, giving her a hug.

"I know, I know. But I'm nervous. I have nerves. I haven't seen Mack in a week, and that makes me feel all jittery and scared." She wrung her hands. She gasped. She bent over. We were definitely in meltdown territory.

"Jules, remember what you love about Mack."

"I love a lot about him. In bed, he's so kind, but he's so passionate. He knows exactly how I like to make love, the pacing, and how I like things different sometimes and sometimes the same, and how he's always a gentleman and he's romantic and whispers sweet things to me so my mind is in it and my body is in it, too. He's so fiery, he makes me feel like a woman, but oh!" She put her hands over her mouth and gasped, again and again.

"Take a breath, honey," my mother said, all fluttery and worried.

"She needs to get her soul aligned with her goals," Aunt Camellia cried.

"She's having a dang panic attack," Aunt Iris said.

"Oh, oh, oh!" Jules said, growing whiter by the second. "I'm getting married! I'm getting married. I'm getting married." She put her hands to her long blonde hair. Then she fiddled with her hoop earrings. She stared at the tattoo of Mack's face, then she burst into tears. I held her as she struggled for breath. Tears and not breathing. Well, we had a problem.

I knew what to do! I hugged her and hurried outside and found Mack, keeping my expression happy so as not to alarm the guests with a suspected freaked-out bride. "Come with me," I told him.

His face instantly leaped to worry. "Is my honey bunch okay? Is my sweetie pie calm?"

"She's nervous. She's scared."

Mack is six foot six inches tall. The kids he works with as a pediatric nurse see the kindness in his heart and they love him, but he looks a little intimidating. He's a mix of a motorcycle gang member and Santa Claus without the white beard. "What's wrong with my pumpkin? She still wants to get married, doesn't she?"

"Please, come upstairs."

His eye flew open wide and he went white. He sprinted to the house and thundered upstairs to her pink room.

"Love muffin," he said. "My sweet rose. My darling cupcake. What is it?"

"Oh, oh, oh!" Jules cried. She wrapped her arms around him and was soon hugged by a giant bear.

"Mom. Aunts." I motioned to them. "Let's leave the two love muffins alone."

They followed me out, hands wringing, chants to the heavens for luck whispered by my aunt Camellia.

My mother said, "My goodness. If she doesn't get married I'm going to drink a whole keg of beer myself."

Aunt Iris muttered, "She'd better walk down the aisle with that young man. Statistically speaking, she has a high chance of being married forever."

I figured they would need fifteen minutes. Mack would not be able to "take his time," this time, as we had a wedding. We waited downstairs. Mack came bounding out on the dot in fifteen minutes and announced, "My sweetheart, my chocolate croissant, is feeling better now, ladies! On with the wedding. I cannot wait to be in that gazebo with my apple pie."

We trooped upstairs, my mother and aunts holding on to their marvelous hats. Jules was much better. Her newly done hair was a mess and her makeup would have to be redone. "He's so sexy," she whispered to me. "He knows exactly what to do for my nerves and my brain and my va va voom. I feel so much better."

I took a deep breath before I walked out of the house in my maid of honor dress and came face-to-face with Marco. He was in a dark blue suit and looked like a cross between Tarzan and a love God. I, however, was not in a traditional maid of honor dress. Picture those silky, fluffy, lacy dresses that maids of honor wear.

That was not me.

Picture the pastel colors.

That was not me.

Picture the matching heels, the hair all done up with curls and whirls.

That was not me.

What was I wearing?

I was in a black leather bustier.

Yes, a *bustier*.

My boobs were almost spilling out the top of said leather bustier. About four inches of my stomach was peeping between the edge of the bustier and my white lace skirt, which fell to above my knees, lined with white satin so it would not be see-through. The white lace skirt had several slits so when I walked my legs showed up to almost midthigh. As a gift, Jules had bought me knee-high black leather boots, so I was wearing those, too. I was also wearing black fishnets and a black bandana around my head that said JULES AND MACK FOREVER.

I was hardly dressed in front of over two hundred people. Cleavage up, thighs showing, even my stomach making an appearance

Curiously, I rather liked it. The wedding dress designer had truly made an eye-catching and unique maid of honor biker-gang dress, but I was nervous about what Marco would say.

Marco did a double take, a shocked expression on his face, then he smiled and looked me up and down, up and down. "Wow. I mean, wow, baby. You look . . . uh, wow."

"I'm a biker chick."

"I can tell."

He smiled, and I smiled back nervously. Oh my. I figured we'd have some fun biker sex tonight. We'd had a lot of fun sex lately. He was holding my bouquet of flowers. They were a mix of pink, red, and white roses, all wrapped in a long black leather ribbon and white lace.

My mother and aunts smiled at me. Their hats bobbed. They had outdone themselves. Their hats were wide brimmed, purple, yellow, and pink, matching their sparkly, ruffled dresses and piled with a mix of fresh and faux flowers. The hats were cocked this way and that, a faux bird here and there, glitter sprayed left and right, a handful of silver sequins, lots of netting and long ribbons trailing down their backs.

"I love you," my mother said to me, and my aunts echoed it. They tried to hug me, but their hats poked me in the face. "You look marvelous, Evie, in your lace and leathers. . . . You should ride a motorcycle. . . . Have you thought about wearing a bustier more often? My goodness you do have our family's bust, don't you? Why do you cover it up?"

And then it was time. My aunts were seated first as a rock band played "Back in Black" by AC/DC. Everyone loved it, especially since many of the guests were in their black leathers for the wedding. Mack's mother, grandma, and great-grandma and their husbands went next. Nine bridesmaids, childhood and motorcycle riding friends of Jules, and the groomsmen walked the aisle arm in arm. The bridesmaids wore summer dresses, knee-high black boots, and the black JULES AND MACK FOREVER headbands, as did the groomsmen.

It was my turn to walk down the aisle, then my sister would follow. My mother was walking Jules down the aisle. My mother held a small, handsome photo of my father so he could walk his daughter down the aisle, too, which made me get all emotional, but I have a feeling that the doors of heaven open up for occasions like this. Henry Lindsay would be watching, and he would see it all.

I winked at Marco on my way down the aisle, then stood at the front of the gazebo and turned around to see Jules, my best friend, my love-sister.

The music changed from rock and roll to a traditional wedding song.

Jules was resplendent. Her wedding dress was white, lacy, and sleeveless, so her shoulders were bare. The layered skirt came to midthigh so her black knee-high leather boots with silver sequins at the top made quite an entrance. She wore her long blonde hair loose like a Viking with a black JULES AND MACK FOREVER headband. A white lace veil was attached to the headband, which created a five-foot train that fluttered in the wind.

She was naturally exquisite.

When she appeared at the end of the aisle, everyone stood, gasped, and started cheering for her. My mother cried next to her, Jules cried. I cried. My aunts cried, even practical Aunt Iris. Mack, dressed in his black leathers with a black bow tie, his arms outstretched at the end of the aisle, had tears racing down his cheeks. "Come on down, my apple pie! I'm waiting for you!" he boomed.

"I'm coming, baby," Jules called back. "I'm coming!"

Whew. What a day.

The wedding was everything Jules and Mack wanted. Mack's best childhood friend, Jay Dove Boy, in his leathers, led the solemn vow ceremony where they promised to be loyal, kind, and devoted and to ride their motorcycles as they explored life and love together until death did they part. A band played a blend of rock/disco/old-time dance music. Everyone loved wearing their own black leather JULES AND MACK FOREVER headbands. It seemed to give everyone a new "wild and rockin'" mentality and the party boomed. The barbeque went over deliciously well.

The cake was made by the Bommarito sisters in Trillium River. It was a three-layer cake painted with exact replicas of the motorcycles that Jules and Mack rode. But on the top layer, using who knew what, they had made two edible motorcycles, exactly patterned off of Jules's and Mack's favorite motorcycles, with Jules and Mack on top. Jules's blonde hair was flying behind her, and they were in their leathers.

The beer and wine flowed like a river. There was dancing and laughing and toasts. The woman they hired to paint fake tattoos on guests was extremely talented.

At one in the morning, Jules and Mack got on his motorcycle to leave for a bed-and-breakfast in town for their honeymoon night, and we all cheered as they sped off. Mack announced to a delighted Jules that they were going to Thailand for their honeymoon.

"I packed perfectly," Jules gushed. "Bikinis and lingerie! I'm ready to go!"

Marco and I, along with a whole bunch of other people, helped to clean up, and then we headed to our beach, made love, and watched the sun come up.

I did feel daringly biker-chickish in my maid of honor dress and Marco adored the leather bustier.

* * *

Marco asked me to marry him shortly thereafter, on one knee, on our beach, in the middle of a sunny, windy Saturday. The ring was exquisite and sparkling, and when he was still on his knee, I was so excited, I hugged him tight and we fell over, me on top of him. I did not bother to get up until I'd kissed that man silly.

I did not want to have a premonition about Marco and me and our future. I simply wanted to live with him, love him, and be like a normal person who doesn't know the good and the bad upcoming. But maybe, because my feelings for him were so intense, it brought it on.

In the premonition I saw two people together. At first I didn't recognize us. We were very, very old. White hair, wrinkled skin, glasses, the works. We were sitting at our beach, in chairs, holding hands, a whole bunch of animals around us. There were at least five dogs. A couple cats. A few grizzled horses in the background, along with alpacas, sheep, and goats.

I had already told him, before he formally asked me to marry him, that because of my family history, I would not have children. "I can't do this to anyone else," I said. "It's clearly in my family line, all the way back." He agreed and said he'd never planned on having children. "I want you, Evie. It'll be you and me and our animals."

We agreed to open up a shelter for animals that cannot find homes. We would call it Sundance's Home. Not all animals are adoptable for one reason or another, and those would stay with us permanently.

"That's a plan," Marco said. "We'll be animal collectors."

Seeing us on the beach, old and smiling, it looked like we'd turned into happy, old animal collectors.

It was my favorite premonition of all time.

ALL ABOUT EVIE

Cathy Lamb

ABOUT THIS GUIDE

The suggested questions are included to enhance
your group's reading of Cathy Lamb's
All About Evie.

DISCUSSION QUESTIONS

1. What did you think of *All About Evie*? Were there scenes that made you laugh or cry? Were there scenes that you, personally, could relate to?

2. Evie Lindsay had premonitions. It was genetic, handed down from mother to daughter in her family line. Do you have premonitions? Do you believe that other people could have premonitions? Would you want to have premonitions?

3. Who was your favorite female character? Betsy, Evie, Jules, Poppy, Aunt Camellia, Aunt Iris, or Tilly? Why?

4. Evie said, "You all knew this secret about me. You've all known how lonely I've often felt, how alone. There was something missing, and I couldn't explain it, couldn't fix it, couldn't deal with it. I thought that it was me, that something was wrong with me. I thought it was my premonitions that were setting me apart, but it wasn't. I had been taken from my biological parents, and somehow, some way, even though I was a baby, I felt it. That separation is what caused the inexplicable hole I have felt, I have battled, my whole life."

   Should Poppy and Henry have told their daughter, Evie, that she was adopted? When should they have told her? Do you understand their reasons for not telling Evie? Do you approve of their reasons?

5. Did Johnny and Betsy deserve to go to jail? Were they right in going to court to gain back custody of Evie when they were released? Should the judge have given them custody of their daughter? If it were you who lost

Evie, would you believe that she should come back to your home, given the same circumstances?

6. Aunt Iris said, regarding the pot they were growing in their greenhouse, "Isn't it better for all of us to die stoned than to die sober? It's a much gentler way to spend your dying time."

"I want to be high as a kite when I die," Aunt Camellia said, her face ecstatic at the thought. "High. As. A. Kite. Flying through the heavens, dipping into the clouds, rolling over rainbows."

How did you feel about the "mowie wowie" growing in the greenhouse?

7. Evie said, "I pulled myself together and went to work, because this is what we do when life falls apart: We buck up and we go to work and we take care of people and our responsibilities.

"Why? Because we must.

"And maybe that answer is, boringly, dully . . . perfect."

What five words would you use to describe Evie? How did she change from the beginning of the book to the end? What would it be like to have her life and to see premonitions?

8. "Jail, Betsy decided, is actually hell.

"It's a hell wrapped in concrete, wire, and steel bars, that has landed on Earth, dangerous and suffocating. She had a metal plank and a sinking, stained, skinny mattress for a bed. She had bars keeping her trapped like an animal; a toilet within her cell with no privacy; and a small, battered sink. She was told what to do and when to do it. The food was horrible, the lack of sunlight graying to life, the lack of freedom deadly to her mind and soul."

Was Betsy's story in jail difficult to read? Did the parallel story line between Evie and Betsy work for you? Did you like Betsy?

9. Rose Bloom Cottage had a huge, thriving garden with a gazebo, paths, willow trees, and a pond, designed by Evie's grandmother. How did the garden, and the flowers, particularly the roses, enhance the story? What were they a metaphor for?

10. Have you had your DNA tested to see where your ancestors are from? If so, were there any surprises, as Evie found out from her test? If you haven't had your DNA tested, are you planning to? Why or why not?

11. Poppy, Camellia, and Iris love their hats. "Hats with feathers, ribbons, birds, pom-pom balls, sequins, and beading. Hats made from straw. Hats with wide brims and tight brims. Hats that are two feet high, and hats that hang over an eye. Hats with netting, gauze, lace, satin, and silk. Hats that look like they came off the British Royal family, and hats from *Alice in Wonderland* and the Kentucky Derby and Dr. Seuss." Draw a hat for yourself.